HENRY MILLER was born on December 26, 1891, in Manhattan and grew up in Brooklyn. After a string of dreary jobs and a disastrous first marriage, Miller left for Paris in 1930. *Tropic of Cancer,* published when he was forty-three and immediately banned in all English-speaking countries, is considered his most important book. Miller's works include *Black Spring* (1936), *Tropic of Capricorn* (1939), *The Cosmological Eye* (1939), *The Colossus of Maroussi* (1941), *The Time of the Assassins* (1946), *The Air-Conditioned Nightmare* (1945), and his autobiographical trilogy, *The Rosy Crucifixion,* comprised of *Sexus* (1949), *Plexus* (1953), and *Nexus* (1960). In 1940, Miller returned to America and settled in Big Sur, California. A lusty romantic, Miller married five times, the last to Japanese singer Hoki Tokuda. His courageous legal battle against the censorship of *Tropic of Cancer* ended with a landmark 1964 Supreme Court decision, which guaranteed a new freedom of expression to all American writers. Generous and supportive of other artists throughout his life, Henry Miller in his final years was surrounded by young admirers and old friends. Writing, painting, and carrying on a voluminous correspondence until the very end, Henry Miller died in June, 1980, in the arms of his housekeeper.

HENRY MILLER

TROPIC OF CANCER

With an Introduction by
Louise DeSalvo

$\mathcal{O}$

A SIGNET CLASSIC

SIGNET CLASSIC
Published by the Penguin Group
Penguin Books USA Inc., 375 Hudson Street,
New York, New York 10014, U.S.A.
Penguin Books Ltd, 27 Wrights Lane,
London W8 5TZ, England
Penguin Books Australia Ltd, Ringwood,
Victoria, Australia
Penguin Books Canada Ltd, 10 Alcorn Avenue,
Toronto, Ontario, Canada M4V 3B2
Penguin Books (N.Z.) Ltd, 182–190 Wairau Road,
Auckland 10, New Zealand

Penguin Books Ltd, Registered Offices:
Harmondsworth, Middlesex, England

Published by Signet Classic, an imprint of Dutton Signet,
a division of Penguin Books USA Inc.

First Signet Classic Printing, August, 1995
10   9   8   7   6   5

Introduction copyright © Louise DeSalvo, 1995
All rights reserved

REGISTERED TRADEMARK—MARCA REGISTRADA

Library of Congress Catalog Card Number: 94–74837

Printed in the United States of America

BOOKS ARE AVAILABLE AT QUANTITY DISCOUNTS WHEN USED TO PROMOTE PRODUCTS OR
SERVICES. FOR INFORMATION PLEASE WRITE TO PREMIUM MARKETING DIVISION, PENGUIN
BOOKS USA INC., 375 HUDSON STREET, NEW YORK, NEW YORK 10014.

"These novels will give way, by and by, to diaries or autobiographies—captivating books, if only a man knew how to choose among what he calls his experiences that which is really his experience, and how to record truth truly."

—RALPH WALDO EMERSON

Introduction to
Henry Miller's *Tropic of Cancer*
by Louise DeSalvo

Henry Miller arrived in Paris on March 4, 1930, to try to become a successful writer.[1] He had ten dollars in his pocket (a loan from his old friend Emil Schnellock), a trunkful of suits (from his tailor father), which he knew he could pawn if he ran out of money, and carbon copies of two novels he had written in New York and hoped to revise—*Moloch* (about his first marriage and his job at Western Union), and *Crazy Cock* (about his second marriage to June Miller and her lesbian love affair, which had tormented him).[2] Though he had been writing seriously for six years, and had published a few small pieces, Miller hadn't yet published a novel, hadn't yet fulfilled his dream of becoming a "working-class Proust," the Proust of Brooklyn.[3] His wife, June, had persuaded him that Paris might be where he could perfect his craft and become financially successful.

What really motivated June to urge her husband to leave New York, though, was that he had become a burden to her and she wanted him (temporarily) out of her life while she pursued another of her schemes to make money for both of them. She was involved in a relationship with an older, wealthy "sugar daddy," who makes a brief appearance in *Tropic of Cancer* as the "fetus with a cigar in its mouth" standing opposite Miller's apartment, watching him leave for Europe.

Though June had persuaded Miller to quit his job at Western Union to become a writer, and had supported him through a variety of jobs—as a hostess, a waitress, and a prostitute—she had lost confidence in him. Despite her efforts, he showed no signs of becoming what she believed he would become: a writer who would immortalize her in his work, who would extol her self-sacrifice, who would reveal her to the world as the semi-mythic *femme fatale* she believed herself to be—a Dostoyevsky heroine, who prowled the streets of New York City in search of adventure.[4]

Miller's life with June formed the foundation of all his mature fiction. On the night of May 21, 1927, in profound despair because June had fled to Paris with her lover Jean Kronski, Miller outlined a *magnum opus* that would recount the agony of his life with June. Though June had kept in touch in her usual desultory way, with a few postcards of the Eiffel Tower, the Arc de Triomphe, and Notre Dame, she hadn't responded to his letters begging her to come back to him, and he sensed that his marriage, if not over, would never be the same again.

Desperate with loneliness, and crazy with jealousy, Miller sat at the typewriter in the office of the Parks Department in Queens where he was working, to outline a novel that would recount his life with June and her betrayal. He was thirty-six years old, and living with his parents because he couldn't afford to live alone. It had been June's idea that he could become a writer. The truth was, though he had always wanted to become a writer, he was "afraid"; he didn't think he had the ability. He wasn't rich or privileged or college educated, though he was extremely well read: he had attended the City College of New York briefly, but soon left, "disgusted with the curriculum" after a "hopeless encounter" with Spenser's *The Fairie Queene*. As a working-class man, the son of first generation German–Americans,[5] who had been born in New York on December 26, 1891, Miller often said to himself, "Who was I to say *I am a writer*?"[6]

On that night, Miller began to type out his notes for what would become a lifelong literary project. The notes came *"without effort"*; he would deal with his and his wife's "battles royal, debauches," her lies and betrayals. He wrote a catalog of the "events and crises" they had endured. He listed the manuscripts in his possession he could cannibalize, letters he had written that he could mine for details. Everything he had lived, everything he had written, would become the source for his art. When he finished, early the next morning, he had a stack of thirty-two closely typed pages, which he labeled *"June."*

He had sketched the basis for much of his life's work, for *Crazy Cock,* portions of *Tropic of Cancer, Tropic of Capricorn,* and *The Rosy Crucifixion.* More importantly, he had fastened upon the intensely autobiographical form that his life's work would take. From now on, he would be both the author and subject of his life's work. He would live his life as if it were the raw material for art; then he would turn the life he had lived into art.[7]

When Henry Miller arrived in Paris in 1930, the city, like New York, was in the midst of the Depression. His Paris was not the Paris of Ernest Hemingway or of F. Scott Fitzgerald. Miller, because of his self-imposed poverty, could describe a side of Paris that tourists (and even the expatriates who lived there before him) never saw. It was a Paris not of exquisite meals, but of hunger, of rancid butter and moldy cheese, of cheap hotels with tattered wallpaper and bloodstained gray sheets crawling with bedbugs, of old women sleeping in doorways, of whores with wooden stumps, of full slop pails, of "*angoisse* and *tristesse*."

Tropic of Cancer recounts the story of Henry Miller's first two years in Paris. It is perhaps the first novel that redefines the creative process for the working-class writer. It is an (un)American, ungenteel, uneducated (but not unlettered), no-holds-barred, middle-aged-man's version of *A Portrait of the Artist as a Young Man* by James Joyce (a writer whom Miller despised, calling him a "pedagogic sadist,"[8] but whom he consciously emulated), or of *Remembrance of Things Past* by Marcel Proust (a writer whom Miller adored). It is a meditation on both the profane and divine aspects of an art that has its source in both lust and longing.

Many critics have commented upon the precedent-shattering descriptions of sexuality in the novel. Yet another subject of *Tropic of Cancer* is even more revolutionary: It shows what a working-class man must go through to live the creative life, and how he must redefine himself to develop the courage to write a novel about his own experiences in his own voice. "A year ago, six months ago," the narrator tells us, "I thought that I was an artist. I no longer think about it, I *am*." It is a work about how to develop self-esteem (which sometimes looks like a compensatory bravado) when you feel like "a zero, ... a cipher, ... a nullity," when you come from a culture that expects you to be a stud and to talk dirty about women, but that devalues you and won't grant you the opportunity to become a writer.

Though Miller's descriptions of sex are surely radical because he wrote down how a certain kind of man talks about sex, what is even more radical are his descriptions of how he seizes for himself the right to do creative work even if it means that he goes hungry, or that he has to invent schemes—like getting well-heeled friends to invite him to dinner—in order to eat. In describing the two-year genesis of *Cancer,* Miller shows us the lonely, perilous, agonizing, yet exhilarating route that he traveled to do his work, and to learn to speak in his own voice. Unlike privileged writers, who have the time, money, and confidence to devote to their art, the working-class writer, Miller tells us, must depend upon others for support. In a patriarchal culture, this dependency "unmans" the male working-class writer. It forces him to use charm, guile, and seduction to keep himself fed, clothed, and housed— attributes ordinarily ascribed to dependent women.

"How the hell can a man write when he doesn't know where he's going to sit the next half-hour," the narrator laments, when he's about to lose his temporary home. "One can sleep almost anywhere but one must have a place to work," he tells us. "Even a bad novel requires a chair to sit on and a bit of privacy." He has to depend upon other people's money (a wife's, a lover's, or friends') for his survival. Or he has to work at demeaning jobs (a houseboy, a proofreader, a tutor) to earn enough just to get by. For if he tries to earn a living in conventional ways, he will dissipate the energy necessary to perfect his craft. He has to learn the art of suffering; he has to give up hope (but eschew despair) and the illusion of safety; if necessary, he must become a predator to survive.

Miller worked steadily on *Tropic of Cancer* from the spring of 1932 through its publication in September 1934. Though his friends remarked upon the spontaneity and directness with which Miller composed the work, changes on the manuscript indicate that Miller revised as he composed, and that he reworked the novel in its entirety at least four times.[9] At one stage, Miller intended to conclude the work with a scene concerning his wife June rather than the portrait of the narrator contemplating the Seine that now ends the work.

An arresting description of Henry Miller at work on *Cancer* is provided by his friends Alfred Perles and Wambly Bald, who describe Miller's apparently limitless sexual and creative energy at the time.[10] He awakened early, often to his friends' distress, for he would awaken them to talk, even if they had worked all night. If Perles's live-in French lover was home, Miller would entertain her with anecdotes in his idiosyncratic brand of French; it was a French spoken with a Brooklyn accent, replete with colloquialisms, but using the inflated syntax of Proust (especially the subjunctive), whom Miller was reading at the time.

In the mornings, he would draft letters and notes. Lunch usually would be taken at the home of a friend, or at a cafe, at someone else's expense. Though Miller has been called a shameless beggar because of this, if he had some money, he would practice what he called "reverse pickpocketing"—putting money in a friend's pocket without telling him.[11] After lunch, he would return home to take a nap, for which he "undressed, put on his pajamas, and went to bed." These daily breaks, he argued, put "velvet in his vertebrae."[12] They also put him in touch with his unconscious and prepared him for an afternoon's work of almost demonic intensity.

When he was writing, he "always managed to knock out his fifteen or twenty pages" in one session. Hunched over his typewriter, a *Gauloise bleue* clenched between his teeth, his head encircled by smoke, his fingers flew over the keyboard in the fastest display of touch typing Perles had ever seen. At times, colored pencils in hand, he stopped to hunt for a passage he wanted to use among the piles of books he had gathered around him; or he consulted a letter he had written (he usually kept a carbon); or he worked from his Paris notebook. At times, he glanced up at a chart tacked onto his wall outlining his work-in-progress to remind himself of what still had to be written. Or he consulted the lists of words he had copied from his dictionary that he wanted to include in his novel. He could work even when other people were present. Often, he typed and talked simultaneously. (It is likely that at times he typed these conversations into the novel.) Sometimes "in the middle of his work he would put on a record and listen to a piece of music. Or he would burst into song himself. His work was done singing."[13]

After, he would go on long walks, taking his notebook with him. He would find new streets to describe, new sights to incorporate, new denizens of the street to include in his work. The "more squalid parts of Paris"[14] fascinated him—the Cité Nortier, for example, near the Place du Combat, with a courtyard bordered by rotting buildings, its flagstones slippery with slime, a "human dump-heap" filled with garbage. Or he would take a bicycle ride to the outlying parts of Paris.

After dinner (again, at the expense of friends), Miller would often go back to work.

Though he was still married to June Miller throughout the composition of *Tropic of Cancer*, this period was also the heyday of Miller's love affair with Anaïs Nin, who was married to the banker Hugh Guiler. Miller was introduced to Anaïs Nin in December 1931 through his friend Richard Osborn.[15]

Miller came into Nin's life when she was ripe for sexual experimentation, soon after she had published a book on D. H. Lawrence. Miller himself had just published a review of Luis Buñuel's *L'Âge d'Or*, and was working on yet another revision of his novel *Crazy Cock*, about the adverse effect of his wife's lesbian love affair upon his sanity.[16] When they met, Nin wrote into her diary: "I saw a man I liked. In his writing he is flamboyant, virile, animal, magnificent. He's a man whom life makes drunk, I thought. He is like me."[17]

At first, the two met to talk about their work, and to exchange ideas. But when Nin met Miller's wife, June, the relationship became immediately complicated. Nin fell in love with June, replicating the love triangle that had caused Miller so much pain.

After June returned to the United States, Nin and Miller became lovers. According to Nin's testimony, he was a wonderful lover, who awakened her sensuality; he was passionate yet considerate, and he satisfied her in ways she had never imagined possible. According to his testimony, she supported him financially, and gave him the peace of mind and the courage to begin *Tropic of Cancer*, the most important novel of his life. She convinced him that his work was more important than Joyce's, and that he should be as explosive and provocative in his work as he was in his talk. She provided the secure base from which Miller felt free to experiment.

Nin and Miller remained lovers for years, spoke of marriage, shared a studio apartment at the Villa Seurat, and conceived a child together (which Nin aborted). Yet Nin never seriously considered leaving her husband for Miller, though she urged Miller to leave June, and helped end his marriage by letting June know that she and Miller were lovers. For one thing, it was Nin's husband's money that financed her freewheeling lifestyle. She realized that Miller could not be counted upon to support a wife. For another, neither Nin nor Miller was inclined to monogamy. During their affair, Nin was sexually involved, not only with Miller, but with her husband, her cousin Eduardo Sanchez, and two of her analysts (Rene Allendy and Otto Rank); Miller continued his dalliances with prostitutes. Though Miller seemed accepting of Nin's behavior, Nin was often angry with Miller for his.

Reading Nin's descriptions of Miller's behavior as a lover and as a man, in her unexpurgated diaries (published as *Henry and June* and *Incest*), and in her fiction (in *Cities of the Interior*) against Miller's description of himself in *Tropic of Cancer* is instructive. It illuminates the distance between the "real" Henry Miller, and the persona Miller created for himself in his work. In Miller's self-portrait, he presents himself as sexually rapacious, rough, tough, woman hating, though he longs for his wife, Mona. In Nin's work, though, Miller is a passionate and tender lover, respectful of her womanhood, though timid, weak, and vulnerable as a man. Her portrait is nothing like the tough-minded persona of *Cancer*, and suggests that Miller's creation was largely compensatory.

Miller was, as Nin put it, "a child in need, ... a victim [of women] seeking solace, ... a weakling seeking sustenance."[18]

Henry Miller developed the narrative of *Tropic of Cancer* from his letters from Paris to his friend Emil Schnellock and those to Anaïs Nin (especially the ones from Dijon describing his wretched teaching experience),[19] from the notes he made as he prowled the streets of Paris, and from his conversations with friends about literature, psychoanalysis (with Anaïs Nin), sex (with Wambly Bald, the Parisian columnist, who appears in the novel as the sex-obsessed Van Norden), death (with Michael Fraenkel), and war. For the first time in his fiction, he used what he called the "first person spectacular."[20] It was a point of view he had studiously avoided in his earlier attempts at fiction, yet it suited him, for he was a magnetic teller and reteller of stories.

In one sense, *Tropic of Cancer* is about the healing of the damaged self through stories, which magnify and mythicize his own and his friends' escapades. Anaïs Nin believed that Miller's work illuminated the workings of the psyche more profoundly than James Joyce's and, in one important sense, she was right. For as James Joyce records the contents of consciousness, Miller's work shows the process by which the contents of consciousness are created by the storytelling self. Miller's avowed aim, as he states it in *Cancer,* is "to put down everything that goes on in my noodle" without self-censorship. Miller shows how, by choosing the way you describe your life, you can create the consciousness that you desire. Without waiting for the world to change, you can change who you are by the stories you tell yourself and others about who you are.

But his stories are not only healing, they are entertaining. Miller adopted the pose of a modern-day *jongleur,* who turned self-display into an art form, into a carnival performance, using a narrative voice uniquely and authentically his, one that had not yet been written down.

Though in his novel *Moloch,* Miller wrote that no successful work of literature could be located in Brooklyn, or have Brooklyn as its subject, *Tropic of Cancer* is written in the voice of the Brooklyn boy. It is the voice of the wise-ass street kid, who hangs out on the corner with his friends, who trades stories with them about his exploits, and who uses one-upsmanship to gain status. It is the voice of the man who hides his pain behind a string of curse words, who vulgarizes women because it is unmanly to admit how much he needs them, and who exaggerates how callous and tough he is so that he will not be victimized. But his longing for Mona (his wife, June) is tenderly and poignantly described, and it forms the emotional core of *Cancer* against which his posture of viciousness toward women must be read. In expressing his disgust at the cunt-obsessed Van Norden, the narrator concludes that having sex without passion is like living in a state of war.

Though a habitué of the streets, a literary *clochard,* Miller's narrator cannot manage to hide how learned he is. In *Cancer,* besides drawing upon his experiences, Miller self-consciously used such models and sources as Knut Hamsun's, D. H. Lawrence's, and Marcel Proust's fiction,[21] Shakespeare's and James Joyce's soliloquies, Francois Rabelais' bawdy humor,[22] Japanese shunga's and Indian sculpture's explicitly profane yet sacred depiction of sex, Walt Whitman's celebratory lists, Brassai's photography, Picasso's nudes, Anaïs Nin's self-reflective diaries, and the techniques of the surrealists (including assemblage),[23] to name but a few. He describes how literature and art can enrich the lives of the members of the working class, of people without university degrees.

Tropic of Cancer was published in a small edition in Paris on September 1, 1934, by Jack Kahane at the Obelisk Press with money provided by Anaïs Nin, given to her by Otto Rank.[24] Obscenity laws in England and the United States prohibited publication, but "potentially 'obscene' books could be published in France if they were in English."[25] The cover of the first edition was designed by Kahane's sixteen-year-old son to save money. It showed "a crab crushing a nude female in its claws,"[26] and Miller thought it was "horrible." The jacket carried a warning to booksellers that *Cancer* "must not be displayed in the window."[27]

At the time, Miller was living in an airy studio at 18 Villa Seurat in Paris, which he shared with Anaïs Nin. When he received his first copy of *Tropic of Cancer,* Miller "felt that he had never been so happy."[28] He celebrated its publication by listening to recordings of American music—"Old Black Joe," "My Old Kentucky Home"—and by giving copies to friends who had helped him—Michael Fraenkel, Richard Osborn, and Anaïs Nin.

Miller became an indefatigable publicist for his work, sending copies of *Cancer* to the most important critics and writers of his time, to John Dos Passos, Herbert Read, Aldous Huxley, T. S. Eliot, and Ezra Pound, among others. His efforts paid off in time, although the book was banned in Britain and the United States and, although, initially, the work did not sell well.[29] Blaise Cendrars, author of *Sutter's Gold* and the *Moravagine,* reviewed the novel in a piece called *"Un Écrivain Américain nous est né."*[30] Lawrence Durrell, living in Greece, was so impressed by the work that he traveled to Paris to meet its author. The "tallish emaciated" George Orwell came to pay his respects and later wrote "Inside the Whale," his landmark essay on Miller. In time, pirated editions of the novel appeared in Vienna, Budapest, Amsterdam, Shanghai, and the United States.[31]

Tropic of Cancer had a steady readership during World War II, and during the Occupation, "when American GIs bought copies and smuggled them home in huge numbers."[32] The 1946 *l'affaire Miller,* in which M. Daniel Parker, President of the Society for Enforcement of Social and Public Morals, brought action against the work and its publishers, prompted a flurry of phenomenal sales for *Cancer.* A committee formed of writers, artists, and intellectuals, such as André Gide, Jean-Paul Sartre, Albert Camus, and Raymond Queneau came to Miller's defense: "not a day passed without articles on Miller filling the daily press."[33] Miller was living in the United States at the time, and he never profited materially from the sales of his work in France.

But it wasn't until May 1961, when Miller was sixty-nine years old, "almost thirty years after it was written," that *"Tropic of Cancer* was legally published in the United States"[34] by Grove Press. By then, because of

Grove's landmark case regarding the publication of D. H. Lawrence's *Lady Chatterley's Lover*, obscenity laws had been liberalized to the extent that any work "*with* social importance *was* guaranteed constitutional protection."[35] The paperback publication of the novel in October 1961, though, prompted a number of censorship cases: "suddenly *Tropic of Cancer* was on trial in fifty-three separate court-rooms across the United States"[36]—at one point, a bench warrant had been issued for his arrest in Brooklyn. Miller did not rest easy until the June 1964 Supreme Court decision finding *Tropic of Cancer* "not obscene."[37]

In 1970, Henry Miller came under attack from Kate Millett in her extremely influential *Sexual Politics*. In it, Millett argues that Miller, among other male authors, promulgated the " 'doctrine of the cave' in which women who are not sexually compliant are properly beaten for it (and women who *are* sexually compliant are also beaten for it)."[38] Yet Anaïs Nin had recorded in her diary that Miller punished women in his work because he let himself be violated by them in his life.[39] She saw *him* as the victim of a woman's mistreatment.

The publication of Nin's unexpurgated diaries and biographies by Jay Martin, Mary V. Dearborn, and Robert Ferguson has done much to enlarge our view of Miller as writer and lover. All illuminate the chaotic, abusive household into which Miller was born. Dearborn describes Miller's sexual abuse by a trusted scout leader;[40] in this context, Miller's machismo can be read as a compensatory defense.

Erica Jong's *The Devil at Large* illuminates Miller's generosity toward young writers, and his impact on Jong's landmark *Fear of Flying* and other precedent-shattering works. For Jong, even more important than Miller's sexual honesty was his struggle to find "the courage to be an individual, no matter what the consequences."[41] And this, surely, is Miller's most significant contribution to American letters. For his work documents, as perhaps no other, what it takes for a working-class man to undertake "the search for the courage to be a writer."[42]

Notes

1. Henry Miller, *Letters to Emil,* ed. by George Wickes (New York: New Directions, 1989), p. 15.

2. Erica Jong, *The Devil at Large* (New York: Turtle Bay, 1993), p. 21; see J. Gerald Kennedy, *Imagining Paris* (New Haven: Yale University Press, 1993).

3. Jay Martin, *Always Merry and Bright* (Santa Barbara: Capra Press, 1978), p. 139; Robert Ferguson, *Henry Miller* (New York: W. W. Norton, 1991), p. 149; Mary V. Dearborn, *Henry Miller* (New York: Simon & Schuster, 1991), p. 108; and the account in Louise DeSalvo, *Conceived with Malice* (New York: Dutton, 1994).

4. Ferguson, p. 81.

5. Jong, p. 55.

6. Martin, p. 18, p. 129; Dearborn, pp. 100–1; Henry Miller, *My Life and Times* (New York: Playboy Press, n.d.), p. 33.

7. For accounts of this event, see Martin, p. 520; Dearborn, p. 323; Miller, *My Life and Times,* p. 50.

8. Henry Miller, *Moloch* (New York: Grove Press, 1992), p. 8.

9. Ferguson, p. 208.

10. Alfred Perles, *My Friend Henry Miller* (New York: John Day, 1956), p. 70; Wambly Bald quoted in Ferguson, pp. 210–11.

11. See the account in Perles.

12. Perles, pp. 70–1.

13. Perles, p. 70.

14. Perles, p. 72.

15. See Noel Riley Fitch, "The Literate Passion of Anaïs Nin & Henry Miller," in Whitney Chadwick and Isabelle de Courtivron, eds., *Significant Others* (New York: Thames and Hudson, 1993), pp. 155–72.

16. Fitch, p. 155; see the account of Miller's writing *Crazy Cock* in DeSalvo.

17. Anaïs Nin, *Henry and June* (New York: Harcourt Brace Jovanovich, 1986), p. 6.

18. Anaïs Nin, *Ladders to Fire,* in *Cities of the Interior* (Athens: Swallow Press/Ohio University Press, 1959, 1975), p. 48.

19. See Dearborn, p. 128, p. 149.

20. Miller, *Moloch,* p. 65.
21. Ferguson, p. 69.
22. Perles, p. 112.
23. Ferguson, p. 181.
24. Martin, p. 303; Dearborn, p. 175.
25. Jong, p. 132.
26. Martin, p. 303.
27. Perles, p. 104.
28. Martin, p. 303.
29. Perles, p. 104; Dearborn, p. 173.
30. Perles, p. 142; Cendrars's review is provided in George Wickes, ed., *Henry Miller and the Critics* (Carbondale: Southern Illinois University Press, 1963).
31. Perles, p. 171; Ferguson, p. 346.
32. Dearborn, p. 241.
33. Perles, pp. 205–6.
34. Ferguson, p. 344.
35. Ferguson, p. 345.
36. Ferguson, p. 348.
37. Ferguson, p. 350.
38. Millett quoted in Jong, p. 29.
39. Anaïs Nin, *The Diary of Anaïs Nin: 1931–1934,* Volume One, ed. and with an Introduction by Gunther Stuhlmann (New York: Harcourt Brace Jovanovich, 1966), p. 66.
40. Dearborn, p. 34.
41. Jong, p. 26.
42. Jong, p. 26.

TROPIC
OF
CANCER

I am living at the Villa Borghese. There is not a crumb of dirt anywhere, nor a chair misplaced. We are all alone here and we are dead.

Last night Boris discovered that he was lousy. I had to shave his armpits and even then the itching did not stop. How can one get lousy in a beautiful place like this? But no matter. We might never have known each other so intimately, Boris and I, had it not been for the lice.

Boris has just given me a summary of his views. He is a weather prophet. The weather will continue bad, he says. There will be more calamities, more death, more despair. Not the slightest indication of a change anywhere. The cancer of time is eating us away. Our heroes have killed themselves, or are killing themselves. The hero, then, is not Time, but Timelessness. We must get in step, a lock step, toward the prison of death. There is no escape. The weather will not change.

It is now the fall of my second year in Paris. I was sent here for a reason I have not yet been able to fathom.

I have no money, no resources, no hopes. I am the happiest man alive. A year ago, six months ago, I thought that I was an artist. I no longer think about it, I *am*. Everything that was literature has fallen from me. There are no more books to be written, thank God.

This then? This is not a book. This is libel, slander, defamation of character. This is not a book, in the ordinary sense of the word. No, this is a prolonged insult, a gob of spit in the face of Art, a kick in the pants to God, Man, Destiny, Time, Love, Beauty . . . what you will. I am going to sing for you, a little off key perhaps, but I will sing. I will sing while you croak, I will dance over your dirty corpse. . . .

To sing you must first open your mouth. You must have a pair of lungs, and a little knowledge of music. It is not necessary to have an accordion, or a guitar. The essential thing is to *want* to sing. This then is a song. I am singing.

It is to you, Tania, that I am singing. I wish that I could sing better, more melodiously, but then perhaps you would never have consented to listen to me. You have heard the others sing and they have left you cold. They sang too beautifully, or not beautifully enough.

It is the twenty-somethingth of October. I no longer keep track of the date. Would you say—my dream of the 14th November last? There are intervals, but they are between dreams, and there is no consciousness of them left. The world around me is dissolving, leaving here and there spots of time. The world is a cancer eating itself away. . . . I am thinking that when the great silence descends upon all and everywhere music will at last triumph. When into the womb of time everything is again withdrawn chaos will be restored and chaos is the score upon which reality is written. You, Tania, are my chaos. It is why I sing. It is not even I, it is the world dying, shedding the skin of time. I am still alive, kicking in your womb, a reality to write upon.

Dozing off. The physiology of love. The whale with his six foot penis, in repose. The bat—*penis libre*. Animals with a bone in the penis. Hence, *a bone on.* . . . "Happily," says Gourmont, "the bony structure is lost in man." Happily? Yes, happily. Think of the human race walking around with a bone on. The kangaroo has a double penis—one for weekdays and one for holidays. Dozing. A letter from a female asking if I have found a title for my book. Title? To be sure: "Lovely Lesbians."

Your anecdotal life! A phrase of M. Borowski's. It is on Wednesdays that I have lunch with Borowski. His wife, who is a dried-up cow, officiates. She is studying English now—her favourite word is "filthy." You can see immediately what a pain in the ass the Borowskis are. But wait. . . .

Borowski wears corduroy suits and plays the accordion. An invincible combination, especially when you consider that he is not a bad artist. He puts on that he is a Pole, but he is not, of course. He is a Jew, Borowski, and his father was a philatelist. In fact, almost all Montparnasse is Jewish, or half Jewish, which is worse. There's Carl and Paula, and Cronstadt and Boris, and Tania and Sylvester, and Moldorf and Lucille. All except Fillmore. Henry Jordan Oswald turned out to be a Jew also. Louis Nichols is a Jew. Even Van Norden and Chérie are Jewish. Frances Blake is a Jew, or a Jewess. Titus is a Jew. The Jews then are snowing me under. I am writing this for my friend Carl whose father is a Jew. All this is important to understand.

Of them all the loveliest Jew is Tania, and for her sake I too would become a Jew. Why not? I already speak like a Jew. And I am as ugly as a Jew. Besides, who hates the Jews more than the Jew?

Twilight hour. Indian blue water of glass, trees glistening and liquescent. The rails fall away into the canal at Jaurès. The long caterpillar with lacquered sides dips like a roller-coaster. It is not Paris. It is not Coney Island. It is a crepuscular melange of all the cities of Europe and Central America. The railroad yards below me, the tracks black, webby, not ordered by the engineer but cataclysmic in design, like those gaunt fissures in the polar ice which the camera registers in degrees of black.

Food is one of the things I enjoy tremendously. And in this beautiful Villa Borghese there is scarcely ever any evidence of food. It is positively appalling at times. I have asked Boris time and again to order bread for breakfast, but he always forgets. He goes out for breakfast, it seems. And when he comes back he is picking his teeth and there is a little egg hanging from his goatee. He eats in the restaurant, out of consideration for me. He says it hurts to eat a big meal and have me watch him.

I like Van Norden but I do not share his opinion of himself. I do not agree, for instance, that he is a philosopher, or a thinker. He is cunt-struck, that's all. And he will never be a writer. Nor will Sylvester ever be a writer, though his name blaze in 50,000 candle power red lights. The only writers about me for whom I have any respect, at present, are Carl and Boris. They are possessed. They glow inwardly with a white flame. They are mad and tone deaf. They are sufferers.

Moldorf, on the other hand, who suffers too in his peculiar way, is not mad. Moldorf is word drunk. He has no veins or blood-vessels, no heart or kidneys. He is a portable trunk filled with innumerable drawers and in the drawers are labels written out in white ink, brown ink, red ink, blue ink, vermilion, saffron, mauve, sienna, apricot, turquoise, onyx, Anjou, herring, Corona, verdigris, gorgonzola. . . .

I have moved the typewriter into the next room where I can see myself in the mirror as I write.

Tania is like Irene. She expects fat letters. But there is another Tania, a Tania like a big seed, who scatters pollen everywhere—or, let us say, a little bit of Tolstoi, a stable scene in which the foetus is dug up. Tania is a fever, too—*les voies urinaires,* Café de la Liberté, Place des Vosges, bright neckties on the Boulevard Montparnasse, dark bathrooms, Porto Sec, Abdullah cigarettes, the adagio sonata pathétique, aural amplificators, anecdotal seances, burnt sienna breasts, heavy garters, what time is it, golden pheasants stuffed with chestnuts, taffeta fingers, vaporish twilights turning to ilex, acromegaly, cancer and delirium, warm veils, poker chips, carpets of blood and soft thighs. Tania says so that every one may hear: "I love him!" And while Boris scalds himself with whisky she says: "Sit down here! O Boris . . . *Russia* . . . what'll I do? I'm bursting with it!"

At night when I look at Boris' goatee lying on the pillow I get hysterical. O Tania, where now is that warm cunt of yours, those fat, heavy garters, those soft, bulging thighs? There is a bone in my prick six inches long. I will ream out every wrinkle in your cunt, Tania, big with seed. I will send you home to your Sylvester with an ache in your belly and your womb turned inside out. Your Sylvester! Yes, he knows how to build a fire, but I know how to inflame a cunt. I shoot hot bolts into you, Tania, I make your ovaries incandescent. Your Sylvester is a little jealous now? He feels something, does he? He feels the remnants of my big prick. I have set the shores a little wider, I have ironed out the wrinkles. After me you can take on stallions, bulls, rams, drakes, St. Bernards. You can stuff toads, bats, lizards up your rectum. You can shit arpeggios if you like, or string a zither across your navel. I am fucking you, Tania, so that you'll stay fucked. And if you are afraid of being fucked publicly I will fuck you privately. I will tear off a few hairs from your cunt and paste them on Boris' chin. I will bite into your clitoris and spit out two franc pieces. . . .

Indigo sky swept clear of fleecy clouds, gaunt trees infinitely extended, their black boughs gesticulating like a sleep-walker. Sombre, spectral trees, their trunks pale as cigar ash. A silence supreme and altogether European. Shutters drawn, shops barred. A red glow here and there to mark a tryst. Brusque the façades, almost forbidding; immaculate except for the splotches of shadow cast by the trees. Passing by the Orangerie I am reminded of another Paris, the Paris of Maugham, of Gauguin, Paris of George Moore. I think of that terrible Spaniard who was then startling the world with his acrobatic leaps from style to style. I think of Spengler and of his terrible pronunciamentos, and I wonder if style, style in the grand manner, is done for. I say that my mind is occupied with these thoughts, but it is not true; it is only later, after I have crossed the Seine, after I have put behind me the carnival of lights, that I allow my mind to play with these ideas. For the moment I can think of nothing—except that I am a sentient being stabbed by the miracle of these waters that reflect a forgotten world. All along the banks the trees lean heavily over the tarnished mirror; when the wind rises and fills them with a rustling murmur they will shed a few tears and shiver as the water swirls by. I am suffocated by it. No one to whom I can communicate even a fraction of my feelings. . . .

The trouble with Irène is that she has a valise instead of a cunt. She wants fat letters to shove in her valise. Immense, *avec des choses inouïes*. Llona now, she had a cunt. I know because she sent us some hairs from down below. Llona—a wild ass snuffing pleasure out of the wind. On every high hill she played the harlot—and

sometimes in telephone booths and toilets. She bought a
bed for King Carol and a shaving mug with his initials on
it. She lay in Tottenham Court Road with her dress pulled
up and fingered herself. She used candles, Roman candles, and door knobs. Not a prick in the land big enough
for her . . . *not one.* Men went inside her and curled up.
She wanted extension pricks, self-exploding rockets, hot
boiling oil made of wax and creosote. She would cut off
your prick and keep it inside her forever, if you gave her
permission. One cunt out of a million, Llona! A laboratory cunt and no litmus paper that could take her color.
She was a liar, too, this Llona. She never bought a bed for
her King Carol. She crowned him with a whiskey bottle
and her tongue was full of lice and tomorrows. Poor
Carol, he could only curl up inside her and die. She drew
a breath and he fell out—like a dead clam.

Enormous, fat letters, *avec des choses inouïes.* A valise
without straps. A hole without a key. She had a German
mouth, French ears, Russian ass. Cunt international.
When the flag waved it was red all the way back to the
throat. You entered on the Boulevard Jules-Ferry and
came out at the Porte de la Villette. You dropped your
sweetbreads into the tumbrils—red tumbrils with two
wheels, naturally. At the confluence of the Ourcq and
Marne, where the water sluices through the dykes and lies
like glass under the bridges. Llona is lying there now and
the canal is full of glass and splinters; the mimosas weep,
and there is a wet, foggy fart on the windowpanes. One
cunt out of a million Llona! All cunt and a glass ass in
which you can read the history of the Middle Ages.

It is the caricature of a man which Moldorf first presents. Thyroid eyes. Michelin lips. Voice like pea-soup.
Under his vest he carries a little pear. However you look
at him it is always the same panorama; netsuke snuffbox,
ivory handle, chess piece, fan, temple motif. He has fer-
mented so long now that he is amorphous. Yeast de-
spoiled of its vitamins. Vase without a rubber plant.

The females were sired twice in the 9th century, and
again during the Renaissance. He was carried through the
great dispersions under yellow bellies and white. Long
before the Exodus a Tatar spat in his blood.

His dilemma is that of the dwarf. With his pineal eye he sees in silhouette projected on a screen of incommensurable size. His voice, synchronized to the shadow of a pinhead, intoxicates him. He hears a roar where others hear only a squeak.

There is his mind. It is an amphitheatre in which the actor gives a protean performance. Moldorf, multiform and unerring, goes through his roles—clown, juggler, contortionist, priest, lecher, mountebank. The amphitheatre is too small. He puts dynamite to it. The audience is drugged. He scotches it.

I am trying ineffectually to approach Moldorf. It is like trying to approach God, for Moldorf *is* God—he has never been anything else. I am merely putting down words. . . .

I have had opinions about him which I have discarded; I have had other opinions which I am revising. I have pinned him down only to find that it was not a dung-beetle I had in my hands, but a dragonfly. He has offended me by his coarseness and then overwhelmed me with his delicacy. He has been voluble to the point of suffocation, then quiet as the Jordan.

When I see him trotting forward to greet me, his little paws outstretched, his eyes perspiring, I feel that I am meeting. . . . No, this is not the way to go about it!

"Comme un oeuf dansant sur un jet d'eau."

He has only one cane—a mediocre one. In his pocket scraps of paper containing prescriptions for Weltschmerz. He is cured now, and the little German girl who washed his feet is breaking her heart. It is like Mr. Nonentity toting his Gujurati dictionary everywhere. *"Inevitable for every one"*—meaning, no doubt, *indispensable*. Borowski would find all this incomprehensible. Borowski has a different cane for each day in the week, and one for Easter.

We have so many points in common that it is like looking at myself in a cracked mirror.

I have been looking over my manuscripts, pages scrawled with revisions. Pages of *literature*. This frightens me a little. It is so much like Moldorf. Only I am a gentile, and gentiles have a different way of suffering. They suffer without neuroses and, as Sylvester says, a man who has never been afflicted with a neurosis does not know the meaning of suffering.

I recall distinctly how I enjoyed my suffering. It was like taking a cub to bed with you. Once in a while he clawed you—and then you really were frightened. Ordinarily you had no fear—you could always turn him loose, or chop his head off.

There are people who cannot resist the desire to get into a cage with wild beasts and be mangled. They go in even without revolver or whip. Fear makes them fearless. . . For the Jew the world is a cage filled with wild beasts. The door is locked and he is there without whip or revolver. His courage is so great that he does not even smell the dung in the corner. The spectators applaud but he does not hear. The drama, he thinks, is going on inside the cage. The cage, he thinks, is the world. Standing there alone and helpless, the door locked, he finds that the lions do not understand his language. Not one lion has ever heard of Spinoza. Spinoza? Why they can't even get their teeth into him. "Give us meat!" they roar, while he stands there petrified, his ideas frozen, his *Weltanschauung* a trapeze out of reach. A single blow of the lion's paw and his cosmogony is smashed.

The lions, too, are disappointed. They expected blood, bones, gristle, sinews. They chew and chew, but the words are chicle and chicle is indigestible. Chicle is a base over which you sprinkle sugar, pepsin, thyme, licorice. Chicle, when it is gathered by chicleros, is O. K. The chicleros came over on the ridge of a sunken continent. They brought with them an algebraic language. In the Arizona desert they met the Mongols of the North, glazed like eggplants. Time shortly after the earth had taken its gyroscopic lean—when the Gulf Stream was parting ways with the Japanese current. In the heart of the soil they found tufa rock. They embroidered the very bowels of the earth with their language. They ate one another's entrails and the forest closed in on them, on their bones and skulls, on their lace tufa. Their language was lost. Here and there one still finds the remnants of a menagerie, a brain plate covered with figures.

* * *

What has all this to do with you, Moldorf? The word in your mouth is anarchy. Say it, Moldorf, I am waiting for it. Nobody knows, when we shake hands, the rivers that pour through our sweat. Whilst you are framing your words, your lips half-parted, the saliva gurgling in your cheeks, I have jumped halfway across Asia. Were I to take your cane, mediocre as it is, and poke a little hole in your side, I could collect enough material to fill the British Museum. We stand on five minutes and devour centuries. You are the sieve through which my anarchy strains, resolves itself into words. Behind the word is chaos. Each word a stripe, a bar, but there are not and never will be enough bars to make the mesh.

In my absence the window-curtains have been hung. They have the appearance of Tyrolian tablecloths dipped in lysol. The room sparkles. I sit on the bed in a daze, thinking about man before his birth. Suddenly bells begin to toll, a weird, unearthly music, as if I had been translated to the steppes of Central Asia. Some ring out with a long, lingering roll, some erupt drunkenly, maudlinly. And now it is quiet again, except for a last note that barely grazes the silence of the night—just a faint, high gong snuffed out like a flame.

I have made a silent compact with myself not to change a line of what I write. I am not interested in perfecting my thoughts, nor my actions. Beside the perfection of Turgeniev I put the perfection of Dostoievski. (Is there anything more perfect than *The Eternal Husband*?) Here, then, in one and the same medium, we have two kinds of perfection. But in Van Gogh's letters there is a perfection beyond either of these. It is the triumph of the individual over art.

There is only one thing which interests me vitally now, and that is the recording of all that which is omitted in books. Nobody, so far as I can see, is making use of those elements in the air which give direction and motivation to our lives. Only the killers seem to be extracting from life some satisfactory measure of what they are putting into it. The age demands violence, but we are getting only abortive explosions. Revolutions are nipped in the bud, or else succeed too quickly. Passion is quickly exhausted. Men fall back on ideas, *comme d'habitude*. Nothing is proposed that can last more than twenty-four hours. We are living a million lives in the space of a generation. In the study of entomology, or of deep sea life, or cellular activity, we derive more. . . .

The telephone interrupts this thought which I should never have been able to complete. Some one is coming to rent the apartment . . .

It looks as though it were finished, my life at the Villa Borghese. Well, I'll take up these pages and move on. Things will happen elsewhere. Things are always happening. It seems wherever I go there is drama. People are like lice—they get under your skin and bury themselves there. You scratch and scratch until the blood comes, but you can't get permanently deloused. Everywhere I go people are making a mess of their lives. Everyone has his private tragedy. It's in the blood now—misfortune, ennui, grief, suicide. The atmosphere is saturated with disaster, frustration, futility. Scratch and scratch—until there's no skin left. However, the effect upon me is exhilarating. Instead of being discouraged, or depressed, I enjoy it. I am crying for more and more disasters, for bigger calamities, for grander failures. I want the whole world to be out of whack, I want every one to scratch himself to death.

So fast and furiously am I compelled to live now that there is scarcely time to record even these fragmentary notes. After the telephone call, a gentleman and his wife arrived. I went upstairs to lie down during the transaction. Lay there wondering what my next move would be. Surely not to go back to the fairy's bed and toss about all night flicking bread crumbs with my toes. That puking little bastard! If there's anything worse than being a fairy it's being a miser. A timid, quaking little bugger who lived in constant fear of going broke some day—the 18th of March perhaps, or the 25th of May precisely. Coffee without milk or sugar. Bread without butter. Meat without gravy, or no meat at all. Without this and without that! The dirty little miser! Open the bureau drawer one day and find money hidden away in a sock. Over two thousand francs—and checks that he hadn't even cashed. Even that I wouldn't have minded so much if there weren't always coffee grounds in my beret and garbage on the floor, to say nothing of the cold cream jars and the greasy towels and the sink always stopped up. I tell you, the little bastard he smelled bad—except when he doused himself with cologne. His ears were dirty, his eyes were dirty, his ass was dirty. He was double-jointed, asthmatic, lousy, picayune, morbid. I could have forgiven him everything if only he had handed me a decent breakfast! But a man who has two thousand francs hidden away in a dirty sock and refuses to wear a clean shirt or smear a little butter over his bread, such a man is not just a fairy, nor even just a miser—he's an imbecile!

But that's neither here nor there, about the fairy. I'm keeping an ear open as to what's going on downstairs. It's a Mr. Wren and his wife who have called to look at the apartment. They're talking about taking it. Only *talking* about it, thank God. Mrs. Wren has a loose laugh—complications ahead. Now *Mister* Wren is talking. His voice is raucous, scraping, booming, a heavy blunt weapon that wedges its way through flesh and bone and cartilage.

Boris calls me down to be introduced. He is rubbing his hands, like a pawnbroker. They are talking about a story Mr. Wren wrote, a story about a spavined horse.

"But I thought Mr. Wren was a painter?"

"To be sure," says Boris, with a twinkle in his eye, "but in the wintertime he writes. And he writes well . . . remarkably well."

I try to induce Mr. Wren to talk, to say something, anything, to talk about the spavined horse, if necessary. But Mr. Wren is almost inarticulate. When he essays to speak of those dreary months with the pen he becomes unintelligible. Months and months he spends before setting a word to paper. (And there are only three months of winter!) What does he cogitate all those months and months of winter? So help me God, I can't see this guy as a writer. Yet Mrs. Wren says that when he sits down to it the stuff *just pours out*.

The talk drifts. It is difficult to follow Mr. Wren's mind because he says nothing. *He thinks as he goes along*—so Mrs. Wren puts it. Mrs. Wren puts everything about Mr. Wren in the loveliest light. "He thinks as he goes

along"—very charming, charming indeed, as Borowski
would say, but really very painful, particularly when the
thinker is nothing but a spavined horse.

Boris hands me money to buy liquor. Going for the liquor I am already intoxicated. I know just how I'll begin
when I get back to the house. Walking down the street it
commences, the grand speech inside me that's gurgling
like Mrs. Wren's loose laugh. Seems to me she had a
slight edge on already. Listens beautifully when she's
tight. Coming out of the wine-shop I hear the urinal gurgling. Everything is loose and splashy. I want Mrs. Wren
to listen . . .

Boris is rubbing his hands again. Mr. Wren is still stuttering and spluttering. I have a bottle between my legs
and I'm shoving the corkscrew in. Mrs. Wren has her
mouth parted expectantly. The wine is splashing between
my legs, the sun is splashing through the bay window,
and inside my veins there is a bubble and splash of a
thousand crazy things that commence to gush out of me
now pell-mell. I'm telling them everything that comes to
mind, everything that was bottled up inside me and which
Mrs. Wren's loose laugh has somehow released. With that
bottle between my legs and the sun splashing through the
window I experience once again the splendor of those
miserable days when I first arrived in Paris, a bewildered,
poverty-stricken individual who haunted the streets like a
ghost at a banquet. Everything comes back to me in a
rush—the toilets that wouldn't work, the prince who
shined my shoes, the Cinema Splendide where I slept on
the patron's overcoat, the bars in the window, the feeling
of suffocation, the fat cockroaches, the drinking and carousing that went on between times, Rose Cannaque and
Naples dying in the sunlight. Dancing the streets on an
empty belly and now and then calling on strange
people—Madame Delorme, for instance. How I ever got
to Madame Delorme's, I can't imagine any more. But I
got there, got inside somehow, past the butler, past the
maid with her little white apron, got right inside the palace with my corduroy trousers and my hunting jacket—
and not a button on my fly. Even now I can taste again
the golden ambiance of that room where Madame
Delorme sat upon a throne in her mannish rig, the gold-

fish in the bowls, the maps of the ancient world, the beautifully bound books; I can feel again her heavy hand resting upon my shoulder, frightening me a little with her
heavy Lesbian air. More comfortable down below in that
thick stew pouring into the Gare St. Lazare, the whores in
the doorways, seltzer bottles on every table; a thick tide
of semen flooding the gutters. Nothing better, between
five and seven than to be pushed around in that throng, to
follow a leg or a beautiful bust, to move along with the
tide and everything whirling in your brain. A weird sort
of contentment in those days. No appointments, no invi-
tations for dinner, no program, no dough. The golden period, when I had not a single friend. Each morning the
dreary walk to the American Express, and each morning
the inevitable answer from the clerk. Dashing here and
there like a bedbug, gathering butts now and then, sometimes furtively, sometimes brazenly; sitting down on a
bench and squeezing my guts to stop the gnawing, or
walking through the Jardin des Tuileries and getting an
erection looking at the dumb statues. Or wandering along
the Seine at night, wandering and wandering, and going
mad with the beauty of it, the trees leaning to, the broken
images in the water, the rush of the current under the
bloody lights of the bridges, the women sleeping in doorways, sleeping on newspapers, sleeping in the rain; everywhere the musty porches of the cathedrals and beggars
and lice and old hags full of St. Vitus' dance; pushcarts
stacked up like wine barrels in the side streets, the smell
of berries in the market-place and the old church surrounded with vegetables and blue arc lights, the gutters
slippery with garbage and women in satin pumps staggering through the filth and vermin at the end of an all-night
souse. The Place St. Sulpice, so quiet and deserted, where
toward midnight there came every night the woman with
the busted umbrella and the crazy veil; every night she
slept there on a bench under her torn umbrella, the ribs
hanging down, her dress turning green, her bony fingers
and the odor of decay oozing from her body; and in the
morning I'd be sitting there myself, taking a quiet snooze
in the sunshine, cursing the goddamned pigeons gathering
up the crumbs everywhere. St. Sulpice! The fat belfries,
the garish posters over the door, the candles flaming in-

side. The Square so beloved of Anatole France, with that
drone and buzz from the altar, the splash of the fountain,
the pigeons cooing, the crumbs disappearing like magic
and only a dull rumbling in the hollow of the guts. Here
I would sit day after day thinking of Germaine and that
dirty little street near the Bastille where she lived, and
that buzz-buzz going on behind the altar, the buses whiz-
zing by, the sun beating down into the asphalt and the asphalt working into me and Germaine, into the asphalt and
all Paris in the big fat belfries.

And it was down the Rue Bonaparte that only a year
before Mona and I used to walk every night, after we had
taken leave of Borowski. St. Sulpice not meaning much
to me then, nor anything in Paris. Washed out with talk.
Sick of faces. Fed up with cathedrals and squares and me-
nageries and what not. Picking up a book in the red bed-
room and the cane chair uncomfortable; tired of sitting on
my ass all day long, tired of red wallpaper, tired of seeing
so many people jabbering away about nothing. The red
bedroom and the trunk always open; her gowns lying
about in a delirium of disorder. The red bedroom with my
goloshes and canes, the notebooks I never touched, the
manuscripts lying cold and dead. Paris! Meaning the Café
Select, the Dôme, the Flea Market, the American Express.
Paris! Meaning Borowski's canes, Borowski's hats,
Borowski's gouaches, Borowski's prehistoric fish—and
prehistoric jokes. In that Paris of '28 only one night
stands out in my memory—the night before sailing for
America. A rare night, with Borowski slightly pickled
and a little disgusted with me because I'm dancing with
every slut in the place. But we're leaving in the morning!
That's what I tell every cunt I grab hold of—*leaving in
the morning!* That's what I'm telling the blonde with
agate-colored eyes. And while I'm telling her she takes
my hand and sqeeezes it between her legs. In the lavatory
I stand before the bowl with a tremendous erection; it
seems light and heavy at the same time, like a piece of
lead with wings on it. And while I'm standing there like
that two cunts sail in—Americans. I greet them cordially,
prick in hand. They give me a wink and pass on. In the
vestibule, as I'm buttoning my fly, I notice one of them
waiting for her friend to come out of the can. The music

is still playing and maybe Mona'll be coming to fetch me, or Borowski with his gold-knobbed cane, but I'm in her arms now and she has hold of me and I don't care who comes or what happens. We wriggle into the cabinet and there I stand her up, slap up against the wall, and I try to get it into her but it won't work and so we sit down on the seat and try it that way but it won't work either. No matter how we try it it won't work. And all the while she's got hold of my prick, she's clutching it like a life-saver, but it's no use, we're too hot, too eager. The music is still playing and so we waltz out of the cabinet into the vestibule again and as we're dancing there in the shit-house I come all over her beautiful gown and she's sore as hell about it. I stumble back to the table and there's Borowski with his ruddy face and Mona with her disap-proving eye. And Borowski says "Let's all go to Brussels tomorrow," and we agree, and when we get back to the hotel I vomit all over the place, in the bed, in the wash-bowl, over the suits and gowns and the goloshes and canes and the notebooks I never touched and the manu-scripts lying cold and dead.

A few months later. The same hotel, the same room. We look out on the courtyard where the bicycles are parked, and there is the little room up above, under the at-tic, where some smart young Alec played the phonograph all day long and repeated clever little things at the top of his voice. I say "we" but I'm getting ahead of myself, be-cause Mona has been away a long time and it's just today that I'm meeting her at the Gare St. Lazare. Toward eve-ning I'm standing there with my face squeezed between the bars, but there's no Mona, and I read the cable over again but it doesn't help any. I go back to the Quarter and just the same I put away a hearty meal. Strolling past the Dôme and a little later suddenly I see a pale, heavy face and burning eyes—and the little velvet suit that I always adored because under the soft velvet there were always her warm breasts, the marble legs, cool, firm, muscular. She rises up out of a sea of faces and embraces me, em-braces me passionately—a thousand eyes, noses, fingers, legs, bottles, windows, purses, saucers all glaring at us and we in each other's arms oblivious. I sit down beside her and she talks—a flood of talk. Wild consumptive notes of histeria, perversion, leprosy. I hear not a word because she is beautiful and I love her and now I am happy and willing to die.

We walk down the Rue du Château, looking for Eugene. Walk over the railroad bridge where I used to watch the trains pulling out and feel all sick inside wondering where the hell she could be. Everything soft and enchanting as we walk over the bridge. Smoke coming up between our legs, the tracks creaking, semaphores in our blood. I feel her body close to mine—all mine now—and I stop to rub my hands over the warm velvet. Everything around us is crumbling, crumbling and the warm body under the warm velvet is aching for me . . .

Back in the very same room and fifty francs to the good, thanks to Eugene. I look out on the court but the phonograph is silent. The trunk is open and her things are lying around everywhere just as before. She lies down on the bed with her clothes on. Once, twice, three times, four times . . . I'm afraid she'll go mad . . . in bed, under the blankets, how good to feel her body again! But for how long? Will it last this time? Already I have a presentiment that it won't.

She talks to me so feverishly—as if there will be no tomorrow. "Be quiet, Mona! Just look at me . . . *don't talk!*" Finally she drops off and I pull my arm from under her. My eyes close. Her body is there beside me . . . it will be there till morning surely . . . It was in February I pulled out of the harbor in a blinding snowstorm. The last glimpse I had of her was in the window waving good-bye to me. A man standing on the other side of the street, at the corner, his hat pulled down over his eyes, his jowls resting on his lapels. A fœtus watching me. A fœtus with a cigar in its mouth. Mona at the window waving good-bye. White heavy face, hair streaming wild. And now it is a heavy bedroom, breathing regularly through the gills, sap still oozing from between her legs, a warm feline odor and her hair in my mouth. My eyes are closed. We breathe warmly into each other's mouth. Close together, America three thousand miles away. I never want to see it again. To have her here in bed with me, breathing on me, her hair in my mouth—I count that something of a miracle. Nothing can happen now till morning . . .

I wake from a deep slumber to look at her. A pale light is trickling in. I look at her beautiful wild hair. I feel something crawling down my neck. I look at her again, closely. Her hair is alive! I pull back the sheet—more of them. They are swarming over the pillow.

It is a little after daybreak. We pack hurriedly and sneak out of the hotel. The cafés are still closed. We walk, and as we walk we scratch ourselves. The day opens in milky whiteness, streaks of salmon-pink sky, snails leaving their shells. Paris. Paris. Everything happens here. Old, crumbling walls and the pleasant sound of water running in the urinals. Men licking their moustaches at the bar. Shutters going up with a bang and little streams purling in the gutters. *Amer Picon* in huge scarlet letters. *Zigzag.* Which way will we go and why or where or what?

Mona is hungry, her dress is thin. Nothing but evening wraps, bottles of perfume, barbaric earrings, bracelets, depilatories. We sit down in a billiard parlor on the Avenue due Maine and order hot coffee. The toilet is out of order. We shall have to sit some time before we can go to another hotel. Meanwhile we pick bedbugs out of each other's hair. Nervous. Mona is losing her temper. Must have a bath. Must have this. Must have that. Must, must, must . . .

"How much money have you left?"

Money! Forgot all about that.

Hôtel des Etats-Unis. An *ascenseur.* We go to bed in broad daylight. When we get up it is dark and the first thing to do is to raise enough dough to send a cable to America. A cable to the fœtus with the long juicy cigar in his mouth. Meanwhile there is the Spanish woman on the Boulevard Raspail—she's always good for a warm meal. By morning something will happen. At least we're going to bed together. No more bedbugs now. The rainy season has commenced. The sheets are immaculate . . .

A new life opening up for me at the Villa Borghese. Only ten o'clock and we have already had breakfast and been out for a walk. We have an Elsa here with us now. "Step softly for a few days," cautions Boris.

The day begins gloriously: a bright sky, a fresh wind, the houses newly washed. On our way to the Post Office Boris and I discussed the book. *The Last Book*—which is going to be written anonymously.

A new day is beginning. I felt it this morning as we stood before one of Dufresne's glistening canvases, a sort of *déjeuner intime* in the 13th century, *sans vin*. A fine, fleshy nude, solid, vibrant, pink as a fingernail, with glistening billows of flesh; all the secondary characteristics, and a few of the primary. A body that sings, that has the moisture of dawn. A still life, only nothing is still, nothing dead here. The table creaks with food; it is so heavy it is sliding out of the frame. A 13th century repast—with all the jungle notes that he has memorized so well. A family of gazelles and zebras nipping the fronds of the palms.

And now we have Elsa. She was playing for us this morning while we were in bed. *Step softly for a few days* . . . Good! Elsa is the maid and I am the guest. And Boris is the big cheese. A new drama is beginning. I'm laughing to myself as I write this. He knows what is going to happen, that lynx, Boris. He has a nose for things too. *Step softly . . .*

Boris is on pins and needles. At any moment now his wife may appear on the scene. She weighs well over 180 pounds, that wife of his. And Boris is only a handful. There you have the situation. He tries to explain it to me on our way home at night. It is so tragic and so ridiculous at the same time that I am obliged to stop now and then and laugh in his face. "Why do you laugh so?" he says gently, and then he commences himself, with that whimpering, hysterical note in his voice, like a helpless wretch who realizes suddenly that no matter how many frock coats he puts on he will never make a man. He wants to run away, to take a new name. "She can have everything, that cow, if only she leaves me alone," he whines. But first the apartment has to be rented, and the deeds signed, and a thousand other details for which his frock coat will come in handy. But the size of her!—that's what really worries him. If we were to find her suddenly standing on the doorstep when we arrive he would faint—that's how much he respects her!

And so we've got to go easy with Elsa for a while. Elsa is only there to make breakfast—and to show the apartment.

But Elsa is already undermining me. That German blood. Those melancholy songs. Coming down the stairs this morning, with the fresh coffee in my nostrils, I was humming softly . . . *"Es wär' so schön gewesen."* For breakfast, that. And in a little while the English boy upstairs with his Bach. As Elsa says—"he needs a woman." And Elsa needs something too. I can feel it. I didn't say anything to Boris about it, but while he was cleaning his teeth this morning Elsa was giving me an earful about Berlin, about the women who look so attractive from behind, and when they turn round—*wow, syphilis!*

It seems to me that Elsa looks at me rather wistfully. Something left over from the breakfast table. This afternoon we were writing, back to back, in the studio. She had begun a letter to her lover who is in Italy. The machine got jammed. Boris had gone to look at a cheap room he will take as soon as the apartment is rented. There was nothing for it but to make love to Elsa. She wanted it. And yet I felt a little sorry for her. She had only written the first line to her lover—I read it out of the corner of my eye as I bent over her. But it couldn't be helped. That damned German music, so melancholy, so sentimental. It undermined me. And then her beady little eyes, so hot and sorrowful at the same time.

After it was over I asked her to play something for me.

She's a musician, Elsa, even though it sounded like broken pots and skulls clanking. She was weeping, too, as she played. I don't blame her. Everywhere the same thing, she says. Everywhere a man, and then she has to leave, and then there's an abortion and then a new job and then another man and nobody gives a fuck about her except to use her. All this after she's played Schumann for me—Schumann, that slobbery, sentimental German bastard! Somehow I feel sorry as hell for her and yet I don't give a damn. A cunt who can play as she does ought to have better sense than be tripped up by every guy with a big putz who happens to come along. But that Schumann gets into my blood. She's still sniffling, Elsa; but my mind is far away. I'm thinking of Tania and how she claws away at her adagio. I'm thinking of lots of things that are gone and buried. Thinking of a summer afternoon in Greenpoint when the Germans were romping over Belgium and we had not yet lost enough money to be concerned over the rape of a neutral country. A time when we were still innocent enough to listen to poets and to sit around a table in the twilight rapping for departed spirits. All that afternoon and evening the atmosphere is saturated with German music; the whole neighborhood is German, more German even than Germany. We were brought up on Schumann and Hugo Wolf and *Sauerkraut* and Kümmel and potato dumplings. Toward evening we're sitting around a big table with the curtains drawn and some fool two-headed wench is rapping for Jesus Christ. We're holding hands under the table and the dame next to me has two fingers in my fly. And finally we lie on the floor, behind the piano, while someone sings a dreary song. The air is stifling and her breath is boozy. The pedal is moving up and down, stiffly, automatically, a crazy, futile movement, like a tower of dung that takes twenty-seven years to build but keeps perfect time. I pull her over me with the sounding board in my ears; the room is dark and the carpet is sticky with the Kümmel that has been spilled about. Suddenly it seems as if the dawn were coming: it is like water purling over ice and the ice is blue with a rising mist, glaciers sunk in emerald green, chamois and antelope, golden groupers, sea-cows mouching along and the amber-jack leaping over the Arctic rim . . .

Elsa is sitting in my lap. Her eyes are like little belly-buttons. I look at her large mouth, so wet and glistening, and I cover it. She is humming now . . . *"Es wär' so schön gewesen . . ."* Ah, Elsa, you don't know yet what that means to me, your *Trompeter von Säckingen.* German Singing Societies, Schwaben Hall, the Turnverein . . . *links um, rechts um* . . . and then a whack over the ass with the end of a rope.

Ah, the Germans! They take you all over like an omnibus. They give you indigestion. In the same night one cannot visit the morgue, the infirmary, the zoo, the signs of the zodiac, the limbos of philosophy, the caves of epistemology, the arcana of Freud and Stekel . . . On the merry-go-round one doesn't get anywhere, whereas with the Germans one can go from Vega to Lope de Vega, all in one night, and come away as foolish as Parsifal.

As I say, the day began gloriously. It was only this morning that I became conscious again of this physical Paris of which I have been unaware for weeks. Perhaps it is because the book has begun to grow inside me. I am carrying it around with me everywhere. I walk through the streets big with child and the cops escort me across the street. Women get up to offer me their seats. Nobody pushes me rudely any more. I am pregnant. I waddle awkwardly; my big stomach pressed against the weight of the world.

It was this morning, on our way to the Post Office, that we gave the book its final *imprimatur*. We have evolved a new cosmogony of literature, Boris and I. It is to be a new Bible—*The Last Book.* All those who have anything to say will say it here—*anonymously*. We will exhaust the age. After us not another book—not for a generation, at least. Heretofore we had been digging in the dark, with nothing but instinct to guide us. Now we shall have a vessel in which to pour the vital fluid, a bomb which, when we throw it, will set off the world. We shall put into it enough to give the writers of tomorrow their plots, their dramas, their poems, their myths, their sciences. The world will be able to feed on it for a thousand years to

come. It is colossal in its pretentiousness. The thought of
it almost shatters us.

For a hundred years or more the world, *our* world, has
been dying. And not one man, in these last hundred years
or so, has been crazy enough to put a bomb up the ass-
hole of creation and set it off. The world is rotting away,
dying piecemeal. But it needs the *coup de grâce*, it needs
to be blown to smithereens. Not one of us is intact, and
yet we have in us all the continents and the seas between
the continents and the birds of the air. We are going to put
it down—the evolution of this world which has died but
which has not been buried. We are swimming on the face
of time and all else has drowned, is drowning, or will
drown. It will be enormous, the Book. There will be
oceans of space in which to move about, to perambulate,
to sing, to dance, to climb, to bathe, to leap somersaults,
to whine, to rape, to murder. A cathedral, a veritable cathedral, in the building of which everybody will assist
who has lost his identity. There will be masses for the
dead, prayers, confessions, hymns, a moaning and a chattering, a sort of murderous insouciance; there will be
rose windows and gargoyles and acolytes and pall-
bearers. You can bring your horses in a gallop through the
aisles. You can butt your head against the walls—they
won't give. You can pray in any language you choose,
or you can curl up outside and go to sleep. It will last a
thousand years, at least, this cathedral, and there will be
no replica, for the builders will be dead and the formula
too. We will have postcards made and organize tours. We
will build a town around it and set up a free commune.
We have no need for genius—genius is dead. We have
need for strong hands, for spirits who are willing to give
up the ghost and put on flesh . . .

The day is moving along at a fine tempo. I am up on
the balcony at Tania's place. The drama is going on down
below in the drawing-room. The dramatist is sick and
from above his scalp looks more scabrous than ever. His
hair is made of straw. His ideas are straw. His wife too is
straw, though still a little damp. The whole house is made
of straw. Here I am up on the balcony, waiting for Boris
to arrive. My last problem—*breakfast*—is gone. I have

simplified everything. If there are any new problems I can carry them in my rucksack, along with my dirty wash. I am throwing away all my sous. What need have I for money? I am a writing machine. The last screw has been added. The thing flows. Between me and the machine there is no estrangement. I am the machine . . .

They have not told me yet what the new drama is about, but I can sense it. They are trying to get rid of me. Yet here I am for my dinner, even a little earlier than they expected. I have informed them where to sit, what to do. I ask them politely if I shall be disturbing them, but what I really mean, and they know it well, is—*will you be disturbing me?* No, you blissful cockroaches, you are not disturbing me. You are *nourishing me*. I see you sitting there close together and I know there is a chasm between you. Your nearness is the nearness of planets. I am the void between you. If I withdraw there will be no void for you to swim in.

Tania is in a hostile mood—I can feel it. She resents my being filled with anything but herself. She knows by the very calibre of my excitement that her value is reduced to zero. She knows that I did not come this evening to fertilize her. She knows there is something germinating inside me which will destroy her. She is slow to realize, but she is realizing it . . .

Sylvester looks more content. He will embrace her this evening at the dinner table. Even now he is reading my manuscript, preparing to inflame my ego, to set my ego against hers.

It will be a strange gathering this evening. The stage is being set. I hear the tinkle of the glasses. The wine is being brought out. There will be bumpers downed and Sylvester who is ill will come out of his illness.

It was only last night, at Cronstadt's, that we projected this setting. It was ordained that the women must suffer, that off-stage there should be more terror and violence, more disasters, more suffering, more woe and misery.

It is no accident that propels people like us to Paris. Paris is simply an artificial stage, a revolving stage that permits the spectator to glimpse all phases of the conflict. Of itself Paris initiates no dramas. They are begun elsewhere. Paris is simply an obstetrical instrument that tears the living embryo from the womb and puts it in the incubator. Paris is the cradle of artificial births. Rocking here in the cradle each one slips back into his soil: one dreams back to Berlin, New York, Chicago, Vienna, Minsk. Vienna is never more Vienna than in Paris. Everything is raised to apotheosis. The cradle gives up its babes and new ones take their places. You can read here on the walls where Zola lived and Balzac and Dante and Strindberg and everybody who ever was anything. Everyone has lived here some time or other. Nobody *dies* here . . .

They are talking downstairs. Their language is symbolic. The word "struggle" enters into it. Sylvester, the sick dramatist, is saying: "I am just reading the *Manifesto.*" And Tania says—*"Whose?"* Yes, Tania, I heard you. I am up here writing about you and you divine it well. *Speak more,* that I may record you. For when we go to table I shall not be able to make any notes . . . Suddenly Tania remarks: "There is no prominent hall in this place." Now what does that mean, if anything?

They are putting up pictures now. That, too, is to impress me. See, they wish to say, we are at home here, living the conjugal life. Making the home attractive. We will even argue a little about the pictures, for *your* benefit. And Tania remarks again: "How the eye deceives one!" Ah, Tania, what things you say! Go on, carry out this farce a little longer. I am here to get the dinner you promised me; I enjoy this comedy tremendously. And now Sylvester takes the lead. He is trying to explain one of Borowski's *gouaches.* "Come here, do you see? One of them is playing the guitar; the other is holding a girl in his lap." True, Sylvester. Very true. Borowski and his guitars! The girls in his lap! Only one never quite knows what it is he holds in his lap, or whether it is really a man playing the guitar . . .

Soon Moldorf will be trotting in on all fours and Boris with that helpless little laugh of his. There will be a golden pheasant for dinner and Anjou and short fat cigars. And Cronstadt, when he gets the latest news, will live a little harder, a little brighter, for five minutes; and then he will subside again into the humus of his ideology and perhaps a poem will be born, a big golden bell of a poem without a tongue.

Had to knock off for an hour or so. Another customer to look at the apartment. Upstairs the bloody Englishman is practising his Bach. It is imperative now, when someone comes to look at the apartment, to run upstairs and ask the pianist to lay off for a while.

Elsa is telephoning the greengrocer. The plumber is putting a new seat on the toilet bowl. Whenever the doorbell rings Boris loses his equilibrium. In the excitement he has dropped his glasses; he is on his hands and knees, his frock coat is dragging the floor. It is a little like the Grand Guignol—the starving poet come to give the butcher's daughter lessons. Every time the phone rings the poet's mouth waters. Mallarmé sounds like a sirloin steak, Victor Hugo like *foie de veau*. Elsa is ordering a delicate little lunch for Boris—"a nice juicy little pork chop," she says. I see a whole flock of pink hams lying cold on the marble, wonderful hams cushioned in white fat. I have a terrific hunger though we've only had breakfast a few minutes ago—it's the lunch that I'll have to skip. It's only Wednesdays that I eat lunch, thanks to Borowski. Elsa is still telephoning—she forgot to order a piece of bacon. "Yes, a nice little piece of bacon, not too fatty," she says . . . *Zut alors!* Throw in some sweetbreads, throw in some mountain oysters and some psst clams! Throw in some fried liverwurst while you're at it; I could gobble up the fifteen hundred plays of Lope de Vega in one sitting.

It is a beautiful woman who has come to look at the apartment. An American, of course. I stand at the window with my back to her watching a sparrow pecking at a fresh turd. Amazing how easily the sparrow is provided for. It is raining a bit and the drops are very big. I used to think a bird couldn't fly if its wings got wet. Amazing how these rich dames come to Paris and find all the swell studios. A little talent and a big purse. If it rains they have a chance to display their brand new slickers. Food is nothing: sometimes they're so busy gadding about that they haven't time for lunch. Just a little sandwich, a wafer, at the Café de la Paix or the Ritz Bar. "For the daugh-

ters of gentlefolk only"—that's what it says at the old
studio of Puvis de Chavannes. Happened to pass there the
other day. Rich American cunts with paint boxes slung
over their shoulders. A little talent and a fat purse.

The sparrow is hopping frantically from one cobble-
stone to another. Truly herculean efforts, if you stop to examine closely. Everywhere there is food lying about—in
the gutter, I mean. The beautiful American woman is in-
quiring about the toilet. The toilet! Let me show you, you
velvet-snooted gazelle! The toilet, you say? *Par ici, Madame. N'oubliez pas que les places numérotées sont
réservées aux mutilés de la guerre.*

Boris is rubbing his hands—he is putting the finishing
touches to the deal. The dogs are barking in the courtyard; they bark like wolves. Upstairs Mrs. Melverness is
moving the furniture around. She had nothing to do all
day, she's bored; if she finds a crumb of dirt anywhere
she cleans the whole house. There's a bunch of green
grapes on the table and a bottle of wine—*vin de choix,* 10
degrees. "Yes," says Boris, "I could make a wash-stand
for you, just come here, please. Yes, this is the toilet.
There is one upstairs too, of course. Yes, a thousand
francs a month. You don't care much for Utrillo, you say?
No, this is it. It needs a new washer, that's all . . ."

She's going in a minute now. Boris hasn't even introduced me this time. The son of a bitch! Whenever it's a
rich cunt he forgets to introduce me. In a few minutes I'll
be able to sit down again and type. Somehow I don't feel
like it any more today. My spirit is dribbling away. She
may come back in an hour or so and take the chair from
under my ass. How the hell can a man write when he
doesn't know where he's going to sit the next half hour?
If this rich bastard takes the place I won't even have a
place to sleep. It's hard to know, when you're in such a
jam which is worse—not having a place to sleep or not
having a place to work. One can sleep almost anywhere,
but one must have a place to work. Even if it's not a mas-
terpiece you're doing. Even a bad novel requires a chair
to sit on and a bit of privacy. These rich cunts never think
of a thing like that. Whenever they want to lower their
soft behinds there's always a chair standing ready for
them . . .

* * *

Last night we left Sylvester and his God sitting together before the hearth. Sylvester in his pajamas, Moldorf with a cigar between his lips. Sylvester is peeling an orange. He puts the peel on the couch-cover. Moldorf draws closer to him. He asks permission to read again that brilliant parody *The Gates of Heaven*. We are getting ready to go, Boris and I. We are too gay for this sick-room atmosphere. Tania is going with us. She is gay because she is going to escape. Boris is gay because the God in Moldorf is dead. I am gay because it is another act we are going to put on.

Moldorf's voice is reverent. "Can I stay with you, Sylvester, until you go to bed?" He has been staying with him for the last six days, buying medicine, running errands for Tania, comforting, consoling, guarding the portals against malevolent intruders like Boris and his scallywags. He is like a savage who has discovered that his idol was mutilated during the night. There he sits, at the idol's feet, with breadfruit and grease and jabberwocky prayers. His voice goes out unctuously. His limbs are already paralyzed.

To Tania he speaks as if she were a priestess who had broken her vows. "You must make yourself worthy. Sylvester is your God." And while Sylvester is upstairs suffering (he has a little wheeze in the chest) the priest and the priestess devour the food. "You are polluting yourself," he says, the gravy dripping from his lips. He has the capacity for eating and suffering at the same time. While he fends off the dangerous ones he puts out his fat little paw and strokes Tania's hair. "I am beginning to fall in love with you. You are like my Fanny."

In other respects it has been a fine day for Moldorf. A letter arrived from America. Moe is getting A's in everything. Murray is learning to ride the bicycle. The victrola was repaired. You can see from the expression on his face that there were other things in the letter besides report cards and velocipedes. You can be sure of it because this afternoon he bought 325 francs worth of jewelry for his Fanny. In addition he wrote her a twenty-page letter. The *garçon* brought him page after page, filled his fountain-pen, served his coffee and cigars, fanned him a little

when he perspired, brushed the crumbs from the table, lit
his cigar when it went out, bought stamps for him, danced
on him, piroutted, salaamed . . . broke his spine damned
near. The tip was fat. Bigger and fatter than a Corona Corona. Moldorf probably mentioned it in his diary. It was
for Fanny's sake. The bracelet and the ear-rings, they
were worth every sou he spent. Better to spend it on
Fanny than waste it on little strumpets like Germaine and
Odette. Yes, he told Tania so. He showed her his trunk. It
is crammed with gifts—for Fanny, and for Moe and Murray.

"My Fanny is the most intelligent woman in the world.
I have been searching and searching to find a flaw in
her—but there's not one.

"She's perfect. I'll tell you what Fanny can do. She
plays bridge like a shark; she's interested in Zionism; you
give her an old hat, for instance, and see what she can do
with it. A little twist here, a ribbon there, and *voilà
quelque chose de beau*! Do you know what is perfect
bliss? To sit beside Fanny, when Moe and Murray have
gone to bed, and listen to the radio. She sits there so
peacefully. I am rewarded for all my struggles and heart-
aches in just watching her. She listens intelligently. When
I think of your stinking Montparnasse and then of my
evenings in Bay Ridge with Fanny after a big meal, I tell
you there is no comparison. A simple thing like food, the
children, the soft lamps, and Fanny sitting there, a little
tired, but cheerful, contented, heavy with bread . . . we
just sit there for hours without saying a word. That's
bliss!

"Today she writes me a letter—not one of those dull
stock report letters. She writes me from the heart, in language that even my little Murray could understand. She's
delicate about everything, Fanny. She says that the children must continue their education but the expense worries her. It will cost a thousand bucks to send little
Murray to school. Moe, of course, will get a scholarship.
But little Murray, that little genius, Murray, what are we
going to do about him? I wrote Fanny not to worry. Send
Murray to school, I said. What's another thousand dollars? I'll make more money this year than ever before. I'll
do it for little Murray—because he's a genius, that kid."

I should like to be there when Fanny opens the trunk. "See, Fanny, this is what I bought in Budapest from an old Jew ... This is what they wear in Bulgaria—it's pure wool ... This belonged to the Duke of something or other—no, you don't wind it, you put it in the sun ... This I want you to wear, Fanny, when we go to the Opera ... wear it with that comb I showed you ... And this, Fanny, is something Tania picked up for me ... she's a little bit on your type ..."

And Fanny is sitting there on the settee, just as she was in the oleograph, with Moe on one side of her and little Murray, Murray the genius, on the other. Her fat legs are a little too short to reach the floor. Her eyes have a dull permanganate glow. Breasts like ripe red cabbage; they bobble a little when she leans forward. But the sad thing about her is that the juice has been cut off. She sits there like a dead storage battery; her face is out of plumb—it needs a little animation, a sudden spurt of juice to bring it back into focus. Moldorf is jumping around in front of her like a fat toad. His flesh quivers. He slips and it is difficult for him to roll over again on his belly. She prods him with her thick toes. His eyes protrude a little further. "Kick me again, Fanny, that was good!" She gives him a good prod this time—it leaves a permanent dent in his paunch. His face is close to the carpet; the wattles are joggling in the nap of the rug. He livens up a bit, flips around, springs from furniture to furniture. "Fanny, you are marvellous!" He is sitting now on her shoulder. He bites a little piece from her ear, just a little tip from the lobe where it doesn't hurt. But she's still dead—all storage battery and no juice. He falls on her lap and lies there quivering like a tooth-ache. He is all warm now and helpless. His belly glistens like a patent-leather shoe. In the sockets of his eyes a pair of fancy vest buttons. "Unbutton my eyes, Fanny, I want to see you better!" Fanny carries him to bed and drops a little hot wax over his eyes. She puts rings around his navel and a thermometer up his ass. She places him and he quivers again. Suddenly he's dwindled, shrunk completely out of sight. She searches all over for him, in her intestines, everywhere. Something is tickling her—she doesn't know where exactly. The bed is full of toads and fancy vest buttons.

"Fanny, where are you?" Something is tickling her—she can't say where. The buttons are dropping off the bed. The toads are climbing the walls. A tickling and a tickling. "Fanny, take the wax out of my eyes! I want to look at you!" But Fanny is laughing, squirming with laughter. There is something inside her, tickling and tickling. She'll die laughing if she doesn't find it. "Fanny, the trunk is full of beautiful things. Fanny, do you hear me?" Fanny is laughing, laughing like a fat worm. Her belly is swollen with laughter. Her legs are getting blue. "O God, Morris, there is something tickling me . . . I can't help it!"

Sunday! Left the Villa Borghese a little before noon, just as Boris was getting ready to sit down to lunch. I left out of a sense of delicacy, because it really pains Boris to see me sitting there in the studio with an empty belly. Why he doesn't invite me to lunch with him I don't know. He says he can't afford it, but that's no excuse. Anyway, I'm delicate about it. If it pains him to eat alone in my presence it would probably pain him more to share his meal with me. It's not my place to pry into his secret affairs.

Dropped in at the Cronstadts' and they were eating too. A young chicken with wild rice. Pretended that I had eaten already, but I could have torn the chicken from the baby's hands. This is not just false modesty—it's a kind of perversion, I'm thinking. Twice they asked me if I wouldn't join them. No! No! Wouldn't even accept a cup of coffee after the meal. I'm *delicat*, I am! On the way out I cast a lingering glance at the bones lying on the baby's plate—there was still meat on them.

Prowling around aimlessly. A beautiful day—so far. The Rue de Buci is alive, crawling. The bars wide open and the curbs lined with bicycles. All the meat and vegetable markets are in full swing. Arms loaded with truck bandaged in newspapers. A fine Catholic Sunday—in the morning, at least.

High noon and here I am standing on an empty belly at the confluence of all these crooked lanes that reek with the odor of food. Opposite me is the Hôtel de Louisiane. A grim old hostelry known to the bad boys of the Rue de Buci in the good old days. Hôtels and food, and I'm walking about like a leper with crabs gnawing at my entrails. On Sunday mornings there's a fever in the streets.

Nothing like it anywhere, except perhaps on the East Side, or down around Chatham Square. The Rue de l'Echaudé is seething. The streets twist and turn, at every angle a fresh hive of activity. Long queues of people with vegetables under their arms, turning in here and there with crisp, sparkling appetites. Nothing but food, food, food. Makes one delirious.

Pass the Square de Furstemberg. Looks different now, at high noon. The other night when I passed by it was deserted, bleak, spectral. In the middle of the square four black trees that have not yet begun to blossom. Intellectual trees, nourished by the paving stones. Like T. S. Eliot's verse. Here, by God, if Marie Laurencin ever brought her Lesbians out into the open, would be the place for them to commune. *Très lesbienne ici.* Sterile, hybrid, dry as Boris' heart.

In the little garden adjoining the Eglise St. Germain are a few dismounted gargoyles. Monsters that jut forward with a terrifying plunge. On the benches other monsters—old people, idiots, cripples, epileptics. Snoozing quietly, waiting for the dinner bell to ring. At the Galerie Zak across the way some imbecile has made a picture of the cosmos—*on the flat.* A painter's cosmos! Full of odds and ends, bric-à-brac. In the lower left-hand corner, however, there's an anchor—and a dinner bell. Salute! Salute, O Cosmos!

Still prowling around. Mid-afternoon. Guts rattling. Beginning to rain now. Notre-Dame rises tomb-like from the water. The gargoyles lean far out over the lace façade. They hang there like an *idée fixe* in the mind of a monomaniac. An old man with yellow whiskers approaches me. Has some Jaworski nonsense in his hand. Comes up to me with his head thrown back and the rain splashing in his face turns the golden sands to mud. Book store with some of Raoul Dufy's drawings in the window. Drawings of charwomen with rose bushes between their legs. A treatise on the philosophy of Joan Miro. The *philosophy,* mind you!

In the same window: *A Man Cut In Slices!* Chapter one: the man in the eyes of his family. Chapter two: the same in the eyes of his mistress. Chapter three:—No chapter three. Have to come back tomorrow for chapters three and four. Every day the window trimmer turns a fresh page. *A man cut in slices* . . . You can't imagine how furious I am not to have thought of a title like that! Where is this bloke who writes "the same in the eyes of his mistress . . . the same in the eyes of . . . the same . . ."? Where is this guy? Who is he? I want to hug him. I wish to Christ I had had brains enough to think of a title like that—instead of *Crazy Cock* and the other fool things I invented. Well, fuck a duck! I congratulate him just the same.

I wish him luck with his fine title. Here's another slice for you—for your next book! Ring me up some day. I'm living at the Villa Borghese. We're all dead, or dying, or about to die. We need good titles. We need meat—slices and slices of meat—juicy tenderloins, porterhouse steaks, kidneys, mountain oysters, sweetbreads. Some day, when I'm standing at the corner of 42nd Street and Broadway, I'm going to remember this title and I'm going to put down everything that goes on in my noodle—caviar, rain drops, axle-grease, vermicelli, liverwurst—slices and slices of it. And I'll tell no one why, after I had put everything down, I suddenly went home and chopped the baby to pieces. *Un acte gratuit pour vous, cher monsieur si bien coupé en tranches!*

How a man can wander about all day on an empty belly, and even get an erection once in a while, is one of those mysteries which are too easily explained by the "anatomists of the soul." On a Sunday afternoon, when the shutters are down and the proletariat possesses the street in a kind of dumb torpor, there are certain thoroughfares which remind one of nothing less than a big chancrous cock laid open longitudinally. And it is just these highways, the Rue St. Denis, for instance, or the Faubourg du Temple—which attract one irresistibly, much as in the old days, around Union Square or the upper reaches of the Bowery, one was drawn to the dime museums where in the show-windows there were displayed wax reproductions of various organs of the body eaten away by syphilis and other venereal diseases. The city sprouts out like a huge organism diseased in every part, the beautiful thoroughfares only a little less repulsive because they have been drained of their pus.

At the Cité Nortier, somewhere near the Place du Combat, I pause a few minutes to drink in the full squalor of the scene. It is a rectangular court like many another which one glimpses through the low passageways that flank the old arteries of Paris. In the middle of the court is a clump of decrepit buildings which have so rotted away that they have collapsed on one another and formed a sort of intestinal embrace. The ground is uneven, the flagging slippery with slime. A sort of human dump-heap which has been filled in with cinders and dry garbage. The sun is setting fast. The colors die. They shift from purple to dried blood, from nacre to bistre, from cool dead grays to pigeon shit. Here and there a lop-sided monster stands in the window blinking like an owl. There is the shrill squawk of children with pale faces and bony limbs, rickety little urchins marked with the forceps. A fetid odor seeps from the walls, the odor of a mildewed mattress Europe—medieval, grotesque, monstrous: a symphony in B mol. Directly across the street the Ciné Combat offers its distinguished clientele *Metropolis*.

Coming away my mind reverts to a book that I was reading only the other day. "The town was a shambles; corpses, mangled by butchers and stripped by plunderers, lay thick in the streets; wolves sneaked from the suburbs to eat them; the black death and other plagues crept in to keep them company, and the English came marching on; the while the *danse macabre* whirled about the tombs in all the cemeteries . . ." Paris during the days of Charles the Silly! A lovely book! Refreshing, appetizing. I'm still enchanted by it. About the patrons and prodromes of the Renaissance I know little, but Madam Pimpernel, *la belle boulangère*, and Maître Jehan Crapotte, *l'orfèvre*, these occupy my spare thoughts still. Not forgetting Rodin, the evil genius of *The Wandering Jew*, who practised his nefarious ways "until the day when he was enflamed and outwitted by the octoroon Cecily." Sitting in the Square du Temple, musing over the doings of the horse-knackers led by Jean Caboche, I have thought long and ruefully over the sad fate of Charles the Silly. A half-wit, who prowled about the halls of his Hôtel St. Paul, garbed in the filthiest rags, eaten away by ulcers and vermin, gnawing a bone, when they flung him one, like a mangy dog. At the Rue des

Lions I looked for the stones of the old menagerie where he once fed his pets. His only diversion, poor dolt, aside from those card games with his "low-born companion," Odette de Champsdivers.

It was a Sunday afternoon, much like this, when I first met Germaine. I was strolling along the Boulevard Beaumarchais, rich by a hundred francs or so which my wife had frantically cabled from America. There was a touch of spring in the air, a poisonous, malefic spring that seemed to burst from the man-holes. Night after night I had been coming back to this quarter, attracted by certain leprous streets which only revealed their sinister splendor when the light of day had oozed away and the whores commenced to take up their posts. The Rue Pasteur-Wagner is one I recall in particular, corner of the Rue Amelot which hides behind the boulevard like a slumbering lizard. Here, at the neck of the bottle, so to speak, there was always a cluster of vultures who croaked and flapped their dirty wings, who reached out with sharp talons and plucked you into a doorway. Jolly, rapacious devils who didn't even give you time to button your pants when it was over. Led you into a little room off the street, a room without a window usually, and, sitting on the edge of the bed with skirts tucked up gave you a quick inspection, spat on your cock, and placed it for you. While you washed yourself another one stood at the door and, holding her victim by one hand, watched nonchalantly as you gave the finishing touches to your toilet.

Germaine was different. There was nothing to tell me so from her appearance. Nothing to distinguish her from the other trollops who met each afternoon and evening at the Café de l'Eléphant. As I say, it was a spring day and the few francs my wife had scraped up to cable me were jingling in my pocket. I had a sort of vague premonition that I would not reach the Bastille without being taken in tow by one of these buzzards. Sauntering along the boulevard I had noticed her verging towards me with that curious trot-about air of a whore and the rundown heels and the cheap jewelry and the pasty look of their kind which the rouge only accentuates. It was not difficult to come to terms with her. We sat in the back of the little *tabac* called *L'Eléphant* and talked it over quickly.

In a few minutes we were in a five-franc room on the Rue Amelot, the curtains drawn and the covers thrown back. She didn't rush things, Germaine. She sat on the *bidet* soaping herself and talked to me pleasantly about this and that; she liked the knickerbockers I was wearing. *Très chic!* she thought. They were once, but I had worn the seat out of them; fortunately the jacket covered my ass. As she stood up to dry herself, still talking to me pleasantly, suddenly she dropped the towel and, advancing towards me leisurely, she commenced rubbing her pussy affectionately, stroking it with her two hands, caressing it, patting it, patting it. There was something about her eloquence at that moment and the way she thrust that rosebush under my nose which remains unforgettable; she spoke of it as if it were some extraneous object which she had acquired at great cost, an object whose value had increased with time and which now she prized above everything in the world. Her words imbued it with a peculiar fragrance; it was no longer just her private organ, but a treasure, a magic, potent treasure, a God-given thing— and none the less so because she traded it day in and day out for a few pieces of silver. As she flung herself on the bed, with legs spread wide apart, she cupped it with her hands and stroked it some more, murmuring all the while in that hoarse, cracked voice of hers that it was good, beautiful, a treasure, a little treasure. And it *was* good, that little pussy of hers! That Sunday afternoon, with its poisonous breath of spring in the air, everything clicked again. As we stepped out of the hotel I looked her over again in the harsh light of day and I saw clearly what a whore she was—the gold teeth, the geranium in her hat, the run-down heels, etc., etc. Even the fact that she had wormed a dinner out of me and cigarettes and taxi hadn't the least disturbing effect upon me. I encouraged it, in fact. I liked her so well that after dinner we went back to the hotel again and took another shot at it. "For love," this time. And again that big, bushy thing of hers worked its bloom and magic. It began to have an independent existence—for me too. There was Germaine and there was that rose-bush of hers. I liked them separately and I liked them together.

As I say, she was different, Germaine. Later, when she

discovered my true circumstances, she treated me nobly—blew me to drinks, gave me credit, pawned my things, introduced me to her friends, and so on. She even apologized for not lending me money, which I understood quite well after her *maquereau* had been pointed out to me. Night after night I walked down the Boulevard Beaumarchais to the little *tabac* where they all congregated and I waited for her to stroll in and give me a few minutes of her precious time.

When, some time later, I came to write about Claude it was not Claude that I was thinking of, but Germaine.... "All the men she's been with and now you, just you, and barges going by, masts and hulls, the whole damned current of life flowing through you, through her, through all the guys behind you and after you, the flowers and the birds and the sun streaming in and the fragrance of it choking you, annihilating you." That was for Germaine! Claude was not the same, though I admired her tremendously—I even thought for a while that I loved her. Claude had a soul and a conscience; she had refinement, too, which is bad—in a whore. Claude always imparted a feeling of sadness; she left the impression, unwittingly, of course, that you were just one more added to the stream which fate had ordained to destroy her. *Unwittingly,* I say, because Claude was the last person in the world who would consciously create such an image in one's mind. She was too delicate, too sensitive for that. At bottom, Claude was just a good French girl of average breed and intelligence whom life had tricked somehow; something in her there was which was not tough enough to withstand the shock of daily experience. For her were meant those terrible words of Louis-Philippe: "and a night comes when all is over, when so many jaws have closed upon us that we no longer have the strength to stand, and our meat hangs upon our bodies, as though it had been masticated by every mouth." Germaine, on the other hand, was a whore from the cradle; she was thoroughly satisfied with her role, enjoyed it in fact, except when her stomach pinched or her shoes gave out, little surface things of no account, nothing that ate into her soul, nothing that created torment. *Ennui!* That was the worst she ever felt. Days there were, no doubt, when she

had a bellyful, as we say—but no more than that! Most of
the time she enjoyed it—or gave the illusion of enjoying
it. It made a difference of course, whom she went
with—or *came* with. But the principal thing was a *man.*
A man! That was what she craved. A man with something
between his legs that could tickle her, that could make her
writhe in ecstasy, make her grab that bushy twat of hers
with both hands and rub it joyfully, boastfully, proudly,
with a sense of connection, a sense of life. That was the
only place where she experienced any life—down there
where she clutched herself with both hands.

Germaine was a whore all the way through, even down
to her good heart, her whore's heart which is not really a
good heart but a lazy one, an indifferent, flaccid heart that
can be touched for a moment, a heart without reference to
any fixed point within, a big, flaccid whore's heart that
can detach itself for a moment from its true center. However vile and circumscribed was that world which she had
created for herself, nevertheless she functioned in it su-
perbly. And that in itself is a tonic thing. When, after we
had become well acquainted, her companions would twit
me, saying that I was in love with Germaine (a situation
almost inconceivable to them), I would say: "Sure! Sure,
I'm in love with her! And what's more, I'm going to be
faithful to her!" A lie, of course, because I could no more
think of loving Germaine than I could think of loving a
spider; and if I *was* faithful, it was not to Germaine but
to that bushy thing she carried between her legs. Whenever I looked at another woman I thought immediately of
Germaine, of that flaming bush which she had left in my
mind and which seemed imperishable. It gave me pleasure to sit on the *terrasse* of the little *tabac* and observe
her as she plied her trade, observe her as she resorted to
the same grimaces, the same tricks, with others as she had
with me. "She's doing her job!"—that's how I felt about
it, and it was with approbation that I regarded her trans-
actions. Later, when I had taken up with Claude, and I
saw her night after night sitting in her accustomed place,
her round little buttocks chubbily ensconced in the plush
settee, I felt a sort of inexpressible rebellion towards her;
a whore, it seemed to me, had no right to be sitting there
like a lady, waiting timidly for some one to approach and

all the while abstemiously sipping her *chocolat*. Germaine was a hustler. She didn't wait for you to come to her—she went out and grabbed you. I remember so well the holes in her stockings, and the torn ragged shoes; I remember too how she stood at the bar and with blind, courageous defiance threw a strong drink down her stomach and marched out again. A hustler! Perhaps it wasn't so pleasant to smell that boozy breath of hers, that breath compounded of weak coffee, cognac, *apéritifs,* pernods and all the other stuff she guzzled between times, what to warm herself and what to summon up strength and courage, but the fire of it penetrated her, it glowed down there between her legs where women ought to glow, and there was established that circuit which makes one feel the earth under his legs again. When she lay there with her legs apart and moaning, even if she did moan that way for any and everybody, it was good, it was a proper show of feeling. She didn't stare up at the ceiling with a vacant look or count the bedbugs on the wall-paper; she kept her mind on her business, she talked about the things a man wants to hear when he's climbing over a woman. Whereas Claude—well, with Claude there was always a certain delicacy, even when she got under the sheets with you. And her delicacy offended me. Who wants a *delicate* whore! Claude would even ask you to turn your face away when she squatted over the *bidet*. All wrong! A man, when he's burning up with passion, wants to see things; he wants to see *everything,* even how they make water. And while it's all very nice to know that a woman has a mind, literature coming from the cold corpse of a whore is the last thing to be served in bed. Germaine had the right idea: she was ignorant and lusty, she put her heart and soul into her work. She was a whore all the way through—and that was her virtue!

Easter came in like a frozen hare—but it was fairly warm in bed. Today it is lovely again and along the Champs-Elysées at twilight it is like an outdoor seraglio choked with dark-eyed houris. The trees are in full foliage and of a verdure so pure, so rich, that it seems as though they were still wet and glistening with dew. From the Palais du Louvre to the Etoile it is like a piece of music for the pianoforte. For five days I have not touched the typewriter nor looked at a book; nor have I had a single idea in my head except to go to the American Express. At nine this morning I was there, just as the doors were being opened, and again at one o'clock. No news. At four-thirty I dash out of the hotel, resolved to make a last minute stab at it. Just as I turn the corner I brush against Walter Pach. Since he doesn't recognize me, and since I have nothing to say to him, I make no attempt to arrest him. Later, when I am stretching my legs in the Tuileries his figure reverts to mind. He was a little stooped, pensive, with a sort of serene yet reserved smile on his face. I wonder, as I look up at this softly enamelled sky, so faintly tinted, which does not bulge today with heavy rain clouds but smiles like a piece of old china, I wonder what goes on in the mind of this man who translated the four thick volumes of the *History of Art* when he takes in this blissful cosmos with his drooping eye.

Along the Champs-Elysées, ideas pouring from me like sweat. I ought to be rich enough to have a secretary to whom I could dictate as I walk, because my best thoughts always come when I am away from the machine.

Walking along the Champs-Elysées I keep thinking of my really superb health. When I say "health" I mean optimism, to be truthful. Incurably optimistic! Still have one foot in the 19th century. I'm a bit retarded, like most Americans. Carl finds it disgusting, this optimism. "I have only to talk about a meal," he says, "and you're radiant!" It's a fact. The mere thought of a meal—*another* meal—rejuvenates me. A meal! That means something to go on—a few solid hours of work, an erection possibly. I don't deny it. I have health, good, solid, animal health. The only thing that stands between me and a future is a meal, *another* meal.

As for Carl, he's not himself these days. He's upset, his nerves are jangled. He says he's ill, and I believe him, but I don't feel badly about it.

I *can't*. In fact, it makes me laugh. And that offends him, of course. Everything wounds him—my laughter, my hunger, my persistence, my insouciance, *everything*. One day he wants to blow his brains out because he can't stand this lousy hole of a Europe any more; the next day he talks of going to Arizona "where they look you square in the eye."

"Do it!" I say. "Do one thing or the other, you bastard, but don't try to cloud my healthy eye with your melancholy breath!"

But that's just it! In Europe one gets used to doing nothing. You sit on your ass and whine all day. You get contaminated. You rot.

Fundamentally Carl is a snob, an aristocratic little prick who lives in a dementia praecox kingdom all his own. "I hate Paris!" he whines. "All these stupid people playing cards all day . . . look at them! And this writing! What's the use of putting words together? I can be a writer without writing, can't I? What does it prove if I write a book? What do we want with books anyway? There are too many books already . . ."

My eye, but I've been all over that ground—years and years ago. I've lived out my melancholy youth. I don't give a fuck any more what's behind me, or what's ahead of me. I'm healthy. Incurably healthy. No sorrows, no regrets. No past, no future. The present is enough for me. Day by day. Today! *Le bel aujourd'hui!*

He has one day a week off, Carl, and on that day he's more miserable, if you can imagine it, than on any other day of the week. Though he professes to despise food, the only way he seems to enjoy himself on his day off is to order a big spread. Perhaps he does it for my benefit—I don't know, and I don't ask. If he chooses to add martyrdom to his list of vices, let him—it's O. K. with me. Anyway, last Tuesday, after squandering what he had on a big spread, he steers me to the Dôme, the last place in the world I would seek on my day off. But one not only gets acquiescent here—one gets supine.

Standing at the Dôme bar is Marlowe, soused to the ears. He's been on a bender, as he calls it, for the last five days. That means a continuous drunk, a peregrination from one bar to another, day and night without interruption, and finally a lay-off at the American Hospital. Marlowe's bony emaciated face is nothing but a skull perforated by two deep sockets in which there are buried a pair of dead clams. His back is covered with sawdust—he has just had a little snooze in the water-closet. In his coat pocket are the proofs for the next issue of his review, he was on his way to the printer with the proofs, it seems, when some one inveigled him to have a drink. He talks about it as though it happened months ago. He takes out the proofs and spreads them over the bar; they are full of coffee stains and dried spittle. He tries to read a poem which he had written in Greek, but the proofs are undecipherable. Then he decides to deliver a speech, in French, but the *gérant* puts a stop to it. Marlowe is piqued: his one ambition is to talk a French which even the *garçon* will understand. Of old French he is a master; of the Surrealists he has made excellent translations; but to say a simple thing like "get the hell out of here, you old prick!"—that is beyond him. Nobody understands Marlowe's French, not even the whores. For that matter, it's difficult enough to understand his English when he's under the weather. He blabbers and spits like a confirmed stutterer . . . no sequence to his phrases. *"You pay!"* that's one thing he manages to get out clearly.

Even if he is fried to the hat some fine preservative instinct always warns Marlowe when it is time to act. If there is any doubt in his mind as to how the drinks are going to be paid he will be sure to put on a stunt. The usual one is to pretend that he is going blind. Carl knows all his tricks by now, and so when Marlowe suddenly claps his hands to his temples and begins to act it out Carl gives him a boot in the ass and says: "Come out of it, you sap! You don't have to do that with me!"

Whether it is a cunning piece of revenge or not, I don't know, but at any rate Marlowe is paying Carl back in good coin. Leaning over us confidentially he relates in a hoarse, croaking voice a piece of gossip which he picked up in the course of his peregrinations from bar to bar. Carl looks up in amazement. He's pale under the gills. Marlowe repeats the story with variations. Each time Carl wilts a little more. "But that's impossible!" he finally blurts out. "No, it ain't!" croaks Marlowe. "You're gonna lose your job . . . I got it straight." Carl looks at me in despair. "Is he shitting me, that bastard?" he murmurs in my ear. And then aloud—"What am I going to do now? I'll never find another job. It took me a year to land this one."

This, apparently, is all that Marlowe has been waiting to hear. At last he has found someone worse off than himself. "They be hard times!" he croaks, and his bony skull glows with a cold, electric fire.

Leaving the Dôme Marlowe explains between hiccups that he's got to return to San Francisco. He seems genuinely touched now by Carl's helplessness. He proposes that Carl and I take over the review during his absence. "I can trust you, Carl," he says. And then suddenly he gets an attack, a real one this time. He almost collapses in the gutter. We haul him to a *bistrot* at the Boulevard Edgar Quinet and sit him down. This time he's really got It—a blinding headache that makes him squeal and grunt and rock himself to and fro like a dumb brute that's been struck by a sledge-hammer. We spill a couple of Fernet-Brancas down his throat, lay him out on the bench and cover his eyes with his muffler. He lies there groaning. In a little while we hear him snoring.

"What about his proposition?" says Carl. "Should we take it up? He says he'll give me a thousand francs when he comes back. I know he won't, but what about it?" He looks at Marlowe sprawled out on the bench, lifts the muffler from his eyes, and puts it back again. Suddenly a mischievous grin lights up his face. "Listen, Joe," he says, beckoning me to move closer, "we'll take him up on it. We'll take his lousy review over and we'll fuck him good and proper."

"What do you mean by that?"

"Why we'll throw out all the other contributors and we'll fill it with our own shit—that's what!"

"Yeah, but what kind of shit?"

"Any kind . . . he won't be able to do anything about it. We'll fuck him good and proper. One good number and after that the magazine'll be finished. Are you game, Joe?"

Grinning and chuckling we lift Marlowe to his feet and haul him to Carl's room. When we turn on the lights there's a woman in the bed waiting for Carl. "I forgot all about her," says Carl. We turn the cunt loose and shove Marlowe into bed. In a minute or so there's a knock at the door. It's Van Norden. He's all aflutter. Lost a plate of false teeth—at the Bal Nègre, he thinks. Anyway, we get to bed, the four of us. Marlowe stinks like a smoked fish.

In the morning Marlowe and Van Norden leave to search for the false teeth. Marlowe is blubbering. He imagines they are *his* teeth.

It is my last dinner at the dramatist's home. They have just rented a new piano, a concert grand. I meet Sylvester coming out of the florist's with a rubber plant in his arms. He asks me if I would carry it for him while he goes for the cigars. One by one I've fucked myself out of all these free meals which I had planned so carefully. One by one the husbands turn against me, or the wives. As I walk along with the rubber plant in my arms I think of that night a few months back when the idea first occurred to me. I was sitting on a bench near the Coupole, fingering the wedding ring which I had tried to pawn off on a *garçon* at the Dôme. He had offered me six francs for it and I was in a rage about it. But the belly was getting the upper hand. Ever since I left Mona I had worn the ring on my pinkie. It was so much a part of me that it had never occurred to me to sell it. It was one of those orange-blossom affairs in white gold. Worth a dollar and a half once, may be more. For three years we went along without a wedding ring and then one day when I was going to the pier to meet Mona I happened to pass a jewelry window on Maiden Lane and the whole window was stuffed with wedding rings. When I got to the pier Mona was not to be seen. I waited for the last passenger to descend the gangplank, but no Mona. Finally I asked to be shown the passenger list. Her name was not on it. I slipped the wedding ring on my pinkie and there it stayed. Once I left it in a public bath, but then I got it back again. One of the orange blossoms had fallen off. Anyway, I was sitting there on the bench with my head down, twiddling the ring, when suddenly someone clapped me on the back. To make it brief, I got a meal and a few francs besides. And then it occurred to me, like

a flash, that no one would refuse a man a meal if only he
had the courage to demand it. I went immediately to a
café and wrote a dozen letters. "Would you let me have
dinner with you once a week? Tell me what day is most
convenient for you." It worked like a charm. I was not
only fed ... I was feasted. Every night I went home
drunk. They couldn't do enough for me, these generous
once-a-week souls. What happened to me between times
was none of their affair. Now and then the thoughtful
ones presented me with cigarettes, or a little pin money.
They were all obviously relieved when they realized that
they would see me only once a week. And they were still
more relieved when I said—"it won't be necessary any
more." They never asked why. They congratulated me,
and that was all. Often the reason was I had found a better host; I could afford to scratch off the ones who were
a pain in the ass. But that thought never occurred to
them. Finally I had a steady, solid program—a fixed
schedule. On Tuesdays I knew it would be this kind of a
meal and on Fridays that kind. Cronstadt, I knew, would
have champagne for me and home-made apple pie. And
Carl would invite me out, take me to a different restaurant each time, order rare wines, invite me to the theatre
afterwards or take me to the Cirque Medrano. They were
curious about one another, my hosts. Would ask me
which place I liked best, who was the best cook, etc. I
think I liked Cronstadt's joint best of all, perhaps because
he chalked the meal up on the wall each time. Not that
it eased my conscience to see what I owed him, because
I had no intention of paying him back nor had he any illusions about being requited. No, it was the odd numbers
which intrigued me. He used to figure it out to the last
centime. If I was to pay in full I would have had to break
a sou. His wife was a marvellous cook and she didn't
give a fuck about those centimes Cronstadt added up.
She took it out of me in carbon copies. A fact! If I hadn't
any fresh carbons for her when I showed up, she was
crestfallen. And for that I would have to take the little
girl to the Luxembourg next day, play with her for two or
three hours, a task which drove me wild because she
spoke nothing but Hungarian and French. They were a
queer lot on the whole, my hosts ...

At Tania's I look down on the spread from the balcony. Moldorf is there, sitting beside his idol. He is warming his feet at the hearth, a monstrous look of gratitude in his watery eyes. Tania is running over the adagio. The adagio says very distinctly: no more words of love! I am at the fountain again, watching the turtles pissing green milk. Sylvester has just come back from Broadway with a heart full of love. All night I was lying on a bench outside the mall while the globe was sprayed with warm turtle piss and the horses stiffened with priapic fury galloped like mad without ever touching the ground. All night long I smell the lilacs in the little dark room where she is taking down her hair, the lilacs that I bought for her as she went to meet Sylvester. He came back with a heart full of love, she said, and the lilacs are in her hair, her mouth, they are choking her armpits. The room is swimming with love and turtle piss and warm lilacs and the horses are galloping like mad. In the morning dirty teeth and scum on the window-panes; the little gate that leads to the mall is locked. People are going to work and the shutters are rattling like coats of mail. In the book-store opposite the fountain is the story of Lake Tchad, the silent lizards, the gorgeous gamboge tints. All the letters I wrote her, drunken ones with a blunt stub, crazy ones with bits of charcoal, little pieces from bench to bench, fire-crackers, doilies, tutti-frutti; they will be going over them now, together, and he will compliment me one day. He will say, as he flicks his cigar ash: "Really, you write quite well. Let's see, you're a Surrealist, aren't you?" Dry, brittle voice, teeth full of dandruff, solo for solar plexus, g for gaga.

Up on the balcony with the rubber plant and the adagio going on down below. The keys are black and white, then black, then white, then white and black. And you want to know if you can play something for me. Yes, play something with those big thumbs of yours. Play the adagio since that's the only god-damned thing you know. Play it, and then cut off your big thumbs.

That adagio! I don't know why she insists on playing it all the time. The old piano wasn't good enough for her; she had to rent a concert grand—for the adagio! When I see her big thumbs pressing the keyboard and that silly

rubber plant beside me I feel like that madman of the
North who threw his clothes away and, sitting naked in
the wintry boughs, threw nuts down into the herring-
frozen sea. There is something exasperating about this
movement, something abortively melancholy about it, as
if it had been written in lava, as if it had the color of lead
and milk mixed. And Sylvester, with his head cocked to
one side like an auctioneer, Sylvester says: "Play that
other one you were practising today." It's beautiful to
have a smoking jacket, a good cigar and a wife who plays
the piano. So relaxing. So lenitive. Between the acts you
go out for a smoke and a breath of fresh air. Yes, her fingers are very supple, extraordinarily supple. She does ba-
tik work too. Would you like to try a Bulgarian cigarette?
I say, pigeon-breast, what's that other movement I like so
well? The scherzo! Ah, yes, the scherzo! Excellent, the
scherzo! Count Waldemar von Schwisseneinzug speaking.
Cool, dandruff eyes. Halitosis. Gaudy socks. And crotons
in the pea soup, if you please. We always have pea soup
Friday nights. Won't you try a little red wine? The red
wine goes with the meat, you know. A dry, crisp voice.
Have a cigar, won't you? Yes, I like my work, but I don't
attach any importance to it. My next play will involve a
pluralistic conception of the universe. Revolving drums
with calcium lights. O'Neill is dead. I think, dear, you
should lift your foot from the pedal more frequently. Yes,
that part is very nice ... *very* nice, don't you think? Yes,
the characters go around with microphones in their trousers. The locale is in Asia, because the atmospheric con-
ditions are more conducive. Would you like to try a little
Anjou? We bought it especially for you ...

All through the meal this patter continues. It feels exactly as if he had taken out that circumcised dick of his
and was peeing on us. Tania is bursting with the strain.
Ever since he came back with a heart full of love this
monologue has been going on. He talks while he's un-
dressing, she tells me—a steady stream of warm piss, as
though his bladder had been punctured. When I think of
Tania crawling into bed with this busted bladder I get enraged. To think that a poor, withered bastard with those
cheap Broadway plays up his sleeve should be pissing on
the woman I love. Calling for red wine and revolving

drums and crotons in his pea soup! The cheek of him! To
think that he can lie beside that furnace I stoked for him
and do nothing but make water! My God, man, you ought
to get down on your knees and thank me. Don't you see
that you have a *woman* in your house now? Can't you
see she's bursting? You telling me with those strangulated
adenoids of yours—"well now, I'll tell you . . . there's
two ways of looking at that . . ." Fuck your two ways of
looking at things! Fuck your pluralistic universe, and
your Asiatic acoustics! Don't hand me your red wine or
your Anjou . . . hand *her* over . . . she belongs to me! You
go sit by the fountain, and let *me* smell the lilacs! Pick
the dandruff from out of your eyes . . . and take that
damned adagio and wrap it in a pair of flannel pants! And
the other little movement too . . . all the little movements
that you make with your weak bladder. You smile at me
so confidently, so calculatingly. I'm flattering the ass off
you, can't you tell? While I listen to your crap she's got
her hand on me—but you don't see that. You think I like
to suffer—that's my role, you say. O. K. Ask her about it!
She'll tell you how I suffer. "You're cancer and delirium," she said over the phone the other day. She's got it
now, the cancer and delirium, and soon you'll have to
pick the scabs. Her veins are bursting, I tell you, and your
talk is all sawdust. No matter how much you piss away
you'll never plug up the holes. What did Mr. Wren say?
Words are loneliness. I left a couple of words for you on
the table-cloth last night—you covered them with your
elbows.

He's put a fence around her as if she were a dirty,
stinking bone of a saint. If he only had the courage to
say "Take her!" perhaps a miracle would occur. Just that.
Take her! and I swear everything would come out all
right. Besides, maybe I wouldn't take her—did that ever
occur to him, I wonder? Or I might take her for a while
and hand her back, *improved.* But putting up a fence
around her, that won't work. You can't put a fence around
a human being. It ain't done any more . . . You think, you
poor, withered bastard, that I'm no good for her, that I
might pollute her, desecrate her. You don't know how
palatable is a polluted woman, how a change of semen
can make a woman bloom! You think a heart full of love

is enough, and perhaps it is, for the right woman, but you
haven't got a heart any more ... you are nothing but a
big, empty bladder. You are sharpening your teeth and
cultivating your growl. You run at her heels like a watch-
dog and you piddle everywhere. She didn't take you for
a watch-dog ... she took you for a poet. You were a poet
once, she said. And now what are you? Courage,
Sylvester, courage! Take the microphone out of your
pants. Put your hind leg down and stop making water everywhere. Courage, I say, because she's ditched you already. She's contaminated, I tell you, and you might as
well take down the fence. No use asking me politely if
the coffee doesn't taste like carbolic acid: that won't
scare me away. Put rat poison in the coffee, and a little
ground glass. Make some boiling hot urine and drop a
few nutmegs in it ...

It is a communal life I have been living for the last few
weeks. I have had to share myself with others, principally
with some crazy Russians, a drunken Dutchman, and a
big Bulgarian woman named Olga. Of the Russians there
are chiefly Eugene and Anatole.

It was just a few days ago that Olga got out of the hospital where she had her tubes burned out and lost a little
excess weight. However she doesn't look as if she had
gone through much suffering. She weighs almost as much
as a camel-backed locomotive; she drips with perspiration, has halitosis, and still wears her Circassian wig that
looks like excelsior. She has two big warts on her chin
from which there sprouts a clump of little hairs; she is
growing a moustache.

The day after Olga was released from the hospital she
commenced making shoes again. At six in the morning
she is at her bench; she knocks out two pairs of shoes a
day. Eugene complains that Olga is a burden, but the truth
is that Olga is supporting Eugene and his wife with her
two pairs of shoes a day. If Olga doesn't work there is no
food. So everyone endeavours to pull Olga to bed on
time, to give her enough food to keep going, etc.

Every meal starts off with soup. Whether it be onion
soup, tomato soup, vegetable soup, or what not, the soup
always tastes the same. Mostly it tastes as if a dish rag

had been stewed in it—slightly sour, mildewed, scummy. I see Eugene hiding it away in the commode after the meal. It stays there, rotting away, until the next meal. The butter, too, is hidden away in the commode; after three days it tastes like the big toe of a cadaver.

The smell of rancid butter frying is not particularly appetizing, especially when the cooking is done in a room in which there is not the slightest form of ventilation. No sooner than I open the door I feel ill. But Eugene, as soon as he hears me coming, usually opens the shutters and pulls back the bed-sheet which is strung up like a fish-net to keep out the sunlight. Poor Eugene! He looks about the room at the few sticks of furniture, at the dirty bed-sheets and the wash basin with the dirty water still in it, and he says: "I am a slave!" Every day he says it, not once, but a dozen times. And then he takes his guitar from the wall and sings.

But about the smell of rancid butter . . . There are good associations too. When I think of this rancid butter, I see myself standing in a little, old-world courtyard, a very smelly, very dreary courtyard. Through the cracks in the shutters strange figures peer out at me . . . old women with shawls, dwarfs, rat-faced pimps, bent Jews, midinettes, bearded idiots. They totter out into the courtyard to draw water or to rinse the slop pails. One day Eugene asked me if I would empty the pail for him. I took it to the corner of the yard. There was a hole in the ground and some dirty paper lying around the hole. The little well was slimy with excrement, which in English is *shit*. I tipped the pail and there was a foul, gurgling spash followed by another and unexpected splash. When I returned the soup was dished out. All through the meal I thought of my toothbrush—it is getting old and the bristles get caught in my teeth.

When I sit down to eat I always sit near the window. I am afraid to sit on the other side of the table—it is too close to the bed and the bed is crawling. I can see blood-stains on the gray sheets if I look that way, but I try not to look that way. I look out on the courtyard where they are rinsing the slop pails.

The meal is never complete without music. As soon as the cheese is passed around Eugene jumps up and reaches for the guitar which hangs over the bed. It is always the same song. He says he has fifteen or sixteen songs in his repertoire, but I have never heard more than three. His favorite is *Charmant poème d'amour.* It is full of *angoisse* and *tristesse.*

In the afternoon we go to the cinema which is cool and dark. Eugene sits at the piano in the big pit and I sit on a bench up front. The house is empty, but Eugene sings as if he had for audience all the crowned heads of Europe. The garden door is open and the odor of wet leaves sops in and the rain blends with Eugene's *angoisse* and *tristesse.* At midnight, after the spectators have saturated the hall with perspiration and foul breath, I return to sleep on a bench. The exit light, swimming in a halo of tobacco smoke, sheds a faint light on the lower corner of the asbestos curtain; I close my eyes every night on an artificial eye . . .

Standing in the courtyard with a glass eye; only half the world intelligible. The stones are wet and mossy and in the crevices are black toads. A big door bars the entrance to the cellar; the steps are slippery and soiled with bat-dung. The door bulges and sags, the hinges are falling off, but there is an enamelled sign on it, in perfect condition, which says: "Be sure to close the door." Why close the door? I can't make it out. I look again at the sign but it is removed; in its place there is a pane of colored glass. I take out my artificial eye, spit on it and polish it with my handkerchief. A woman is sitting on a dais above an immense carven desk; she has a snake around her neck. The entire room is lined with books and strange fish swimming in colored globes; there are maps and charts on the wall, maps of Paris before the plague, maps of the antique world, of Knossus and Carthage, of Carthage before and after the salting. In a corner of the room I see an iron bedstead and on it a corpse is lying; the woman gets up wearily, removes the corpse from the bed and absent-mindedly throws it out the window. She returns to the huge carven desk, takes a goldfish from the bowl and swallows it. Slowly the room begins to revolve and one by one the continents slide into the sea; only the woman is left, but her body is a mass of geography. I lean out the window and the Eiffel Tower is fizzing champagne; it is built entirely of numbers and shrouded in black lace. The sewers are gurgling furiously. There are nothing but roofs everywhere, laid out with execrable geometric cunning.

I have been ejected from the world like a cartridge. A deep fog has settled down, the earth is smeared with frozen grease. I can feel the city palpitating, as if it were a heart just removed from a warm body. The windows of my hotel are festering and there is a thick, acrid stench as of chemicals burning. Looking into the Seine I see mud and desolation, street lamps drowning, men and women choking to death, the bridges covered with houses, slaughter-houses of love. A man is standing against a wall with an accordion strapped to his belly; his hands are cut off at the wrists, but the accordion writhes between his stumps like a sack of snakes. The universe has dwindled; it is only a block long and there are no stars, no trees, no rivers. The people who live here are dead; they make chairs which other people sit on in their dreams. In the middle of the street is a wheel and in the hub of the wheel a gallows is fixed. People already dead are trying frantically to mount the gallows, but the wheel is turning too fast . . .

Something was needed to put me right with myself. Last night I discovered it: *Papini*. It doesn't matter to me whether he's a chauvinist, a little Christer, or a near-sighted pedant. As a failure he's marvellous . . .

The books he read—at eighteen! Not only Homer, Dante, Goethe, not only Aristotle, Plato, Epictetus, not only Rabelais, Cervantes, Swift, not only Walt Whitman, Edgar Allan Poe, Baudelaire, Villon, Carducci, Manzoni, Lope de Vega, not only Nietzsche, Schopenhauer, Kant, Hegel, Darwin, Spencer, Huxley—not only these but all the small fry in between. This on page 18. *Alors,* on page 232 he breaks down and confesses. I know nothing, he admits. I know the titles, I have compiled bibliographies, I have written critical essays, I have maligned and defamed . . . I can talk for five minutes or for five days, but then I give out, I am squeezed dry.

Follows this: "Everybody wants to see me. Everybody insists on talking to me. People pester me and they pester others with inquiries about what I am doing. How am I? Am I quite well again? Do I still go for my walks in the country? Am I working? Have I finished my book? Will I begin another soon?

"A skinny monkey of a German wants me to translate his works. A wild-eyed Russian girl wants me to write an account of my life for her. An American lady wants the *very latest* news about me. An American gentleman will send his carriage to take me to dinner—just an intimate, confidential talk, you know. An old schoolmate and chum of mine, of ten years ago, wants me to read him all that I write as fast as I write it. A painter friend I know expects me to pose for him by the hour. A newspaper man wants my present address. An acquaintance, a mystic, inquires about the state of my soul; another, more practical, about the state of my pocketbook. The president of my club wonders if I will make a speech for the boys! A lady, spiritually inclined, hopes I will come to her house for tea as often as possible. She wants to have my opinion of Jesus Christ, and—what do I think of that new medium? . . .

"Great God! what have I turned into? What right have you people to clutter up my life, steal my time, probe my soul, suckle my thoughts, have me for your companion, confidant, and information bureau? What do you take me for? Am I an entertainer on salary, required every evening to play an intellectual farce under your stupid noses? Am I a slave, bought and paid for, to crawl on my belly in front of you idlers and lay at your feet all that I do and all that I know? Am I a wench in a brothel who is called upon to lift her skirts or take off her chemise at the bidding of the first man in a tailored suit who comes along?

"I am a man who would live an heroic life and make the world more endurable in his own sight. If, in some moment of weakness, of relaxation, of need, I blow off steam—a bit of red-hot rage cooled off in words—a passionate dream, wrapped and tied in imagery—well, take it or leave it . . . *but don't bother me!*

"I am a free man—and I need my freedom. I need to be alone. I need to ponder my shame and my despair in seclusion; I need the sunshine and the paving stones of the streets without companions, without conversation, face to face with myself, with only the music of my heart

for company. What do you want of me? When I have
something to say, I put it in print. When I have something
to give, I give it. Your prying curiosity turns my stomach!
Your compliments humiliate me! Your tea poisons me! I
owe nothing to any one. I would be responsible to God
alone—if He existed!"

It seems to me Papini misses something by a hair's
breadth when he talks of the need to be alone. It is not
difficult to be alone if you are poor and a failure. An artist is always alone—if he *is* an artist. No, what the artist
needs is *loneliness*.

The artist, I call myself. So be it. A beautiful nap this
afternoon that put velvet between my vertebrae. Gener-
ated enough ideas to last me three days. Chock full of energy and nothing to do about it. Decide to go for a walk.
In the street I change my mind. Decide to go to the movies. Can't go to the movies—short a few sous. A walk
then. At every movie house I stop and look at the bill-
boards, then at the price list. Cheap enough, these opium
joints, but I'm short just a few sous. If it weren't so late
I might go back and cash an empty bottle.

By the time I get to the Rue Amélie I've forgotten all
about the movies. The Rue Amélie is one of my favorite
streets. It is one of those streets which by good fortune
the municipality has forgotten to pave. Huge cobblestones
spreading convexly from one side of the street to the
other. Only one block long and narrow. The Hôtel Pretty
is on this street. There is a little church, too, on the Rue
Amélie. It looks as though it were made especially for the
President of the Republic and his private family. It's good
occasionally to see a modest little church. Paris is full of
pompous cathedrals.

Pont Alexandre III. A great wind-swept space approaching the bridge. Gaunt bare trees mathematically
fixed in their iron grates; the gloom of the Invalides
welling out of the dome and overflowing the dark streets
adjacent to the Square. The morgue of poetry. They have
him where they want him now, the great warrior, the last
big man of Europe. He sleeps soundly in his granite bed.
No fear of him turning over in his grave. The doors are
well bolted, the lid is on tight. Sleep, Napoleon! It was
not your ideas they wanted, it was only your corpse!

The river is still swollen, muddy, streaked with lights. I don't know what it is rushes up in me at the sight of this dark, swift-moving current, but a great exultation lifts me up, affirms the deep wish that is in my never to leave this land. I remember passing this way the other morning on my way to the American Express, knowing in advance that there would be no mail for me, no check, no cable, nothing, nothing. A wagon from the Galeries Lafayette was rumbling over the bridge. The rain had stopped and the sun breaking through the soapy clouds touched the glistening rubble of roofs with a cold fire. I recall now how the driver leaned out and looked up the river towards Passy way. Such a healthy, simple, approving glance, as if he were saying to himself: "Ah, spring is coming!" And God knows, when spring comes to Paris the humblest mortal alive must feel that he dwells in paradise. But it was not only this—it was the intimacy with which his eye rested upon the scene. It was *his* Paris. A man does not need to be rich, nor even a citizen, to feel this way about Paris. Paris is filled with poor people—the proudest and filthiest lot of beggars that ever walked the earth, it seems to me. And yet they give the illusion of being at home. It is that which distinguishes the Parisian from all other metropolitan souls.

When I think of New York I have a very different feeling. New York makes even a rich man feel his unimportance. New York is cold, glittering, malign. The buildings dominate. There is a sort of atomic frenzy to the activity going on; the more furious the pace, the more diminished the spirit. A constant ferment, but it might just as well be going on in a test-tube. Nobody knows what it's all about. Nobody directs the energy. Stupendous. Bizarre. Baffling. A tremendous reactive urge, but absolutely uncoordinated.

When I think of this city where I was born and raised, this Manhattan that Whitman sang of, a blind, white rage licks my guts. New York! The white prisons, the sidewalks swarming with maggots, the bread lines, the opium joints that are built like palaces, the kikes that are there, the lepers, the thugs, and above all, the *ennui,* the monotony of faces, streets, legs, houses, skyscrapers, meals, posters, jobs, crimes, loves . . . A whole city erected over a hollow pit of nothingness. Meaningless. Absolutely meaningless. And Forty-Second Street! The top of the world, they call it. Where's the bottom then? You can walk along with your hand out and they'll put cinders in your cap. Rich or poor, they walk along with head thrown back and they almost break their necks looking up at their beautiful white prisons. They walk along like blind geese and the searchlights spray their empty faces with flecks of ecstasy.

"Life," said Emerson, "consists in what a man is thinking all day." If that be so, then my life is nothing but a big intestine. I not only think about food all day, but I dream about it at night.

But I don't ask to go back to America, to be put in double harness again, to work the treadmill. No, I prefer to be a poor man of Europe. God knows, I am poor enough; it only remains to be a man. Last week I thought the problem of living was about to be solved, thought I was on the way to becoming self-supporting. It happened that I ran across another Russian—Serge is his name. He lives in Suresnes where there is a little colony of *émigrés* and run-down artists. Before the revolution Serge was a captain in the Imperial Guard; he stands six foot three in his stockinged feet and drinks vodka like a fish. His father was an admiral, or something like that, on the battleship Potemkin.

I met Serge under rather peculiar circumstances. Sniffing about for food I found myself towards noon the other day in the neighborhood of the Folies Bergère—the back entrance, that is to say, in the narrow little lane with an iron gate at one end. I was dawdling about the stage entrance, hoping vaguely for a casual brush with one of the butterflies, when an open truck pulls up to the sidewalk. Seeing me standing there with my hands in my pockets the driver, who was Serge, asks me if I would give him a hand unloading the iron barrels. When he learns that I am an American and that I'm broke he almost weeps with joy. He has been looking high and low for an English teacher, it seems. I help him roll the barrels of insecticide inside and I look my fill at the butterflies fluttering about the wings. The incident takes on strange proportions to me—the empty house, the sawdust dolls bouncing in the wings, the barrels of germicide, the battleship Potemkin—above all, Serge's gentleness. He is big and tender, a man every inch of him, but with a woman's heart.

In the café nearby—Café des Artistes—he proposes immediately to put me up; says he will put a mattress on the floor in the hallway. For the lessons he says he will give me a meal every day, a big Russian meal, or if for any reason the meal is lacking then five francs. It sounds wonderful to me—*wonderful*. The only question is, how will I get from Suresnes to the American Express every day.

Serge insists that we begin at once—he gives me the car fare to get out to Suresnes in the evening. I arrive a little before dinner, with my knapsack, in order to give Serge a lesson. There are some guests on hand already— seems as though they always eat in a crowd, everybody chipping in.

There are eight of us at the table—and three dogs. The dogs eat first. They eat oatmeal. Then we commence. We eat oatmeal too—as an hors-d'oeuvre. *"Chez nous,"* says Serge, with a twinkle in his eye, *"c'est pour les chiens, les Quaker Oats. Ici pour le gentleman. Ca va."* After the oatmeal, mushroom soup and vegetables; after that bacon omelette, fruit, red wine, vodka, coffee, cigarettes. Not bad, the Russian meal. Everyone talks with his mouth full. Toward the end of the meal Serge's wife who is a lazy slut of an Armenian, flops on the couch and begins to nibble bonbons. She fishes around in the box with her fat fingers, nibbles a tiny piece to see if there is any juice inside, and then throws it on the floor for the dogs.

The meal over, the guests rush away. They rush away precipitously, as if they feared a plague. Serge and I are left with the dogs—his wife has fallen asleep on the couch. Serge moves about unconcernedly, scraping the garbage together for the dogs. "Dogs like very much," he says. "Very good for dogs. Little dog he has worms . . . he too young yet." He bends down to examine some white worms lying on the carpet between the dog's paws. Tries to explain about the worms in English, but his vocabulary is lacking. Finally he consults the dictionary.

"Ah," he says, looking at me exultantly, *"tape-worms!"*
My response is evidently not very intelligent. Serge is
confused. He gets down on his hands and knees to examine them better. He picks one up and lays it on the table
beside the fruit. "Huh, him not very beeg," he grunts.
"Next lesson you learn me worms, no? You are gude
teacher. I make progress with you . . ."

Lying on the mattress in the hallway the odor of the
germicide stifles me. A pungent, acrid odor that seems to
invade every pore of my body. The food begins to repeat
on me—the quaker oats, the mushrooms, the bacon, the
fried apples. I see the little tape-worm lying beside the
fruit and all the varieties of worms that Serge drew on
the tablecloth to explain what was the matter with the
dog. I see the empty pit of the Folies Bergère and in every crevice there are cockroaches and lice and bedbugs; I
see people scratching themselves frantically, scratching
and scratching until the blood comes. I see the worms
crawling over the scenery like an army of red ants, devouring everything in sight. I see the chorus girls throwing away their gauze tunics and running through the
aisles naked; I see the spectators in the pit throwing off
their clothes also and scratching each other like monkeys.

I try to quiet myself. After all, this is a home I've
found, and there's a meal waiting for me every day. And
Serge is a brick, there's no doubt about that. But I can't
sleep. It's like going to sleep in a morgue. The mattress
is saturated with embalming fluid. It's a morgue for lice,
bedbugs, cockroaches, tape-worms. I can't stand it. I
won't stand it. After all I'm a man, not a louse.

In the morning I wait for Serge to load the truck. I ask
him to take me in to Paris. I haven't the heart to tell him
I'm leaving. I leave the knapsack behind, with the few
things that were left me. When we get to the Place
Pereire I jump out. No particular reason for getting off
here. No particular reason for anything. *I'm free*—that's
the main thing . . .

Light as a bird I flit about from one quarter to another.
It's as though I had been released from prison. I look at
the world with new eyes. Everything interests me profoundly. Even trifles. On the Rue du Faubourg Poisson-
nière I stop before the window of a physical culture

establishment. There are photographs showing specimens of manhood "before and after." All frogs. Some of them are nude, except for a pince-nez or a beard. Can't understand how these birds fall for parallel bars and dumb-bells. A frog should have just a wee bit of a paunch, like the Baron de Charlus. He should wear a beard and a pince-nez, but he should never be photographed in the nude. He should wear twinkling patent-leather boots and in the breast pocket of his sack coat there should be a white handkerchief protruding about three-quarters of an inch above the vent. If possible, he should have a red ribbon in his lapel, through the button-hole. He should wear pajamas on going to bed.

Approaching the Place Clichy toward evening I pass the little whore with the wooden stump who stands opposite the Gaumont Palace day in and day out. She doesn't look a day over eighteen. Has her regular customers, I suppose. After midnight she stands there in her black rig rooted to the spot. Back of her is the little alleyway that blazes like an inferno. Passing her now with a light heart she reminds me somehow of a goose tied to a stake, a goose with a diseased liver, so that the world may have its *pâte de foie gras*. Must be strange taking that wooden stump to bed with you. One imagines all sorts of things—splinters, etc. However, every man to his taste!

Going down the Rue des Dames I bump into Peckover, another poor devil who works on the paper. He complains of getting only three or four hours' sleep a night—has to get up at eight in the morning to work at a dentist's office. It isn't for the money he's doing it, so he explains—it's for to buy himself a set of false teeth. "It's hard to read proof when you're dropping with sleep," he says. "The wife, she thinks I've got a cinch of it. What would we do if you lost your job? she says." But Peckover doesn't give a damn about the job; it doesn't even allow him spending money. He has to save his cigarette butts and use them for pipe tobacco. His coat is held together with pins. He has halitosis and his hands sweat. And only three hours' sleep a night. "It's no way to treat a man," he says. "And that boss of mine, he bawls the piss out of me if I miss a semi-colon." Speaking of his wife he adds:

"That woman of mine, she's got no fucking gratitude, I tell you!"

In parting I manage to worm a franc fifty out of him. I try to squeeze another fifty centimes out of him but it's impossible. Anyway I've got enough for a coffee and *croissants.* Near the Gare St. Lazare there's a bar with reduced prices.

As luck would have it I find a ticket in the *lavabo* for a concert. Light as a feather now I go there to the Salle Gaveau. The usher looks ravaged because I overlook giving him his little tip. Every time he passes me he looks at me inquiringly, as if perhaps I will suddenly remember.

It's so long since I've sat in the company of well dressed people that I feel a bit panic-stricken. I can still smell the formaldehyde. Perhaps Serge makes deliveries here too. But nobody is scratching himself, thank God. A faint odor of perfume . . . very faint. Even before the music begins there is that bored look on people's faces. A polite form of self-imposed torture, the concert. For a moment, when the conductor raps with his little wand, there is a tense spasm of concentration followed almost immediately by a general slump, a quiet vegetable sort of repose induced by the steady, uninterrupted drizzle from the orchestra. My mind is curiously alert; it's as though my skull had a thousand mirrors inside it. My nerves are taut, vibrant! the notes are like glass balls dancing on a million jets of water. I've never been to a concert before on such an empty belly. Nothing escapes me, not even the tiniest pin falling. It's as though I had no clothes on and every pore of my body was a window and all the windows open and the light flooding my gizzards. I can feel the light curving under the vault of my ribs and my ribs hang there over a hollow nave trembling with reverberations. How long this lasts I have no idea; I have lost all sense of time and place. After what seems like an eternity there follows an interval of semiconsciousness balanced by such a calm that I feel a great lake inside me, a lake of iridescent sheen, cool as jelly; and over this lake, rising in great swooping spirals, there emerge great flocks of birds, huge birds of passage with long slim legs and brilliant plumage. Flock after flock surge up from the cool, still surface of the lake and, passing under my clavicles, lose themselves in the white sea of space. And then slowly, very slowly, as if an old woman in a white cap were going the rounds of my body, slowly the windows are closed and my organs drop back into place. Suddenly the lights flare up and the man in the white box whom I had taken for a Turkish officer turns out to be a woman with a flower-pot on her head.

There is a buzz now and all those who want to cough cough to their heart's content. There is the noise of feet shuffling and seats slamming, the steady, frittering noise of people moving about aimlessly, of people fluttering their programs and pretending to read and then dropping their programs and scuffling under their seats, thankful for even the slightest accident which will prevent them from asking themselves what they were thinking about because if they knew they were thinking about nothing they would go mad. In the harsh glare of the lights they look at each other vacuously and there is a strange tenseness with which they stare at one another. And the moment the conductor raps again they fall back into a cataleptic state—they scratch themselves unconsciously or they remember suddenly a show-window in which there was displayed a scarf or a hat; they remember every detail of that window with amazing clarity, but where it was exactly, that they can't recall; and that bothers them, keeps them wide awake, restless, and they listen now with redoubled attention because they are wide awake and no matter how wonderful the music is they will not lose consciousness of that show-window and that scarf that was hanging there, or the hat.

And this fierce attentiveness communicates itself; even the orchestra seems galvanized into an extraordinary alertness. The second number goes off like a top—so fast indeed that when suddenly the music ceases and the lights go up some are stuck in their seats like carrots, their jaws working convulsively, and if you suddenly shouted in their ear *Brahms, Beethoven, Mendeleieff, Herzegovina,* they would answer without thinking—4, 967, 289.

By the time we get to the Debussy number the atmosphere is completely poisoned. I find myself wondering what it feels like, during intercourse, to be a woman— whether the pleasure is keener, etc. Try to imagine something penetrating my groin, but have only a vague sensation of pain. I try to focus, but the music is too slippery. I can think of nothing but a vase slowly turning and the figures dropping off into space. Finally there is only light turning, and how does light turn, I ask myself. The man next to me is sleeping soundly. He looks like a broker, with his big paunch and his waxed moustache. I like him thus. I like especially that big paunch and all that went into the making of it. Why shouldn't he sleep soundly? If he wants to listen he can always rustle up the price of a ticket. I notice that the better dressed they are the more soundly they sleep. They have an easy conscience, the rich. If a poor man dozes off, even for a few seconds, he feels mortified; he imagines that he has committed a crime against the composer.

In the Spanish number the house was electrified. Everybody sat on the edge of his seat—the drums woke them up. I thought when the drums started it would keep up forever. I expected to see people fall out of the boxes or throw their hats away. There was something heroic about it and he could have driven us stark mad, Ravel, if he had wanted to. But that's not Ravel. Suddenly it all died down. It was as if he remembered, in the midst of his antics, that he had on a cut-away suit. He arrested himself. A great mistake, in my humble opinion. Art consists in going the full length. If you start with the drums you have to end with dynamite, or TNT. Ravel sacrificed something for form, for a vegetable that people must digest before going to bed.

My thoughts are spreading. The music is slipping away from me, now that the drums have ceased. People everywhere are composed to order. Under the exit light is a Werther sunk in despair; he is leaning on his two elbows, his eyes are glazed. Near the door, huddled in a big cape, stands a Spaniard with a sombrero in his hand. He looks as if he were posing for the Balzac of Rodin. From the neck up he suggests Buffalo Bill. In the gallery opposite me, in the front row, sits a woman with her legs spread wide apart; she looks as though she had lock-jaw, with her neck thrown back and dislocated. The woman with the red hat who is dozing over the rail—marvellous if she were to have a hemorrhage! if suddenly she spilled a bucketful on those stiff shirts below. Imagine these bloody no-accounts going home from the concert with blood on their dickies!

Sleep is the keynote. No one is listening any more. Impossible to think and listen. Impossible to dream even when the music itself is nothing but a dream. A woman with white gloves holds a swan in her lap. The legend is that when Leda was fecundated she gave birth to twins. Everybody is giving birth to something—everybody but the Lesbian in the upper tier. Her head is uptilted, her throat wide open; she is all alert and tingling with the shower of sparks that burst from the radium symphony. Jupiter is piercing her ears. Little phrases from California, whales with big fins, Zanzibar, the Alcazar. *When along the Guadalquivir there were a thousand mosques a-shimmer.* Deep in the icebergs and the days all lilac. The Money Street with two white hitching-posts. The gargoyles ... the man with the Jaworski nonsense ... the river lights ... the ...

In America I had a number of Hindu friends, some good, some bad, some indifferent. Circumstances had placed me in a position where fortunately I could be of aid to them; I secured jobs for them, I harbored them, and I fed them when necessary. They were very grateful, I must say, so much so, in fact, that they made my life miserable with their attentions. Two of them were saints, if I know what a saint is; particularly Gupte who was found one morning with his throat cut from ear to ear. In a little boarding-house in Greenwich Village he was found one morning stretched out stark naked on the bed, his flute beside him, and his throat gashed, as I say, from ear to ear. It was never discovered whether he had been murdered or whether he had committed suicide. But that's neither here nor there …

I'm thinking back to the chain of circumstances which has brought me finally to Nanantatee's place. Thinking how strange it is that I should have forgotten all about Nanantatee until the other day when lying in a shabby hotel room on the Rue Cels. I'm lying there on the iron bed thinking what a zero I have become, what a cipher, what a nullity, when, bango! out pops the word: NONENTITY! That's what we called him in New York—Nonentity. *Mister* Nonentity.

I'm lying on the floor now in that gorgeous suite of rooms he boasted of when he was in New York. Nanantatee is playing the good Samaritan; he has given me a pair of itchy blankets, horse blankets they are, in which I curl up on the dusty floor. There are little jobs to do every hour of the day—that is, if I am foolish enough to remain indoors. In the morning he wakes me rudely in order to have me prepare the vegetables for his lunch: onions, garlic, beans, etc. His friend, Kepi, warns me not to eat the food—he says it's bad. Bad or good what difference? *Food!* That's all that matters. For a little food I am quite willing to sweep his carpets with a broken broom, to wash his clothes and to scrape the crumbs off the floor as soon as he has finished eating. He's become absolutely immaculate since my arrival: everything has to be dusted now, the chairs must be arranged a certain way, the clock must ring, the toilet must flush properly ... A crazy Hindu if ever there was one! And parsimonious as a string bean. I'll have a great laugh over it when I get out of his clutches, but just now I'm a prisoner, a man without caste, an untouchable ...

If I fail to come back at night and roll up in the horse blankets he says to me on arriving: "Oh, so you didn't die then? I thought you had died." And though he knows I'm absolutely penniless he tells me every day about some cheap room he has just discovered in the neighborhood. "But I can't take a room yet, you know that," I say. And then, blinking his eyes like a Chink, he answers smoothly: "Oh, yes, I forgot that you had no money. I am always forgetting, Endree ... But when the cable comes ... when Miss Mona sends you the money, then you will come with me to look for a room, eh?" And in the next breath he urges me to stay as long as I wish—"six months ... seven months, Endree ... you are very good for me here."

Nanantatee is one of the Hindus I never did anything for in America. He represented himself to me as a wealthy merchant, a pearl merchant, with a luxurious suite of rooms on the Rue Lafayette, Paris, a villa in Bombay, a bungalow in Darjeeling. I could see from the first glance that he was a half-wit, but then half-wits sometimes have the genius to amass a fortune. I didn't know that he paid his hotel bill in New York by leaving a couple of fat pearls in the proprietor's hands. It seems amusing to me now that this little duck once swaggered about the lobby of that hotel in New York with an ebony cane, bossing the bell-hops around, ordering luncheons for his guests, calling up the porter for theatre tickets, renting a taxi by the day, etc., etc., all without a sou in his pocket. Just a string of fat pearls around his neck which he cashed one by one as time wore on. And the fatuous way he used to pat me on the back, thank me for being so good to the Hindu boys—"they are all very intelligent boys, Endree . . . very intelligent!" Telling me that the good lord so-and-so would repay me for my kindness. That explains now why they used to giggle so, these intelligent Hindu boys, when I suggested that they touch Nanantatee for a five-spot.

Curious now how the good lord so-and-so is requiting me for my benevolence. I'm nothing but a slave to this fat little duck. I'm at his beck and call continually. He needs me here—he tells me so to my face. When he goes to the crap-can he shouts: "Endree, bring me a pitcher of water, please. I must wipe myself." He wouldn't think of using toilet paper, Nanantatee. Must be against his religion. No, he calls for a pitcher of water and a rag. He's *delicate,* the fat little duck. Sometimes when I'm drinking a cup of pale tea in which he has dropped a rose-leaf he comes alongside of me and lets a loud fart, right in my face. He never says "Excuse me!" The word must be missing from his Gujurati dictionary.

The day I arrived at Nanantatee's apartment he was in the act of performing his ablutions, that is to say, he was standing over a dirty bowl trying to work his crooked arm around toward the back of his neck. Beside the bowl was a brass goblet which he used to change the water. He requested me to be silent during the ceremony. I sat there silently, as I was bidden, and watched him as he sang and prayed and spat now and then into the wash-bowl. So this is the wonderful suite of rooms he talked about in New York! The Rue Lafayette! It sounded like an important street to me back there in New York. I thought only millionaires and pearl merchants inhabited the street. It sounds wonderful, the Rue Lafayette, when you're on the other side of the water. So does Fifth Avenue, when you're over here. One can't imagine what dumps there are on these swell streets. Anyway, here I am at last, sitting in the gorgeous suite of rooms on the Rue Lafayette. And this crazy duck with his crooked arm is going through the ritual of washing himself. The chair on which I'm sitting is broken, the bedstead is falling apart, the wall-paper is in tatters, there is an open valise under the bed crammed with dirty wash. From where I sit I can glance at the miserable courtyard down below where the aristocracy of the Rue Lafayette sit and smoke their clay pipes. I wonder now, as he chants the doxology, what that bungalow in Darjeeling looks like. It's interminable, his chanting and praying.

He explains to me that he is obliged to wash in a certain prescribed way—his religion demands it. But on Sundays he takes a bath in the tin tub—the Great I AM will wink at that, he says. When he's dressed he goes to the cupboard, kneels before a little idol on the third shelf, and repeats the mumbojumbo. If you pray like that every day, he says, nothing will happen to you. The good lord what's his name never forgets an obedient servant. And then he shows me the crooked arm which he got in a taxi accident on a day doubtless when he had neglected to rehearse the complete song and dance. His arm looks like a broken compass; it's not an arm any more, but a knuckle-bone with a shank attached. Since the arm has been repaired he has developed a pair of swollen glands in the armpit—fat little glands, exactly like a dog's testicles. While bemoaning his plight he remembers suddenly that the doctor had recommended a more liberal diet. He begs me at once to sit down and make up a menu with plenty of fish and meat. "And what about oysters, Endree—for *le petit frère?*" But all this is only to make an impression on me. He hasn't the slightest intention of buying himself oysters, or meat, or fish. Not as long as I am there, at least. For the time being we are going to nourish ourselves on lentils and rice and all the dry foods he has stored away, in the attic. And the butter he bought last week, that won't go to waste either. When he commences to cure the butter the smell is unbearable. I used to run out at first, when he started frying the butter, but now I stick it out. He'd be only too delighted if he could make me vomit up my meal—that would be something else to put away in the cupboard along with the dry bread and the mouldy cheese and the little grease cakes that he makes himself out of the stale milk and the rancid butter.

For the last five years, so it seems, he hasn't done a stroke of work, hasn't turned over a penny. Business has gone to smash. He talks to me about pearls in the Indian

ocean—big fat ones on which you can live for a lifetime.
The Arabs are ruining the business, he says. But meanwhile he prays to the lord so-and-so every day, and that
sustains him. He's on a marvellous footing with the deity:
knows just how to cajole him, how to wheedle a few sous
out of him. It's a pure commercial relationship. In exchange for that flummery before the cabinet every day he
gets his ration of beans and garlic, to say nothing of the
swollen testicles under his arm. He is confident that everything will turn out well in the end. The pearls will sell
again some day, maybe five years hence, maybe twenty—
when the Lord Boomaroom wishes it. "And when the
business goes, Endree, you will get ten per cent—for
writing the letters. But first, Endree, you must write the
letter to find out if we can get credit from India. It will
take about six months for an answer, maybe seven
months ... the boats are not fast in India." He has no
conception of time at all, the little duck. When I ask him
if he has slept well he will say: "Ah, yes, Endree, I sleep
very well ... I sleep sometimes ninety-two hours in three
days."

Mornings he is usually too weak to do any work. His
arm! That poor broken crutch of an arm! I wonder sometimes when I see him twisting it around the back of his
neck how he will ever get it into place again. If it weren't
for that little paunch he carries he'd remind me of one of
those contortionists at the Cirque Medrano. All he needs
is to break a leg. When he sees me sweeping the carpet,
when he sees what a cloud of dust I raise, he begins to
cluck like a pygmy. "Good! Very good, Endree. And now
I will pick up the knots." That means that there are a few
crumbs of dust which I have overlooked; it is a polite
way he has of being sarcastic.

Afternoons there are always a few cronies from the
pearl market dropping in to pay him a visit. They're all
very suave, butter-tongued bastards with soft, doelike
eyes; they sit around the table drinking the perfumed tea
with a loud, hissing noise while Nanantatee jumps up and
down like a jack-in-the-box or points to a crumb on the
floor and says in his smooth slippery voice—"Will you

please to pick that up, Endree." When the guests arrive he goes unctuously to the cupboard and gets out the dry crusts of bread which he toasted maybe a week ago and which taste strongly now of the mouldy wood. Not a crumb is thrown away. If the bread gets too sour he takes it downstairs to the concierge who, so he says, has been very kind to him. According to him, the concierge is delighted to get the stale bread—she makes bread pudding with it.

One day my friend Anatole came to see me. Nanantatee was delighted. Insisted that Anatole stay for tea. Insisted that he try little grease cakes and the stale bread. "You must come every day," he says, "and teach me Russian. Fine language, Russian . . . I want to speak it. How do you say that again, Endree—*borscht*? You will write that down for me, please, Endree . . ." And I must write it on the typewriter, no less, so that he can observe my technique. He bought the typewriter, after he had collected on the bad arm, because the doctor recommended it as a good exercise. But he got tired of the typewriter shortly—it was an *English* typewriter.

When he learned that Anatole played the mandolin he said: "Very good! You must come every day and teach me the music. I will buy a mandolin as soon as business is better. It is good for my arm." The next day he borrows a phonograph from the concierge. "You will please teach me to dance, Endree. My stomach is too big." I am hoping that he will buy a porterhouse steak some day so that I can say to him: "You will please bite it for me, *Mister* Nonentity. My teeth are not strong!"

As I said a moment ago, ever since my arrival he has become extraordinarily meticulous. "Yesterday," he says, "you made three mistakes, Endree. First, you forgot to close the toilet door and so all night it makes boom-boom; second, you left the kitchen window open and so the window is cracked this morning. And you forgot to put out the milk bottle! Always you will put out the milk bottle please, before you go to bed, and in the morning you will please bring in the bread."

Every day his friend Kepi drops in to see if any visitors have arrived from India. He waits for Nanantatee to go out and then he scurries to the cupboard and devours the sticks of bread that are hidden away in a glass jar. The food is no good, he insists, but he puts it away like a rat. Kepi is a scrounger, a sort of human tick who fastens himself to the hide of even the poorest compatriot. From Kepi's standpoint they are all nabobs. For a Manila cheroot and the price of a drink he will suck any Hindu's ass. A Hindu's mind you, but not an Englishman's. He has the address of every whore-house in Paris, and the rates. Even from the ten-franc points he gets his little commission. And he knows the shortest way to any place you want to go. He will ask you first if you want to go by taxi; if you say no, he will suggest the bus, and if that is too high then the tramway or the metro. Or he will offer to walk you there and save a franc or two, knowing very well that it will be necessary to pass a *tabac* on the way and that you will please be so good as to buy me a little cheroot.

Kepi is interesting, in a way, because he has absolutely no ambition except to get a fuck every night. Every penny he makes, and they are damned few, he squanders in the dance-halls. He has a wife and eight children in Bombay, but that does not prevent him from proposing marriage to any little *femme de chambre* who is stupid and credulous enough to be taken in by him. He has a little room on the Rue Condorcet for which he pays sixty francs a month. He papered it all himself. Very proud of it, too. He uses violet-colored ink in his fountain-pen because it lasts longer. He shines his own shoes, presses his own pants, does his own laundry. For a little cigar, a cheroot, if you please, he will escort you all over Paris. If you stop to look at a shirt or a collar-button his eyes flash. "Don't buy it here," he will say. "They ask too much. I will show you a cheaper place." And before you have time to think about it he will whisk you away and deposit you before another shop-window where there are the same ties and shirts and collar-buttons—maybe it's the very same store! but you don't know the difference. When Kepi hears that you want to buy something his soul becomes animated. He will ask you so many questions and drag you to so many places that you are bound to get thirsty and ask him to have a drink, whereupon you will discover to your amazement that you are again standing in a *tabac*—maybe the same *tabac*!—and Kepi is saying again in that small unctuous voice: "Will you please be so good as to buy me a little cheroot?" No matter what you propose doing, even if it's only to walk around the corner, Kepi will economize for you. Kepi will show you the shortest way, the cheapest place, the biggest dish, because whatever you have to do you *must* pass a *tabac*, and whether there is a revolution or a lock-out or a quarantine Kepi must be at the Moulin Rouge or the Olympia or the Ange Rouge when the music strikes up.

The other day he brought a book for me to read. It was about a famous suit between a holy man and the editor of an Indian paper. The editor, it seems, had openly accused the holy man of leading a scandalous life; he went further, and accused the holy man of being diseased. Kepi says it must have been the great French pox, but Nanantatee avers that it was the Japanese clap. For Nanantatee everything has to be a little exaggerated. At any rate, says Nanantatee cheerily: "You will please tell me what it says, Endree. I can't read the book—it hurts my arm." Then, by way of encouraging me—"it is a fine book about the fucking, Endree. Kepi has brought it for you. He thinks about nothing but the girls. So many girls he fucks—just like Krishna. We don't believe in that business, Endree . . ."

A little later he takes me upstairs to the attic which is loaded down with tin cans and crap from India wrapped in burlap and firecracker paper. "Here is where I bring the girls," he says. And then rather wistfully: "I am not a very good fucker, Endree. I don't screw the girls any more. I hold them in my arms and I say the words. I like only to say the words now." It isn't necessary to listen any further: I know that he is going to tell me about his arm. I can see him lying there with that broken hinge dangling from the side of the bed. But to my surprise he adds: "I am no good for the fucking, Endree. I never was a very good fucker. My brother, he is good! Three times a day, every day! And Kepi, he is good—just like Krishna."

His mind is fixed now on the "fucking business." Downstairs, in the little room where he kneels before the open cabinet, he explains to me how it was when he was

rich and his wife and children were here. On holidays he
would take his wife to the House of All Nations and hire
a room for the night. Every room was appointed in a different style. His wife liked it there very much. "A wonderful place for the fucking, Endree. I know all the
rooms . . ."

The walls of the little room in which we are sitting are
crammed with photographs. Every branch of the family is
represented, it is like a cross-section of the Indian empire.
For the most part the members of this genealogical tree
look like withered leaves: the women are frail and they
have a startled, frightened look in their eyes: the men
have a keen, intelligent look, like educated chimpanzees.
They are all there, about ninety of them, with their white
bullocks, their dung-cakes, their skinny legs, their old-
fashioned spectacles; in the background, now and then,
one catches a glimpse of the parched soil, of a crumbling
pediment, of an idol with crooked arms, a sort of human
centipede. There is something so fantastic, so incongruous about this gallery that one is reminded inevitably of
the great spawn of temples which stretch from the Himalayas to the tip of Ceylon, a vast jumble of architecture,
staggering in beauty and at the same time monstrous, hid-
eously monstrous because the fecundity which seethes
and ferments in the myriad ramifications of design seems
to have exhausted the very soil of India itself. Looking at
the seething hive of figures which swarm the façades of
the temples one is overwhelmed by the potency of these
dark, handsome people who mingled their mysterious
streams in a sexual embrace that has lasted thirty centuries or more. These frail men and women with piercing
eyes who stare out of the photographs seem like the emaciated shadows of those virile, massive figures who incar-
nated themselves in stone and fresco from one end of
India to the other in order that the heroic myths of the
races who here intermingled should remain forever en-
twined in the hearts of their countrymen. When I look at
only a fragment of these spacious dreams of stone, these
toppling, sluggish edifices studded with gems, coagulated
with human sperm, I am overwhelmed by the dazzling
splendor of those imaginative flights which enabled half

a billion people of diverse origins to thus incarnate the most fugitive expressions of their longing.

It is a strange, inexplicable medley of feelings which assails me now as Nanantatee prattles on about the sister who died in child-birth. There she is on the wall, a frail, timid thing of twelve or thirteen clinging to the arm of a dotard. At ten years of age she was given in wedlock to this old roué who had already buried five wives. She had seven children, only one of whom survived her. She was given to the aged gorilla in order to keep the pearls in the family. As she was passing away, so Nanantatee puts it, she whispered to the doctor: "I am tired of this fucking ... I don't want to fuck any more, doctor." As he relates this to me he scratches his head solemnly with his withered arm. "The fucking business is bad, Endree," he says. "But I will give you a word that will always make you lucky; you must say it every day, over and over, a million times you must say it. It is the best word there is, Endree ... say it now ... OOMAHARUMOOMA!"

"OOMARABOO ..."

"No, Endree ... like this ... OOMAHARUMOOMA!"

"OOMAMABOOMBA ..."

"No, Endree ... like this ...

"... but what with the murky light, the botchy print, the tattered cover, the jigjagged page, the fumbling fingers, the foxtrotting fleas, the lie-a-bed lice, the scum on his tongue, the drop in his eye, the lump in his throat, the drink in his pottle, the itch in his palm, the wail of his wind, the grief from his breath, the fog of his brainfag, the tic of his conscience, the height of his rage, the gush of his fundament, the fire in his gorge, the tickle of his tail, the rats in his garret, the hullabaloo and the dust in his ears, since it took him a month to steal a march, he was hardset to memorize more than a word a week."

I suppose I would never have gotten out of Nanantatee's clutches if fate hadn't intervened. One night, as luck would have it, Kepi asked me if I wouldn't take one of his clients to a whore-house near by. The young man had just come from India and he had not very much money to spend. He was one of Gandhi's men, one of that little band who made the historic march to the sea during the salt trouble. A very gay disciple of Gandhi's I must say, despite the vows of abstinence he had taken. Evidently he hadn't looked at a woman for ages. It was all I could do to get him as far as the Rue Laferrière; he was like a dog with his tongue hanging out. And a pompous, vain little devil to boot! He had decked himself out in a corduroy suit, a beret, a cane, a Windsor tie; he had bought himself two fountain-pens, a kodak, and some fancy underwear. The money he was spending was a gift from the merchants of Bombay; they were sending him to England to spread the gospel of Gandhi.

Once inside Miss Hamilton's joint he began to lose his *sang-froid.* When suddenly he found himself surrounded by a bevy of naked women he looked at me in consternation. "Pick one out," I said. "You can have your choice." He had become so rattled that he could scarcely look at them. "You do it for me," he murmured, blushing violently. I looked them over coolly and picked out a plump young wench who seemed full of feathers. We sat down in the reception room and waited for the drinks. The madame wanted to know why I didn't take a girl also. "Yes, you take one too," said the young Hindu. "I don't want to be alone with her." So the girls were brought in again and I chose one for myself, a rather tall, thin one with melancholy eyes. We were left alone, the four of us, in the reception room. After a few moments my young Gandhi leans over and whispers something in my ear. "Sure, if you like her better, take her," I said, and so, rather awkwardly and considerably embarrassed, I explained to the girls that we would like to switch. I saw at once that we had made a *faux pas,* but by now my young friend had become gay and lecherous and nothing would do but to get upstairs quickly and have it over with.

We took adjoining rooms with a connecting door between. I think my companion had in mind to make another switch once he had satisfied his sharp, gnawing hunger. At any rate, no sooner had the girls left the room to prepare themselves than I hear him knocking on the door. "Where is the toilet, please?" he asks. Not thinking that it was anything serious I urge him to do in the *bidet.* The girls return with towels in their hands. I hear him giggling in the next room.

As I'm putting on my pants suddenly I hear a commotion in the next room. The girl is bawling him out, calling him a pig, a dirty little pig. I can't imagine what he has done to warrant such an outburst. I'm standing there with one foot in my trousers listening attentively. He's trying to explain to her in English, raising his voice louder and louder until it becomes a shriek.

I hear a door slam and in another moment the madame bursts into my room, her face as red as a beet, her arms gesticulating wildly. "You ought to be ashamed of yourself," she screams, "bringing a man like that to my place! He's a barbarian ... he's a pig ... he's a ... !" My companion is standing behind her, in the doorway, a look of utmost discomfiture on his face. "What did you do?" I ask.

"What did he do?" yells the madame. "I'll show you ... Come here!" And grabbing me by the arm she drags me into the next room. "There! There!" she screams, pointing to the bidet.

"Come on, let's get out," says the Hindu boy.

"Wait a minute, you can't get out as easily as all that."

The madame is standing by the *bidet,* fuming and spitting. The girls are standing there too, with towels in their hands. The five of us are standing there looking at the *bidet.* There are two enormous turds floating in the water. The madame bends down and puts a towel over it. "Frightful! Frightful!" she wails. "Never have I seen anything like this! A pig! A dirty little pig!"

The Hindu boy looks at me reproachfully. "You should have told me!" he says. "I didn't know it wouldn't go down. I asked you where to go and you told me to use that." He is almost in tears.

Finally the madame takes me to one side. She has become a little more reasonable now. After all, it was a mistake. Perhaps the gentlemen would like to come downstairs and order another drink—for the girls. It was a great shock to the girls. They are not used to such things. And if the good gentlemen will be so kind as to remember the *femme de chambre* ... It is not so pretty for the *femme de chambre*—that mess, that ugly mess. She shrugs her shoulders and winks her eye. A lamentable incident. But an accident. If the gentlemen will wait here a few moments the maid will bring the drinks. Would the gentlemen like to have some champagne? Yes?

"I'd like to get out of here," says the Hindu boy weakly.

"Don't you feel so badly about it," says the madame. "It is all over now. Mistakes will happen sometimes. Next time you will ask for the toilet." She goes on about the toilet—one on every floor, it seems. And a bathroom too. "I have lots of English clients," she says. "They are all gentlemen. The gentleman is a Hindu? Charming people, the Hindus. So intelligent. So handsome."

When we get into the street the charming young gentleman is almost weeping. He is sorry now that he bought a corduroy suit and the cane and the fountain-pens. He talks about the eight vows that he took, the control of the palate, etc. On the march to Dandi even a plate of ice cream it was forbidden to take. He tells me about the spinning wheel—how the little band of Satyagrahists imitated the devotion of their master. He relates with pride how he walked beside the master and conversed with him. I have the illusion of being in the presence of one of the twelve disciples.

During the next few days we see a good deal of each other; there are interviews to be arranged with the newspaper men and lectures to be given to the Hindus of Paris. It is amazing to see how these spineless devils order one another about; amazing also to see how ineffectual they are in all that concerns practical affairs. And the jealousy and the intrigues, the petty, sordid rivalries. Wherever there are ten Hindus together there is India with her sects and schisms, her racial, lingual, religious, political antagonisms. In the person of Gandhi they are experiencing for a brief moment the miracle of unity, but when he goes there will be a crash, an utter relapse into that strife and chaos so characteristic of the Indian people.

The young Hindu, of course, is optimistic. He has been to America and he has been contaminated by the cheap idealism of the Americans, contaminated by the ubiquitous bath-tub, the five and ten cent store bric-à-brac, the bustle, the efficiency, the machinery, the high wages, the free libraries, etc., etc. His ideal would be to americanize India. He is not at all pleased with Gandhi's retrogressive mania. *Forward,* he says, just like a Y. M. C. A. man. As I listen to his tales of America I see how absurd it is to expect of Gandhi that miracle which will deroute the trend of destiny. India's enemy is not England, but America. India's enemy is the time spirit, the hand which cannot be turned back. Nothing will avail to offset this virus which is poisoning the whole world. America is the very incarnation of doom. She will drag the whole world down to the bottomless pit.

He thinks the Americans are a very gullible people. He tells me about the credulous souls who succored him there—the Quakers, the Unitarians, the Theosophists, the New Thoughters, the Seventh Day Adventists, etc. He knew where to sail his boat, this bright young man. He knew how to make the tears come to his eyes at the right moment; he knew how to take up a collection, how to appeal to the minister's wife, how to make love to the mother and daughter at the same time. To look at him you would think him a saint. And he is a saint, in the modern fashion; a contaminated saint who talks in one breath of love, brotherhood, bath-tubs, sanitation, efficiency, etc.

The last night of his sojourn in Paris is given up to "the fucking business." He has had a full program all day—conferences, cablegrams, interviews, photographs for the newspapers, affectionate farewells, advice to the faithful, etc., etc. At dinner time he decides to lay aside his troubles. He orders champagne with the meal, he snaps his fingers at the *garçon* and behaves in general like the boorish little peasant that he is. And since he has had a bellyful of all the good places he suggests now that I show him something more primitive. He would like to go to a very cheap place, order two or three girls at once. I steer him along the Boulevard de la Chapelle, warning him all the while to be careful of his pocket-book. Around Aubervilliers we duck into a cheap dive and immediately we've got a flock of them on our hands. In a few minutes he's dancing with a naked wench, a huge blonde with creases in her jowls. I can see her ass reflected a dozen times in the mirrors that line the room—and those dark, bony fingers of his clutching her tenaciously. The table is full of beer glasses, the mechanical piano is wheezing and gasping. The girls who are unoccupied are sitting placidly on the leather benches, scratching themselves peacefully just like a family of chimpanzees. There is a sort of subdued pandemonium in the air, a note of repressed violence, as if the awaited explosion required the advent of some utterly minute detail, something microscopic but thoroughly unpremeditated, completely unexpected. In that sort of half-reverie which permits one to participate in an event and yet remain quite aloof, the little detail which was lacking began obscurely but insistently to coagulate, to assume a freakish, crystalline form, like the frost which gathers on the window-pane. And like those frost patterns which seem so bizarre, so utterly free and fantastic in design, but which are nevertheless determined by the most rigid laws, so this sensation which commenced to take form inside me seemed also to be giving obedience to ineluctable laws. My whole being was responding to the dictates of an ambiance which it had never before experienced; that which I could call myself seemed to be contracting, condensing, shrinking from the stale, customary boundaries of the flesh whose perimeter knew only the modulations of the nerve ends.

And the more substantial, the more solid the core of me became, the more delicate and extravagant appeared the close, palpable reality out of which I was being squeezed. In the measure that I became more and more metallic, in the same measure the scene before my eyes became inflated. The state of tension was so finely drawn now that the introduction of a single foreign particle, even a microscopic particle, as I say, would have shattered everything. For the fraction of a second perhaps I experienced that utter clarity which the epileptic, it is said, is given to know. In that moment I lost completely the illusion of time and space: the world unfurled its drama simultaneously along a meridian which had no axis. In this sort of hair-trigger eternity I felt that everything was justified, supremely justified; I felt the wars inside me that had left behind this pulp and wrack; I felt the crimes that were seething here to emerge tomorrow in blatant screamers; I felt the misery that was grinding itself out with pestle and mortar, the long dull misery that dribbles away in dirty handkerchiefs. On the meridian of time there is no injustice: there is only the poetry of motion creating the illusion of truth and drama. If at any moment anywhere one comes face to face with the absolute that great sympathy which makes men like Gautama and Jesus seem divine freezes away; the monstrous thing is not that men have created roses out of this dung-heap, but that, for some reason or other, they should *want* roses. For some reason or other man looks for the miracle, and to accomplish it he will wade through blood. He will debauch himself with ideas, he will reduce himself to a shadow if for only one second of his life he can close his eyes to the hideousness of reality. Everything is endured, disgrace, humiliation, poverty, war, crime, *ennui*—in the belief that overnight something will occur, a miracle, which will render life tolerable. And all the while a meter is running inside and there is no hand that can reach in there and shut it off. All the while someone is eating the bread of life and drinking the wine, some dirty fat cockroach of a priest who hides away in the cellar guzzling it, while up above in the light of the street a phantom host touches the lips and the blood is pale as water. And out of the endless torment and misery no miracle comes forth, no microscopic vestige even of relief. Only ideas, pale, attenuated ideas which have to be fattened by slaughter; ideas which come forth like bile, like the guts of a pig when the carcass is ripped open.

And so I think what a miracle it would be if this miracle which man attends eternally should turn out to be nothing more than these two enormous turds which the faithful disciple dropped in the *bidet*. What if at the last moment, when the banquet table is set and the cymbals clash, there should appear suddenly, and wholly without warning, a silver platter on which even the blind could see that there is nothing more, and nothing less, than two enormous lumps of shit. That, I believe would be more miraculous than anything which man has looked forward to. It would be miraculous because it would be undreamed of. It would be more miraculous than even the wildest dream because *anybody* could imagine the possibility but nobody ever has, and probably nobody ever again will.

Somehow the realization that nothing was to be hoped

for had a salutary effect upon me. For weeks and months, for years, in fact, all my life I had been looking forward to something happening, some extrinsic event that would alter my life, and now suddenly, inspired by the absolute hopelessness of everything, I felt relieved felt as though a great burden had been lifted from my shoulders. At dawn I parted company with the young Hindu, after touching him for a few francs, enough for a room. Walking toward Montparnasse I decided to let myself drift with the tide, to make not the least resistance to fate, no matter in what form it presented itself. Nothing that had happened to me thus far had been sufficient to destroy me; nothing had been destroyed except my illusions. I myself was intact. The world was intact. Tomorrow there might be a revolution, a plague, an earthquake; tomorrow there might not be left a single soul to whom one could turn for sympathy, for aid, for faith. It seemed to me that the great calamity had already manifested itself, that I could be no more truly alone than at this very moment. I made up my mind that I would hold on to nothing, that I would expect nothing, that henceforth I would live as an animal, a beast of prey, a rover, a plunderer. Even if war were declared, and it were my lot to go, I would grab the bayonet and plunge it, plunge it up to the hilt. And if rape were the order of the day then rape I would, and with a vengeance. At this very moment, in the quiet dawn of a new day, was not the earth giddy with crime and distress? Had one single element of man's nature been altered, vitally, fundamentally altered, by the incessant march of history? By what he calls the better part of his nature, man has been betrayed, that is all. At the extreme limits of his spiritual being man finds himself again naked as a savage. When he finds God, as it were, he has been picked clean: he is a skeleton. One must burrow into life again in order to put on flesh. The word must become flesh; the soul thirsts. On whatever crumb my eye fastens, I will pounce and devour. If to live is the paramount thing, then I will live, even if I must become a cannibal. Heretofore I have been trying to save my precious hide, trying to preserve the few pieces of meat that hid my bones. I am done with that. I have reached the limits of endurance. My back is to the wall; I can retreat no further. As far as history goes I am dead. If there is something beyond I shall have to bounce back. I have found God, but he is insufficient. I am only spiritually dead. Physically I am alive. Morally I am free. The world which I have departed is a menagerie. The dawn is breaking on a new world, a jungle world in which the lean spirits roam with sharp claws. If I am a hyena I am a lean and hungry one: I go forth to fatten myself.

At one-thirty I called on Van Norden, as per agreement. He had warned me that if he didn't answer it would mean that he was sleeping with some one, probably his Georgia cunt.

Anyway, there he was, tucked away comfortably, but with an air of weariness as usual. He wakes up, cursing himself, or cursing the job, or cursing life. He wakes up utterly bored and discomfited, chagrined to think that he did not die overnight.

I sit down by the window and give him what encouragement I can. It is tedious work. One has to actually coax him out of bed. Mornings—he means by mornings anywhere between one and five p.m.—mornings, as I say, he gives himself up to reveries. Mostly it is about the past he dreams. About his "cunts." He endeavors to recall how they felt, what they said to him at certain critical moments, where he laid them, and so on. And as he lies there, grinning and cursing, he manipulates his fingers in that curious, bored way of his, as though to convey the impression that his disgust is too great for words. Over the bedstead hangs a douche-bag which he keeps for emergencies—for the *virgins* whom he tracks down like a sleuth. Even after he has slept with one of these mythical creatures he will still refer to her as a virgin, and almost never by name. "My virgin," he will say, just as he says "my Georgia cunt." When he goes to the toilet he says: "If my Georgia cunt calls tell her to wait. Say I said so. And listen, you can have her if you like. I'm tired of her."

He takes a squint at the weather and heaves a deep sigh. If it's rainy he says: "God damn this fucking climate, it makes one morbid." And if the sun is shining brightly he says: "God damn that fucking sun, it makes you blind." As he starts to shave he suddenly remembers that there is no clean towel. "God damn this fucking hotel, they're too stingy to give you a clean towel every day!" No matter what he does or where he goes things are out of joint. Either it's the fucking country or the fucking job, or else it's some fucking cunt who's put him on the blink.

"My teeth are all rotten," he says, gargling his throat. "It's the fucking bread they give you to eat here." He opens his mouth wide and pulls his lower lip down. "See that? Pulled out six teeth yesterday. Soon I'll have to get another plate. That's what you get working for a living. When I was on the bum I had all my teeth, my eyes were bright and clear. Look at me now! It's a wonder I can make a cunt any more. Jesus, what I'd like is to find some rich cunt—like that cute little prick, Carl. Did he ever show you the letters she sends him? Who is she, do you know? He wouldn't tell me her name, the bastard . . . he's afraid I might take her away from him." He gargles his throat again and then he takes a long look at the cavities. "You're lucky," he says ruefully. "You've got friends, at least. I haven't anybody, except that cute little prick who drives me bats about his rich cunt."

"Listen," he says, "do you happen to know a cunt by the name of Norma? She hangs around the Dôme all day. I think she's queer. I had her up here yesterday, tickling her ass. She wouldn't let me do a thing. I had her on the bed . . . I even had her drawers off . . . and then I got disgusted. Jesus, I can't bother struggling that way any more. It isn't worth it. Either they do or they don't—it's foolish to waste time wrestling with them. While you're struggling with a little bitch like that there may be a dozen cunts on the *terrasse* just dying to be laid. It's a fact. They all come over here to get laid. They think it's sinful here . . . *the poor boobs!* Some of these schoolteachers from out West, they're honestly virgins . . . I mean it! They sit around on their can all day thinking about it. You don't have to work over them very much. They're dying for it. I had a married woman the other day who told me she hadn't had a lay for six months. Can you imagine that? Jesus, she was hot! I thought she'd tear the cock off me. And groaning all the time. *'Do you? Do you?'* She kept saying that all the time, like she was nuts. And you know what that bitch wanted to do? She wanted to move in here. Imagine that! Asking me if I loved her. I didn't even know her name. I never know their names . . . I don't want to. The married ones! Christ, if you saw all the married cunts I bring up here you'd never have any more illusions. They're worse than the virgins, the married ones. They don't wait for you to start things—they fish it out for you themselves. And then they talk about love afterwards. It's disgusting. I tell you, I'm actually beginning to hate cunt!"

He looks out the window again. It's drizzling. It's been drizzling this way for the last five days.

"Are we going to the Dôme, Joe?" I call him Joe because he calls me Joe. When Carl is with us he is Joe too. Everybody is Joe because it's easier that way. It's also a pleasant reminder not to take yourself too seriously. Anyway, Joe doesn't want to go to the Dôme—he owes too much money there. He wants to go to the Coupole. Wants to take a little walk first around the block.

"But it's raining, Joe."

"I know, but what the hell! I've got to have my constitutional. I've got to wash the dirt out of my belly." When he says this I have the impression that the whole world is wrapped up there inside his belly, and that it's rotting there.

As he's putting on his things he falls back again into a semi-comatose state. He stands there with one arm in his coat sleeve and his hat on ass-ways and he begins to dream aloud—about the Riviera, about the sun, about lazing one's life away. "All I ask of life," he says, "is a bunch of books, a bunch of dreams, and a bunch of cunt." As he mumbles this meditatively he looks at me with the softest, the most insidious smile. "Do you like that smile?" he says. And then disgustedly—"Jesus, if I could only find some rich cunt to smile at that way!"

"Only a rich cunt can save me now," he says with an air of utmost weariness. "One gets tired of chasing after new cunts all the time. It gets mechanical. The trouble is, you see, I can't fall in love. I'm too much of an egoist. Women only help me to dream, that's all. It's a vice, like drink or opium. I've got to have a new one every day; if

I don't I get morbid. I think too much. Sometimes I'm amazed at myself, how quick I pull it off—and how little it really means. I do it automatically like. Sometimes I'm not thinking about a woman at all, but suddenly I notice a woman looking at me and then bango! it starts all over again. Before I know what I'm doing I've got her up to the room. I don't even remember what I say to them. I bring them up to the room, give them a pat on the ass and before I know what it's all about it's over. It's like a dream ... Do you know what I mean?"

He hasn't much use for the French girls. Can't stand them. "Either they want money or they want you to marry them. At bottom they're all whores. I'd rather wrestle with a virgin," he says. "They give you a little illusion They put up a fight at least." Just the same, as we glance over the *terrasse* there is hardly a whore in sight whom he hasn't fucked at some time or other. Standing at the bar he points them out to me, one by one, goes over them anatomically, describes their good points and their bad. "They're all frigid," he says. And then begins to mould his hands, thinking of the nice, juicy virgins who are just dying for it.

In the midst of his reveries he suddenly arrests himself, and grabbing my arm excitedly he points to a whale of a woman who is just lowering herself into a seat. "There's my Danish cunt," he grunts. "See that ass? *Danish.* How that woman loves it! She just begs me for it. Come over here ... look at her now, from the side! Look at that ass, will you? It's enormous. I tell you, when she climbs over me I can hardly get my arms around it. It blots out the whole world. She makes me feel like a little bug crawling inside her I don't know why I fall for her—I suppose it's that ass. It's so incongruous like. And the creases in it! You can't forget an ass like that. It's a fact ... a solid fact. The others, they may bore you, or they may give you a moment's illusion, but this one—with her ass!—zowie, you can't obliterate her ... it's like going to bed with a monument on top of you."

The Danish cunt seems to have electrified him. He's lost all his sluggishness now. His eyes are popping out of his head. And of course one thing reminds him of another. He wants to get out of the fucking hotel because the noise bothers him. He wants to write a book too so as to have something to occupy his mind. But then the god-damned job stands in the way. "It takes it out of you, that fucking job! I don't want to write about Montparnasse . . . I want to write my life, my thoughts. I want to get the dirt out of my belly . . . Listen, get that one over there! I had her a long time ago. She used to be down near Les Halles. A funny bitch. She lay on the edge of the bed and pulled her dress up. Ever try it that way? Not bad. She didn't hurry me either. She just lay back and played with her hat while I slugged away at her. And when I come she says sort of bored like—Are you through? Like it didn't make any difference at all. Of course, it doesn't make any difference, I know that god-damn well . . . but the cold blooded way she had . . . I sort of liked it . . . it was fas-cinating, you know? When she goes to wipe herself she begins to sing. Going out of the hotel she was still sing-ing. Didn't even say *Au revoir!* Walks off swinging her hat and humming to herself like. That's a whore for you! A good lay though. I think I liked her better than my vir-gin. There's something depraved about screwing a woman who doesn't give a fuck about it. It heals your blood . . ." And then, after a moment's meditation—"Can you imag-ine what she'd be like if she had any feelings?"

"Listen," he says, "I want you to come to the Club with me tomorrow afternoon . . . there's a dance on."

"I can't tomorrow, Joe. I promised to help Carl out . . ."

"Listen, forget that prick! I want you to do me a favor. It's like this"—he commences to mould his hands again. "I've got a cunt lined up . . . she promised to stay with me on my night off. But I'm not positive about her yet. She's got a mother you see . . . some shit of a painter, she chews my ear off every time I see her. I think the truth is, the mother's jealous. I don't think she'd mind so much if I gave her a lay first. You know how it is . . . Anyway, I thought maybe you wouldn't mind taking the mother . . . she's not so bad . . . if I hadn't seen the daughter I might have considered her myself. The daughter's nice and young, fresh like, you know what I mean? There's a clean smell to her . . ."

"Listen, Joe, you'd better find somebody else . . ."

"Aw, don't take it like that! I know how you feel about

it. It's only a little favor I'm asking you to do for me. I don't know how to get rid of the old hen. I thought first I'd get her drunk and ditch her—but I don't think the young one'd like that. They're sentimental like. They come from Minnesota or somewhere. Anyway, come around tomorrow and wake me up, will you? Otherwise I'll oversleep. And besides, I want you to help me find a room. You know I'm helpless. Find me a room in a quiet street, somewhere near here. I've got to stay around here . . . I've got credit here. Listen, promise me you'll do that for me. I'll buy you a meal now and then. Come around anyway, because I go nuts talking to these foolish cunts. I want to talk to you about Havelock Ellis. Jesus, I've had the book out for three weeks now and I haven't looked at it. You sort of rot here. Would you believe it, I've never been to the Louvre—nor the Comédie Française. Is it worth going to those joints? Still, it sort of takes your mind off things, I suppose. What do you do with yourself all day? Don't you get bored? What do you do for a lay? Listen . . . come here! Don't run away yet . . . I'm lonely. Do you know something—if this keeps up another year I'll go nuts. I've got to get out of this fucking country. There's nothing for me here. I know it's lousy now, in America, but just the same . . . You go queer over here . . . all these cheap shits sitting on their ass all day bragging about their work and none of them is worth a stinking damn. They're all failures—that's why they come over here. Listen, Joe, don't you ever get homesick? You're a funny guy . . . you seem to like it over here. What do you see in it . . . I wish you'd tell me. I wish to Christ I could stop thinking about myself. I'm all twisted up inside . . . it's like a knot in there . . . Listen, I know I'm boring the shit out of you, but I've got to talk to someone. I can't talk to those guys upstairs . . . you know what those bastards are like . . . they all take a by-line. And Carl, the little prick, he's so god-damned selfish. I'm an egotist, but I'm not selfish. There's a difference. I'm a neurotic, I guess. I can't stop thinking about myself. It isn't that I think myself so important. . . . I simply can't think about anything else, that's all. If I could fall in love with a woman that might help some. But I can't find a woman who interests me. I'm in a mess,

you can see that can't you? What do you advise me to
do? What would you do in my place? Listen, I don't want
to hold you back any longer, but wake me up
tomorrow—at one-thirty—will you? I'll give you something extra if you'll shine my shoes. And listen, if you've
got an extra shirt, a clean one, bring it along, will you?
Shit, I'm grinding my balls off on that job, and it doesn't
even give me a clean shirt. They've got us over here like
a bunch of niggers. Ah, well, shit! I'm going to take a
walk . . . wash the dirt out of my belly. Don't forget, *to-
morrow*!"

For six months or more it's been going on, this correspondence with the rich cunt, Irene. Recently I've been
reporting to Carl every day in order to bring the affair to
a head, because as far as Irene is concerned this thing
could go on indefinitely. In the last few days there's been
a perfect avalanche of letters exchanged; the last letter we
dispatched was almost forty pages long, and written in
three languages. It was a *pot-pourri,* the last letter—tag
ends of old novels, slices from the Sunday supplement,
reconstructed versions of old letters to Llona and Tania,
garbled transliterations of Rabelais and Petronius—in
short, we exhausted ourselves. Finally Irene decides to
come out of her shell. Finally a letter arrives giving a
rendez-vous at her hotel. Carl is pissing in his pants. It's
one thing to write letters to a woman you don't know; it's
another thing entirely to call on her and make love to her.
At the last moment he's quaking so that I almost fear I'll
have to substitute for him. When we get out of the taxi in
front of her hotel he's trembling so much that I have to
walk him around the block first. He's already had two
Pernods, but they haven't made the slightest impression
on him. The sight of the hotel itself is enough to crush
him: it's a pretentious place with one of those huge empty
lobbies in which Englishwomen sit for hours with a blank
look. In order to make sure that he wouldn't run away I
stood by while the porter telephoned to announce him.
Irene was there, and she was waiting for him. As he got
into the lift he threw me a last despairing glance, one of
those mute appeals which a dog makes when you put a

noose around its neck. Going through the revolving door I thought of Van Norden . . .

I go back to the hotel and wait for a telephone call. He's only got an hour's time and he's promised to let me know the results before going to work. I look over the carbons of the letters we sent her. I try to imagine the situation as it actually is, but it's beyond me. Her letters are much better than ours—they're sincere, that's plain. By now they've sized each other up. I wonder if he's still pissing in his pants.

The telephone rings. His voice sounds queer, squeaky, as though he were frightened and jubilant at the same time. He asks me to substitute for him at the office. "Tell the bastard anything! Tell him I'm dying . . ."

"Listen, Carl . . . can you tell me . . .?"

"Hello! Are you Henry Miller?" It's a woman's voice. It's Irene. She's saying hello to me. Her voice sounds beautiful over the phone . . . beautiful. For a moment I'm in a perfect panic. I don't know what to say to her. I'd like to say: "Listen, Irene, I think you're beautiful . . . I think you're *wonderful*." I'd like to say one true thing to her, no matter how silly it would sound, because now that I hear her voice everything is changed. But before I can gather my wits Carl is on the phone again and he's saying in that queer squeaky voice: "She likes you, Joe. I told her all about you . . ."

At the office I have to hold copy for Van Norden. When it comes time for the break he pulls me aside. He looks glum and ravaged.

"So he's dying, is he, the little prick? Listen, what's the low-down on this?"

"I think he went to see his rich cunt," I answer calmly.

"*What!* You mean he called on her?" He seems beside himself. "Listen, where does she live? What's her name?" I pretend ignorance. "Listen," he says, "you're a decent guy. Why the hell don't you let me in on this racket?"

In order to appease him I promise finally that I'll tell him everything as soon as I get the details from Carl. I can hardly wait myself until I see Carl.

Around noon next day I knock at his door. He's up already and lathering his beard. Can't tell a thing from the expression on his face. Can't even tell whether he's going to tell me the truth. The sun is streaming in through the open window, the birds are chirping, and yet somehow, why it is I don't know, the room seems more barren and poverty-stricken than ever. The floor is slathered with lather, and on the rack there are the two dirty towels which are never changed. And somehow Carl isn't changed either, and that puzzles me more than anything. This morning the whole world ought to be changed, for bad or good, but changed, radically changed. And yet Carl is standing there lathering his face and not a single detail is altered.

"Sit down ... sit down there on the bed," he says. "You're going to hear everything ... but wait first ... wait a little." He commences to lather his face again, and then to hone his razor. He even remarks about the water ... no hot water again.

"Listen, Carl, I'm on tenter-hooks. You can torture me afterwards, if you like, but tell me now, tell me one thing ... was it good or bad?"

He turns away from the mirror with brush in hand and gives me a strange smile. "Wait! I'm going to tell you everything ..."

"That means it was a failure."

"No," he says, drawing out his words. "It wasn't a failure, and it wasn't a success either ... By the way, did you fix it up for me at the office? What did you tell them?"

I see it's no use trying to pull it out of him. When he gets good and ready he'll tell me. Not before. I lie back on the bed, silent as a clam. He goes on shaving.

Suddenly, apropos of nothing at all, he begins to talk— disconnectedly at first, and then more and more clearly, emphatically, resolutely. It's a struggle to get it out, but he seems determined to relate everything; he acts as if he were getting something off his conscience. He even reminds me of the look he gave me as he was going up the elevator shaft. He dwells on that lingeringly, as though to imply that everything were contained in that last moment, as though, if he had to the power to alter things, he would never have put foot outside the elevator.

She was in her dressing sack when he called. There was a bucket of champagne on the dresser. The room was rather dark and her voice was lovely. He gives me all the details about the room, the champagne, how the *garçon* opened it, the noise it made, the way her dressing sack rustled when she came forward to greet him—he tells me everything but what I want to hear.

It was about eight when he called on her. At eight-thirty he was nervous, thinking about the job. "It was about nine when I called you, wasn't it?" he says.

"Yes, about that."

"I was nervous, see . . ."

"I know that. Go on . . ."

I don't know whether to believe him or not, especially after those letters we concocted. I don't even know whether I've heard him accurately, because what he's telling me sounds utterly fantastic. And yet it sounds true too, knowing the sort of guy he is. And then I remember his voice over the telephone, that strange mixture of fright and jubilation. But why isn't he more jubilant now? He keeps smiling all the time, smiling like a rosy little bed-bug that has had its fill. "It was nine o'clock," he says once again, "when I called you up, wasn't it?" I nod my head wearily. Yes, it was nine o'clock. He is certain now that it was nine o'clock because he remembers having taken out his watch. Anyway, when he looked at his watch again it was ten o'clock. At ten o'clock she was lying on the divan with her boobies in her hands. That's the way he gives it to me—in driblets. At eleven o'clock it was all settled; they were going to run away, to Borneo. Fuck the husband! She never loved him anyway. She would never have written the first letter if the husband wasn't old and passionless. "And then she says to me: 'But listen, dear, how do you know you won't grow tired of me?' "

At this point I burst out laughing. This sounds preposterous to me, I can't help it.

"And you said?"

"What did you expect me to say? I said: how could anyone ever grow tired of *you*?"

And then he describes to me what happened after that, how he bent down and kissed her breasts, and how, after he had kissed them fervidly, he stuffed them back into her corsage, or whatever it is they call these things. And after that another *coupe* of champagne.

Around midnight the *garçon* arrives with beer and sandwiches—caviar sandwiches. And all the while, so he says, he has been dying to take a leak. He had one hard-on, but it faded out. All the while his bladder is fit to burst, but he imagines, the cute little prick that he is, that the situation calls for delicacy.

At one-thirty she's for hiring a carriage and driving through the Bois. He has only one thought in his head—how to take a leak? "I love you . . . I adore you," he says. "I'll go anywhere you say—Istamboul, Singapore, Honolulu. Only I must go now . . . It's getting late."

He tells me all this in his dirty little room, with the sun pouring in and the birds chirping away like mad. I don't yet know whether she was beautiful or not. He doesn't know himself, the imbecile. He rather thinks she wasn't. The room was dark and then there was the champagne and his nerves all frazzled.

"But you ought to know something about her—if this isn't all a god-damned lie!"

"Wait a minute," he says. "Wait . . . let me think! No, she wasn't beautiful. I'm sure of that now. She had a streak of gray hair over her forehead . . . I remember that. But that wouldn't be so bad—I had almost forgotten it you see. No, it was her arms—they were thin . . . they were thin and brittle." He begins to pace back and forth.—Suddenly, he stops dead. "If she were only ten years younger!" he exclaims. "If she were ten years younger I might overlook the streak of gray hair . . . and even the brittle arms. But she's too old. You see, with a cunt like that every year counts now. She won't be just one year older next year—she'll be ten years older. Another year hence and she'll be twenty years older. And I'll be getting younger looking all the time—at least for another five years . . ."

"But how did it end?" I interrupt.

"That's just it . . . it didn't end. I promised to see her Tuesday around five o'clock. That's bad, you know! There were lines in her face which will look much worse in daylight. I suppose she wants me to fuck her Tuesday. Fucking in the day-time—you don't do it with a cunt like that. Especially in a hotel like that. I'd rather do it on my night off ... but Tuesday's not my night off. And that's not all. I promised her a letter in the meantime. How am I going to write her a letter now? I haven't anything to say ... Shit! If only she were ten years younger. Do you think I should go with her ... to Borneo or wherever it is she wants to take me? What would I do with a rich cunt like that on my hands? I don't know how to shoot. I am afraid of guns and all that sort of thing. Besides, she'll be wanting me to fuck her night and day ... nothing but hunting and fucking all the time ... I can't do it!"

"Maybe it won't be so bad as you think. She'll buy you ties and all sorts of things ..."

"Maybe you'll come along with us, eh? I told her all about you ..."

"Did you tell her I was poor? Did you tell her I needed things?"

"I told her everything. Shit, everything would be fine, if she were just a few years younger. She said she was turning forty. That means fifty or sixty. It's like fucking your own mother ... you can't do it ... it's impossible."

"But she must have had some attractiveness ... you were kissing her breasts, you said."

"Kissing her breasts—what's that? Besides it was dark, I'm telling you."

Putting on his pants a button falls off. "Look at that, will you. It's falling apart, the god-damned suit. I've worn it for seven years now ... I never paid for it either. It was a good suit once, but it stinks now. And that cunt would buy me suits too, all I wanted most likely. But that's what I don't like, having a woman shell out for me. I never did that in my life. That's *your* idea. I'd rather live alone. Shit, this is a good room, isn't it? What's wrong with it? Its a damned sight better than her room, isn't it? I don't like her fine hotel. I'm against hotels like that. I told her so. She said she didn't care where she lived ... said she'd come and live with me if I wanted her to. Can you picture her moving in here with her big trunks and her hat-boxes and all that crap she drags around with her? She has too many things—too many dresses and bottles and all that. It's like a clinic, her room. If she gets a little scratch on her finger it's serious.

And then she has to be massaged and her hair has to be waved and she mustn't eat this and she mustn't eat that. Listen, Joe, she'd be all right if she were just a little younger. You can forgive a young cunt anything. A young cunt doesn't have to have any brains. They're better without brains. But an old cunt, even if she's brilliant, even if she's the most charming woman in the world, nothing makes any difference. A young cunt is an investment; an old cunt is a dead loss. All they can do for you is buy you things. But that doesn't put meat on their arms or juice between the legs. She isn't bad, Irene. In fact, I think you'd like her. With you it's different. You don't have to fuck her. You can afford to like her. Maybe you wouldn't like all those dresses and the bottles and what not, but you could be tolerant. She wouldn't bore you, that I can tell you. She's even interesting, I might say. But she's withered. Her breasts are all right yet—but her arms! I told her I'd bring you around some day. I talked a lot about you ... I didn't know what to say to her. Maybe you'd like her, especially when she's dressed. I don't know ..."

"Listen, she's rich, you say? I'll like her! I don't care how old she is, so long as she's not a hag ..."

"She's not a hag! What are you talking about? She's charming, I tell you. She talks well. She looks well too ... only her arms ..."

"All right, if that's how it is, *I'll* fuck her—if you don't want to. Tell her that. Be subtle about it, though. With a woman like that you've got to do things slowly. You bring me around and let things work out for themselves. Praise the shit out of me. Act jealous like ... Shit, maybe we'll fuck her together ... and we'll go places and we'll eat together ... and we'll drive and hunt and wear nice things. If she wants to go to Borneo let her take us along. I don't know how to shoot either, but that doesn't matter. She doesn't care about that either. She just wants to be fucked that's all. You're talking about her arms all the time. You don't have to look at her arms all the time, do you? Look at this bedspread! Look at the mirror! Do you call this living? Do you want to go on being delicate and live like a louse all your life? You can't even pay your hotel bill ... and you've got a job too. This is no way to live. I don't care if she's seventy years old—it's better than this ..."

"Listen, Joe, you fuck her for me ... then everything'll be fine. Maybe I'll fuck her once in a while too ... on my night off. It's four days now since I've had a good shit. There's something sticking to me, like grapes ..."

"You've got the piles, that's what."

"My hair's falling out too ... and I ought to see the dentist. I feel as though I were falling apart. I told her what a good guy you are ... You'll do things for me, eh? You're not too delicate, eh? If we go to Borneo I won't have haemorrhoids any more. Maybe I'll develop something else ... something worse ... fever perhaps ... or cholera. Shit, it is better to die of a good disease like that than to piss your life away on a newspaper with grapes up your ass and buttons falling off your pants. I'd like to be rich, even if it were only for a week, and then go to a hospital with a good disease, a fatal one, and have flowers in the room and nurses dancing around and telegrams coming. They take good care of you if you're rich. They wash you with cotton batting and they comb your hair for you. Shit, I know all that. Maybe I'd be lucky and not die at all. Maybe I'd be a cripple all my life ... maybe I'd be paralyzed and have to sit in a wheel-chair. But then I'd be taken care of just the same ... even if I had no more money. If you're an invalid—a *real* one—they don't let you starve. And you get a clean bed to lie in ... and they change the towels every day. This way nobody gives a fuck about you, especially if you have a job. They think a man should be happy if he's got a job. What would you rather do—be a cripple all your life, or have a job ... or marry a rich cunt? You'd rather marry a rich cunt, I can see that. You only think about food. But supposing you married her and then you couldn't get a hard-on any more—that happens sometimes—what would you do then? You'd be at her mercy. You'd have to eat out of her hand, like a little poodle dog. You'd like that, would you? Or maybe you don't think of those things? *I think of everything.* I think of the suits I'd pick out and the places I'd like to go to, but I also think of the other thing. That's the important thing. What good are the fancy ties and the fine suits if you can't get a hard-on any more? You

couldn't even betray her—because she'd be on your heels
all the time. No, the best thing would be to marry her and
then get a disease right away. Only not syphilis. Cholera,
let's say, or yellow fever. So that if a miracle did happen
and your life was spared you'd be a cripple for the rest of
your days. Then you wouldn't have to worry about
fucking her any more, and you wouldn't have to worry
about the rent either. She'd probably buy you a fine
wheel-chair with rubber tires and all sorts of levers and
what not. You might even be able to use your hands—I
mean enough to be able to write. Or you could have a
secretary, for that matter. That's it—that's the best solu-
tion for a writer. What does a guy want with his arms and
legs? He doesn't need arms and legs to write with. He
needs security . . . peace . . . protection. All those heroes
who parade in wheel-chairs—it's too bad they're not writers. If you could only be sure, when you go off to war,
that you'd have only your legs blown off . . . if you could
be sure of that I'd say let's have a war tomorrow. I
wouldn't give a fuck about the medals—they could keep
the medals. All I'd want is a good wheel-chair and three
meals a day. Then I'd give them something to read, those
pricks!"

The following day, at one-thirty, I call on Van Norden.
It's his day off, or rather his night off. He has left word
with Carl that I am to help him move today.

I find him in a state of unusual depression. He hasn't
slept a wink all night, he tells me. There's something on
his mind, something that's eating him up. It isn't long before I discover what it is; he's been waiting impatiently
for me to arrive in order to spill it.

"That guy," he begins, meaning Carl, "that guy's an
artist. He described every detail minutely. He told it to
me with such accuracy that I know it's all a god-damned
lie . . . but I can't dismiss it from my mind. You know
how my minds works!"

He interrupts himself to inquire if Carl has told me the
whole story. There isn't the least suspicion in his mind
that Carl may have told me one thing and him another. He
seems to think that the story was invented expressly to
torture him. He doesn't seem to mind so much that it's a

fabrication. It's the "images," as he says, which Carl left
in his mind, that get him. The images are real, even if the
whole story is false. And besides, the fact that there actually is a rich cunt on the scene and that Carl actually paid
her a visit, that's undeniable. What actually happened is
secondary; he takes it for granted that Carl put the boots
to her. But what drives him desperate is the thought that
what Carl has described to him might have been *possible*.

"It's just like that guy," he says, "to tell me he put it
to her six or seven times. I know that's a lot of shit and
I don't mind that so much, but when he tells me that she
hired a carriage and drove him out to the Bois and that
they used the husband's fur-coat for a blanket, that's too
much. I suppose he told you about the chauffeur waiting
respectfully . . . and listen, did he tell you how the engine
purred all the time? Jesus, he built that up wonderfully.
It's just like him to think of a detail like that . . . it's one
of those little details which makes a thing psychologically
real . . . you can't get it out of your head afterwards. And
he tells it to me so smoothly, so naturally . . . I wonder,
did he think it up in advance or did it just pop out of his
head like that, spontaneously? He's such a cute little liar
you can't walk away from him . . . it's like he's writing
you a letter, one of those flower-pots that he makes overnight. I don't understand how a guy can write such
letters . . . I don't get the mentality behind it . . . it's a
form a masturbation . . . what do you think?"

But before I have an opportunity to venture an opinion,
or even to laugh in his face, Van Norden goes on with his
monologue.

"Listen, I suppose he told you everything . . . did he
tell you how he stood on the balcony in the moonlight
and kissed her? That sounds banal when you repeat it, but
the way that guy describes it . . . I can just see the little
prick standing there with the woman in his arms and already he's writing another letter to her, another flower-pot
about the roof-tops and all that crap he steals from his
French authors. That guy never says a thing that's original, I found that out. You have to get a clue like . . . find
out whom he's been reading lately . . . and it's hard to do
that because he's so damned secretive. Listen, if I didn't
know that you went there with him, I wouldn't believe

that the woman existed. A guy like that could write letters to himself. And yet he's lucky . . . he's so damned tiny, so frail, so romantic-looking, that women fall for him now and then . . . they sort of adopt him . . . they feel sorry for him, I guess. And some cunts like to receive flower-pots . . . it makes them feel important . . . But this woman's an intelligent woman, so he says. You ought to know, you've seen her letters. What do you suppose a woman like that saw in him? I can understand her falling for the letters . . . but how do you suppose she felt when she *saw* him?

"But listen, all that's beside the point. What I'm getting at is the way he tells it to me. You know how he embroiders things . . . well, after that scene on the balcony—he gives me that like an hors d'oeuvre, you know—after that, so he says, they went inside and he unbuttoned her pajamas. What are you smiling for? Was he shitting me about that?"

"No, no! You're giving it to me exactly as he told me. Go ahead . . ."

"After that"—here Van Norden has to smile himself—"after that, mind you, he tells me how she sat in the chair with her legs up . . . not a stitch on . . . and he's sitting on the floor looking up at her, telling her how beautiful she looks . . . did he tell you that she looked like a Matisse . . . Wait a minute . . . I'd like to remember exactly what he said. He had some cute little phrase there about an odalisque . . . what the hell's an odalisque anyway? He said it in French, that's why it's hard to remember the fucking thing . . . but it sounded good. It sounded just like the sort of thing he might say. And she probably thought it was original with him . . . I suppose she thinks he's a poet or something. But listen, all this is nothing . . . I make allowance for his imagination. It's what happened after that that drives me crazy. All night long I've been tossing about, playing with these images he left in my mind. I can't get it out of my head. It sounds so real to me that if it didn't happen I could strangle the bastard. A guy has no right to invent things like that. Or else he's diseased . . .

"What I'm getting at is that moment when, he says, he got down on his knees and with those two skinny fingers of his he spread her cunt open. You remember that? He says she was sitting there with her legs dangling over the arms of the chair and suddenly, he says, he got an inspiration. This was after he had given her a couple of lays already ... after he had made that little spiel about Matisse. He gets down on his knees—*get this!*—and with his two fingers ... just the tips of them, mind you ... he opens the little petals ... *squish-squish* ... just like that. A sticky little sound ... almost inaudible. *Squish-squish!* Jesus, I've been hearing it all night long! And then he says—as if that weren't enough for me—then he tells me he buried his head in her muff. And when he did that, so help me Christ, if she didn't swing her legs around his neck and lock him there. *That finished me!* Imagine it! Imagine a fine, sensitive woman like that swinging her legs around *his neck*! There's something poisonous about it. It's so fantastic that it sounds convincing. If he had only told me about the champagne and the ride in the Bois and even that scene on the balcony I could have dismissed it. But this thing is so incredible that it doesn't sound like a lie, any more. I can't believe that he ever read anything like that anywhere, and I can't see what could have put the idea into his head unless there was some truth in it. With a little prick like that, you know, anything can happen. He may not have fucked her at all, but she may have let him diddle her ... you never know with these rich cunts what they might expect you to do ..."

When he finally pulls himself out of bed and starts to shave the afternoon is already well advanced. I've finally succeeded in switching his mind to other things, to the moving principally. The maid comes in to see if he's ready—he's supposed to have vacated the room by noon. He's just in the act of slipping into his trousers. I'm a little surprised that he doesn't excuse himself, or turn away. Seeing him standing there nonchalantly buttoning his fly as he gives her orders I begin to titter. "Don't mind her," he says, throwing her a look of supreme contempt, "she's just a big sow. Give her a pinch in the ass, if you like. She won't say anything." And then addressing her, in English, he says: "Come here, you bitch, put your hand on this!" At this I can't restrain myself any longer. I burst out laughing, a fit of hysterical laughter which infects the maid also, though she doesn't know what it's all about.

The maid commences to take down the pictures and photographs, mostly of himself, which line the walls. *"You,"* he says, jerking his thumb, "come here! Here's something to remember me by"—ripping a photograph off the wall—"when I go you can wipe your ass with it. See," he says, turning to me, "she's a dumb bitch. She wouldn't look any more intelligent if I said it in French." The maid stands there with her mouth open; she is evidently convinced that he is cracked. "Hey!" he yells at her as if she were hard of hearing. "Hey, *you*! Yes, *you*! Like this . . . !" and he takes the photograph, his own photograph, and wipes his ass with it. *"Comme ça!* Savvy? You've got to draw pictures for her," he says, thrusting his lower lip forward in absolute disgust.

He watches her helplessly as she throws his things into the big valises. "Here, put these in too," he says, handing her a tooth-brush and the douche-bag. Half of his belongings are lying on the floor. The valises are crammed full and there is nowhere to put the paintings and the books and the bottles that are half empty. "Sit down a minute," he says. "We've got plenty of time. We've got to think this thing out. If you hadn't come around I'd never have gotten out of here. You see how helpless I am. Don't let me forget to take the bulbs out . . . they belong to me. That waste-basket belongs to me too. They expect you to live like pigs, these bastards." The maid has gone downstairs to get some twine . . . "Wait till you see . . . she'll charge me for the twine even if it's only three sous. They wouldn't sew a button on your pants here without charging for it. The lousy, dirty scroungers!" He takes a bottle of Calvados from the mantelpiece and nods to me to grab the other. "No use carrying these to the new place. Let's finish them off now. But don't give *her* a drink! That bastard, I wouldn't leave her a piece of toilet-paper. I'd like to ruin the joint before I go. Listen . . . piss on the floor, if you like. I wish I could take a crap in the bureau drawer." He feels so utterly disgusted with himself and everything else that he doesn't know what to do by way of venting his feelings. He walks over to the bed with the bottle in his hand and pulling back the covers he sprinkles Calvados over the mattress. Not content with that he digs his heel into the mattress. Unfortunately there's no mud on his heels. Finally he takes the sheet and cleans his shoes with it. "That'll give them something to do," he mutters vengefully. Then, taking a good swig, he throws his head back and gargles his throat, and after he's gargled it good and proper he spits it out on the mirror. "There, you cheap bastards! Wipe that off when I go!" He walks back and forth mumbling to himself. Seeing his torn socks lying on the floor he picks them up and tears them to bits. The paintings enrage him too. He picks one up—a portrait of himself done by some Lesbian he knew and he puts his foot through it. "That bitch! You know what she had the nerve to ask me? She asked me to turn over my cunts to her after I was through with them. She never gave me a sou for writing her up. She thought I honestly admired her work. I wouldn't have gotten that painting out of her if I hadn't promised to fix her up with that cunt from Minnesota. She was nuts about her ... used to follow us around like a dog in heat ... we couldn't get rid of the bitch! She bothered the life out of me. I got so that I was almost afraid to bring a cunt up here for fear that she'd bust in on me. I used to creep up here like a burglar and lock the door behind me as soon as I got inside ... She and that Georgia cunt—they drive me nuts. The one is always in heat and the other is always hungry. I hate fucking a woman who's hungry. It's like you push a feed inside her and then you push it out again ... Jesus, that reminds me of something ... where did I put that blue ointment? That's important. Did you ever have those things? It's worse than having a dose. And I don't know where I got them from either. I've had so many women up here in the last week or so I've lost track of them. Funny too, because they all smelled so fresh. But you know how it is ..."

The maid has piled his things up on the sidewalk. The *patron* looks on with a surly air. When everything has been loaded into the taxi there is only room for one of us inside. As soon as we commence to roll Van Norden gets out a newspaper and starts bundling up his pots and pans; in the new place all cooking is strictly forbidden. By the time we reach our destination all his luggage has come undone; it wouldn't be quite so embarrassing if the madame had not stuck her head out of the doorway just as we rolled up. "My God!" she exclaims, "what in the devil is all this? What does it mean?" Van Norden is so intimidated that he can think of nothing more to say than *"C'est moi ... c'est moi, madame!"* And turning to me he mumbles savagely: "That cluck! Did you notice her face? She's going to make it hard for me."

The hotel lies back of a dingy passage and forms a rectangle very much on the order of a modern penitentiary. The bureau is large and gloomy, despite the brilliant reflections from the tile walls. There are bird cages hanging in the windows and little enamel signs everywhere begging the guests in an obsolete language not to do this and not to forget that. It is almost immaculately clean but absolutely poverty-stricken, threadbare, woe-begone. The upholstered chairs are held together with wired thongs; they remind one unpleasantly of the electric chair. The room he is going to occupy is on the fifth floor. As we climb the stairs Van Norden informs me that Maupassant once lived here. And in the same breath he remarks that there is a peculiar odor in the hall. On the fifth floor a few window-panes are missing; we stand a moment gazing at the tenants across the court. It is getting toward dinner-time and people are straggling back to their rooms with that weary, dejected air which comes from earning a living honestly. Most of the windows are wide open: the dingy rooms have the appearance of so many yawning mouths. The occupants of the rooms are yawning too, or else scratching themselves. They move about listlessly and apparently without much purpose; they might just as well be lunatics.

As we turn down the corridor towards room 57, a door suddenly opens in front of us and an old hag with matted hair and the eyes of a maniac peers out. She startles us so that we stand transfixed. For a full minute the three of us stand there powerless to move or even to make an intelligent gesture. Back of the old hag I can see a kitchen table and on it lies a baby all undressed, a puny little brat no bigger than a plucked chicken. Finally the old one picks up a slop-pail by her side and makes a move forward. We stand aside to let her pass and as the door closes behind her the baby lets out a piercing scream. It is room number 56, and between 56 and 57 is the toilet where the old hag is emptying her slops.

Ever since we have mounted the stairs Van Norden has kept silence. But his looks are eloquent. When he opens the door of 57 I have for a fleeting moment the sensation of going mad. A huge mirror covered with green gauze and tipped at an angle of 45 degrees hangs directly opposite the entrance over a baby-carriage which is filled with books. Van Norden doesn't even crack a smile; instead he walks nonchalantly over to the baby-carriage and picking up a book begins to skim it through, much as a man would enter the public library and go unthinkingly to the rack nearest to hand. And perhaps this would not seem so ludicrous to me if I had not espied at the same time a pair of handle-bars resting in the corner. They look so absolutely peaceful and contented, as if they had been dozing there for years, that suddenly it seems to me as if we had been standing in this room, in exactly this position, for an incalculably long time, that it was a pose we had struck in a dream from which we never emerged, a dream which the least gesture, the wink of an eye even, will shatter. But more remarkable still is the remembrance that suddenly floats up of an actual dream which occurred only the other night, a dream in which I saw Van Norden in just such a corner as is occupied now by the handle-bars, only instead of the handle-bars there was a woman crouching with her legs drawn up. I see him standing over the woman with that alert, eager look in his eye, which comes when he wants something badly. The street in which this is going on is blurred—only the angle made by two walls is clear, and the cowering figure of the woman. I can see him going at her in that quick, animal way of his, reckless of what's going on about him, determined only to have his way. And a look in his eye as though to say—"you can kill me afterwards, but just let me get it in . . . I've got to get it in!" And there he is, bent over her, their heads knocking against the wall, he has such a tremendous erection that it's simply impossible to get it in her. Suddenly, with that disgusted air which he knows so well how to summon, he picks himself up and adjusts his clothes. He is about to walk away when suddenly he notices that his penis is lying on the sidewalk. It

is about the size of a sawed-off broom-stick. He picks it
up nonchalantly and slings it under his arm. As he walks
off I notice two huge bulbs, like tulip bulbs, dangling
from the end of the broom-stick, and I can hear him muttering to himself "flower-pots ... flower-pots."

The *garçon* arrives panting and sweating. Van Norden
looks at him uncomprehendingly. The madame now
marches in and walking straight up to Van Norden she
takes the book out of his hand, thrusts it in the baby-
carriage, and without saying a word, wheels the baby-
carriage into the hallway.

"This is a bug-house," says Van Norden, smiling
distressedly. It is such a faint, indescribable smile that for
a moment the dream feeling comes back and it seems to
me that we are standing at the end of a long corridor at
the end of which is a corrugated mirror. And down this
corridor, swinging his distress like a dingy lantern, Van
Norden staggers, staggers in and out as here and there a
door opens and a hand yanks him in or a hoof pushes him
out. And the further off he wanders the more lugubrious
is his distress; he wears it like a lantern which the cyclists hold between their teeth on a night when the pavement is wet and slippery. In and out of the dingy rooms
he wanders, and when he sits down the chair collapses,
when he opens his valise there is only a tooth-brush inside. In every room there is a mirror before which he
stands attentively and chews his rage, and from the constant chewing, from the grumbling and mumbling and the
muttering and cursing his jaws have gotten unhinged and
they sag badly and, when he rubs his beard, pieces of his
jaw crumble away and he's so disgusted with himself that
he stamps on his own jaw, grinds it to bits with his big
heels.

Meanwhile the luggage is being hauled in. And things
begin to look crazier even than before—particularly when
he attaches his exerciser to the bedstead and begins his
Sandow exercises. "I like this place," he says, smiling at
the *garçon*. He takes his coat and vest off. The *garçon* is
watching him with a puzzled air; he has a valise in one
hand and the douche-bag in the other. I'm standing apart
in the ante-chamber holding the mirror with the green
gauze. Not a single object seems to possess a practical

use. The ante-chamber itself seems useless, a sort of vestibule to a barn. It is exactly the same sort of sensation which I get when I enter the Comédie Française or the Palais Royal Theatre; it is a world of bric-à-brac, of trap-doors, of arms and busts and waxed floors, of candelabras and men in armor, of statues without eyes and love letters lying in glass cases. Something is going on, but it makes no sense; it's like finishing the half-empty bottle of Calvados because there's no room in the valise.

Climbing up the stairs, as I said a moment ago, he had mentioned the fact that Maupassant used to live here. The coincidence seems to have made an impression upon him. He would like to believe that it was in this very room that Maupassant gave birth to some of those gruesome tales on which his reputation rests. "They lived like pigs, those poor bastards," he says. We are sitting at the round table in a pair of comfortable old arm-chairs that have been trussed up with thongs and braces; the bed is right beside us, so close indeed that we can put our feet on it. The *armoire* stands in a corner behind us, also conveniently within reach. Van Norden has emptied his dirty wash on the table; we sit here with our feet buried in his dirty socks and shirts, and smoke contentedly. The sordidness of the place seems to have worked a spell on him: he is content here. When I get up to switch on the light he suggests that we play a game of cards before going out to eat. And so we sit there by the window, with the dirty wash strewn over the floor and the Sandow exerciser hanging from the chandelier, and we play a few rounds of two-handed pinochle. Van Norden has put away his pipe and packed a wad of snuff on the under side of his lower lip. Now and then he spits out of the window, big healthy gobs of brown juice which resound with a smack on the pavement below. He seems content now.

"In America," he says, "you wouldn't dream of living in a joint like this. Even when I was on the bum I slept in better rooms than this. But here it seems natural—it's like the books you read. If I ever go back there I'll forget all about this life, just like you forget a bad dream. I'll probably take up the old life again just where I left off . . . if I ever get back. Sometimes I lie in bed dreaming about the past and it's so vivid to me that I have to shake my-

self in order to realize where I am. Especially when I
have a woman beside me; a woman can set me off better
than anything. That's all I want of them—to forget myself. Sometimes I get so lost in my reveries that I can't
remember the name of the cunt or where I picked her up.
That's funny, eh? It's good to have a fresh warm body beside you when you wake up in the morning. It gives you
a clean feeling. You get spiritual like . . . until they start
pulling that mushy crap about love et cetera. Why do all
these cunts talk about love so much, can you tell me that?
A good lay isn't enough for them apparently . . . they
want your soul too . . ."

Now this word soul, which pops up frequently in Van
Norden's soliloquies, used to have a droll effect upon me
at first. Whenever I heard the word soul from his lips I
would get hysterical; somehow it seemed like a false
coin, more particularly because it was usually accompanied by a gob of brown juice which left a trickle down
the corner of his mouth. And as I never hesitated to laugh
in his face it happened invariably that when this little
word bobbed up Van Norden would pause just long
enough for me to burst into a cackle and then, as if nothing had happened, he would resume his monologue, repeating the word more and more frequently and each time
with a more caressing emphasis. It was the soul of him
that women were trying to possess—that he made clear to
me. He had explained it over and over again, but he
comes back to it afresh each time like a paranoiac to his
obsession. In a sense Van Norden is mad, of that I'm convinced. His one fear is to be left alone, and this fear is so
deep and so persistent that even when he is on top of a
woman, even when he has welded himself to her, he cannot escape the prison which he has created for himself. "I
try all sorts of things," he explains to me. "I even count
sometimes, or I begin to think of a problem in philosophy, but it doesn't work. It's like I'm two people, and one
of them is watching me all the time. I get so god-damned
mad at myself that I could kill myself . . . and in a way,
that's what I do every time I have an orgasm. For one
second like I obliterate myself. There's not even one me
then . . . there's nothing . . . not even the cunt. It's like re-
ceiving communion. Honest, I mean that. For a few sec-

onds afterwards I have a fine spiritual glow ... and maybe it would continue that way indefinitely—how can you tell?—if it weren't for the fact that there's a woman beside you and then the douche-bag and the water running ... all those little details that make you desperately self-conscious, desperately lonely. And for that one moment of freedom you have to listen to all that love crap ... it drives me nuts sometimes ... I want to kick them out immediately ... I do now and then. But that doesn't keep them away. They like it, in fact. The less you notice them the more they chase after you. There's something perverse about women ... they're all masochists at heart."

"But what is it you want of a woman, then?" I demand.

He begins to mould his hands; his lower lip droops. He looks completely frustrated. When eventually he succeeds in stammering out a few broken phrases it's with the conviction that behind his words lies an overwhelming futility. "I want to be able to surrender myself to a woman," he blurts out. "I want her to take me out of myself. But to do that, she's got to be better than I am; she's got to have a mind, not just a cunt. She's got to make me believe that I need her, that I can't live without her. Find me a cunt like that, will you? If you could do that I'd give you my job. I wouldn't care then what happened to me: I wouldn't need a job or friends or books or anything. If she could only make me believe that there was something more important on earth than myself. Jesus, I hate myself! But I hate these bastardly cunts even more—because they're none of them any good.

"You think I like myself," he continues. "That shows how little you know about me. I know I'm a great guy ... I wouldn't have these problems if there weren't something to me. But what eats me up is that I can't express myself. People think I'm a cunt-chaser. That's how shallow they are, these high-brows who sit on the *terrasse* all day chewing the psychologic cud ... That's not so bad, eh—psychologic cud? Write it down for me. I'll use it in my column next week ... By the way, did you ever read Stekel? Is he any good? It looks like nothing but case histories to me. I wish to Christ I could get up enough nerve to visit an analyst ... a good one, I mean. I don't want to see these little shysters with goatees and frock coats, like your friend Boris. How do you manage to tolerate those guys? Don't they bore you stiff? You talk to anybody, I notice. You don't give a god-damn. Maybe you're right. I wish I weren't so damned critical. But these dirty little Jews who hang around the Dôme, Jesus, they give me the creeps. They sound just like textbooks. If I could talk to you every day maybe I could get things off my chest. You're a good listener. I know you don't give a damn about me, but you're patient. And you don't have any theories to exploit. I suppose you put it all down afterwards in that notebook of yours. Listen, I don't mind what you say about me, but don't make me out to be a cunt-chaser—it's too simple. Some day I'll write a book about myself, about my thoughts. I don't mean just a piece of introspective analysis . . . I mean that I'll lay myself down on the operating table and I'll expose my whole guts . . . every god-damned thing. Has anybody ever done that before?—What the hell are you smiling at? Does it sound naïf?"

I'm smiling because whenever we touch on the subject of this book which he is going to write some day things assume an incongruous aspect. He has only to say "my book" and immediately the world shrinks to the private dimensions of Van Norden and Co. The book must be absolutely original, absolutely perfect. That is why, among other things, it is impossible for him to get started on it. As soon as he gets an idea he begins to question it. He remembers that Dostoievski used it, or Hamsun, or somebody else. "I'm not saying that I want to be better than them, but I want to be different," he explains. And so, instead of tackling his book, he reads one author after another in order to make absolutely certain that he is not going to tread on their private property. And the more he reads the more disdainful he becomes. None of them are satisfying; none of them arrive at that degree of perfection which he has imposed on himself. And forgetting completely that he has not written as much as a chapter he talks about them condescendingly, quite as though there existed a shelf of books bearing his name, books which everyone is familiar with and the titles of which it is therefore superfluous to mention. Though he has never overtly lied about this fact, nevertheless it is obvious that the people whom he buttonholes in order to air his private philosophy, his criticism, and his grievances, take it for granted that behind his loose remarks there stands a solid body of work. Especially the young and foolish virgins whom he lures to his room on the pretext of reading to them his poems, or on the still better pretext of asking their advice. Without the least feeling of guilt or self-consciousness he will hand them a piece of soiled paper on which he has scribbled a few lines—the basis of a new poem, as he puts it—and with absolute seriousness demand of them an honest expression of opinion. As they usually have nothing to give by way of comment, wholly bewildered as they are by the utter senselessness of the lines, Van Norden seizes the occasion to expound to them his view of art, a view, needless to say, which is spontaneously created to suit the event. So expert has he become in this role that the transition from Ezra Pound's cantos to the bed is made as simply and naturally as a modulation from one key to another; in fact, if it were not made there would be a discord, which is what happens now and then when he makes a mistake as regards those nit-wits whom he refers to as "push-overs." Naturally, constituted as he is, it is with reluctance that he refers to these fatal errors of judgment. But when he does bring himself to confess to an error of this kind it is with absolute frankness; in fact, he seems to derive a perverse pleasure in dwelling upon his inaptitude. There is one woman, for example, whom he has been trying to make for almost ten years now—first in America, and finally here in Paris. It is the only person of the opposite sex with whom he has a cordial, friendly relationship. They seem not only to like each other, but to understand each other. At first it seemed to me that if he could really make this creature his problem might be solved. All the elements for a successful union were there—except the fundamental one. Bessie was almost as unusual in her way as himself. She had as little concern about giving herself to a man as she has about the dessert which follows the meal. Usually she singled out the object of her choice and made the proposition herself. She was not bad-looking, nor could one say that she was good-looking either. She had a fine body, that was the chief thing—and she liked it, as they say.

They were so chummy, these two, that sometimes, in order to gratify her curiosity (and also in the vain hope of inspiring her by his prowess), Van Norden would arrange to hide her in his closet during one of his seances. After it was over Bessie would emerge from her hiding-place and they would discuss the matter casually, that is to say, with an almost total indifference to everything except "technique." Technique was one of her favorite terms, at least in those discussions which I was privileged to enjoy. "What's wrong with my technique?" he would say. And Bessie would answer: "You're too crude. If you ever expect to make me you've got to become more subtle."

There was such a perfect understanding between them, as I say, that often when I called for Van Norden at one-thirty, I would find Bessie sitting on the bed, the covers thrown back and Van Norden inviting her to stroke his penis ... "just a few silken strokes," he would say, "so as I'll have the courage to get up." Or else he would urge her to blow on it, or failing that, he would grab hold of himself and shake it like a dinner-bell, the two of them laughing fit to die. "I'll never make this bitch," he would say. "She has no respect for me. That's what I get for taking her into my confidence." And then abruptly he might add: "What do you make of that blonde I showed you yesterday?" Talking to Bessie, of course. And Bessie would jeer at him, telling him he had no taste. "Aw, don't give me that line," he would say. And then playfully, perhaps for the thousandth time, because by now it had become a standing joke between them—"Listen, Bessie, what about a quick lay? Just one little lay ... no." And when this had passed off in the usual manner he would add, in the same tone: "Well, what about *him*? Why don't you give *him* a lay?"

The whole point about Bessie was that she couldn't, or just wouldn't, regard herself as a lay. She talked about passion, as if it were a brand new word. She was passionate about things, even a little thing like a lay. She had to put her soul into it.

"I get passionate too sometimes," Van Norden would say.

"Oh, *you*," says Bessie. You're just a worn-out satyr. You don't know the meaning of passion. When you get an erection you think you're passionate."

"All right, maybe it's not passion . . . but you can't get passionate without having an erection, that's true isn't it?"

All this about Bessie, and the other women whom he drags to this room day in and out, occupies my thoughts as we walk to the restaurant. I have adjusted myself so well to his monologues that without interrupting my own reveries I make whatever comment is required automatically, the moment I hear his voice die out. It is a duet, and like most duets moreover in that one listens attentively only for the signal which announces the advent of one's own voice. As it is his night off, and as I have promised to keep him company, I have already dulled myself to his queries. I know that before the evening is over I shall be thoroughly exhausted; if I am lucky, that is, if I can worm a few francs out of him on some pretext or other, I will duck him the moment he goes to the toilet. But he knows my propensity for slipping away, and, instead of being insulted, he simply provides against the possibility by guarding his sous. If I ask him for money to buy cigarettes he insists on going with me to purchase them. He will not be left alone, not for a second. Even when he has succeeded in grabbing off a woman, even then he is terrified to be left alone with her. If it were possible he would have me sit in the room while he puts on the performance. It would be like asking me to wait while he took a shave.

On his night off Van Norden generally manages to have at least fifty francs in his pocket, a circumstance which does not prevent him from making a touch whenever he encounters a prospect. "Hello," he says, "give me twenty francs . . . I need it." He has a way of looking panic-stricken at the same time. And if he meets with a rebuff he becomes insulting. "Well, you can buy a drink at least." And when he gets his drink he says more graciously—"Listen, give me five francs then . . . give me *two* francs . . ." We go from bar to bar looking for a little excitement and always accumulating a few more francs.

At the Coupole we stumble into a drunk from the newspaper. One of the upstairs guys. There's just been an accident at the office, he informs us. One of the proof-readers fell down the elevator shaft. Not expected to live.

At first Van Norden is shocked, deeply shocked. But when he learns that it was Peckover, the Englishman, he looks relieved. "The poor bastard," he says, "he's better off dead than alive. He just got his false teeth the other day too . . ."

The allusion to the false teeth moves the man upstairs to tears. He relates in a slobbery way a little incident connected with the accident. He is upset about it, more upset about this little incident than about the catastrophe itself. It seems that Peckover, when he hit the bottom of the shaft, regained consciousness before anyone could reach him. Despite the fact that his legs were broken and his ribs busted, he had managed to rise to all fours and grope about for his false teeth. In the ambulance he was crying out in his delirium for the teeth he had lost. The incident was pathetic and ludicrous at the same time. The guy from upstairs hardly knew whether to laugh or to weep as he related it. It was a delicate moment because with a drunk like that one false move and he'd crash a bottle over your skull. He had never been particularly friendly with Peckover—as a matter of fact, he had scarcely ever set foot in the proof-reading department: there was an invisible wall between the guys upstairs and the guys down below. But now, since he had felt the touch of death, he wanted to display his comradeship. He wanted to weep, if possible, to show that he was a regular guy. And Joe and I, who knew Peckover well and who knew also that he wasn't worth a good god-damn, even a few tears, we felt annoyed with this drunken sentimentality. We wanted to tell him so too, but with a guy like that you can't afford to be honest; you have to buy a wreath and go to the funeral and pretend that you're miserable. And you have to congratulate him too for the delicate obituary he's written. He'll be carrying his delicate little obituary around with him for months, praising the shit out of himself for the way he handled the situation. We felt all that, Joe and I, without saying a word to each other. We just stood there and listened with a murderous, silent contempt. And as soon as we could break away we did so; we left him there at the bar blubbering to himself over his Pernod.

Once out of his sight we began to laugh hysterically. The false teeth! No matter what we said about the poor devil, and we said some good things about him too, we always came back to the false teeth. There are people in this world who cut such a grotesque figure that even death renders them ridiculous. And the more horrible the death the more ridiculous they seem. It's no use trying to invest the end with a little dignity—you have to be a liar and a hypocrite to discover anything tragic in their going. And since we didn't have to put on a false front we could laugh about the incident to our heart's content. We laughed all night about it, and in between times, we vented our scorn and disgust for the guys upstairs, the fat-heads who were trying to persuade themselves, no doubt, that Peckover was a fine fellow and that his death was a catastrophe. All sorts of funny recollections came to our minds—the semicolons that he overlooked and for which they bawled the piss out of him. They made his life miserable with their fucking little semi-colons and the fractions which he always got wrong. They were even going to fire him once because he came to work with a boozy breath. They despised him because he always looked so miserable and because he had eczema and dandruff. He was just a nobody, as far as they were concerned, but, now that he was dead, they would all chip in lustily and buy him a huge wreath and they'd put his name in big type in the obituary column. Anything to throw a little reflection on themselves; they'd make him out to be a *big* shit if they could. But unfortunately, with Peckover, there was little they could invent about him. He was a zero, and even the fact that he was dead wouldn't add a cipher to his name.

"There's only one good aspect to it," says Joe. "You may get his job. And if you have any luck, maybe you'll fall down the elevator shaft and break your neck too. We'll buy you a nice wreath, I promise you that."

Towards dawn we're sitting on the *terrasse* of the Dôme. We've forgotten about poor Peckover long ago.

We've had a little excitement at the Bal Nègre and Joe's mind has slipped back to the eternal preoccupation: cunt. It's at this hour, when his night off is almost concluded, that his restlessness mounts to a fever pitch. He thinks of the women he passed up earlier in the evening and of the steady ones whom he might have had for the asking, if it weren't that he was fed up with them. He is reminded inevitably of his Georgia cunt—she's been hounding him lately, begging him to take her in, at least until she can find herself a job. "I don't mind giving her a feed once in a while," he says, "but I couldn't take her on as a steady thing . . . she'd ruin it for my other cunts." What gripes him most about her is that she doesn't put on any flesh. "It's like taking a skeleton to bed with you," he says. "The other night I took her on—out of pity—and what do you think the crazy bitch had done to herself? She had shaved it clean . . . not a speck of hair on it! Did you ever have a woman who shaved her twat? It's repulsive, ain't it? And it's funny, too. Sort of mad like. It doesn't look like a twat any more: it's like a dead clam or something." He describes to me how, his curiosity aroused, he got out of bed and searched for his flashlight. "I made her hold it open and I trained the flashlight on it. You should have seen me . . . it was comical. I got so worked up about it that I forgot all about her. I never in my life looked at a cunt so seriously. You'd imagine I'd never seen one before. And the more I looked at it the less interesting it became. It only goes to show that there's nothing to it after all, especially when it's shaved. It's the hair that makes it mysterious. That's why a statue leaves you cold. Only once I saw real cunt on a statue—that was by Rodin. You ought to see it some time . . . she has her legs spread wide apart . . . I don't think there was any head on it. Just a cunt you might say. Jesus, it looked ghastly. The thing is this—they all look alike. When you look at them with their clothes on you imagine all sorts of things; you give them an individuality like, which they haven't got, of course. There's just a crack there between the legs and you get all steamed up about it—you don't even look at it half the time. You know it's there and all you think about is getting your ramrod inside; it's as though your penis did the thinking for you. It's an illusion! You get all burned up about nothing … about a crack with hair on it, or without hair. It's so absolutely meaningless that it fascinated me to look at it. I must have studied it for ten minutes or more. When you look at it that way, sort of detached like, you get funny notions in your head. All that mystery about sex and then you discover that it's nothing, just a blank. Wouldn't it be funny if you found a harmonica inside … or a calendar? But there's nothing there … nothing at all. It's disgusting. It almost drove me mad … Listen, do you know what I did afterwards? I gave her a quick lay and then I turned my back on her. Yeah, I picked up a book and I read. You can get something out of a book, even a bad book … but a cunt, it's just a sheer loss of time …"

It just so happened that as he was concluding his speech a whore gave us the eye. Without the slightest transition he says to me abruptly: "Would you like to give her a tumble? It won't cost much … she'll take the two of us on." And without waiting for a reply he staggers to his feet and goes over to her. In a few minutes he comes back. "It's all fixed," he says. "Finish your beer. She's hungry. There's nothing doing any more at this hour … she'll take the both of us for fifteen francs. We'll go to my room … it'll be cheaper."

On the way to the hotel the girl is shivering so that we have to stop and buy her a coffee. She's a rather gentle sort of creature and not at all bad to look at. She evidently knows Van Norden, knows there's nothing to expect from him but the fifteen francs. "You haven't got any dough," he says, mumbling to me under his breath. As I haven't a centime in my pocket I don't quite see the point of this, until he bursts out "For Christ's sake, remember that we're broke. Don't get tenderhearted when we get upstairs. She's going to ask you for a little extra—I know this cunt! I could get her for ten francs, if I wanted to. There's no use spoiling them …"

"Il est méchant, celui-là," she says to me, gathering the drift of his remarks in her dull way.

"Non, il n'est pas méchant, il est très gentil."

She shakes her head laughingly. *"Je le connais bien, ce*

type." And then she commences a hard luck story, about the hospital and the back rent and the baby in the country. But she doesn't overdo it. She knows that our ears are stopped; but the misery is there inside her, like a stone, and there's no room for any other thoughts. She isn't trying to make an appeal to our sympathies—she's just shifting this big weight inside her from one place to another. I rather like her. I hope to Christ she hasn't got a disease . . .

In the room she goes about her preparations mechanically. "There isn't a crust of bread about by any chance?" she inquires, as she squats over the *bidet*. Van Norden laughs at this. "Here, take a drink," he says, shoving a bottle at her. She doesn't want anything to drink; her stomach's already on the bum, she complains.

"That's just a line with her," says Van Norden. "Don't let her work on your sympathies. Just the same, I wish she'd talk about something else. How the hell can you get up any passion when you've got a starving cunt on your hands?"

Precisely! We haven't any passion either of us. And as for her, one might as well expect her to produce a diamond necklace as to show a spark of passion. But there's the fifteen francs and something has to be done about it. It's like a state of war; the moment the condition is precipitated nobody thinks about anything but peace, about getting it over with. And yet nobody has the courage to lay down his arms, to say, "I'm fed up with it . . . I'm through." No, there's fifteen francs somewhere, which nobody gives a damn about any more and which nobody is going to get in the end anyhow, but the fifteen francs is like the primal cause of things and rather than listen to one's own voice, rather than walk out of the primal cause, one surrenders to the situation, one goes on butchering and butchering and the more cowardly one feels the more heroically does he behave, until a day when the bottom drops out and suddenly all the guns are silenced and the stretcher-bearers pick up the maimed and bleeding heroes and pin medals on their chest. Then one has the rest of his life to think about the fifteen francs. One hasn't any eyes or arms or legs, but he has the consolation of dreaming for the rest of his days about the fifteen francs which everybody has forgotten.

It's exactly like a state of war—I can't get it out of my head. The way she works over me, to blow a spark of passion into me, makes me think what a damned poor soldier I'd be if I was ever silly enough to be trapped like this and dragged to the front. I know for my part that I'd surrender everything, honor included, in order to get out of the mess. I haven't any stomach for it, and that's all there is to it. But she's got her mind set on the fifteen francs and if I don't want to fight about it she's going to make me fight. But you can't put fight into a man's guts if he hasn't any fight in him. There are some of us so cowardly that you can't even make heroes of us, not even if you frighten us to death. We know too much, maybe. There are some of us who don't live in the moment, who live a little ahead, or a little behind. My mind is on the peace treaty all the time. I can't forget that it was the fifteen francs which started all the trouble. Fifteen francs! What does fifteen francs mean to me, particularly since it's not my fifteen francs?

Van Norden seems to have a more normal attitude about it. He doesn't care a rap about the fifteen francs either now; it's the situation itself which intrigues him. It seems to call for a show of mettle—his manhood is involved. The fifteen francs are lost, whether we succeed or not. There's something more involved—not just manhood perhaps, but will. It's like a man in the trenches again: he doesn't know any more why he should go on living, because if he escapes now he'll only be caught later, but he goes on just the same, and even though he has the soul of a cockroach and has admitted as much to himself, give him a gun or a knife or even just his bare nails, and he'll go on slaughtering and slaughtering, he'd slaughter a million men rather than stop and ask himself why.

As I watch Van Norden tackle her, it seems to me that I'm looking at a machine whose cogs have slipped. Left to themselves, they could go on this way forever, grinding and slipping, without ever anything happening. Until a hand shuts the motor off. The sight of them coupled like a pair of goats without the least spark of passion, grinding and grinding away for no reason except the fifteen francs, washes away every bit of feeling I have, except the inhuman one of satisfying my curiosity. The girl is lying on

the edge of the bed and Van Norden is bent over her like
a satyr with his two feet solidly planted on the floor. I am
sitting on a chair behind him, watching their movements
with a cool, scientific detachment; it doesn't matter to me
if it should last forever. It's like watching one of those
crazy machines which throw the newspaper out, millions
and billions and trillions of them with their meaningless
head-lines. The machine seems more sensible, crazy as it
is, and more fascinating to watch, than the human beings
and the events which produced it. My interest in Van
Norden and the girl is nil; if I could sit like this and
watch every single performance going on at this minute
all over the world my interest would be even less than nil.
I wouldn't be able to differentiate between this phenom-
enon and the rain falling or a volcano erupting. As long
as that spark of passion is missing there is no human sig-
nificance in the performance. The machine is better to
watch. And these two are like a machine which has
slipped its cogs. It needs the touch of a human hand to set
it right. It needs a mechanic.

I get down on my knees behind Van Norden and I examine the machine more attentively. The girl throws her
head on one side and gives me a despairing look. "It's
no use," she says. "It's impossible." Upon which Van
Norden sets to work with renewed energy, just like an old
billy goat. He's such an obstinate cuss that he'll break his
horns rather than give up. And he's getting sore now because I'm tickling him in the rump.

"For God's sake, Joe, give it up! You'll kill the poor
girl."

"Leave me alone," he grunts. "I almost got it in that
time."

The posture and the determined way in which he blurts
this out suddenly brings to my mind, for the second time,
the remembrance of my dream. Only now it seems as
though that broomstick, which he had so nonchalantly
slung under his arm, as he walked away, is lost forever.
It is like the sequel to the dream—the same Van Norden,
but minus the primal cause. He's like a hero come back
from the war, a poor maimed bastard living out the reality
of his dreams. Wherever he sits himself the chair collapses; whatever door he enters the room is empty; what-

ever he puts in his mouth leaves a bad taste. Everything is just the same as it was before; the elements are unchanged, the dream is no different than the reality. Only, between the time he went to sleep and the time he woke up, his body was stolen. He's like a machine throwing out newspapers, millions and billions of them every day, and the front page is loaded with catastrophes, with riots, murders, explosions, collisions, but he doesn't feel anything. If somebody doesn't turn the switch off he'll never know what it means to die; you can't die if your own proper body has been stolen. You can get over a cunt and work away like a billy-goat until eternity; you can go to the trenches and be blown to bits; nothing will create that spark of passion if there isn't the intervention of a human hand. Somebody has to put his hand into the machine and let it be wrenched off if the cogs are to mesh again. Somebody has to do this without hope of reward, without concern over the fifteen francs; somebody whose chest is so thin that a medal would make him hunchbacked. And somebody has to throw a feed into a starving cunt without fear of pushing it out again. Otherwise this show'll go on forever. There's no way out of the mess . . .

After sucking the boss's ass for a whole week—it's the thing to do here—I managed to land Peckover's job. He died all right, the poor devil, a few hours after he hit the bottom of the shaft. And just as I predicted, they gave him a fine funeral, with solemn mass, huge wreaths, and everything. *Tout compris.* And after the ceremonies they regaled themselves, the upstairs guys, at a *bistrot.* It was too bad Peckover couldn't have had just a little snack—he would have appreciated it so much to sit with the men upstairs and hear his own name mentioned so frequently.

I must say, right at the start, that I haven't a thing to complain about. It's like being in a lunatic asylum, with permission to masturbate for the rest of your life. The world is brought right under my nose and all that is requested of me is to punctuate the calamities. There is nothing in which these slick guys upstairs do not put their fingers: no joy, no misery passes unnoticed. They live among the hard facts of life, reality, as it is called. It is the reality of a swamp and they are like frogs who have nothing better to do than to croak. The more they croak the more real life becomes. Lawyer, priest, doctor, politician, newspaper man—these are the quacks who have their fingers on the pulse of the world. A constant atmosphere of calamity. It's marvellous. It's as if the barometer never changed, as if the flag were always at half-mast. One can see now how the idea of heaven takes hold of men's consciousness, how it gains ground even when all the props have been knocked from under it. There must be another world beside this swamp in which everything is dumped pell-mell. It's hard to imagine what it can be like, this heaven that men dream about. A frog's heaven, no doubt. Miasma, scum, pond lilies, stagnant water. Sit on a lily-pad unmolested and croak all day. Something like that, I imagine.

They have a wonderful therapeutic effect upon me, these catastrophes which I proof-read. Imagine a state of perfect immunity, a charmed existence, a life of absolute security in the midst of poison bacilli. Nothing touches me, neither earthquakes nor explosions nor riots nor famine nor collisions nor wars nor revolutions. I am inoculated against every disease, every calamity, every sorrow and misery. It's the culmination of a life of fortitude. Seated at my little niche all the poisons which the world gives off each day pass through my hands. Not even a finger-nail gets stained. I am absolutely immune. I am even better off than a laboratory attendant, because there are no bad odors here, just the smell of lead burning. The world can blow up—I'll be here just the same to put in a comma or a semi-colon. I may even touch a little overtime, for with an event like that there's bound to be a final extra. When the world blows up and the final edition has gone to press the proof-readers will quietly gather up all commas, semi-colons, hyphens, asterisks, brackets, parentheses, periods, exclamation marks, etc., and put them in a little box over the editorial chair. *Comme, ça tout est réglé* ...

None of my companions seem to understand why I appear so contented. They grumble all the time, they have ambitions, they want to show their pride and spleen. A good proof-reader has no ambitions, no pride, no spleen. A good proof-reader is a little like God Almighty, he's in the world but not of it. He's for Sundays only. Sunday is his night off. On Sundays he steps down from his pedestal and shows his ass to the faithful. Once a week he listens in on all the private grief and misery of the world; it's enough to last him for the rest of the week. The rest of the week he remains in the frozen winter marshes, an absolute, an impeccable absolute, with only a vaccination mark to distinguish him from the immense void.

The greatest calamity for a proof-reader is the threat of losing his job. When we get together in the break the question that sends a shiver down our spines is: what'll you do if you lose your job? For the man in the paddock, whose duty it is to sweep up the manure, the supreme terror is the possibility of a world without horses. To tell him that it is disgusting to spend one's life shoveling up hot turds is a piece of imbecility. A man can get to love shit if his livelihood depends on it, if his happiness is involved.

This life which, if I were still a man with pride, honor, ambition and so forth, would seem like the bottom rung of degradation, I welcome now, as an invalid welcomes death. It's a negative reality, just like death—a sort of heaven without the pain and terror of dying. In this chthonian world the only thing of importance is orthography and punctuation. It doesn't matter what the nature of the calamity is, only whether it is spelled right. Everything is on one level, whether it be the latest fashion for evening gowns, a new battleship, a plague, a high explosive, an astronomic discovery, a bank run, a railroad wreck, a bull market, a hundred to one shot, an execution, a stick-up, an assassination, or what. Nothing escapes the proof-reader's eye, but nothing penetrates his bullet-proof vest. To the Hindoo Agha Mir, Madame Scheer (formerly Miss Esteve) writes saying she is quite satisfied with his work. "I was married June 6th and I thank you. We are very happy and I hope that thanks to your power it will be so forever. I am sending you by telegraph money order the sum of ... to reward you ..." The Hindoo Agha Mir foretells your future and reads all your thoughts in a precise and inexplicable way. He will advise you, will help you rid yourself of all your worries and troubles of all kinds, etc. *Call or write 20 Avenue Mac-Mahon, Paris.*

He reads all your thoughts in a marvellous way! I take it, that means without exception, from the most trivial thoughts to the most shameless. He must have a lot of time on his hands, this Agha Mir. Or does he only concentrate on the thoughts of those who send money by telegraph money order? In the same edition I notice a headline announcing that "the universe is expanding so fast it may burst" and underneath it is the photograph of a splitting headache. And then there is a spiel about the pearl, signed Tecla. The oyster produces both, he informs all and sundry. Both the "wild" or Oriental pearl, and the "cultured" pearl. On the same day, at the Cathedral of Trier, the Germans are exhibiting the Coat of Christ; it's the first time it's been taken out of the moth-balls in forty-two years. Nothing said about the pants and vest. In Salzburg, also the same day, two mice were born in a man's stomach, believe it or not. A famous movie actress is shown with her legs crossed: she is taking a rest in Hyde Park, and underneath a well-known painter remarks "I'll admit that Mrs. Coolidge has such charm and personality that she would have been one of the 12 famous Americans, even had her husband not been President." From an interview with Mr. Humhal, of Vienna, I glean the following ... "Before I stop," said Mr. Humhal, "I'd like to say that faultless cut and fit does not suffice; the proof of good tailoring is seen in the wearing. A suit must bend to the body, yet keep its line when the wearer is walking or sitting." And whenever there is an explosion in a coal mine—a *British* coal mine—notice please that the King and Queen always send their condolences promptly, *by telegraph*. And they always attend the important races, though the other day, according to the copy, it was at the Derby, I believe, "heavy rains began to fall, much to the surprise of the King and Queen." More heart-rending, however, is an item like this: "It is claimed in Italy that the persecutions are not against the Church, but nevertheless they are conducted against the most exquisite parts of the Church. It is claimed that they are not against the Pope, but they are against the very heart and eyes of the Pope."

I had to travel precisely all around the world to find just such a comfortable, agreeable niche as this. It seems incredible almost. How could I have foreseen, in America, with all those firecrackers they put up your ass to give you pep and courage, that the ideal position for a man of my temperament was to look for orthographic mistakes? Over there you think of nothing but becoming President of the United States some day. Potentially every man is presidential timber. Here it's different. Here every man is potentially a zero. If you become something or somebody it is an accident, a miracle. The chances are a thousand to one that you will never leave your native village. The chances are a thousand to one that you'll have your legs shot off or your eyes blown out. Unless the miracle happens and you find yourself a general or a rearadmiral.

But it's just because the chances are all against you, just because there is so little hope, that life is sweet over here. Day by day. No yesterdays and no to-morrows. The barometer never changes, the flag is always at halfmast. You wear a piece of black crape on your arm, you have a little ribbon in your button-hole, and, if you are lucky enough to afford it, you buy yourself a pair of artificial light-weight limbs, aluminium preferably. Which does not prevent you from enjoying an *apéritif* or looking at the animals in the zoo or flirting with the vultures who sail up and down the boulevards always on the alert for fresh carrion. Time passes. If you're a stranger and your papers are in order you can expose yourself to infection without fear of being contaminated. It is better, if possible, to have a proof-reader's job. *Comme ça, tout s'arrange.* That means, that if you happen to be strolling home at three in the morning and you are intercepted by the bicycle cops, you can snap your fingers at them. In the morning, when the market is in swing, you can buy Belgian eggs, at fifty centimes a piece. A proof-reader doesn't get up usually until noon, or a little after. It's well to choose a hotel near a cinema, because if you have a tendency to oversleep the bells will wake you up in time for the matinée. Or if you can't find a hotel near a cinema, choose one near a cemetery, it comes to the same thing. Above all, never despair. *Il ne faut jamais désespérer.*

Which is what I try to din into Carl and Van Norden every night. A world without hope, but no despair. It's as

though I had been converted to a new religion, as though
I were making an annual novena every night to Our Lady
of Solace. I can't imagine what there would be to gain if
I were made editor of the paper, or even President of the
United States. I'm up a blind alley, and it's cosy and comfortable. With a piece of copy in my hand I listen to the
music around me, the hum and drone of voices, the tinkle
of the linotype machines, as if there were a thousand silver bracelets passing through a wringer; now and then a
rat scurries past our feet or a cockroach descends the wall
in front of us, moving nimbly and gingerly on his delicate
legs. The events of the day are slid under your nose, quietly, unostentatiously, with, now and then, a by-line to
mark the presence of a human hand, an ego, a touch of
vanity. The procession passes serenely, like a cortège entering the cemetery gates. The paper under the copy desk
is so thick that it almost feels like a carpet with a soft
nap. Under Van Norden's desk it is stained with brown
juice. Around eleven o'clock the peanut vendor arrives, a
half-wit of an Armenian who is also content with his lot
in life.

Now and then I get a cablegram from Mona saying that
she's arriving on the next boat. "Letter following," it always says. It's been going on like this for nine months,
but I never see her name in the list of boat arrivals, nor
does the *garçon* ever bring me a letter on a silver platter.
I haven't any more expectations in that direction either. If
she ever does arrive she can look for me downstairs, just
behind the lavatory. She'll probably tell me right away
that it's unsanitary. That's the first thing that strikes an
American woman about Europe—that it's unsanitary. Impossible for them to conceive of a Paradise without modern plumbing. If they find a bed-bug they want to write
a letter immediately to the Chamber of Commerce. How
am I ever going to explain to her that I'm contented here?
She'll say I've become a degenerate. I know her line from
beginning to end. She'll want to look for a studio with a
garden attached—and a bath-tub to be sure. She wants to
be poor in a romantic way. I know her. But I'm prepared
for her this time.

There are days, nevertheless, when the sun is out and
I get off the beaten path and think about her hungrily.

Now and then, despite my grim satisfaction, I get to thinking about another way of life, get to wondering if it would make a difference having a young, restless creature by my side. The trouble is I can hardly remember what she looks like, nor even how it feels to have my arms around her. Everything that belongs to the past seems to have fallen into the sea; I have memories, but the images have lost their vividness, they seem dead and desultory, like time-bitten mummies stuck in a quagmire. If I try to recall my life in New York I get a few splintered fragments, nightmarish and covered with verdigris. It seems as if my own proper existence had come to an end somewhere, just where exactly I can't make out. I'm not an American any more, nor a New Yorker, and even less a European, or a Parisian. I haven't any allegiance, any responsibilities, any hatreds, any worries, any prejudices, any passion. I'm neither for nor against. I'm neutral.

When we walk home of a night, the three of us, it often happens after the first spasms of disgust that we get to talking about the condition of things with the enthusiasm which only those who bear no active part in life can muster. What seems strange to me sometimes, when I crawl into bed, is that all this enthusiasm is engendered just to kill time, just to annihilate the three-quarters of an hour which it requires to walk from the office to Montparnasse. We might have the most brilliant, the most feasible ideas for the amelioration of this or that, but there is no vehicle to hitch them to. And what is more strange is that the absence of any relationship between ideas and living causes us no anguish, no discomfort. We have become so adjusted that, if to-morrow we were ordered to walk on our hands, we would do so without the slightest protest. Provided, of course, that the paper came out as usual. And that we touched our pay regularly. Otherwise nothing matters. Nothing. We have become Orientalized. We have become coolies, white collar coolies, silenced by a handful of rice each day. A special feature in American skulls, I was reading the other day, is the presence of the epactal bone, or *os Incae,* in the occiput. The presence of this bone, so the savant went on to say, is due to a persistence of the transverse occipital suture which is usually closed in foetal life. Hence it is a sign of arrested development and indicative of an inferior race. "The average cubical capacity of the American skull," so he went on to say, "falls below that of the white, and rises above that of the black race. Taking both sexes, the Parisians of to-day have a cranial capacity of 1.448 cubic centimeters; the Negroes 1.344 centimeters: the American Indians 1.376." From all of which I deduce nothing because I am an American and not an Indian. But it's cute to explain things that way, by a bone, an *os Incae*, for example. It doesn't disturb his theory at all to admit that single examples of Indian skulls have yielded the extraordinary capacity of 1.920 cubic centimeters, a cranial capacity not exceeded in any other race. What I note with satisfaction is that the Parisians, of both sexes, seem to have a normal cranial capacity. The transverse occipital suture is evidently not so persistent with them. They know how to enjoy an *apéritif* and they don't worry if the houses are unpainted. There's nothing extraordinary about their skulls, so far as cranial indices go. There must be some other explanation for the art of living which they have brought to such a degree of perfection.

At Monsieur Paul's, the *bistrot* across the way, there is a back room reserved for the newspapermen where we can eat on credit. It is a pleasant little room with saw-dust on the floor and flies in season and out. When I say that it is reserved for the newspapermen I don't mean to imply that we eat in privacy; on the contrary, it means that we have the privilege of associating with the whores and pimps who form the more substantial element of Monsieur Paul's clientèle. The arrangement suits the guys upstairs to a T, because they're always on the look-out for tail, and even those who have a steady little French girl are not averse to making a switch now and then. The principal thing is not to get a dose; at times it would seems as if an epidemic had swept the office, or perhaps it might be explained by the fact that they all sleep with the same woman. Anyhow, it's gratifying to observe how miserable they can look when they are obliged to sit beside a pimp who, despite the little hardships of his profession, lives a life of luxury by comparison.

I'm thinking particularly now of one tall, blonde fellow who delivers the Havas messages by bicycle. He is always a little late for his meal, always perspiring profusely and his face covered with grime. He has a fine, awkward way of strolling in, saluting everybody with two fingers and making a bee line for the sink which is just between the toilet and the kitchen. As he wipes his face he gives the edibles a quick inspection; if he sees a nice steak lying on the slab he picks it up and sniffs it, or he will dip the ladle into the big pot and try a mouthful of soup. He's like a fine bloodhound, his nose to the ground all the time. The preliminaries over, having made pipi and blown his nose vigorously, he walks nonchalantly over to his wench and gives her a big, smacking kiss together with an affectionate pat on the rump. Her, the wench, I've never seen look anything but immaculate—even at three a.m., after an evening's work. She looks exactly as if she had just stepped out of a Turkish Bath. It's a pleasure to look at such healthy brutes, to see such repose, such affection, such appetite as they display. It's the evening meal I'm speaking of now, the little snack that she takes before entering upon her duties. In a little while she will be obliged to take leave of her big blonde brute, to flop somewhere on the boulevard and sip her *digestif*. If the job is irksome or wearing or exhaustive, she certainly doesn't show it. When the big fellow arrives, hungry as a wolf, she puts her arms around him and kisses him hungrily—his eyes, nose, cheeks, hair, the back of his neck ... she'd kiss his ass if it could be done publicly. She's grateful to him, that's evident. She's no wage-slave. All through the meal she laughs convulsively. You wouldn't think she had a care in the world. And now and then, by way of affection, she gives him a resounding slap in the face, such a whack as would knock a proof-reader spinning.

They don't seem to be aware of anything but themselves and the food that they pack away in shovelsful. Such perfect contentment, such harmony, such mutual understanding, it drives Van Norden crazy to watch them. Especially when she slips her hand in the big fellow's fly and caresses it, to which he generally responds by grabbing her teat and squeezing it playfully.

There is another couple who arrive usually about the same time and they behave just like two married people.

They have their spats, they wash their linen in public and after they've made things disagreeable for themselves and everybody else, after threats and curses and reproaches and recriminations, they make up for it by billing and cooing, just like a pair of turtle doves. Lucienne, as he calls her, is a heavy, platinum blonde with a cruel, saturnine air. She has a full under-lip which she chews venomously when her temper runs away with her. And a cold, beady eye, a sort of faded china blue, which makes him sweat when she fixes him with it. But she's a good sort, Lucienne, despite the condor-like profile which she presents to us when the squabbling begins. Her bag is always full of dough, and if she deals it out cautiously, it is only because she doesn't want to encourage him in his bad habits. He has a weak character; that is, if one takes Lucienne's tirades seriously. He will spend fifty francs of an evening while waiting for her to get through. When the waitress comes to take his order he has no appetite. "Ah, you're not hungry again!" growls Lucienne. "Humpf! You were waiting for me, I suppose, on the Faubourg Montmartre. You had a good time, I hope, while I slaved for you. *Speak, imbecile, where were you?*"

When she flares up like that, when she gets enraged, he looks up at her timidly and then, as if he had decided that silence was the best course, he lets his head drop and he fiddles with his napkin. But this little gesture, which she knows so well and which of course is secretly pleasing to her because she is convinced now that he is guilty, only increases Lucienne's anger. *"Speak, imbecile!"* she shrieks. And with a squeaky, timid little voice he explains to her woefully that while waiting for her he got so hungry that he was obliged to stop off for a sandwich and glass of beer. It was just enough to ruin his appetite—he says it dolefully, though it's apparent that food just now is the least of his worries. "But"—and he tries to make his voice sound more convincing—"I was waiting for you all the time," he blurts out.

"Liar!" she screams. "Liar! Ah, fortunately, I too am a liar . . . a *good liar*. You make me ill with your petty little lies. Why don't you tell me a big lie?"

He hangs his head again and absent-mindedly he gathers a few crumbs and puts them to his mouth. Whereupon she slaps his hand. "Don't do that! You make me tired. You're such an imbecile. Liar! Just you wait! I have more to say. I am a liar too, but I am not an imbecile."

In a little while, however, they are sitting close together, their hands locked, and she is murmuring softly: "Ah, my little rabbit, it is hard to leave you now. Come here, kiss me! What are you going to do this evening? Tell me the truth, my little one ... I am sorry that I have such an ugly temper." He kisses her timidly, just like a little bunny with long pink ears; gives her a little peck on the lips as if he were nibbling a cabbage leaf. And at the same time his bright round eyes fall caressingly on her purse which is lying open beside her on the bench. He is only waiting for the moment when he can graciously give her the slip; he is itching to get away, to sit down in some quiet café on the Rue du Faubourg-Montmartre.

I know him, the innocent little devil, with his round, frightened eyes of a rabbit. And I know what a devil's street is the Faubourg Montmartre with its brass plates and rubber goods, the lights twinkling all night and sex running through the street like a sewer. To walk from the Rue Lafayette to the boulevard is like running the gauntlet; they attach themselves to you like barnacles, they eat into you like ants, they coax, wheedle, cajole, implore, beseech, they try it out in German, English, Spanish, they show you their torn hearts and their busted shoes, and long after you've chopped the tentacles away, long after the fizz and sizzle has died out, the fragrance of the *lavabo* clings to your nostrils—it is the odor of the *Parfum de Dansé* whose effectiveness is guaranteed only for a distance of twenty centimeters. One could piss away a whole lifetime in that little stretch between the boulevard and the Rue Lafayette. Every bar is alive, throbbing, the dice loaded; the cashiers are perched like vultures on their high stools and the money they handle has a human stink to it. There is no equivalent in the Banque de France for the blood money that passes currency here, the money that glistens with human sweat, that passes like a forest fire from hand to hand and leaves behind it a smoke and stench. A man who can walk through the Faubourg Montmartre at night without panting or sweating, without a prayer or a curse on his lips, a man like that has no balls, and if he has, then he ought to be castrated.

Supposing the timid little rabbit does spend fifty francs of an evening while waiting for his Lucienne? Supposing he does get hungry and buy a sandwich and a glass of beer, or stop and chat with somebody else's trollop? You think he ought to be weary of that round night after night? You think it ought to weigh on him, oppress him, bore him to death? You don't think that a pimp is inhuman, I hope? A pimp has his private grief and misery too, don't you forget. Perhaps he would like nothing better than to stand on the corner every night with a pair of white dogs and watch them piddle. Perhaps he would like it if, when he opened the door, he would see her there reading the *Paris-Soir,* her eyes already a little heavy with sleep. Perhaps it isn't so wonderful, when he bends over his Lucienne, to taste another man's breath. Better maybe to have only three francs in your pocket and a pair of white dogs that piddle on the corner than to taste those bruised lips. Bet you, when she squeezes him tight, when she begs for that little package of love which only he knows how to deliver, bet you he fights like a thousand devils to pump it up, to wipe out that regiment that has marched between her legs. Maybe when he takes her body and practises a new tune, maybe it isn't all passion and curiosity with him, but a fight in the dark, a fight singlehanded against the army that rushed the gates, the army that walked over her, trampled her, that left her with such a devouring hunger that not even a Rudolph Valentino could appease her. When I listen to the reproaches that are levelled against a girl like Lucienne, when I hear her being denigrated or despised because she is cold and mercenary, because she is too mechanical, or because she's in too great a hurry, or because this or because that, I say to myself, hold on there bozo, not so fast! Remember that you're far back in the procession; remember that a whole army corps has laid siege to her, that she's been laid waste, plundered and pillaged. I say to myself, listen, bozo, don't begrudge the fifty francs you hand her because you know her pimp is pissing it away in the Faubourg Montmartre. It's *her* money and *her* pimp. It's blood money. It's money that'll never be taken out of circulation because there's nothing in the Banque de France to redeem it with.

That's how I think about it often when I'm seated in my little niche juggling the Havas reports or untangling the cables from Chicago, London, and Montreal. In between the rubber and silk markets and the Winnipeg grains there oozes a little of the fizz and sizzle of the Faubourg Montmartre. When the bonds go weak and spongy and the pivotals balk and the volatiles effervesce, when the grain market slips and slides and the bulls commence to roar, when every fucking calamity, every ad, every sport item and fashion article, every boat arrival, every travelogue, every tag of gossip has been punctuated, checked, revised, pegged and wrung through the silver bracelets, when I hear the front page being hammered into whack and see the frogs dancing around like drunken squibs, I think of Lucienne sailing down the boulevard with her wings outstretched, a huge silver condor suspended over the sluggish tide of traffic, a strange bird from the tips of the Andes with a rose-white belly and a tenacious little knob. Sometimes I walk home alone and I follow her through the dark streets, follow her through the court of the Louvre, over the Pont des Arts, through the arcade, through the fents and slits, the somnolence, the drugged whiteness, the grill of the Luxembourg, the tangled boughs, the snores and groans, the green slats, the strum and tinkle, the points of the stars, the spangles, the jetties, the blue and white striped awnings that she brushed with the tips of her wings.

In the blue of an electric dawn the peanut shells look wan and crumpled; along the beach at Montparnasse the waterlilies bend and break. When the tide is on the ebb and only a few syphilitic mermaids are left stranded in the muck, the Dome looks like a shooting gallery that's been struck by a cyclone. Everything is slowly dribbling back to the sewer. For about an hour there is a death-like calm during which the vomit is mopped up. Suddenly the trees begin to screech. From one end of the boulevard to the other a demented song rises up. It is like the signal that announces the close of the exchange. What hopes there were are swept up. The moment has come to void the last bagful of usine. The day is sneaking in like a leper . . .

One of the things to guard against when you work nights is not to break your schedule; if you don't get to bed before the birds begin to screech it's useless to go to bed at all. This morning, having nothing better to do, I visited the *Jardin des Plantes*. Marvellous pelicans here from Chapultepec and peacocks with studded fans that look at you with silly eyes. Suddenly it began to rain.

Returning to Montparnasse in the bus I noticed a little French woman opposite me who sat stiff and erect as if she were getting ready to preen herself. She sat on the edge of the seat as if she feared to crush her gorgeous tail. Marvellous, I thought, if suddenly she shook herself and from her *derrière* there sprung open a huge studded fan with long silken plumes.

At the Café de l'Avenue, where I stop for a bite, a woman with a swollen stomach tries to interest me in her condition. She would like me to go to a room with her and while away an hour or two. It is the first time I have ever been propositioned by a pregnant woman: I am almost tempted to try it. As soon as the baby is born and handed over to the authorities she will go back to her trade, she says. She makes hats. Observing that my interest is waning she takes my hand and puts it on her abdomen, I feel something stirring inside. It takes my appetite away.

I have never seen a place like Paris for varieties of sexual provender. As soon as a woman loses a front tooth or an eye or a leg she goes on the loose. In America she'd starve to death if she had nothing to recommend her but a mutilation. Here it is different. A missing tooth or a nose eaten away or a fallen womb, any misfortune that aggravates the natural homeliness of a female, seems to be regarded as an added spice, a stimulant for the jaded appetites of the male.

I am speaking naturally of that world, which is peculiar to the big cities, the world of men and women whose last drop of juice has been squeezed out by the machine—the martyrs of modern progress. It is this mass of bones and collar buttons which the painter finds so difficult to put flesh on.

It is only later, in the afternoon, when I find myself in an art gallery on the Rue de Sèze, surrounded by the men and women of Matisse, that I am drawn back again to the proper precincts of the human world. On the threshold of that big hall whose walls are now ablaze, I pause a moment to recover from the shock which one experiences when the habitual gray of the world is rent asunder and the color of life splashes forth in song and poem. I find myself in a world so natural, so complete, that I am lost. I have the sensation of being immersed in the very plexus of life, focal from whatever place, position or attitude I take my stance. Lost as when once I sank into the quick of a budding grove and seated in the dining room of that enormous world of Balbec, I caught for the first time the profound meaning of those interior stills which manifest their presence through the exorcism of sight and touch. Standing on the threshold of that world which Matisse has created I re-experienced the power of that revelation which had permitted Proust to so deform the picture of life that only those who, like himself, are sensible to the alchemy of sound and sense, are capable of transforming the negative reality of life into the substantial and significant outlines of art. Only those who can admit the light into their gizzards can translate what is there in the heart. Vividly now I recall how the glint and sparkle of light caroming from the massive chandeliers splintered and ran blood, flecking the tips of the waves that beat monotonously on the dull gold outside the windows. On the beach, masts and chimneys interlaced, and like a fuliginous shadow the figure of Albertine gliding through the surf, fusing into the mysterious quick and prism of a protoplasmic realm, uniting her shadow to the dream and harbinger of death. With the close of day, pain rising like a mist from the earth, sorrow closing in, shuttering the endless vista of sea and sky. Two waxen hands lying listlessly on the bedspread and along the pale veins the fluted murmur of a shell repeating the legend of its birth.

In every poem by Matisse there is the history of a particle of human flesh which refused the consummation of death. The whole run of flesh, from hair to nails, ex-

presses the miracle of breathing, as if the inner eye, in its
thirst for a greater reality, had converted the pores of the
flesh into hungry seeing mouths. By whatever vision one
passes there is the odor and the sound of voyage. It is impossible to gaze at even a corner of his dreams without
feeling the lift of the wave and the cool of the flying
spray. He stands at the helm peering with steady blue
eyes into the portfolio, of time. Into what distant corners
has he not thrown his long, slanting gaze? Looking down
the vast promontory of his nose he has beheld
everything—the Cordilleras falling away into the Pacific,
the history of the diaspora done in vellum, shutters fluting
the froufrou of the beach, the piano curving like a conch,
corollas giving out diapasons of light, chameleons
squirming under the book-press, seraglios expiring in
oceans of dust, music issuing like fire from the hidden
chromosphere of pain, spore and madrepore fructify-
ing the earth, navels vomiting their bright spawn of
anguish ... He is a bright sage, a dancing seer who, with
a sweep of the brush, removes the ugly scaffold to which
the body of a man is chained by the incontrovertible facts
of life. He it is, if any man to-day possesses the gift, who
knows where to dissolve the human figure, who has the
courage to sacrifice an harmonious line in order to detect
the rhythm and murmur of the blood, who takes the light
that has been refracted inside him and lets it flood the
keyboard of color. Behind the minutiae, the chaos, the
mockery of life, he detects the invisible pattern; he announces his discoveries in the metaphysical pigment of
space. No searching for formulae, no crucifixion of ideas,
no compulsion other than to create. Even as the world
goes to smash there is one man who remains at the core,
who becomes more solidly fixed and anchored, more cen-
trifugal as the process of dissolution quickens.

More and more the world resembles an entomologist's
dream. The earth is moving out of its orbit, the axis has
shifted; from the north the snow blows down in huge
knife-blue drifts. A new ice age is setting in, the transverse sutures are closing up and everywhere throughout
the corn belt the foetal world is dying, turning to dead
mastoid. Inch by inch the deltas are drying out and the
river-beds are smooth as glass. A new day is dawning, a

metallurgical day, when the earth shall clink with showers of bright yellow ore. As the thermometer drops, the form of the world grows blurred; osmosis there still is, and here and there articulation, but at the periphery the veins are all varicose, at the periphery the light-waves bend and the sun bleeds like a broken rectum.

At the very hub of this wheel which is falling apart, is Matisse. And he will keep on rolling until everything that has gone to make up the wheel has disintegrated. He has already rolled over a goodly portion of the globe, over Persia and India and China, and like a magnet he has attached to himself microscopic particles from Kurd, Beluchistan, Timbuctoo, Somaliland, Angkor, Tierra del Fuego. The odalisques he has studded with malachite and jasper, their flesh veiled with a thousand eyes, perfumed eyes dipped in the sperm of whales. Wherever a breeze stirs there are breasts as cool as jelly, white pigeons come to flutter and rut in the ice-blue veins of the Himalayas.

The wallpaper with which the men of science have covered the world of reality is falling to tatters. The grand whorehouse which they have made of life requires no decoration; it is essential only that the drains function adequately. Beauty, that feline beauty which has us by the balls in America, is finished. To fathom the new reality it is first necessary to dismantle the drains, to lay open the gangrened ducts which compose the genito-urinary system that supplies the excreta of art. The odor of the day is permanganate and formaldehyde. The drains are clogged with strangled embryos.

The world of Matisse is still beautiful in an old-fashioned bedroom way. There is not a ball-bearing in evidence, nor a boiler-plate, nor a piston, nor a monkey-wrench. It is the same old world that went gayly to the Bois in the pastoral days of wine and fornication. I find it soothing and refreshing to move amongst these creatures with live, breathing pores whose background is stable and solid as light itself. I feel it poignantly when I walk along the Boulevard de la Madeleine and the whores rustle beside me, when just to glance at them causes me to tremble. Is it because they are exotic or well-nourished? No, it is rare to find a beautiful woman along the Boulevard de la Madeleine. But in Matisse, in the ex-

ploration of his brush, there is the trembling glitter of a
world which demands only the presence of the female to
crystallize the most fugitive aspirations. To come upon a
woman offering herself outside a urinal, where there are
advertised cigarette papers, rum, acrobats, horse-races,
where the heavy foliage of the trees breaks the heavy
mass of walls and roofs, is an experience that begins
where the boundaries of the known world leave off. In the
evening now and then, skirting the cemetery walls, I
stumble upon the phantom odalisques of Matisse fastened
to the trees, their tangled manes drenched with sap. A few
feet away, removed by incalculable aeons of time, lies the
prone and mummy-swathed ghost of Baudelaire, of a
whole world that will belch no more. In the dusky corners
of cafés are men and women with hands locked, their
loins slather-flecked; nearby stands the garçon with his
apron full of sous, waiting patiently for the entr'acte in
order to fall upon his wife and gouge her. Even as the
world falls apart the Paris that belongs to Matisse shud-
ders with bright, gasping orgasms, the air itself is steady
with a stagnant sperm, the trees tangled like hair. On its
wobbly axle the wheel rolls steadily downhill; there are
no brakes, no ball-bearings, no balloon tires. The wheel is
falling apart, but the revolution is intact . . .

Out of a clear sky there comes one day a letter from Boris whom I have not seen for months and months. It is a strange document and I don't pretend to understand it all clearly. "What happened between us—at any rate, as far as I go—is that you touched me, touched my life, that is, at the one point where I am still alive: my death. By the emotional flow I went through another immersion. I lived again, alive. No longer by reminiscence, as I do with others, but alive."

That's how it began. Not a word of greeting, no date, no address. Written in a thin, pompous scrawl on ruled paper torn out of a blank book. "That is why, whether you like me or not—deep down I rather think you hate me—you are very close to me. By you I know how I died: I see myself dying again: I *am* dying. That is something. More than to be dead simply. That may be the reason why I am so afraid to see you: you may have played the trick on me, and died. Things happen so fast nowadays."

I'm reading it over, line by line, standing by the stones. It sounds nutty to me, all this palaver about life and death and things happening so fast. Nothing is happening that I can see, except the usual calamities on the front page. He's been living all by himself for the last six months, tucked away in a cheap little room—probably holding telepathic communication with Cronstadt. He talks about the line falling back, the sector evacuated, and so on and so forth, as though he were dug into a trench and writing a report to headquarters. He probably had his frock coat on when he sat down to pen his missive, and he probably rubbed his hands a few times as he used to do when a customer was calling to rent the apartment. "The reason

I wanted you to commit suicide . . ." he begins again. At that I burst out laughing. He used to walk up and down with one hand stuck in the tail-flap of his frock coat at the Villa Borghese, or at Cronstadt's—wherever there was deck space, as it were—and reel off this nonsense about living and dying to his heart's content. I never understood a word of it, I must confess, but it was a good show and, being a Gentile, I was naturally interested in what went on in that menagerie of a brain-pan. Sometimes he would lie on his couch full length, exhausted by the surge of ideas that swept through his noodle. His feet just grazed the book rack where he kept his Plato and Spinoza—he couldn't understand why I had no use for them. I must say he made them sound interesting, though what it was all about I hadn't the least idea. Sometimes I would glance at a volume furtively, to check up on these wild ideas which he imputed to them—but the connection was frail, tenuous. He had a language all his own, Boris, that is, when I had him alone; but when I listened to Cronstadt it seemed to me that Boris had plagiarized his wonderful ideas. They talked a sort of higher mathematics, these two. Nothing of flesh and blood ever crept in; it was weird, ghostly, ghoulishly abstract. When they got on to the dying business it sounded a little more concrete: after all, a cleaver or a meat-axe has to have a handle. I enjoyed those sessions immensely. It was the first time in my life that death had ever seemed fascinating to me—all these abstract deaths which involved a bloodless sort of agony. Now and then they would compliment me on being alive, but in such a way that I felt embarrassed. They made me feel that I was alive in the nineteenth century, a sort of atavistic remnant, a romantic shred, a soulful *pithecanthropus erectus.* Boris especially seemed to get a great kick out of touching me: he wanted me to be alive so that he could die to his heart's content. You would think that all those millions in the street were nothing but dead cows the way he looked at me and touched me. But the letter . . . I'm forgetting the letter . . .

"The reason why I wanted you to commit suicide that evening at the Cronstadts', when Moldorf became God, was that I was very close to you then. Perhaps closer than I shall ever be. And I was afraid, terribly afraid, that some day you'd go back on me, die on my hands. And I would be left high and dry with my idea of you simply, and nothing to sustain it. I should never forgive you for that."

Perhaps you can visualize him saying a thing like that! Myself it's not clear what his idea of me was, or at any rate, it's clear that I was just pure idea, an idea that kept itself alive without food. He never attached much importance, Boris, to the food problem. He tried to nourish me with ideas. Everything was idea. Just the same, when he had his heart set on renting the apartment, he wouldn't forget to put a new washer in the toilet. Anyway, he didn't want me to die on his hands. "You must be life for me to the very end," so he writes. "That is the only way in which you can sustain my idea of you. Because you have gotten, as you see, tied up with something so vital to me, I do not think I shall ever shake you off. Nor do I wish to. I want you to live more vitally every day, as I am dead. That is why, when I speak of you to others, I am just a bit ashamed. It's hard to talk of one's self so intimately."

You would imagine perhaps that he was anxious to see me, or that he would like to know what I was doing—but no, not a line about the concrete or the personal, except in this living-dying language, nothing but this little message from the trenches, this whiff of poison gas to apprise all and sundry that the war was still on. I sometimes ask myself how it happens that I attract nothing but crackbrained individuals, neurasthenics, neurotics, psychopaths—and Jews especially. There must be something in a healthy Gentile that excites the Jewish mind, like when he sees sour black bread. There was Moldorf, for example, who had made himself God, according to Boris and Cronstadt. He positively hated me, the little viper—yet he couldn't stay away from me. He came round regularly for his little dose of insults—it was like a tonic to him. In the beginning, it's true, I was lenient with him; after all, he was paying me to listen to him. And though I never displayed much sympathy I knew how to be silent when it involved a meal and a little pin money. After a while, however, seeing what a masochist he was, I permitted myself to laugh in his face now and then; that was like a whip for him, it made the grief and agony gush forth with renewed vigor. And perhaps everything would have gone smoothly between us if he had not felt it his duty to protect Tania. But Tania being a Jewess, that brought up a moral question. He wanted me to stick to Mlle. Claude for whom, I must admit, I had a genuine affection. He even gave me money occasionally to sleep with her. Until he realized that I was a hopeless lecher.

I mention Tania now because she's just got back from Russia—just a few days ago. Sylvester remained behind to worm his way into a job. He's given up literature entirely. He's dedicated himself to the new Utopia. Tania wants me to go back there with her, to the Crimea preferably, and start a new life. We had a fine drinking bout up in Carl's room the other day, discussing the possibilities. I wanted to know what I could do for a living back there—if I could be a proof-reader, for example. She said I didn't need to worry about what I would do—they would find a job for me as long as I was earnest and sincere. I tried to look earnest, but I only succeeded in looking pathetic. They don't want to see sad faces, in Russia; they want you to be cheerful, enthusiastic, light-hearted, optimistic. It sounded very much like America to me. I wasn't born with this kind of enthusiasm. I didn't let on to her, of course, but secretly I was praying to be left alone, to go back to my little niche, and to stay there until the war breaks out. All this hocus-pocus about Russia disturbed me a little. She got so excited about it, Tania, that we finished almost a half dozen bottles of *vin ordinaire*. Carl was jumping about like a cockroach. He has just enough Jew in him to lose his head over an idea like Russia. Nothing would do but to marry us off—immediately. "Hitch up!" he says, "you have nothing to lose!" And then he pretends to run a little errand so that we can pull off a fast one. And while she wanted it all right, Tania, still that Russia business had gotten so solidly planted in her skull that she pissed the interval away chewing my ear off, which made me somewhat grumpy and ill at ease. Anyway, we had to think about eating and getting to the office, so we piled into a taxi on the Boulevard Edgar-Quinet, just a stone's throw away from the cemetery, and off we whizzed. It was just a nice hour to spin through

Paris in an open cab, and the wine rolling around in our tanks made it seem even more lovely than usual. Carl was sitting opposite us, on the *strapontin,* his face as red as a beet. He was happy, the poor bastard, thinking what a glorious new life he would lead on the other side of Europe. And at the same time he felt a bit wistful, too—I could see that. He didn't really want to leave Paris, any more than I did. Paris hadn't been good to him, any more than it had to me, or to anybody, for that matter, but when you've suffered and endured things here it's then that Paris takes hold of you, grabs you by the balls, you might say, like some lovesick bitch who'd die rather than let you get out of her hands. That's how it looked to him, I could see that. Rolling over the Seine he had a big foolish grin on his face and he looked around at the buildings and the statues as though he were seeing them in a dream. To me it was like a dream too: I had my hand in Tania's bosom and I was squeezing her titties with all my might and I noticed the water under the bridge and the barges and Notre Dame down below, just like the post-cards show it, and I was thinking drunkenly to myself that's how one gets fucked, but I was sly about it too and I knew I wouldn't ever trade all this whirling about my head for Russia or heaven or anything on earth. It was a fine afternoon, I was thinking to myself, and soon we'd be pushing a feed down our bellies and what could we order as a special treat, some good heavy wine that would drown out all this Russia business. With a woman like Tania, full of sap and everything, they don't give a damn what happens to you once they get an idea in their heads. Let them go far enough and they'll pull the pants off you, right in the taxi. It was grand though, milling through the traffic, our faces all smudged with rouge and the wine gurgling like a sewer inside us, especially when we swung into the Rue Laffitte which is just wide enough to frame the little temple at the end of the street and above it the Sacré-Coeur, a kind of exotic jumble of architecture, a lucid French idea that gouges right through your drunkenness and leaves you swimming helplessly in the past, in a fluid dream that makes you wide awake and yet doesn't jar your nerves.

* * *

With Tania back on the scene, a steady job, the drunken talk about Russia, the walks home at night, and Paris in full summer, life seems to lift its head a little higher. That's why perhaps, a letter such as Boris sent me seems absolutely cock-eyed. Most every day I meet Tania around five o'clock, to have a Porto with her, as she calls it. I let her take me to places I've never seen before, the swell bars around the Champs-Elysées where the sound of jazz and baby voices crooning seems to soak right through the mahogany woodwork. Even when you go to the *lavabo* these pulpy, sappy strains pursue you, come floating into the cabinet through the ventilators and make life all soft soap and iridescent bubbles. And whether it's because Sylvester is away and she feels free now, or whatever it is, Tania certainly tries to behave like an angel. "You treated me lousy just before I went away," she says to me one day. "Why did you want to act that way? I never did anything to hurt you, did I?" We were getting sentimental, what with the soft lights and that creamy, mahogany music seeping through the place. It was getting near time to go to work and we hadn't eaten yet. The stubs were lying there in front of us—six francs, four-fifty, seven francs, two-fifty—I was counting them up mechanically and wondering too at the same time if I would like it better being a bartender. Often like that, when she was talking to me, gushing about Russia, the future, love, and all that crap, I'd get to thinking about the most irrelevant things, about shining shoes or being a lavatory attendant, particularly I suppose because it was so cosy in these joints that she dragged me to and it never occurred to me that I'd be stone sober and perhaps old and bent . . . no, I imagined always that the future, however modest, would be in just this sort of ambiance, with the same tunes playing through my head and the glasses clinking and behind every shapely ass a trail of perfume a yard wide that would take the stink out of life, even downstairs in the *lavabo*.

The strange thing is it never spoiled me trotting around to the swell bars with her like that. It was hard to leave her, certainly. I used to lead her around to the porch of a church near the office and standing there in the dark we'd take a last embrace, she whispering to me "Jesus, what am I going to do now?" She wanted me to quit the job so as I could make love night and day; she didn't even care about Russia any more, just so long as we were together. But the moment I left her my head cleared. It was another kind of music, not so croony but good just the same, which greeted my ears when I pushed through the swinging door. And another kind of perfume, not just a yard wide, but omnipresent, a sort of sweat and patchouli that seemed to come from the machines. Coming in with a skinful, as I usually did, it was like dropping suddenly to a low altitude. Generally I made a beeline for the toilet—that braced me up rather. It was a little cooler there, or else the sound of water running made it seem so. It was always a cold douche, the toilet. It was real. Before you got inside you had to pass a line of Frenchmen peeling off their clothes. Ugh! but they stank, those devils! And they were well paid for it, too. But there they were, stripped down, some in long underwear, some with beards, most of them pale, skinny rats with lead in their veins. Inside the toilet you could take an inventory of their idle thoughts. The walls were crowded with sketches and epithets, all of them jocosely obscene, easy to understand, and on the whole rather jolly and sympathetic. It must have required a ladder to reach certain spots, but I suppose it was worth while doing it even looking at it from just the psychological viewpoint. Sometimes, as I stood there taking a leak, I wondered what an impression it would make on those swell dames whom I observed passing in and out of the beautiful lavatories on the Champs-Elysées. I wondered if they would carry their tails so high if they could see what was thought of an ass here. In their world, no doubt, everything was gauze and velvet—or they made you think so with the fine scents they gave out, swishing past you. Some of them hadn't always been such fine ladies either; some of them swished up and down like that just to advertise their trade. And maybe, when they were left alone with themselves, when they talked out loud in the privacy of their boudoirs, maybe some strange things fell out of their mouths too; because in that world, just as in every world, the greater part of what happens is just muck and filth, sordid as any garbage can, only they are lucky enough to be able to put covers over the can.

As I say, that afternoon life with Tania never had any bad effect upon me. Once in a while I'd get too much of a skinful and I'd have to stick my finger down my throat—because it's hard to read proof when you're not all there. It requires more concentration to detect a missing comma than to epitomize Nietzsche's philosophy. You can be brilliant sometimes, when you're drunk, but brilliance is out of place in the proof-reading department. Dates, fractions, semi-colons—these are the things that count. And these are the things that are most difficult to track down when your mind is all ablaze. Now and then I made some bad blunders, and if it weren't that I had learned how to kiss the boss's ass, I would have been fired, that's certain. I even got a letter one day from the big mogul upstairs, a guy I never even met, so high up he was, and between a few sarcastic phrases about my more than ordinary intelligence, he hinted pretty plainly that I'd better learn my place and toe the mark or there'd be what's what to pay. Frankly, that scared the shit out of me. After that I never used a polysyllabic word in conversation; in fact, I hardly ever opened my trap all night. I played the high-grade moron, which is what they wanted of us. Now and then, to sort of flatter the boss, I'd go up to him and ask him politely what such and such a word might mean. He liked that. He was a sort of dictionary and time-table, that guy. No matter how much beer he guzzled during the break—and he made his own private breaks too, seeing as how he was running the show—you could never trip him up on a date or a definition. He was born to the job. My only regret was that I knew too much. It leaked out now and then, despite all the precautions I took. If I happened to come to work with a book under my arm this boss of ours would notice it, and if it were a good book it made him venomous. But I never did anything intentionally to displease him; I liked the job too well to put a noose around my neck. Just the same it's hard to talk to a man when you have nothing in common with him; you betray yourself, even if you use only monosyllabic words. He knew god-damn well, the boss, that I didn't take the least bit of interest in his yarns; and yet, explain it how you will, it gave him pleasure to wean me away from my dreams and fill me full of dates and historical events. It was his way of taking revenge, I suppose.

The result was that I developed a bit of a neurosis. As soon as I hit the air I became extravagant. It wouldn't matter what the subject of conversation happened to be, as we started back to Montparnasse in the early morning, I'd soon turn the fire-hose on it, squelch it, in order to trot out my perverted dreams. I liked best talking about those things which none of us knew anything about. I had cultivated a mild sort of insanity, echolalia, I think it's called. All the tag-ends of a night's proofing danced on the tip of my tongue. *Dalmatia*—I had held copy on an ad for that beautiful jewelled resort. All right, *Dalmatia*. You take a train and in the morning your pores are perspiring and the grapes are bursting their skins. I could reel it off about Dalmatia from the grand boulevard to Cardinal Mazarin's palace, further, if I chose to. I don't even know where it is on the map, and I don't want to know ever, but at three in the morning with all that lead in your veins and your clothes saturated with sweat and patchouli and the clink of bracelets passing through the wringer and those beer yarns that I was braced for, little things like geography, costume, speech, architecture don't mean a god-damn thing. Dalmatia belongs to a certain hour of the night when those high goings are snuffed out and the court of the Louvre seems so wonderfully ridiculous that you feel like weeping for no reason at all, just because it's so beautifully silent, so empty, so totally unlike the front page and the guys upstairs rolling the dice. With that little piece of Dalmatia resting on my throbbing nerves like a cold knife-blade I could experience the most wonderful sensations of voyage. And the funny thing is again that I could travel all around the globe but America would never enter my mind; it was even further lost than a lost continent, because with the lost continents I felt some mysterious attachment, whereas with America I felt nothing, nothing at all. Now and then, it's true, I did think of Mona, not as of a person in a definite aura of time and space, but separately, detached, as though she had blown up into a great cloud-like form that blotted out the past. I couldn't allow myself to think about her very long; if I had I would have jumped off the bridge. It's strange. I had become so reconciled to this life without her, and yet if I thought about her only for a minute it was enough to pierce the bone and marrow of my contentment and shove me back again into the agonizing gutter of my wretched past.

For seven years I went about, day and night, with only one thing on my mind—*her.* Were there a Christian so faithful to his God as I was to her we would all be Jesus Christs to-day. Day and night I thought of her, even when I was deceiving her. And now sometimes, in the very midst of things, sometimes when I feel that I am absolutely free of it all, suddenly, in rounding a corner perhaps, there will bob up a little square, a few trees and a bench, a deserted spot where we stood and had it out, where we drove each other crazy with bitter, jealous scenes. Always some deserted spot, like the Place de l'Estrapade, for example, or those dingy, mournful streets off the Mosque or along that open tomb of an Avenue de Breteuil which at ten o'clock in the evening is so silent, so dead, that it makes one think of murder or suicide, anything that might create a vestige of human drama. When I realize that she is gone, perhaps gone forever, a great void opens up and I feel that I am falling, falling, falling into deep, black space. And this is worse than tears, deeper than regret or pain or sorrow; it is the abyss into which Satan was plunged. There is no climbing back, no ray of light, no sound of human voice or human touch of hand.

How many thousand times, in walking through the streets at night, have I wondered if the day would ever come again when she would be at my side: all those yearning looks I bestowed on the buildings and statues, I had looked at them so hungrily, so desperately, that by now my thoughts must have become a part of the very buildings and statues, they must be saturated with my anguish. I could not help but reflect also that when we had walked side by side through these mournful, dingy streets now so saturated with my dream and longing, she had observed nothing, felt nothing: they were like any other streets to her, a little more sordid perhaps, and that is all. She wouldn't remember that at a certain corner I had stopped to pick up her hairpin, or that, when I bent down to tie her laces, I remarked the spot on which her foot had rested and that it would remain there forever, even after the cathedrals had been demolished and the whole Latin civilization wiped out forever and ever.

Walking down the Rue Lhomond one night in a fit of unusual anguish and desolation, certain things were revealed to me with poignant clarity. Whether it was that I had so often walked this street in bitterness and despair or whether it was the remembrance of a phrase which she had dropped one night as we stood at the Place Lucien-Herr I do not know. "Why don't you show me that Paris," she said, "that you have written about?" One thing I know, that at the recollection of these words I suddenly realized the impossibility of ever revealing to her that Paris which I had gotten to know, the Paris whose *arrondissements* are undefined, a Paris that has never existed except by virtue of my loneliness, my hunger for her. Such a huge Paris! It would take a lifetime to explore it again. This Paris, to which I alone had the key, hardly lends itself to a tour, even with the best of intentions; it is a Paris that has to be lived, that has to be experienced each day in a thousand different forms of torture, a Paris that grows inside you like a cancer, and grows and grows until you are eaten away by it.

Stumbling down the Rue Mouffetard, with these reflections stirring in my brain, I recalled another strange item out of the past, out of that guide-book whose leaves she had asked me to turn but which, because the covers were so heavy, I then found impossible to pry open. For no reason at all—because at the moment my thoughts were occupied with Salavin in whose sacred precincts I was now meandering—for no reason at all, I say, there came to mind the recollection of a day when, inspired by the plaque which I passed day in and day out, I impulsively entered the Pension Orfila and asked to see the room Strindberg had occupied. Up to that time nothing very terrible had befallen me, though I had already lost all my worldly possessions and had known what it was to walk the streets in hunger and in fear of the police. Up to then I had not found a single friend in Paris, a circumstance which was not so much depressing as bewildering, for wherever I have roamed in this world the easiest thing for me to discover has been a friend. But in reality, nothing very terrible had happened to me yet. One can live without friends, as one can live without love, or even without money, that supposed *sine qua non*. One can live in Paris—I discovered that!—on just grief and anguish. A bitter nourishment—perhaps the best there is for certain people. At any rate, I had not yet come to the end of my rope. I was only flirting with disaster. I had time and sentiment enough to spare to peep into other people's lives, to dally with the dead stuff of romance which, however morbid it may be, when it is wrapped between the covers of a book, seems deliciously remote and anonymous. As I was leaving the place I was conscious of an ironic smile hovering over my lips, as though I were saying to myself "Not yet, the Pension Orfila!"

Since then, of course, I have learned what every madman in Paris discovers sooner or later—that there are no ready-made infernos for the tormented.

It seems to me I understand a little better now why she took such huge delight in reading Strindberg. I can see her looking up from her book after reading a *delicious* passage and, with tears of laughter in her eyes, saying to me: "You're just as mad as he was ... you *want* to be punished!" What a delight that must be to the sadist when she discovers her own proper masochist! When she bites herself, as it were, to test the sharpness of her teeth. In those days, when I first knew her, she was saturated with Strindberg. That wild carnival of maggots which he revelled in, that eternal duel of the sexes, that spiderish ferocity which had endeared him to the sodden oafs of the northland, it was that which had brought us together. We came together in a dance of death and so quickly was I sucked down into the vortex that when I came to the surface again I could not recognize the world. When I found myself loose the music had ceased; the carnival was over and I had been picked clean ...

After leaving the Pension Orfila that afternoon I went to the library and there, after bathing in the Ganges and pondering over the signs of the zodiac, I began to reflect on the meaning of that inferno which Strindberg had so mercilessly depicted. And, as I ruminated, it began to grow clear to me, the mystery of his pilgrimage, the flight which the poet makes over the face of the earth and then, as if he had been ordained to re-enact a lost drama, the heroic descent to the very bowels of the earth, the dark and fearsome sojourn in the belly of the whale, the bloody struggle to liberate himself, to emerge clean of the past, a bright, gory sun-god cast up on an alien shore. It was no mystery to me any longer why he and others (Dante, Rabelais, Van Gogh, etc., etc.) had made their pilgrimage to Paris. I understood then why it is that Paris attracts the tortured, the hallucinated, the great maniacs of love. I understood why it is that here, at the very hub of the wheel, one can embrace the most fantastic, the most impossible theories, without finding them in the least strange; it is here that one reads again the books of his youth and the enigmas take on new meanings, one for every white hair. One walks the streets knowing that he is mad, possessed, because it is only too obvious that these cold, indifferent faces are the visages of one's keepers. Here all boundaries fade away and the world reveals itself for the mad slaughter-house that it is. The treadmill stretches away to infinitude, the hatches are closed down tight, logic runs rampant, with bloody cleaver flashing. The air is chill and stagnant, the language apocalyptic. Not an exit sign anywhere; no issue save death. A blind alley at the end of which is a scaffold.

An eternal city, Paris! More eternal than Rome, more splendorous than Nineveh. The very navel of the world to which, like a blind and faltering idiot, one crawls back on hands and knees. And like a cork that has drifted finally to the dead center of the ocean, one floats here in the scum and wrack of the seas, listless, hopeless, heedless even of a passing Columbus. The cradles of civilization are the putrid sinks of the world, the charnel-house to which the stinking wombs confide their bloody packages of flesh and bone.

The streets were my refuge. And no man can understand the glamor of the streets until he is obliged to take refuge in them, until he has become a straw that is tossed here and there by every zephyr that blows. One passes along a street on a wintry day and, seeing a dog for sale, one is moved to tears. While across the way, cheerful as a cemetery, stands a miserable hut that calls itself "Hôtel du Tombeau des Lapins." That makes one laugh, laugh fit to die. Until one notices that there are hotels everywhere, for rabbits, dogs, lice, emperors, cabinet ministers, pawnbrokers, horse-knackers, and so on. And almost every other one is an "Hôtel de l'Avenir." Which makes one more hysterical still. So many hotels of the future! No hotels in the past participle, no subjunctive modes, no conjunctivitis. Everything is hoary, grisly, bristling with merriment, swollen with the future, like a gumboil. Drunk with this lecherous eczema of the future, I stagger over to the Place Violet, the colors all mauve and slate, the doorways so low that only dwarfs and goblins could hobble in; over the dull cranium of Zola the chimneys are belching pure coke, while the Madonna of Sandwiches listens with cabbage ears to the bubbling of the gas tanks, those beautiful bloated toads which squat by the roadside.

Why do I suddenly recollect the Passage des Thermopyples? Because that day a woman addressed her puppy in the apocalyptic language of the slaughter-house, and the little bitch, she understood what this greasy slut of a midwife was saying. How that depressed me! More even than the sight of those whimpering curs that were being sold on the Rue Brancion, because it was not the dogs which filled me so with pity, but the huge iron railing, those rusty spikes which seemed to stand between me and my rightful life. In the pleasant little lane near the Abattoir de Vaugirard (Abattoir Hippophagique), which is called the Rue des Périchaux, I had noticed here and there signs of blood. Just as Strindberg in his madness had recognized omens and portents in the very flagging of the Pension Orfila, so, as I wandered aimlessly through this muddy lane bespattered with blood, fragments of the past detached themselves and floated listlessly before my eyes, taunting me with the direst forebodings. I saw my own blood being spilled, the muddy road stained with it, as far back as I could remember, from the very beginning doubtless. One is ejected into the world like a dirty little mummy; the roads are slippery with blood and no one knows why it should be so. Each one is travelling his own way and, though the earth be rotting with good things, there is no time to pluck the fruits; the procession scrambles toward the exit sign, and such a panic is there, such a sweat to escape, that the weak and the helpless are trampled into the mud and their cries are unheard.

My world of human beings had perished; I was utterly alone in the world and for friends I had the streets, and the streets spoke to me in that sad, bitter language compounded of human misery, yearning, regret, failure, wasted effort. Passing under the viaduct along the Rue Broca, one night after I had been informed that Mona was ill and starving, I suddenly recalled that it was here in the squalor and gloom of this sunken street, terrorized perhaps by a premonition of the future, that Mona clung to me and with a quivering voice begged me to promise that I would never leave her, never, no matter what happened. And, only a few days later, I stood on the platform of the Gare St. Lazare and I watched the train pull out, the train that was bearing her away; she was leaning out of the window, just as she had leaned out of the window when I left her in New York, and there was that same, sad, incrustable smile on her face, the last-minute look which is intended to convey so much, but which is only a mask that is twisted by a vacant smile. Only a few days before, she had clung to me desperately and then something happened, something which is not even clear to me now, and of her own volition she boarded the train and she was looking at me again with that sad, enigmatic smile which baffles me, which is unjust, unnatural, which I distrust with all my soul. And now it is I, standing in the shadow of the viaduct, who reach out for her, who cling to her desperately and there is that same inexplicable smile on my lips, the mask that I have clamped down over my grief. I can stand here and smile vacantly, and no matter how fervid my prayers, no matter how desperate my longing, there is an ocean between us; there she will stay and starve, and here I shall walk from one street to the next, the hot tears scalding my face.

It is that sort of cruelty which is embedded in the streets, it is *that* which stares out from the walls and terrifies us when suddenly we respond to a nameless fear, when suddenly our souls are invaded by a sickening panic. It is *that* which gives the lampposts their ghoulish twists, which makes them beckon to us and lure us to their strangling grip; it is *that* which makes certain houses appear like the guardians of secret crimes and their blind windows like the empty sockets of eyes that have seen too much. It is that sort of thing, written into the human physiognomy of the streets which makes me flee when overhead I suddenly see inscribed "Impasse Satan." That which makes me shudder when at the very entrance to the Mosque I observe that it is written: "Mondays and Thursdays *tuberculosis;* Wednesdays and Fridays *syphilis.*" In every Metro station there are grinning skulls that greet you with *"Défendez-vous contre la syphilis!"* Wherever there are walls, there are posters with bright venomous crabs heralding the approach of cancer. No matter where you go, no matter what you touch, there is cancer and syphilis. It is written in the sky; it flames and dances, like an evil portent. It has eaten into our souls and we are nothing but a dead thing like the moon.

I think it was the fourth of July when they took the chair from under my ass again. Not a word of warning. One of the big mucky-mucks from the other side of the water had decided to make economies; cutting down on proof-readers and helpless little *dactylos* enabled him to pay the expenses of his trips back and forth and the palatial quarters he occupied at the Ritz. After paying what little debts I had accumulated among the linotype operators and a good-will token at the *bistrot* across the way, in order to preserve my credit, there was scarcely anything left out of my final pay. I had to notify the *patron* of the hotel that I would be leaving; I didn't tell him why because he'd have been worried about his measly two hundred francs.

"What'll you do if you lose your job?" That was the phrase that rung in my ears continually. *Ça y est maintenant! Ausgespielt!* Nothing to do but get down into the street again, walk, hang around, sit on benches, kill time. By now, of course, my face was familiar in Montparnasse; for a while I could pretend that I was still working on the paper. That would make it a little easier to bum a breakfast or a dinner. It was Summer time and the tourists were pouring in. I had schemes up my sleeve for mulcting them. "What'll you do . . . ?" Well, I wouldn't starve, that's one thing. If I should do nothing else but concentrate on food that would prevent me from falling to pieces. For a week or two I could still go to Monsieur Paul's and have a square meal every evening; he wouldn't know whether I was working or not. The main thing is to eat. Trust to Providence for the rest!

Naturally, I kept my ears open for anything that sounded like a little dough. And I cultivated a whole new set of acquaintances—bores whom I had sedulously avoided heretofore, drunks whom I loathed, artists who had a little money, Guggenheim prize men, etc. It's not hard to make friends when you squat on a *terrasse* twelve hours a day. You get to know every sot in Montparnasse. They cling to you like lice, even if you have nothing to offer them but your ears.

Now that I had lost my job Carl and Van Norden had a new phrase for me: "What if your wife should arrive now?" Well, what of it? Two mouths to feed, instead of one. I'd have a companion in misery. And, if she hadn't lost her good looks, I'd probably do better in double harness than alone: the world never permits a good-looking woman to starve. Tania I couldn't depend on to do much for me; she was sending money to Sylvester. I had thought at first that she might let me share her room, but she was afraid of compromising herself; besides, she had to be nice to her boss.

The first people to turn to when you're down and out are the Jews. I had three of them on my hands almost at once. Sympathetic souls. One of them was a retired fur merchant who had an itch to see his name in the papers; he proposed that I write a series of articles under his name for a Jewish daily in New York. I had to scout around the Dome and the Coupole searching for prominent Jews. The first man I picked on was a celebrated mathematician; he couldn't speak a word of English. I had to write about the theory of shock from the diagrams he left on the paper napkins; I had to describe the movements of the astral bodies and demolish the Einsteinian conception at the same time. All for twenty-five francs. When I saw my articles in the newspaper I couldn't read them; but they looked impressive, just the same, especially with the pseudonym of the fur merchant attached.

I did a lot of pseudonymous writing during this period. When the big new whorehouse opened up on the Boulevard Edgar-Quinet, I got a little rake-off, for writing the pamphlets. That is to say, a bottle of champagne and a free fuck in one of the Egyptian rooms. If I succeeded in bringing a client I was to get my commission, just like Kepi got his in the old days. One night I brought Van Norden; he was going to let me earn a little money by enjoying himself upstairs. But when the *Madame* learned that he was a newspaper man she wouldn't hear of taking money from him; it was a bottle of champagne again and a free fuck. I got nothing out of it. As a matter of fact, I had to write the story for him because he couldn't think how to get round the subject without mentioning the kind of place it was. One thing after another like that. I was getting fucked good and proper.

The worst job of all was a thesis I undertook to write for a deaf and dumb psychologist. A treatise on the care of crippled children. My head was full of diseases and braces and work-benches and fresh air theories; it took about six weeks off and on, and then, to rub it in, I had to proof-read the god-damned thing. It was in French, such a French as I've never in my life seen or heard. But it brought me in a good breakfast every day, an American breakfast, with orange juice, oatmeal, cream, coffee, now and then, ham and eggs for a change. It was the only period of my Paris days that I ever indulged in a decent breakfast, thanks to the crippled children of Rockaway Beach, the East Side, and all the coves and inlets bordering on these sore points.

Then one day I fell in with a photographer; he was making a collection of the slimy joints of Paris for some degenerate in Munich. He wanted to know if I would pose for him with my pants down, and in other ways. I thought of those skinny little runts, who look like bell-hops and messenger boys, that one sees on pornographic post-cards in little book-shop windows occasionally, the mysterious phantoms who inhabit the Rue de la Lune and other malodorous quarters of the city. I didn't like very much the idea of advertising my physog in the company of these élite. But, since I was assured that the photographs were for a strictly private collection, and since it was destined for Munich, I gave my consent. When you're not in your home town you can permit yourself little liberties, particularly for such a worthy motive as earning your daily bread. After all, I hadn't been so squeamish, come to think of it, even in New York. There were nights when I was so damned desperate, back there, that I had to go out right in my own neighborhood and panhandle.

We didn't go to the show places familiar to the tourists,

but to the little joints where the atmosphere was more congenial, where we could play a game of cards in the afternoon before getting down to work. He was a good companion, the photographer. He knew the city inside out, the walls particularly; he talked to me about Goethe often, and the days of the Hohenstaufen, and the massacre of the Jews during the reign of the Black Death. Interesting subjects, and always related in some obscure way to the things he was doing. He had ideas for scenarios too, astounding ideas, but nobody had the courage to execute them. The sight of a horse split-open like a saloon door, would inspire him to talk of Dante or Leonardo da Vinci or Rembrandt; from the slaughter-house at Villette he would jump into a cab and rush me to the Trocadéro Museum, in order to point out a skull or a mummy that had fascinated him. We explored the 5th, the 13th, the 19th and the 20th *arrondissements* thoroughly. Our favorite resting places were lugubrious little spots such as the Place Nationale, Place des Peupliers, Place Contrescarpe, Place Paul-Verlaine. Many of these places were already familiar to me, but all of them I now saw in a different light owing to the rare flavor of his conversation. If today I should happen to stroll down the Rue du Château-des-Rentiers, for example, inhaling the fetid stench of the hospital beds with which the 13th *arrondissement* reeks, my nostrils would undoubtedly expand with pleasure, because, compounded with that odor of stale piss and formaldehyde, there would be the odors of our imaginative voyages through the charnel house of Europe which the Black Death had created.

Through him I got to know a spiritual-minded individual named Kruger, who was a sculptor and painter. Kruger took a shine to me for some reason or other; it was impossible to get away from him once he discovered that I was willing to listen to his "esoteric" ideas. There are people in this world for whom the word "esoteric" seems to act as a divine ichor. Like "settled" for Herr Peeperkorn of the *Magic Mountain*. Kruger was one of those saints who have gone wrong, a masochist, an anal type whose law is scrupulousness, rectitude and conscientiousness, who on an off day would knock a man's teeth down his throat without a qualm. He seemed to think I was ripe to move on to another plane, "a *higher* plane," as he put it. I was ready to move on to any plane he designated, provided that one didn't eat less or drink less. He chewed my head off about the "threadsoul," the "causal body," "ablation," the Upanishads, Plotinus, Krishnamurti, "the Karmic vestiture of the soul," "the nirvanic consciousness," all that flapdoodle which blows out of the East like a breath from the plague. Sometimes he would go into a trance and talk about his previous incarnations, how he imagined them to be, at least. Or he would relate his dreams which, so far as I could see, were thoroughly insipid, prosaic, hardly worth even the attention of a Freudian, but, for him, there were vast esoteric marvels hidden in their depths which I had to aid him to decipher. He had turned himself inside out, like a coat whose nap is worn off.

Little by little, as I gained his confidence, I wormed my way into his heart. I had him at such a point that he would come running after me, in the street, to inquire if he could lend me a few francs. He wanted to hold me together in order to survive the transition to a higher plane. I acted like a pear that is ripening on the tree. Now and then I had relapses and I would confess my need for more earthly nourishment—a visit to the Sphinx or the Rue St. Apolline where I knew he repaired in weak moments when the demands of the flesh had become too vehement.

As a painter he was nil; as a sculptor less than nil. He was a good housekeeper, that I'll say for him. And an economical one to boot. Nothing went to waste, not even the paper that meat was wrapped in. Friday nights he threw open his studio to his fellow artists; there was always plenty to drink and good sandwiches, and if by chance there was anything left over I would come round the next day to polish it off.

Back of the Bal Bullier was another studio I got into the habit of frequenting—the studio of Mark Swift. If he was not a genius he was certainly an eccentric, this caustic Irishman. He had for a model a Jewess whom he had been living with for years; he was now tired of her and was searching for a pretext to get rid of her. But as he had eaten up the dowry which she had originally brought with her, he was puzzled as to how to disembarrass himself of

her without making restitution. The simplest thing was to
so antagonize her that she would choose starvation rather
than support his cruelties.

  She was rather a fine person, his mistress; the worst
that one could say against her was that she had lost her
shape, *and* her ability to support him any longer. She was
a painter herself and, among those who professed to
know, it was said that she had far more talent than he. But
no matter how miserable he made life for her she was
just; she would never allow anyone to say that he was not
a great painter. It was because he really has genius, she
said, that he was such a rotten individual. One never saw
her canvases on the wall—only his. Her things were stuck
away in the kitchen. Once it happened, in my presence,
that someone insisted on seeing her work. The result was
painful. "You see this figure," said Swift, pointing to one
of her canvases with his big foot. "The man standing in
the doorway there is just about to go out for a leak. He
won't be able to find his way back because his head is on
wrong ... Now take that nude over there ... It was all
right until she started to paint the cunt. I don't know what
she was thinking about, but she made it so big that her
brush slipped and she couldn't get it out again."

  By way of showing us what a nude ought to be like he
hauls out a huge canvas which he had recently completed.
It was a picture of *her,* a splendid piece of vengeance inspired by a guilty conscience. The work of a madman—
vicious, petty, malign, brilliant. You had the feeling that he
had spied on her through the keyhole, that he had caught
her in an off moment, when she was picking her nose
absent-mindedly, or scratching her ass. She sat there on the
horsehair sofa, in a room without ventilation, an enormous
room without a window; it might as well have been the an-
terior lobe of the pineal gland. Back of her ran the zigzag
stairs leading to the balcony; they were covered with a
bilious-green carpet, such a green as could only emanate
from a universe that had been pooped out. The most prominent thing was her buttocks, which were lop-sided and full
of scabs; she seemed to have slightly raised her ass from
the sofa, as if to let a loud fart. Her face he had idealized:
it looked sweet and virginal, pure as a cough-drop. But her
bosom was distended, swollen with sewer-gas; she seemed

to be swimming in a menstrual sea, an enlarged foetus with the dull, syrupy look of an angel.

Nevertheless one couldn't help but like him. He was an indefatigable worker, a man who hadn't a single thought in his head but paint. And cunning as a lynx withal. It was he who put it into my head to cultivate the friendship of Fillmore, a young man in the diplomatic service who had found his way into the little group that surrounded Kruger and Swift. "Let him help you," he said. "He doesn't know what to do with his money."

When one spends what he has on himself, when one has a thoroughly good time with his own money, people are apt to say "he doesn't know what to do with his money." For my part, I don't see any better use to which one can put money. About such individuals one can't say that they're generous or stingy. They put money into circulation—that's the principal thing. Fillmore knew that his days in France were limited; he was determined to enjoy them. And as one always enjoys himself better in the company of a friend it was only natural that he should turn to one like myself, who had plenty of time on his hands, for that companionship which he needed. People said he was a bore, and so he was, I suppose, but when you're in need of your food you can put up with worse things than being bored. After all, despite the fact that he talked incessantly, and usually about himself or the authors whom he admired slavishly—such birds as Anatole France and Joseph Conrad—he nevertheless made my nights interesting in other ways. He liked to dance, he liked good wines, and he liked women. That he liked Byron also, and Victor Hugo, one could forgive; he was only a few years out of college and he had plenty of time ahead of him to be cured of such tastes. What he had that I liked was a sense of adventure.

We got even better acquainted, more intimate, I might say, due to a peculiar incident that occurred during my brief sojourn with Kruger. It happened just after the arrival of Collins, a sailor whom Fillmore had got to know on the way over from America. The three of us used to meet regularly on the *terrasse* of the Rotonde before going to dinner. It was always Pernod, a drink which put Collins in good humor and provided a base, as it were, for the wine and beer and *fines,* etc., which had to be guzzled afterwards. All during Collins's stay in Paris I lived like a duke; nothing but fowl and good vintages and desserts that I hadn't even heard of before. A month of this regimen and I should have been obliged to go to Baden-Baden or Vichy or Aix-les-Bains. Meanwhile Kruger was putting me up at his studio. I was getting to be a nuisance because I never showed up before three a.m. and it was difficult to rout me out of bed before noon. Overtly Kruger never uttered a word of reproach but his manner indicated plainly enough that I was becoming a bum.

One day I was taken ill. The rich diet was taking effect upon me. I don't know what ailed me, but I couldn't get out of bed. I had lost all my stamina, and with it whatever courage I possessed. Kruger had to look after me, had to make broths for me, and so on. It was a trying period for him, more particularly because he was just on the verge of giving an important exhibition at his studio, a private showing to some wealthy connoisseurs from whom he was expecting aid. The cot on which I lay was in the studio; there was no other room to put me in.

The morning of the day he was to give his exhibition, Kruger awoke thoroughly disgruntled. If I had been able to stand on my feet I know he would have given me a clout in the jaw and kicked me out. But I was prostrate, and weak as a cat. He tried to coax me out of bed, with the idea of locking me up in the kitchen upon the arrival of his visitors. I realized that I was making a mess of it for him. People can't look at pictures and statues with enthusiasm when a man is dying before their eyes. Kruger honestly thought I was dying. So did I. That's why, despite my feeling of guilt, I couldn't muster any enthusiasm when he proposed calling for the ambulance and having me shipped to the American Hospital. I wanted to die there, comfortably, right in the studio; I didn't want to be urged to get up and find a better place to die in. I didn't care where I died, really, so long as it wasn't necessary to get up.

When he heard me talk this way Kruger became alarmed. Worse than having a sick man in his studio should the visitors arrive, was to have a dead man. That would completely ruin his prospects, slim as they were. He didn't put it that way to me, of course, but I could see from his agitation that that was what worried him. And that made me stubborn. I refused to let him call the hospital. I refused to let him call a doctor. I refused everything.

He got so angry with me finally that, despite my protestations, he began to dress me. I was too weak to resist. All I could do was to murmur weakly—"you bastard, you!" Though it was warm outdoors I was shivering like a dog.—After he had completely dressed me he flung an overcoat over me and slipped outside to telephone. "I won't go! I won't go!" I kept saying but he simply slammed the door on me. He came back in a few minutes and, without addressing a word to me, busied himself about the studio. Last minute preparations. In a little while there was a knock on the door. It was Fillmore. Collins was waiting downstairs, he informed me.

The two of them, Fillmore and Kruger, slipped their arms under me and hoisted me to my feet. As they dragged me to the elevator Kruger softened up. "It's for your own good," he said. "And besides, it wouldn't be fair to me. You know what a struggle I've had all these years. You ought to think about me too." He was actually on the point of tears.

Wretched and miserable as I felt, his words almost made me smile. He was considerably older than I, and even though he was a rotten painter, a rotten artist all the way through, he deserved a break—at least once in a lifetime.

"I don't hold it against you," I muttered. "I understand how it is."

"You know I always liked you," he responded. "When you get better you can come back here again . . . you can stay as long as you like."

"Sure, I know . . . I'm not going to croak yet," I managed to get out.

Somehow, when I saw Collins down below my spirits revived. If ever any one seemed to be thoroughly alive, healthy, joyous, magnanimous, it was he. He picked me up as if I were a doll and laid me out on the seat of the cab—gently too, which I appreciated after the way Kruger had manhandled me.

When we drove up to the hotel—the hotel that Collins was stopping at—there was a bit of a discussion with the proprietor, during which I lay stretched out on the sofa in the bureau. I could hear Collins saying to the *patron* that it was nothing . . . just a little breakdown . . . be all right in a few days. I saw him put a crisp bill in the man's hands and then, turning swiftly and lithely, he came back to where I was and said: "Come on, buck up! Don't let him think you're croaking." And with that, he yanked me to my feet and, bracing me with one arm, escorted me to the elevator.

Don't let him think you're croaking! Obviously it was bad taste to die on people's hands. One should die in the bosom of his family, in private, as it were. His words were encouraging. I began to see it all as a bad joke. Upstairs, with the door closed, they undressed me and put me between the sheets. "You can't die now, god-damn it!" said Collins warmly. "You'll put me in a hole . . . Besides, what the hell's the matter with you? Can't stand good living? Keep your chin up! You'll be eating a porterhouse steak in a day or two. You think you're ill! Wait, by Jesus until you get a dose of syphilis! That's something to make you worry . . ." And he began to relate, in a humorous way, his trip down the Yangtsze-Kaing, with hair falling out and teeth rotting away. In the feeble state that I was in, the yarn that he spun had an extraordinarily soothing effect upon me. It took me completely out of myself. He had guts, this guy. Perhaps he put it on a bit thick, for my benefit, but I wasn't listening to him critically at the moment. I was all ears and eyes. I saw the dirty yellow mouth of the river, the lights going up at Hankow, the sea of yellow faces, the sampans shooting down through the gorges and the rapids flaming with the sulphurous breath of the dragon. What a story! The coolies swarming around the boat each day, dredging for the garbage that was flung overboard, Tom Slattery rising up on his death-bed to take a last look at the lights of Hankow, the beautiful Eurasian who lay in a dark room and filled his veins with poison, the monotony of blue jackets and yellow faces, millions and millions of them hollowed out by famine, ravaged by disease, subsisting on rats and dogs and roots, chewing the grass off the earth, devouring their own children. It was hard to imagine that this man's body had once been a mass of sores, that he had been shunned like a leper; his voice was so quiet and gentle, it was as though his spirit had been cleansed by all the suffering he had endured. As he reached for his drink his face grew more and more soft and his words actually seemed to caress me. And all the while China hanging over us like Fate itself. A China rotting away, crumbling to dust like a huge dinosaur, yet preserving to the very end the glamor, the enchantment, the mystery, the cruelty of her hoary legends.

I could no longer follow his story; my mind had slipped back to a Fourth of July when I bought my first package of firecrackers and with it the long pieces of punk which break so easily, the punk that you blow on to get a good red glow, the punk whose smell sticks to your fingers for days and makes you dream of strange things. The Fourth of July the streets are littered with bright red paper stamped with black and gold figures and everywhere there are tiny firecrackers which have the most curious intestines; packages and packages of them, all strung together by their thin, flat, little gutstrings, the color of human brains. All day long there is the smell of powder and punk and the gold dust from the bright red wrappers sticks to your fingers. One never thinks of China, but it is there all the time on the tips of your fingers and it makes your nose itchy; and long afterwards, when you have forgotten almost what a firecracker smells like, you wake up one day with gold-leaf choking you and the broken pieces of punk waft back their pungent odor and the bright red wrappers give you a nostalgia for a people and a soil you have never known, but which is in your blood, mysteriously there in your blood, like the sense of time or space, a fugitive, constant value to which you turn more and more as you get old, which you try to seize with your mind, but ineffectually, because in everything Chinese there is wisdom and mystery and you can never grasp it with two hands or with your mind but you must let it rub off, let it stick to your fingers, let it slowly infiltrate your veins.

A few weeks later, upon receipt of a pressing invitation from Collins who had returned to Le Havre, Fillmore and I boarded the train one morning, prepared to spend the week-end with him. It was the first time I had been out-side of Paris since my arrival here. We were in fine fettle, drinking Anjou all the way to the coast. Collins had given us the address of a bar where we were to meet; it was a place called Jimmie's Bar, which everyone in Le Havre was supposed to know.

We got into an open barouche at the station and started on a brisk trot for the rendez-vous; there was still a half bottle of Anjou left which we polished off as we rode along. Le Havre looked gay, sunny; the air was bracing, with that strong salty tang which almost made me home-sick for New York. There were masts and hulls cropping up everywhere, bright bits of bunting, big open squares and high-ceilinged cafés such as one only sees in the provinces. A fine impression immediately; the city was welcoming us with open arms.

Before we ever reached the bar we saw Collins coming down the street on a trot, heading for the station, no doubt, and a little late as usual. Fillmore immediately suggested a Pernod; we were all slapping each other on the back, laughing and spitting, drunk already from the sunshine and the salt sea air. Collins seemed undecided about the Pernod at first. He had a little dose of clap, he informed us. Nothing very serious—"a strain" most likely. He showed us a bottle he had in his pocket—"Vénétienne" it was called, if I remember rightly. The sailors' remedy for clap.

We stopped off at a restaurant to have a little snack be-fore repairing to Jimmie's place. It was a huge tavern with big, smoky rafters and tables creaking with food. We drank copiously of the wines that Collins recommended. Then we sat down on a *terrasse* and had coffee and li-queurs. Collins was talking about the Baron de Charlus, a man after his own heart, he said. For almost a year now he had been staying at Le Havre, going through the money that he had accumulated during his bootlegging days. His tastes were simple—food, drink, women and books. And a private bath! That he insisted on.

We were still talking about the Baron de Charlus when we arrived at Jimmie's Bar. It was late in the afternoon and the place was just beginning to fill up. Jimmie was there, his face red as a beet, and beside him was his spouse, a fine, buxom Frenchwoman with glittering eyes. We were given a marvellous reception all around. There were Pernods in front of us again, the gramophone was shrieking, people were jabbering away in English and French and Dutch and Norwegian and Spanish, and Jimmie and his wife, both of them looking very brisk and dapper, were slapping and kissing each other heartily and raising their glasses and clinking them—altogether such a bubble and blabber of merriment that you felt like pulling off your clothes and doing a war dance. The women at the bar had gathered around like flies. If we were friends of Collins that meant we were rich. It didn't matter that we had come in our old clothes; all *Anglais* dressed like that. I hadn't a sou in my pocket, which didn't matter, of course, since I was the guest of honor. Nevertheless I felt somewhat embarrassed with two stunning-looking whores hanging on my arms waiting for me to order something. I decided to take the bull by the horns. You couldn't tell any more which drinks were on the house and which were to be paid for. I had to be a *gentleman,* even if I didn't have a sou in my pocket.

Yvette—that was Jimmie's wife—was extraordinarily gracious and friendly with us. She was preparing a little spread in our honor. It would take a little while yet. We were not to get too drunk—she wanted us to enjoy the meal. The gramophone was going like wild and Fillmore had begun to dance with a beautiful mulatto who had on a tight velvet dress that revealed all her charms. Collins slipped over to my side and whispered a few words about the girl at my side. "The *madame* will invite her to dinner," he said, "if you'd like to have her." She was an ex-whore who owned a beautiful home on the outskirts of the city. The mistress of a sea captain now. He was away and there was nothing to fear. "If she likes you she'll invite you to stay with her," he added.

That was enough for me. I turned at once to Marcelle and began to flatter the ass off her. We stood at the corner of the bar, pretending to dance, and mauled each other ferociously. Jimmie gave me a big horse-wink and nodded his head approvingly. She was a lascivious bitch, this Marcelle, and pleasant at the same time. She soon got rid of the other girl, I noticed, and then we settled down for a long and intimate conversation which was interrupted unfortunately by the announcement that dinner was ready.

There were about twenty of us at the table, and Marcelle and I were placed at one end opposite Jimmie and his wife. It began with the popping of champagne corks and was quickly followed by drunken speeches, during the course of which Marcelle and I played with each other under the table. When it came my turn to stand up and deliver a few words I had to hold the napkin in front of me. It was painful and exhilarating at the same time. I had to cut the speech very short because Marcelle was tickling me in the crotch all the while.

The dinner lasted until almost midnight. I was looking forward to spending the night with Marcelle in that beautiful home up on the cliff. But it was not to be. Collins had planned to show us about and I couldn't very well refuse. "Don't worry about her," he said. "You'll have a bellyful of it before you leave. Tell her to wait here for you until we get back."

She was a bit peeved at this, Marcelle, but when we informed her that we had several days ahead of us she brightened up. When we got outdoors Fillmore very solemnly took us by the arm and said he had a little confession to make. He looked pale and worried.

"Well, what is it?" said Collins cheerfully. "Spit it out!"

Fillmore couldn't spit it out like that, all at once. He hemmed and hawed and finally he blurted out—"Well, when I went to the closet just a minute ago I noticed something ..."

"Then you've got it!" said Collins triumphantly, and with that he flourishes the bottle of "Vénétienne." "Don't go to a doctor," he added venomously. "They'll bleed you to death, the greedy bastards. And don't stop drinking either. That's all hooey. Take this twice a day ... shake it well before using. And nothing's worse than worry, do you understand? Come on now. I'll give you a syringe and some permanganate when we get back."

And so we started out into the night, down towards the waterfront where there was the sound of music and shouts and drunken oaths, Collins talking quietly all the while about this and that, about a boy he had fallen in love with, and the devil's time he had to get out of the scrape when the parents got wise to it. From that he switched back to the Baron de Charlus and then to Kurtz who had gone up the river and got lost. His favorite theme. I liked the way Collins moved against this background of literature continuously; it was like a millionaire who never stepped out of his Rolls Royce. There was no intermediate realm for him between reality and ideas. When we entered the whorehouse on the Quai Voltaire, after he had flung himself on the divan and rung for girls and for drinks, he was still paddling up the river with Kurtz, and only when the girls had flopped on the bed beside him and stuffed his mouth with kisses did he cease his divagations. Then, as if he had suddenly realized where he was, he turned to the old mother who ran the place and gave her an eloquent spiel about his two friends who had come down from Paris expressly to see the joint. There were about half a dozen girls in the room, all naked and all beautiful to look at, I must say. They hopped about like birds while the three of us tried to maintain a conversation with the grandmother. Finally the latter excused herself and told us to make ourselves at home. I was altogether taken in by her, so sweet and amiable she was, so thoroughly gentle and maternal. And what manners! If she had been a little younger I would have made overtures to her. Certainly you would not have thought that we were in a "den of vice," as it is called.

Anyway we stayed there an hour or so, and as I was the only one in condition to enjoy the privileges of the house, Collins and Fillmore remained downstairs chattering with the girls. When I returned I found the two of them stretched out on the bed; the girls had formed a semi-circle about the bed and were singing with the most angelic voices the chorus of *Roses in Picardy*. We were sentimentally depressed when we left the house—Fillmore particularly. Collins swiftly steered us to a rough joint which was packed with drunken sailors on shore leave and there we sat awhile enjoying the homosexual rout that was in full swing. When we sallied out we had to pass through the red-light district where there were more grandmothers with shawls about their necks sitting on the doorsteps fanning themselves and nodding pleasantly to the passersby. All such good-looking, kindly souls, as if they were keeping guard over a nursery. Little groups of sailors came swinging along and pushed their way noisily inside the gaudy joints. Sex everywhere: it was slopping over, a neap-tide that swept the props from under the city. We piddled along at the edge of the basin where everything was jumbled and tangled; you had the impression that all these ships, these trawls and yachts and schooners and barges, had been blown ashore by a violent storm.

In the space of forty-eight hours so many things had happened that it seemed as if we had been in Le Havre a month or more. We were planning to leave early Monday morning, as Fillmore had to be back on the job. We spent Sunday drinking and carousing, clap or no clap. That afternoon Collins confided to us that he was thinking of returning to his ranch in Idaho; he hadn't been home for eight years and he wanted to have a look at the mountains again before making another voyage East. We were sitting in a whorehouse at the time, waiting for a girl to appear; he had promised to slip her some cocaine. He was fed up with Le Havre, he told us. Too many vultures hanging around his neck. Besides, Jimmie's wife had fallen in love with him and she was making things hot for him with her jealous fits. There was a scene almost every night. She had been on her good behavior since we arrived, but it wouldn't last, he promised us. She was particularly jealous of a Russian girl who came to the bar now and then when she got tight. A troublemaker. On top of it all he was desperately in love with this boy whom he had told us about the first day. "A boy can break your heart," he said. "He's so damned beautiful! And so cruel!" We had to laugh at this. It sounded preposterous. But Collins was in earnest.

Around midnight Sunday Fillmore and I retired; we had been given a room upstairs over the bar. It was sultry as the devil, not a breath of air stirring. Through the open windows we could hear them shouting downstairs and the gramophone going continually. All of a sudden a storm broke—a regular cloudburst. And between the thunderclaps and the squalls that lashed the window-panes there came to our ears the sound of another storm raging downstairs at the bar. It sounded frightfully close and sinister; the women were shrieking at the tops of their lungs, bottles were crashing, tables were upset and there was that familiar, nauseating thud that the human body makes when it crashes to the floor.

About six o'clock Collins stuck his head in the door. His face was all plastered and one arm was stuck in a sling. He had a big grin on his face.

"Just as I told you," he said. "She broke loose last night. Suppose you heard the racket?"

We got dressed quickly and went downstairs to say good-bye to Jimmie. The place was completely demolished, not a bottle left standing, not a chair that wasn't broken. The mirror and the show-window were smashed to bits. Jimmie was making himself an egg-nog.

On the way to the station we pieced the story together. The Russian girl had dropped in after we toddled off to bed and Yvette had insulted her promptly, without even waiting for an excuse. They had commenced to pull each other's hair and in the midst of it a big Swede had stepped in and given the Russian girl a sound slap in the jaw—to bring her to her senses. That started the fireworks. Collins wanted to know what right this big stiff had to interfere in a private quarrel. He got a poke in the jaw for an answer, a good one that sent him flying to the other end of the bar. "Serves you right!" screamed Yvette, taking advantage of the occasion to swing a bottle at the Russian girl's head. And at that moment the thunderstorm broke loose. For a while there was a regular pandemonium, the women all hysterical and hungry to seize the opportunity to pay off private grudges. Nothing like a nice bar-room brawl ... so easy to stick a knife in a man's back or club him with a bottle when he's lying under a table. The poor Swede had found himself in a hornet's nest; everyone in the place hated him, particularly his shipmates. They wanted to see him done in. And so they locked the door and pushing the tables aside they made a little space in front of the bar where the two of them could have it out. And they had it out! They had to carry the poor devil to the hospital when it was over. Collins had come off rather lucky—nothing more than a

sprained wrist and a couple of fingers out of joint, a
bloody nose and a black eye. Just a few scratches, as he
put it. But if he ever signed up with that Swede he was
going to murder him. It wasn't finished yet. He promised
us that.

And that wasn't the end of the fracas either. After that
Yvette had to go out and get liquored up at another bar.
She had been insulted and she was going to put an end
to things. And so she hires a taxi and orders the driver to
ride out to the edge of the cliff overlooking the water. She
was going to kill herself, that's what she was going to do.
But then she was so drunk that when she tumbled out of
the cab she began to weep and before any one could stop
her she had begun to peel her clothes off. The driver
brought her home that way, half-naked, and when Jimmie
saw the condition she was in he was so furious with her
that he took his razorstrop and he belted the piss out of
her, and she liked it, the bitch that she was. "Do it some
more!" she begged, down on her knees as she was and
clutching him around the legs with her two arms. But
Jimmie had enough of it. "You're a dirty old sow!" he
said and with his foot he gave her a shove in the guts that
took the wind out of her and—a bit of her sexy nonsense
too.

It was high time we were leaving. The city looked different in the early morning light. The last thing we talked
about, as we stood there waiting for the train to pull out,
was Idaho. The three of us were Americans. We came
from different places, each of us, but we had something
in common—a whole lot, I might say. We were getting
sentimental, as Americans do when it comes time to part.
We were getting quite foolish about the cows and sheep
and the big open spaces where men are men and all that
crap. If a boat had swung along instead of the train we'd
have hopped aboard and said good-bye to it all. But Collins was never to see America again, as I learned later;
and Fillmore . . . well, Fillmore had to take his punish-
ment too, in a way that none of us could have suspected
then. It's best to keep America just like that, always in
the background, a sort of picture post-card which you
look at in a weak moment. Like that, you imagine it's always there waiting for you, unchanged, unspoiled, a big

patriotic open space with cows and sheep and tender-hearted men ready to bugger everything in sight, man, woman or beast. It doesn't exist, America. It's a name you give to an abstract idea . . .

Paris is like a whore. From a distance she seems ravishing, you can't wait until you have her in your arms. And five minutes later you feel empty, disgusted with yourself. You feel tricked.

I returned to Paris with money in my pocket—a few hundred francs, which Collins had shoved in my pocket just as I was boarding the train. It was enough to pay for a room and at least a week's good rations. It was more than I had had in my hands at one time for several years. I felt elated, as though perhaps a new life was opening before me. I wanted to conserve it too, so I looked up a cheap hotel over a bakery on the Rue du Château, just off the Rue de Vanves, a place that Eugène had pointed out to me once. A few yards away was the bridge that spans the Montparnasse tracks. A familiar quarter.

I could have had a room here for a hundred francs a month, a room without any conveniences to be sure—without even a window—and perhaps I would have taken it, just to be sure of a place to flop for a while, had it not been for the fact that in order to reach this room I would have been obliged to first pass through the room of a blind man. The thought of passing his bed every night had a most depressing effect upon me. I decided to look elsewhere. I went over to the Rue Cels, just behind the cemetery, and I looked at a sort of rat-trap there with balconies, running around the court-yard. There were bird-cages suspended from the balcony too, all along the lower tier. A cheerful sight perhaps, but to me it seemed like the public ward in a hospital. The proprietor didn't seem to have all his wits either. I decided to wait for the night, to have a good look around, and then choose some attractive little joint in a quiet side street.

At dinner time I spent fifteen francs for a meal, just about twice the amount I had planned to allot myself. That made me so wretched that I wouldn't allow myself to sit down for a coffee, even despite the fact that it had begun to drizzle. No, I would walk about a bit and then go quietly to bed, at a reasonable hour. I was already miserable, trying to husband my resources this way. I had never in my life done it; it wasn't in my nature.

Finally it began to come down in bucketsful. I was glad. That would give me the excuse I needed to duck somewhere and stretch my legs out. It was still too early to go to bed. I began to quicken my pace, heading back towards the Boulevard Raspail. Suddenly a woman comes up to me and stops me, right in the pouring rain. She wants to know what time it is. I told her I didn't have a watch. And then she bursts out, just like this: "Oh, my good sir, do you speak English by chance?" I nod my head. It's coming down in torrents now. "Perhaps, my dear good man, you would be so kind as to take me to a café. It is raining so and I haven't the money to sit down anywhere. You will excuse me, my dear sir, but you have such a kind face ... I knew you were English right away." And with this she smiles at me, a strange, half-demented smile. "Perhaps you could give me a little advice, dear sir. I am all alone in the world ... my God, it is terrible to have no money ..."

This "dear sir" and "kind sir" and "my good man," etc., had me on the verge of hysteria. I felt sorry for her and yet I had to laugh. I did laugh. I laughed right in her face. And then she laughed too, a weird, high-pitched laugh, off-key, an altogether unexpected piece of cachinnation. I caught her by the arm and we made a bolt for it to the nearest café. She was still giggling when we entered the *bistrot*. "My dear good sir," she began again, "perhaps you think I am not telling you the truth. I am a good girl ... I come of a good family. Only"—and here she gave me that wan, broken smile again—"only I am so misfortunate as not to have a place to sit down." At this I began to laugh again. I couldn't help it—the phrases she used, the strange accent, the crazy hat she had on, that demented smile ...

"Listen," I interrupted, "what nationality are you?"

"I'm English," she replied. "That is, I was born in Po-
land, but my father is Irish."

"So that makes you English?"

"Yes," she said, and she began to giggle again, sheep-
ishly, and with a pretense of being coy.

"I suppose you know a nice little hotel where you
could take me?" I said this, not because I had any intention of going with her, but just to spare her the usual preliminaries.

"Oh, my dear sir," she said, as though I had made the
most grievous error, "I'm sure you don't mean that! I'm
not that kind of a girl. You were joking with me, I see
that. You're so good . . . you have such a kind face. I
would not dare to speak to a Frenchman as I did to you.
They insult you right away . . ."

She went on in this vein for some time. I wanted to
break away from her. But she didn't want to be left alone.
She was afraid—her papers were not in order. Wouldn't I
be good enough to walk her to her hotel? Perhaps I could
"lend" her fifteen or twenty francs, to quiet the *patron*? I
walked her to the hotel where she said she was stopping
and I put a fifty francs bill in her hand. Either she was
very clever, or very innocent—it's hard to tell sometimes—but, at any rate, she wanted me to wait until she
ran to the *bistrot* for change. I told her not to bother. And
with that she seized my hand impulsively and raised it to
her lips. I was flabbergasted. I felt like giving her every
damned thing I had. That touched me, that crazy little
gesture. I thought to myself, it's good to be rich once in
a while, just to get a new thrill like that. Just the same,
I didn't lose my head. Fifty francs! That was quite
enough to squander on a rainy night. As I walked off she
waved to me with that crazy little bonnet which she
didn't know how to wear. It was as though we were old
playmates. I felt foolish and giddy. "My dear kind sir . . .
you have such a gentle face . . . you are so good, etc." I
felt like a saint.

When you feel all puffed up inside it isn't so easy to go
to bed right away. You feel as though you ought to atone
for such unexpected bursts of goodness. Passing the "Jungle" I caught a glimpse of the dance floor; women with
bare backs and ropes of pearls choking them—or so it

looked—were wiggling their beautiful bottoms at me. Walked right up to the bar and ordered a *coupe* of champagne. When the music stopped, a beautiful blonde—she looked like a Norwegian—took a seat right beside me. The place wasn't as crowded or as gay as it had appeared from outside. There were only a half dozen couples in the place—they must have all been dancing at once. I ordered another *coupe* of champagne in order not to let my courage dribble away.

When I got up to dance with the blonde there was no one on the floor but us. Any other time I would have been self-conscious, but the champagne and the way she clung to me, the dimmed lights and the solid feeling of security which the few hundred francs gave me, well . . . We had another dance together, a sort of private exhibition, and then we fell into conversation. She had begun to weep— that was how it started. I thought possibly she had had too much to drink, so I pretended not to be concerned. And meanwhile I was looking around to see if there was any other timber available. But the place was thoroughly deserted.

The thing to do when you're trapped is to breeze—at once. If you don't, you're lost. What retained me, oddly enough, was the thought of paying for a hat check a second time. One always lets himself in for it because of a trifle.

The reason she was weeping, I discovered soon enough, was because she had just buried her child. She wasn't Norwegian either, but French, and a midwife to boot. A chic midwife, I must say, even with the tears running down her face. I asked her if a little drink would help to console her, whereupon she very promptly ordered a whisky and tossed it off in the wink of an eye. "Would you like another?" I suggested gently. She thought she would, she felt so rotten, so terribly dejected. She thought she would like a package of Camels too. "No, wait a minute," she said, "I think I'd rather have *les* Pall Mall." Have what you like, I thought, but stop weeping, for Christ's sake, it gives me the willies. I jerked her to her feet for another dance. On her feet she seemed to be another person. Maybe grief makes one more lecherous, I don't know. I murmured something about breaking away. "Where to?" she said eagerly. "Oh, anywhere. Some quiet place where we can talk."

I went to the toilet and counted the money over again. I hid the hundred franc notes in my fob pocket and kept a fifty franc note and the loose change in my trousers pocket. I went back to the bar determined to talk turkey.

She made it easier for me because she herself introduced the subject. She was in difficulties. It was not only that she had just lost her child, but her mother was home, ill, very ill, and there was the doctor to pay and medicine to be bought, and so on and so forth. I didn't believe a word of it, of course. And since I had to find a hotel for myself, I suggested that she come along with me and stay the night. A little economy there, I thought to myself. But she wouldn't do that. She insisted on going home, said she had an apartment to herself—and besides she had to look after her mother. On reflection I decided that it would be still cheaper sleeping at her place, so I said yes and let's go immediately. Before going, however, I decided it was best to let her know just how I stood, so that there wouldn't be any squawking at the last minute. I thought she was going to faint when I told her how much I had in my pocket. "The likes of it!" she said. Highly insulted she was. I thought there would be a scene ... Undaunted, however, I stood my ground. "Very well, then, I'll leave you," I said quietly. "Perhaps I've made a mistake."

"I should say you have!" she exclaimed, but clutching me by the sleeve at the same time. *"Ecoute, chéri ... sois raisonnable!"* When I heard that all my confidence was restored. I knew that it would be merely a question of promising her a little extra and everything would be O. K. "All right," I said wearily, "I'll be nice to you, you'll see."

"You were lying to me, then?" she said.

"Yes," I smiled, "I was just lying ..."

Before I had even put my hat on she had hailed a cab. I heard her give the Boulevard de Clichy for an address. That was more than the price of a room, I thought to myself. Oh well, there was time yet ... we'd see. I don't know how it started any more but soon she was raving to me about Henry Bordeaux. (I have yet to meet a whore who doesn't know of Henry Bordeaux!) But this one was genuinely inspired; her language was beautiful now, so tender, so discerning, that I was debating how much to give her. It seemed to me that I had heard her say— *"quand il n'y aura plus de temps."* It sounded like that, anyway. In the state I was in, a phrase like that was worth a hundred francs. I wondered if it was her own or if she had pulled it from Henry Bordeaux. Little matter. It was just the right phrase with which to roll up to the foot of Montmartre. "Good evening, mother," I was saying to myself, "daughter and I will look after you—*quand il n'y aura plus de temps!*" She was going to show me her diploma, too, I remembered that.

She was all aflutter, once the door had closed behind us. Distracted. Wringing her hands and striking Sarah Bernhardt poses, half undressed too, and pausing between times to urge me to hurry, to get undressed, to do this and do that. Finally, when she had stripped down and was poking about with a chemise in her hand, searching for her kimono, I caught hold of her and gave her a good squeeze. She had a look of anguish on her face when I released her. "My God! My God! I must go downstairs and have a look at mother!" she exclaimed. "You can take a bath if you like, *chéri.* There! I'll be back in a few minutes." At the door I embraced her again. I was in my underclothes and I had a tremendous erection. Somehow all this anguish and excitement, all the grief and histrionics, only whetted my appetite. Perhaps she was just going downstairs to quiet her *maquereau.* I had a feeling that something unusual was happening, some sort of drama which I would read about in the morning paper. I gave the place a quick inspection. There were two rooms and a bath, not badly furnished. Rather coquettish. There was her diploma on the wall—"first class," as they all read. And there was the photograph of a child, a little girl with beautiful locks, on the dresser. I put the water on for a bath, and then I changed my mind. If something were to happen and I were found in the tub ... I didn't like the idea. I paced back and forth, getting more and more uneasy as the minutes rolled by.

When she returned she was even more upset than before. "She's going to die ... she's going to die!" she kept wailing. For a moment I was almost on the point of leaving. How the hell can you climb over a woman when her mother's dying downstairs, perhaps right beneath you? I put my arms around her, half in sympathy and half determined to get what I had come for. As we stood thus she murmured, as if in real distress, her need for the money I had promised her. It was for *"maman."* Shit, I didn't have the heart to haggle about a few francs at that moment. I walked over to the chair where my clothes were lying and I wiggled a hundred franc note out of my fob pocket, carefully keeping my back turned to her just the same. And, as a further precaution, I placed my pants on the side of the bed where I knew I was going to flop. The hundred francs wasn't altogether satisfactory to her, but I could see from the feeble way that she protested that it was quite enough. Then, with an energy that astonished me, she flung off her kimono and jumped into bed. As soon as I had put my arms around her and pulled her to me she reached for the switch and out went the lights. She embraced me passionately, and she groaned as all French cunts do when they get you in bed. She was getting me frightfully roused with her carrying-on; that business of turning out the lights was a new one to me ... it seemed like the real thing. But I was suspicious too, and as soon as I could manage conveniently I put my hand out to feel if my trousers were still there on the chair.

I thought we were settled for the night. The bed felt very comfortable, softer than the average hotel bed—and the sheets were clean, I had noticed that. If only she wouldn't squirm so! You would think she hadn't slept with a man for a month. I wanted to stretch it out. I wanted full value for my hundred francs. But she was mumbling all sorts of things in that crazy bed language which goes to your blood even more rapidly when it's in the dark. I was putting up a stiff fight, but it was impossible with her groaning and gasping going on, and her muttering: *"Vite chéri! Vite chéri! Oh, c'est bon! Oh, oh! Vite, vite, chéri!"* I tried to count but it was like a fire alarm going off. *"Vite, chéri!"* and this time she gave such a gasping shudder that bango! I heard the stars chiming and there was my hundred francs gone and the fifty that I had forgotten all about and the lights were on again and with the same alacrity that she had bounced into bed she was bouncing out again and grunting and squealing like an old sow. I lay back and puffed a cigarette, gazing ruefully at my pants the while; they were terribly wrinkled. In a moment she was back again, wrapping the kimono around her, and telling me in that agitated way which was getting on my nerves that I should make myself at home. "I'm going downstairs to see mother," she said. *"Mais faites comme chez vous, chéri. Je reviens tout de suite."*

After a quarter of an hour had passed I began to feel thoroughly restless. I went inside and I read through a letter that was lying on the table. It was nothing on any account—a love letter. In the bathroom I examined all the bottles on the shelf; she had everything a woman requires to make herself smell beautiful. I was still hoping that she would come back and give me another fifty francs' worth. But time dragged on and there was no sign of her. I began to grow alarmed. Perhaps there *was* someone dying downstairs. Absent-mindedly, out of a sense of self-preservation, I suppose, I began to put my things on. As I was buckling my belt it came to me like a flash how she had stuffed the hundred franc note into her purse. In the excitement of the moment she had thrust the purse in the wardrobe, on the upper shelf. I remembered the gesture she made—standing on her tip-toes and reaching for the shelf. It didn't take me a minute to open the wardrobe and feel around for the purse. It was still there. I opened it hurriedly and saw my hundred franc note lying snugly between the silk coverlets. I put the purse back just as it was, slipped into my coat and shoes, and then I went to the landing and listened intently. I couldn't hear a sound. Where she had gone to, Christ only knows. In a jiffy I was back at the wardrobe and fumbling with her purse. I pocketed the hundred francs and all the loose change besides. Then, closing the door silently, I tip-toed down the stairs and when once I had hit the street I walked just as fast as my legs would carry me. At the Café Boudon I stopped for a bite. The whores there having a gay time pelting a fat man who had fallen asleep over his meal. He was sound asleep; snoring, in fact, and yet his jaws were working away mechanically. The place was in an uproar.

There were shouts of "All aboard!" and then a concerted banging of knives and forks. He opened his eyes for a moment, blinked stupidly, and then his head rolled forward again on his chest. I put the hundred franc bill carefully away in my fob pocket and counted the change. The din around me was increasing and I had difficulty to recall exactly whether I had seen "first-class" on her diploma or not. It bothered me. About her mother I didn't give a damn. I hoped she had croaked by now. It would be strange if what she had said were true. Too good to believe. *Vite chéri ... vite, vite!* And that other half-wit with her "my good sir" and "you have such a kind face"! I wondered if she had really taken a room in that hotel we stopped by.

It was along toward the close of Summer when Fillmore invited me to come and live with him. He had a studio apartment overlooking the cavalry barracks just off the Place Dupleix. We had seen a lot of each other ever since the little trip to Le Havre. If it hadn't been for Fillmore I don't know where I should be to-day—dead, most likely.

"I would have asked you long before," he said, "if it hadn't been for that little bitch Jackie. I didn't know how to get her off my hands."

I had to smile. It was always like that with Fillmore. He had a genius for attracting homeless bitches. Anyway, Jackie had finally cleared out of her own accord.

The rainy season was coming on the long, dreary stretch of grease and fog and squirts of rain that make you damp and miserable. An execrable place in the winter, Paris! A climate that eats into your soul, that leaves you bare as the Labrador coast. I noticed with some anxiety that the only means of heating the place was the little stove in the studio. However, it was still comfortable. And the view from the studio window was superb.

In the morning Fillmore would shake me roughly and leave a ten franc note on the pillow. As soon as he had gone I would settle back for a final snooze. Sometimes I would lie abed till noon. There was nothing pressing, except to finish the book, and that didn't worry me much because I was already convinced that nobody would accept it anyway. Nevertheless, Fillmore was much impressed by it. When he arrived in the evening with a bottle under his arm the first thing he did was to go to the table and see how many pages I had knocked off. At first I enjoyed the show of enthusiasm but later, when I was running dry, it made me devilishly uneasy to see him poking around, searching for the pages that were supposed to trickle out of me like water from a tap. When there was nothing to show I felt exactly like some bitch whom he had harbored. He used to say about Jackie, I remembered—"it would have been all right if only she had slipped me a piece of ass once in a while." If I had been a woman I would have been only too glad to slip him a piece of ass: it would have been much easier than to feed him the pages which he expected.

Nevertheless, he tried to make me feel at ease. There was always plenty of food and wine, and now and then he would insist that I accompany him to a *dancing*. He was fond of going to a nigger joint on the Rue d'Odessa where there was a good-looking mulatto who used to come home with us occasionally. The one thing that bothered him was that he couldn't find a French girl who liked to drink. They were all too sober to satisfy him— He liked to bring a woman back to the studio and guzzle it with her before getting down to business. He also liked to have her think that he was an artist. As the man from whom he had rented the place was a painter, it was not difficult to create an impression; the canvases which we had found in the *armoire* were soon stuck about the place and one of the unfinished ones conspicuously mounted on the easel. Unfortunately they were all of a Surrealistic quality and the impression they created was usually unfavorable. Between a whore, a concierge and a cabinet minister there is not much difference in taste where pictures are concerned. It was a matter of great relief to Fillmore when Mark Swift began to visit us regularly with the intention of doing my portrait. Fillmore had a great admiration for Swift. He was a genius, he said. And though there was something ferocious about everything he tackled nevertheless when he painted a man or an object you could recognize it for what it was.

At Swift's request I had begun to grow a beard. The shape of my skull, he said, required a beard. I had to sit by the window with the Eiffel Tower in back of me because he wanted the Eiffel Tower in the picture too. He also wanted the typewriter in the picture. Kruger got the habit of dropping in too about this time; he maintained that Swift knew nothing about painting. It exasperated him to see things out of proportion. He believed in Nature's laws, implicitly. Swift didn't give a fuck about Nature; he wanted to paint what was inside his head. Anyway, there was Swift's portrait of me stuck on the easel now, and though everything was out of proportion, even a cabinet minister could see that it was a human head, a man with a beard. The concierge, indeed, began to take a great interest in the picture; she thought the likeness was striking. And she liked the idea of showing the Eiffel Tower in the background.

Things rolled along this way peacefully for about a month or more. The neighborhood appealed to me, particularly at night when the full squalor and lugubriousness of it made itself felt. The little Place, so charming and tranquil at twilight, could assume the most dismal, sinister character when darkness came on. There was that long, high wall covering one side of the barracks against which there was always a couple embracing each other furtively—often in the rain. A depressing sight to see two lovers squeezed against a prison wall under a gloomy street light: as if they had been driven right to the last bounds. What went on inside the enclosure was also depressing. On a rainy day I used to stand by the window and look down on the activity below, quite as if it were something going on on another planet. It seemed incomprehensible to me. Everything done according to schedule, but a schedule that must have been devised by a lunatic. There they were, floundering around in the mud, the bugles blowing, the horses charging—all within four walls. A sham battle. A lot of tin soldiers who hadn't the least interest in learning how to kill or how to polish their boots or curry-comb the horses. Utterly ridiculous the whole thing, but part of the scheme of things. When they had nothing to do they looked even more ridiculous; they scratched themselves, they walked about with their hands in their pockets, they looked up at the sky. And when an officer came along they clicked their heels and saluted. A madhouse, it seemed to me. Even the horses looked silly. And then sometimes the artillery was dragged out and they went clattering down the street on parade and people stood and gaped and admired the fine uniforms. To me they always looked like an army corps in retreat; something shabby, bedraggled, crestfallen about them, their uniforms too big for their bodies, all the alertness, which as individuals they possess to such a remarkable degree, gone now.

When the sun came out, however, things looked different. There was a ray of hope in their eyes, they walked more elastically, they showed a little enthusiasm. Then the color of things peeped out graciously and there was that fuss and bustle so characteristic of the French; at the *bistrot* on the corner they chattered gaily over their drinks and the officers seemed more human, more French, I might say. When the sun comes out, any spot in Paris can look beautiful; and if there is a *bistrot* with an awning rolled down, a few tables on the sidewalk and colored drinks in the glasses, then people look altogether human. And they *are* human—the finest people in the world when the sun shines! So intelligent, so indolent, so care-free! It's a crime to herd such a people into barracks, to put them through exercises, to grade them into privates and sergeants and colonels and what not.

As I say, things were rolling along smoothly. Now and then Carl came along with a job for me, travel articles which he hated to do himself. They only paid fifty francs a piece, but they were easy to do because I had only to consult the back issues and revamp the old articles. People only read these things when they were sitting on a toilet or killing time in a waiting room. The principal thing was to keep the adjectives well furbished—the rest was a matter of dates and statistics. If it was an important article the head of the department signed it himself; he was a half-wit who couldn't speak any language well, but who knew how to find fault. If he found a paragraph that seemed to him well written he would say—"Now that's the way I want you to write! That's beautiful. You have my permission to use it in your book." These beautiful paragraphs we sometimes lifted from the encyclopaedia or an old guide book. Some of them Carl did put into his book—they had a Surrealistic character.

Then one evening, after I had been out for a walk, I open the door and a woman springs out of the bed-room. "So you're the writer!" she exclaims at once, and she looks at my beard as if to corroborate her impression. "What a horrid beard!" she says. "I think you people must be crazy around here." Fillmore is trailing after her with a blanket in his hand. "She's a princess," he says, smacking his lips as if he had just tasted some rare caviar. The two of them were dressed for the street; I couldn't understand what they were doing with the bed-clothes. And then it occurred to me immediately that Fillmore must have dragged her into the bed-room to show her his laundry bag. He always did that with a new woman, especially if she was a *Française*. "No tickee, no shirtee!" that's what was stitched on the laundry bag, and somehow Fillmore had an obsession for explaining this motto to every female who arrived. But this dame was not a *Française*—he made that clear to me at once. She was Russian—and a princess, no less.

He was bubbling over with excitement, like a child that has just found a new toy. "She speaks five languages!" he said, obviously overwhelmed by such an accomplishment.

"Non, *four!*" she corrected promptly.

"Well, four then ... Anyway, she's a damned intelligent girl. You ought to hear her speak."

The princess was nervous—she kept scratching her thigh and rubbing her nose. "Why does he want to make his bed now?" she asked me abruptly. "Does he think he will get me that way? He's a big child. He behaves disgracefully. I took him to a Russian restaurant and he danced like a nigger." She wiggled her bottom to illustrate. "And he talks too much. Too loud. He talks nonsense." She swished about the room, examining the paintings and the books, keeping her chin well up all the time but scratching herself intermittently. Now and then she wheeled around like a battleship and delivered a broadside. Fillmore kept following her about with a bottle in one hand and a glass in the other. "Stop following me like that!" she exclaimed. "And haven't you anything to drink but this? Can't you get a bottle of champagne? I must have some champagne. My nerves! My nerves!"

Fillmore tries to whisper a few words in my ear. "An actress ... a movie star ... some guy jilted her and she can't get over it ... I'm going to get her cockeyed ..."

"I'll clear out then," I was saying, when the princess

interrupted us with a shout. "Why do you whisper like that?" she cried, stamping her foot. "Don't you know that's not polite? And *you,* I thought you were going to take me out? I must get drunk to-night, I have told you that already."

"Yes, yes," said Fillmore, "we're going in a minute. I just want another drink."

"You're a pig!" she yelled. "But you're a nice boy too. Only you're loud. You have no manners." She turned to me. "Can I trust him to behave himself? I must get drunk to-night but I don't want him to disgrace me. Maybe I will come back here afterwards. I would like to talk to you. You seem more intelligent."

As they were leaving the princess shook my hand cordially and promised to come for dinner some evening—"when I will be sober," she said.

"Fine!" I said. "Bring another princess along—or a countess, at least. We change the sheets every Saturday."

About three in the morning Fillmore staggers in ... alone. Lit up like an ocean liner, and making a noise like a blind man with his cracked cane. Tap, tap, tap, down the weary lane ... "Going straight to bed," he says, as he marches past me. "Tell you all about it to-morrow." He goes inside to his room and throws back the covers. I hear him groaning—"what a woman! what a woman!" In a second he's out again, with his hat on and the cracked cane in his hand. "I knew something like that was going to happen. She's crazy!"

He rummages around in the kitchen a while and then comes back to the studio with a bottle of Anjou. I have to sit up and down a glass with him.

As far as I can piece the story together the whole thing started at the Rond-Point des Champs Elysées where he had dropped off for a drink on his way home. As usual at that hour the *terrasse* was crowded with buzzards. This one was sitting right on the aisle with a pile of saucers in front of her; she was getting drunk quietly all by herself when Fillmore happened along and caught her eye. "I'm drunk," she giggled, "won't you sit down?" And then, as though it were the most natural thing in the world to do, she began right off the bat with the yarn about her movie director, how he had given her the go-by and how she had thrown herself in the Seine and so forth and so on. She couldn't remember any more which bridge it was, only that there was a crowd around when they fished her out of the water. Besides, she didn't see what difference it made which bridge she threw herself from—why did he ask such questions? She was laughing hysterically about it, and then suddenly she had a desire to be off—she wanted to dance. Seeing him hesitate she opens her bag impulsively and pulls out a hundred francs note. The next moment, however, she decided that a hundred francs wouldn't go very far. "Haven't you any money at all?" she said. No, he hadn't very much in his pocket, but he had a checkbook at home. So they made a dash for the checkbook and then, of course, I had to happen in just as he was explaining to her the "No tickee, no shirtee" business.

On the way home they had stopped off at the Poisson d'Or for a little snack which she had washed down with a few vodkas. She was in her element there with everyone kissing her hand and murmuring *Princesse, Princesse*. Drunk as she was, she managed to collect her dignity. "Don't wiggle your behind like that!" she kept saying, as they danced.

It was Fillmore's idea, when he brought her back to the studio, to stay there. But, since she was such an intelligent girl and so erratic, he had decided to put up with her whims and postpone the grand event. He had even visualized the prospect of running across another princess and bringing the two of them back. When they started out for the evening, therefore, he was in a good humor and prepared, if necessary, to spend a few hundred francs on her. After all, one doesn't run across a princess every day.

This time she dragged him to another place, a place where she was still better known and where there would be no trouble in cashing a check, as she said. Everybody was in evening clothes and there was more spine-breaking, hand-kissing nonsense as the waiter escorted them to a table.

In the middle of a dance she suddenly walks off the floor, with tears in her eyes. "What's the matter?" he said, "what did I do this time?" and instinctively he put his hand to his backside, as though perhaps it might still be wiggling. "It's nothing," she said. "You didn't do anything. Come, you're a nice boy," and with that she drags him on to the floor again and begins to dance with abandon. "But what's the matter with you?" he murmured. "It's nothing," she repeated. "I saw somebody, that's all." And then, with a sudden spurt of anger—"why do you get me drunk? Don't you know it makes me crazy?"

"Have you got a check?" she says. "We must get out of here." She called the waiter over and whispered to him in Russian. "Is it a good check?" she asked, when the waiter had disappeared. And then, impulsively: "Wait for me downstairs in the cloak-room. I must telephone somebody."

After the waiter had brought the change Fillmore sauntered leisurely downstairs to the cloak-room to wait for her. He strode up and down, humming and whistling softly, and smacking his lips in anticipation of the caviar to come. Five minutes passed. Ten minutes. Still whistling softly. When twenty minutes had gone by and still no princess he at last grew suspicious. The cloak-room attendant said that she had left long ago. He dashed outside. There was a nigger in livery standing there with a big grin on his face. Did the nigger know where she had breezed to? Nigger grins. Nigger says: "Ah heerd Coupole, dassall sir!"

At the Coupole, downstairs, he finds her sitting in front of a cocktail with a dreamy, trance-like expression on her face. She smiles when she sees him.

"Was that a decent thing to do," he says, "to run away like that? You might have told me that you didn't like me . . ."

She flared up at this, got theatrical about it. And after a lot of gushing she commenced to whine and slobber. "I'm crazy," she blubbered. "And you're crazy too. You want me to sleep with you, and I don't want to sleep with you." And then she began to rave about her lover, the movie director whom she had seen on the dance floor. That's why she had to run away from the place. That's why she took drugs and got drunk every night. That's why she threw herself in the Seine. She babbled on this way about how crazy she was and then suddenly she had an idea. "Let's go to

Bricktop's!" There was a man there whom she knew . . . he had promised her a job once. She was certain he would help her.

"What's it going to cost?" asked Fillmore cautiously.

It would cost a lot, she let him know that immediately. "But listen, if you take me to Bricktop's, I promise to go home with you." She was honest enough to add that it might cost him five or six hundred francs. "But I'm worth it! You don't know what a woman I am. There isn't another woman like me in all Paris . . ."

"That's what *you* think!" His Yankee blood was coming to the fore. "But I don't see it. I don't see that you're worth anything. You're just a poor crazy son-of-a-bitch. Frankly, I'd rather give fifty francs to some poor French girl; at least they give you something in return."

She hit the ceiling when he mentioned the French girls. "Don't talk to me about those women! I hate them! They're stupid . . . they're ugly . . . they're mercenary. Stop it, I tell you!"

In a moment she had subsided again. She was on a new tack. "Darling," she murmured, "you don't know what I look like when I'm undressed. I'm *beautiful*!" And she held her breasts with her two hands.

But Fillmore remained unimpressed. "You're a bitch!" he said coldly. "I wouldn't mind spending a few hundred francs on you, but you're crazy. You haven't even washed your face. Your breath stinks. I don't give a damn whether you're a princess or not . . . I don't want any of your high-assed Russian variety. You ought to get out in the street and hustle for it. You're no better than any little French girl. You're not as good. I wouldn't piss away another sou on you. You ought to go to America—that's the place for a blood-sucking leech like you . . ."

She didn't seem to be at all put out by this speech. "I think you're just a little afraid of me," she said.

"Afraid of you? Of *you?*"

"You're just a little boy," she said. "You have no manners. When you know me better you will talk differently . . . Why don't you try to be nice? If you don't want to go with me to-night, very well. I will be at the Rond-Point to-morrow between five and seven. I like you."

"I don't intend to be at the Rond-Point to-morrow, or

any other night. I don't want to see you again ... ever.
I'm through with you. I'm going out and find myself a
nice little French girl. You can go to hell!"

She looked at him and smiled wearily. "That's what
you say now. But wait! Wait until you've slept with me.
You don't know yet what a beautiful body I have. You
think the French girls know how to make love ... wait!
I will make you crazy about me. I like you. Only you're
uncivilized. You're just a boy. You talk too much ..."

"You're crazy," said Fillmore. "I wouldn't fall for you
if you were the last woman on earth. Go home and wash
your face." He walked off without paying for the drinks.

In a few days, however, the princess was installed.
She's a genuine princess, of that we're pretty certain. But
she has the clap. Anyway, life is far from dull here.
Fillmore had bronchitis, the princess, as I was saying, has
the clap, and I have the piles. Just exchanged six empty
bottles at the Russian *épicerie* across the way. Not a drop
went down my gullet. No meat, no wine, no rich game,
no women. Only fruit and paraffin oil, arnica drops and
adenalin ointment. And not a chair in the joint that's comfortable enough. Right now, looking at the princess, I'm
propped up like a pasha. Pasha! That reminds me of her
name: Macha. Doesn't sound so damned aristocratic to
me. Reminds me of *The Living Corpse.*

At first I thought it was going to be embarrassing, a
ménage à trois, but not at all. I thought when I saw her
move in that it was all up with me again, that I should
have to find another place, but Fillmore soon gave me to
understand that he was only putting her up until she got
on her feet. With a woman like her I don't know what an
expression like that means; as far as I can see she's been
standing on her head all her life. She says the revolution
drove her out of Russia, but I'm sure if it hadn't been the
revolution it would have been something else. She's
under the impression that she's a great actress; we never
contradict her in anything she says because it's time
wasted. Fillmore finds her amusing. When he leaves for
the office in the morning he drops ten francs on her pillow and ten francs on mine; at night the three of us go to
the Russian restaurant down below. The neighborhood is
full of Russians and Macha has already found a place

where she can run up a little credit. Naturally ten francs a day isn't anything for a princess; she wants caviar now and then and champagne, and she needs a complete new wardrobe in order to get a job in the movies again. She has nothing to do now except to kill time. She's putting on fat.

This morning I had quite a fright. After I had washed my face I grabbed her towel by mistake. We can't seem to train her to put her towel on the right hook. And when I bawled her out for it she answered smoothly: "My dear, if one can become blind from that I would have been blind years ago."

And then there's the toilet, which we all have to use. I try speaking to her in a fatherly way about the toilet seat. "Oh zut!" she says. "If you are so afraid I'll go to a café." But it's not necessary to do that, I explain. Just use ordinary precautions. "Tut tut!" she says, "I won't sit down then . . . I'll stand up."

Everything is cockeyed with her around. First she wouldn't come across because she had the monthlies. For eight days that lasted. We were beginning to think she was faking it. But no, she wasn't faking. One day, when I was trying to put the place in order, I found some cotton batting under the bed and it was stained with blood. With her everything goes under the bed: orange peel, wadding, corks, empty bottles, scissors, used condoms, books, pillows . . . She makes the bed only when it's time to retire. Most of the time she lies abed reading her Russian papers. "My dear," she says to me, "if it weren't for my papers I wouldn't get out of bed at all." That's it precisely! Nothing but Russian newspapers. Not a scratch of toilet paper around—nothing but Russian newspapers with which to wipe your ass.

Anyway, speaking of her idiosyncrasies, after the menstrual flow was over, after she had rested properly and put a nice layer of fat around her belt, still she wouldn't come across. Pretended that she only liked women. To take on a man she had to first be properly stimulated. Wanted us to take her to a bawdy house where they put on the dog and man act. Or better still, she said, would be Leda and the swan: the flapping of the wings excited her terribly.

One night, to test her out, we accompanied her to a

place that she suggested. But before we had a chance to broach the subject to the madame, a drunken Englishman, who was sitting at the next table, fell into a conversation with us. He had already been upstairs twice but he wanted another try at it. He had only about twenty francs in his pocket, and not knowing any French, he asked us if we would help him to bargain with the girl he had his eye on. Happened she was a negress, a powerful wench from Martinique, and beautiful as a panther. Had a lovely disposition too. In order to persuade her to accept the Englishman's remaining sous, Fillmore had to promise to go with her himself soon as she got through with the Englishman. The princess looked on, heard everything that was said, and then got on her high horse. She was insulted. "Well," said Fillmore, "you wanted some excitement—you can watch me do it!" She didn't want to watch him—she wanted to watch a drake. "Well, by Jesus," he said, "I'm as good as a drake any day ... maybe a little better." Like that, one word led to another, and finally the only way we could appease her was to call one of the girls over and let them tickle each other ... When Fillmore came back with the negress her eyes were smouldering. I could see from the way Fillmore looked at her that she must have given an unusual performance and I began to feel lecherous myself. Fillmore must have sensed how I felt, and what an ordeal it was to sit and look on all night, for suddenly he pulled a hundred franc note out of his pocket and slapping it in front of me, he said: "Look here, you probably need a lay more than any of us. Take that and pick someone out for yourself." Somehow that gesture endeared him more to me than anything he had ever done for me, and he had done considerable. I accepted the money in the spirit it was given and promptly signalled to the negress to get ready for another lay. That enraged the Princess more than anything, it appeared. She wanted to know if there wasn't anyone in the place good enough for us except this negress. I told her bluntly NO. And it was so—the negress was the queen of the harem. You had only to look at her to get an erection. Her eyes seemed to be swimming in sperm. She was drunk with all the demands made upon her. She couldn't walk straight any more—at least, it seemed that

way to me. Going up the narrow winding stairs behind
her I couldn't resist the temptation to slide my hand up
her crotch; we continued up the stairs that way, she looking back at me with a cheerful smile and wiggling her ass
a bit when it tickled her too much.

It was a good session all around. Everyone was happy.
Macha seemed to be in a good mood too. And so the next
evening, after she had had her ration of champagne and
caviar, after she had given us another chapter out of the
history of her life, Fillmore went to work on her. It
seemed as though he was going to get his reward at last.
She had ceased to put up a fight any more. She lay back
with her legs apart and she let him fool around and fool
around and then, just as he was climbing over her, just as
he was going to slip it in, she informs him nonchalantly
that she has a dose of clap. He rolled off her like a log.
I heard him fumbling around in the kitchen for the black
soap he used on special occasions, and in a few moments
he was standing by my bed with a towel in his hands and
saying—"can you beat that? that son-of-a-bitch of a princess has the clap!" He seemed pretty well scared about it.
The princess meanwhile was munching an apple and calling for her Russian newspapers. It was quite a joke to her.
"There are worse things than that," she said, lying there
in her bed and talking to us through the open door. Finally Fillmore began to see it as a joke too and opening
another bottle of Anjou he poured out a drink for himself
and quaffed it down. It was only about one in the morning and so he sat there talking to me for a while. He
wasn't going to be put off by a thing like that, he told me.
Of course, he had to be careful . . . there was the old dose
which had come on in Le Havre. He couldn't remember
any more how that happened. Sometimes when he got
drunk he forgot to wash himself. It wasn't anything very
terrible, but you never knew what might develop later. He
didn't want any one massaging his prostate gland. No,
that he didn't relish. The first dose he ever got was at college. Didn't know whether the girl had given it to him or
he to the girl; there was so much funny work going on
about the campus you didn't know whom to believe.
Nearly all the co-eds had been knocked up some time or
other. Too damned ignorant . . . even the profs were igno-

rant. One of the profs had himself castrated, so the rumor went . . .

Anyway, the next night he decided to risk it—with a condom. Not much risk in that, unless it breaks. He had bought himself some of the long fish-skin variety—they were the most reliable, he assured me. But then, that didn't work either. She was too tight. "Jesus, there's nothing abnormal about me," he said. "How do you make that out? Somebody got inside her all right to give her that dose. He must have been abnormally small."

So, one thing after another failing, he just gave it up altogether. They lie there now like brother and sister, with incestuous dreams. Says Macha, in her philosophic way: "In Russia it often happens that a man sleeps with a woman without touching her. They can go on that way for weeks and weeks and never think anything about it. Until paff! once he touches her . . . paff! paff! After that it's paff, paff, paff!"

All efforts are concentrated now on getting Macha into shape. Fillmore thinks if he cures her of the clap she may loosen up. A strange idea. So he's bought her a douche bag, a stock of permanganate, a whirling syringe and other little things which were recommended to him by a Hungarian doctor, a little quack of an abortionist over near the Place d'Aligre. It seems his boss had knocked up a sixteen year old girl once and she had introduced him to the Hungarian; and then after that the boss had a beautiful chancre and it was the Hungarian again. That's how one gets acquainted in Paris—genito-urinary friendships. Anyway, under our strict supervision, Macha is taking care of herself. The other night, though, we were in a quandary for a while. She stuck the suppository inside her and then she couldn't find the string attached to it. "My God!" she was yelling, "where is that string? My God! I can't find the string!"

"Did you look under the bed?" said Fillmore.

Finally she quieted down. But only for a few minutes. The next thing was: "My God! I'm bleeding again. I just had my period and now there are *gouttes* again. It must be that cheap champagne you buy. My God, do you want me to bleed to death?" She comes out with a kimono on and a towel stuck between her legs, trying to look dignified as usual. "My whole life is just like that," she says. "I'm a neurasthenic. The whole day running around and at night I'm drunk again. When I came to Paris I was still an innocent girl. I read only Villon and Beaudelaire. But as I had then 300,000 Swiss francs in the bank I was crazy to enjoy myself, because in Russia they were always strict with me. And as I was even more beautiful then than I am now I had all the men falling at my feet." Here she hitched up the slack which had accumulated around her belt. "You mustn't think I had a stomach like that when I came here . . . that's from all the poison I was given to drink . . . those horrible *apéritifs* which the French are so crazy to drink . . . So then I met my movie director and he wanted that I should play a part for him. He said I was the most gorgeous creature in the world and he was begging me to sleep with him every night. I was a foolish young virgin and so I permitted him to rape me one night. I wanted to be a great actress and I didn't know that he was full of poison. So he gave me the clap . . . and now I want that he should have it back again. It's all his fault that I committed suicide in the Seine . . . Why are you laughing? Don't you believe that I committed suicide? I can show you the newspapers . . . there is my picture in all the papers. I will show you the Russian papers some day . . . they wrote about me wonderfully . . . But darling, you know that first I must have a new dress. I can't vamp this man with these dirty rags I am in. Besides, I still owe my dressmaker 12,000 francs . . ."

From here on it's a long story about the inheritance which she is trying to collect. She has a young lawyer, a Frenchman, who is rather timid, it seems, and he is trying to win back her fortune. From time to time he used to give her a hundred francs or so on account. "He's stingy, like all the French people," she says. "And I was so beautiful, too, that he couldn't keep his eyes off me. He kept begging me always to fuck him. I got so sick and tired of listening to him that one night I said yes, just to keep him quiet, and so as I wouldn't lose my hundred francs now and then." She paused a moment to laugh hysterically. "My dear," she continued, "it was too funny for words what happened to him. He calls me up on the phone one

day and he says: "I must see you right away . . . it's very
important." And when I see him he shows me a paper
from the doctor—and it's gonorrhea! My dear, I laughed
in his face. How should I know that I still had the clap?
"You wanted to fuck me and so I fucked you!" That made
him quiet. That's how it goes in life: you don't suspect
anything, and then all of a sudden paff, paff, paff! He was
such a fool that he fell in love with me all over again.
Only he begged me to behave myself and not run around
Montparnasse all night drinking and fucking. He said I
was driving him crazy. He wanted to marry me and then
his family heard about me and they persuaded him to go
to Indo-China . . ."

From this Macha calmly switches to an affair she had
with a Lesbian. "It was very funny, my dear, how she
picked me up one night. I was at the 'Fétiche' and I was
drunk as usual. She took me from one place to the other
and she made love to me under the table all night until I
couldn't stand it any more. Then she took me to her
apartment and for two hundred francs I let her suck me
off. She wanted me to live with her but I didn't want to
have her suck me off every night . . . it makes you too
weak. Besides, I can tell you that I don't care so much for
Lesbians as I used to. I would rather sleep with a man
even though it hurts me. When I get terribly excited I
can't hold myself back any more . . . three, four, five
times . . . just like that! Paff, paff, paff! And then I bleed
and that is very unhealthy for me because I am inclined
to be anaemic. So you see why once in a while I must let
myself be sucked by a Lesbian . . ."

When the cold weather set in the princess disappeared. It was getting uncomfortable with just a little coal stove in the studio; the bed-room was like an ice-box and the kitchen was hardly any better. There was just a little space around the stove where it was actually warm. So Macha had found herself a sculptor who was castrated. She told us about him before she left. After a few days she tried coming back to us, but Fillmore wouldn't hear of it. She complained that the sculptor kept her awake all night kissing her. And then there was no hot water for her douches. But finally she decided that it was just as well she didn't come back. "I won't have that candle-stick next to me any more," she said. "Always that candle-stick . . . it made me nervous. If you had only been a fairy I would have stayed with you . . ."

With Macha gone our evenings took on a different character. Often we sat by the fire drinking hot toddies and discussing the life back there in the States. We talked about it as if we never expected to go back there again. Fillmore had a map of New York City which he had tacked on the wall; we used to spend whole evenings discussing the relative virtues of Paris and New York. And inevitably there always crept into our discussions the figure of Whitman, that one lone figure which America has produced in the course of her brief life. In Whitman the whole American scene comes to life, her past and her future, her birth and her death. Whatever there is of value in America Whitman has expressed, and there is nothing more to be said. The future belongs to the machine, to the robots. He was the Poet of the Body and the Soul, Whitman. The first and the last poet. He is almost undecipherable today, a monument covered with rude hieroglyphs for which there is no key. It seems strange almost to mention his name over here. There is no equivalent in the languages of Europe for the spirit which he immortalized. Europe is saturated with art and her soil is full of dead bones and her museums are bursting with plundered treasures, but what Europe has never had is a free, healthy spirit, what you might call a MAN. Goethe was the nearest approach, but Goethe was a stuffed shirt, by comparison. Goethe was a respectable citizen, a pedant, a bore, a universal spirit, but stamped with the German trade-mark, with the double eagle. The serenity of Goethe, the calm, Olympian attitude, is nothing more than the drowsy stupor of a German bourgeois deity. Goethe is an end of something, Whitman is a beginning.

After a discussion of this sort I would sometimes put on my things and go for a walk, bundled up in a sweater, a spring overcoat of Fillmore's and a cape over that. A foul, damp cold against which there is no protection except a strong spirit. They say America is a country of extremes, and it is true that the thermometer registers degrees of cold which are practically unheard of here; but the cold of a Paris winter is a cold unknown to America, it is psychological, an inner as well as an outer cold. If it never freezes here it never thaws either. Just as the people protect themselves against the invasion of their privacy, by their high walls, their bolts and shutters, their growling, evil-tongued, slatternly concierges, so they have learned to protect themselves against the cold and heat of a bracing, vigorous climate. They have fortified themselves: protection is the keyword. Protection and security. In order that they may rot in comfort. On a damp winter's night it is not necessary to look at the map to discover the latitude of Paris. It is a northern city, an outpost erected over a swamp filled in with skulls and bones. Along the boulevards there is a cold electrical imitation of heat. *Tout Va Bien* in ultraviolet rays that make the clients of the Dupont chain cafés look like gangrened cadavers. *Tout Va Bien!* That's the motto that nourishes the forlorn beggars who walk up and down all night under the drizzle of the violet rays. Wherever there are lights there is a little heat. One gets warm from watching the fat, secure bastards down their grogs, their steaming black coffees.

Where the lights are there are people on the sidewalks, jostling one another, giving off a little animal heat through their dirty underwear and their foul, cursing breaths. Maybe for a stretch of eight or ten blocks there is a semblance of gaiety, and then it tumbles back into night, dismal, foul, black night like frozen fat in a soup tureen. Blocks and blocks of jagged tenements, every window closed tight, every shop front barred and bolted. Miles and miles of stone prisons without the faintest glow of warmth; the dogs and the cats are all inside with the canary birds. The cockroaches and the bedbugs too are safely incarcerated. *Tout Va Bien.* If you haven't a sou why just take a few old newspapers and make yourself a bed on the steps of a cathedral. The doors are well bolted and there will be no draughts to disturb you. Better still is to sleep outside the Metro doors; there you will have company. Look at them on a rainy night, lying there stiff as mattresses—men, women, lice, all huddled together and protected by the newspapers against spittle and the vermin that walks without legs. Look at them under the bridges or under the market sheds. How vile they look in comparison with the clean, bright vegetables stacked up like jewels. Even the dead horses and the cows and sheep hanging from the greasy hooks look more inviting. At least we will eat these to-morrow and even the intestines will serve a purpose. But these filthy beggars lying in the rain, what purpose do they serve? what good can they do us? They make us bleed for five minutes, that's all.

Oh, well, these are night thoughts produced by walking in the rain after two thousand years of Christianity. At least now the birds are well provided for, and the cats and dogs. Every time I pass the concierge's window and catch the full icy impact of her glance I have an insane desire to throttle all the birds in creation. At the bottom of every frozen heart there is a drop or two of love—just enough to feed the birds.

Still I can't get it out of my mind what a discrepancy there is between ideas and living. A permanent disloca-tion, though we try to cover the two with a bright awning. And it won't go. Ideas have to be wedded to action; if there is no sex, no vitality in them, there is no action. Ideas cannot exist alone in the vacuum of the mind. Ideas are related to living: liver ideas, kidney ideas, interstitial ideas, etc. If it were only for the sake of an idea Copernicus would not have smashed the existent macrocosm and Columbus would have foundered in the Sargasso Sea. The aesthetics of the idea breeds flower-pots and flower-pots you put on the window-sill. But if there be no rain or sun of what use putting flower-pots outside the window?

Fillmore is full of ideas about gold. The "mythos" of gold, he calls it. I like "mythos" and I like the idea of gold, but I am not obsessed by the subject and I don't see why we should make flower-pots, even of gold. He tells me that the French are hoarding their gold away in watertight compartments deep below the surface of the earth; he tells me that there is a little locomotive which runs around in these subterranean vaults and corridors. I like the idea enormously. A profound, uninterrupted silence in which the gold softly snoozes at a temperature of 17 ¼ degrees Centigrade. He says an army working 46 days and 37 hours would not be sufficient to count all the gold that is sunk beneath the Bank of France, and that there is a reserve supply of false teeth, bracelets, wedding rings, etc. Enough food also to last for eighty days and a lake on top of the gold pile to resist the shock of high explosives. Gold, he says, tends to become more and more invisible, a myth, and no more defalcations. Excellent! I am wondering what will happen to the world when we go off the gold standard in ideas, dress, morals, etc. *The gold standard of love!*

Up to the present, my idea in collaborating with myself has been to get off the gold standard of literature. My idea briefly has been to present a resurrection of the emotions, to depict the conduct of a human being in the stratosphere of ideas, that is, in the grip of delirium. To paint a pre-Socratic being, a creature part goat, part Titan. In short, to erect a world on the basis of the *omphalos,* not on an abstract idea nailed to a cross. Here and there you may have come across neglected statues, oases untapped, windmills overlooked by Cervantes, rivers that run uphill, women with five and six breasts ranged longitudinally along the torso. (Writing to Gauguin, Strindberg said: *"J'ai vu des arbres que ne retrouverait aucun*

*botaniste, des animaux que Cuvier n'a jamais soupçonnés
et des hommes que vous seul avez pu créer."*)

When Rembrandt hit par he went below with the gold
ingots and the pemmican and the portable beds. Gold is
a night word belonging to the chthonian mind: it has
dream in it and mythos. We are reverting to alchemy, to
that fake Alexandrian wisdom which produced our inflated symbols. Real wisdom is being stored away in the
sub-cellars by the misers of learning. The day is coming
when they will be circling around in the middle air with
magnetizers; to find a piece of ore you will have to go up
ten thousand feet with a pair of instruments—in a cold
latitude preferably—and establish telepathic communication with the bowels of the earth and the shades of the
dead. No more Klondikes. No more bonanzas. You will
have to learn to sing and caper a bit, to read the zodiac
and study your entrails. All the gold that is being tucked
away in the pockets of the earth will have to be re-mined;
all this symbolism will have to be dragged out again from
the bowels of men. But first the instruments must be per-
fected. First it is necessary to invent better airplanes, to
distinguish *where* the noise comes from and not go daffy
just because you hear an explosion under your ass. And
secondly it will be necessary to get adapted to the cold
layers of the stratosphere, to become a cold-blooded fish
of the air. No reverence. No piety. No longing. No regrets. No hysteria. Above all, as Philippe Datz
says—"NO DISCOURAGEMENT!"

These are sunny thoughts inspired by a Vermouth Cas-
sis at the Place de la Trinité. A Saturday afternoon and a
"misfire" book in my hands. Everything swimming in a
divine mucopus. The drink leaves a bitter herbish taste in
my mouth, the lees of our great Western civilization, rotting now like the toe-nails of the saints. Women are passing by—regiments of them—all swinging their asses in
front of me; the chimes are ringing and the buses are
climbing the sidewalk and bussing one another. The
garçon wipes the table with a dirty rag while the *patronne*
tickles the cash-register with fiendish glee. A look of va-
cuity on my face, blotto, vague in acuity, biting the asses
that brush by me. In the belfry opposite a hunchback
strikes with a golden mallet and the pigeons scream

alarum. I open the book—the book which Nietzsche called "the best German book there is"—and it says:

"MEN WILL BECOME MORE CLEVER AND MORE ACUTE; BUT NOT BETTER, HAPPIER, AND STRONGER IN ACTION—OR, AT LEAST, ONLY AT EPOCHS. I FORESEE THE TIME WHEN GOD WILL HAVE NO MORE JOY IN THEM, BUT WILL BREAK UP EVERYTHING FOR A RENEWED CREATION. I AM CERTAIN THAT EVERYTHING IS PLANNED TO THIS END, AND THAT THE TIME AND HOUR IN THE DISTANT FUTURE FOR THE OCCURRENCE OF THIS RENOVATING EPOCH ARE ALREADY FIXED. BUT A LONG TIME WILL ELAPSE FIRST, AND WE MAY STILL FOR THOUSANDS AND THOUSANDS OF YEARS AMUSE OURSELVES ON THIS DEAR OLD SURFACE."

Excellent! At least a hundred years ago there was a man who had vision enough to see that the world was pooped out. *Our Western world!*—When I see the figures of men and women moving listlessly behind their prison walls, sheltered, secluded for a few brief hours, I am appalled by the potentialities for drama that are still contained in these feeble bodies. Behind the gray walls there are human sparks, and yet never a conflagration. Are these men and women, I ask myself, or are these shadows, shadows of puppets dangled by invisible strings? They move in freedom apparently, but they have nowhere to go. In one realm only are they free and there they may roam at will—but they have not yet learned how to take wing. So far there have been no dreams that have taken wing. Not one man has been born light enough, *gay* enough, to leave the earth! The eagles who flapped their mighty pinions for a while came crashing heavily to earth. They made us dizzy with the flap and whir of their wings. Stay on the earth, you eagles of the future! The heavens have been explored and they are empty. And what lies under the earth is empty too, filled with bones and shadows. Stay on the earth and swim another few hundred thousand years!

And now it is three o'clock in the morning and we have a couple of trollops here who are doing somersaults on the bare floor. Fillmore is walking around naked with a goblet in his hand, and that paunch of his is drumtight, hard as a fistula. All the Pernod and champagne and cognac and Anjou which he guzzled from three in the afternoon on, is gurgling in his trap like a sewer. The girls are

putting their ears to his belly as if it were a music-box.
Open his mouth with a button-hook and drop a slug in the
slot. When the sewer gurgles I hear the bats flying out of
the belfry and the dream slides into artifice.

The girls have undressed and we are examining the
floor to make sure that they won't get any splinters in
their ass. They are still wearing their high-heeled shoes.
But the ass! The ass is worn down, scraped, sandpapered,
smooth, hard, bright as a billiard ball or the skull of a
leper. On the wall is Mona's picture: she is facing north-
east on a line with Cracow written in green ink. To the
left of her is the Dordogne, encircled with a red pencil.
Suddenly I see a dark, hairy crack in front of me set in a
bright, polished billiard ball; the legs are holding me like
a pair of scissors. A glance at that dark, unstitched wound
and a deep fissure in my brain opens up: all the images
and memories that had been laboriously or absent-
mindedly assorted, labelled, documented, filed, sealed
and stamped break forth pellmell like ants pouring out of
a crack in the sidewalk; the world ceases to revolve, time
stops, the very nexus of my dreams is broken and dis-
solved and my guts spill out in a grand schizophrenic
rush, an evacuation that leaves me face to face with the
Absolute. I see again the great sprawling mothers of
Picasso, their breasts covered with spiders, their legend
hidden deep in the labyrinth. And Molly Bloom lying on
a dirty mattress for eternity. On the toilet door red chalk
cocks and the madonna uttering the diapason of woe. I
hear a wild, hysterical laugh, a room full of lockjaw, and
the body that was black glows like phosphorus. Wild,
wild, utterly uncontrollable laughter, and that crack
laughing at me too, laughing through the mossy whiskers,
a laugh that creases the bright, polished surface of the billiard ball. Great whore and mother of man with gin in her
veins. Mother of all harlots, spider rolling us in your log-
arithmic grave, insatiable one, fiend whose laughter rives
me! I look down into that sunken crater, world lost and
without traces, and I hear the bells chiming, two nuns at
the Palace Stanislas and the smell of rancid butter under
their dresses, manifesto never printed because it was
raining, war fought to further the cause of plastic surgery,
the Prince of Wales flying around the world decorating

the graves of unknown heroes. Every bat flying out of the belfry a lost cause, every whoop-la a groan over the radio from the private trenches of the damned. Out of that dark, unstitched wound, that sink of abominations, that cradle of black-thronged cities where the music of ideas is drowned in cold fat, out of strangled Utopias is born a clown, a being divided between beauty and ugliness, between light and chaos, a clown who when he looks down and sidelong is Satan himself and when he looks upward sees a buttered angel, a snail with wings.

When I look down into that crack I see an equation sign, the world at balance, a world reduced to zero and no trace of remainder. Not the zero on which Van Norden turned his flashlight, not the empty crack of the prematurely disillusioned man, but an Arabian zero rather, the sign from which spring endless mathematical worlds, the fulcrum which balances the stars and the light dreams and the machines lighter than air and the light-weight limbs and the explosives that produced them. Into that crack I would like to penetrate up to the eyes, make them waggle ferociously, dear, crazy, metallurgical eyes. When the eyes waggle then will I hear again Dostoievski's words, hear them rolling on page after page, with minutest observation, with maddest introspection, with all the undertones of misery now lightly, humorously touched, now swelling like an organ note until the heart bursts and there is nothing left but a blinding, scorching light, the radiant light that carries off the fecundating seeds of the stars. The story of art whose roots lie in massacre.

When I look down into this fucked-out cunt of a whore I feel the whole world beneath me, a world tottering and crumbling, a world used up and polished like a leper's skull. If there were a man who dared to say all that he thought of this world there would not be left him a square foot of ground to stand on. When a man appears the world bears down on him and breaks his back. There are always too many rotten pillars left standing, too much festering humanity for man to bloom. The superstructure is a lie and the foundation is a huge quaking fear. If at intervals of centuries there does appear a man with a desperate, hungry look in his eye, a man who would turn the world upside down in order to create a new race, the love that he brings to the world is turned to bile and he becomes a scourge. If now and then we encounter pages that explode, pages that wound and sear, that wring groans and tears and curses, know that they come from a man with his back up, a man whose only defense left are his words and his words are always stronger than the lying, crushing weight of the world, stronger than all the racks and wheels which the cowardly invent to crush out the miracle of personality. If any man ever dared to translate all that is in his heart, to put down what is really his experience, what is truly his truth, I think then the world would go to smash, that it would be blown to smithereens and no god, no accident, no will could ever again assemble the pieces, the atoms, the indestructible elements that have gone to make up the world.

In the four hundred years since the last devouring soul appeared, the last man to know the meaning of ecstasy, there has been a constant and steady decline of man in art, in thought, in action. The world is pooped out: there isn't a dry fart left. Who that has a desperate, hungry eye can have the slightest regard for these existent governments, laws, codes, principles, ideals, ideas, totems, and taboos? If anyone knew what it meant to read the riddle of that thing which to-day is called a "crack" or a "hole," if any one had the least feeling of mystery about the phenomena which are labelled "obscene," this world would crack asunder. It is the obscene horror, the dry, fucked-out aspect of things which makes this crazy civilization look like a crater. It is this great yawning gulf of nothingness which the creative spirits and mothers of the race carry between their legs. When a hungry, desperate spirit appears and makes the guinea pigs squeal it is because he knows where to put the live wire of sex, because he knows that beneath the hard carapace of indifference there is concealed the ugly gash, the wound that never heals. And he puts the live wire right between the legs; he hits below the belt, scorches the very gizzards. It is no use putting on rubber gloves; all that can be coolly and intellectually handled belongs to the carapace and a man who is intent on creation always dives beneath, to the open wound, to the festering obscene horror. He hitches his dynamo to the tenderest parts; if only blood and pus gush forth, it is something. The dry, fucked-out crater is obscene. More obscene than anything is inertia. More blasphemous than the bloodiest oath is paralysis. If there is only a gaping wound left then it must gush forth though it produce nothing but toads and bats and homunculi.

Everything is packed into a second which is either consummated or not consummated. The earth is not an arid plateau of health and comfort, but a great sprawling female with velvet torso that swells and heaves with ocean billows; she squirms beneath a diadem of sweat and anguish. Naked and sexed she rolls among the clouds in the violet light of the stars. All of her, from the generous breasts to her gleaming thighs, blazes with furious ardor. She moves amongst the seasons and the years with a grand whoop-la that seizes the torso with paroxysmal fury, that shakes the cobwebs out of the sky; she subsides on her pivotal orbits with volcanic tremors. She is like a doe at times, a doe that has fallen into a snare and lies waiting with beating heart for the cymbals to crash and the dogs to bark. Love and hate, despair, pity, rage, disgust—what are these amidst the fornications of the planets? What is war, disease, cruelty, terror, when night presents the ecstasy of myriad blazing suns? What is this chaff we chew in our sleep if it is not the remembrance of fang-whorl and star cluster?

She used to say to me, Mona, in her fits of exaltation, "you're a great human being," and though she left me here to perish, though she put beneath my feet a great howling pit of emptiness, the words that lie at the bottom of my soul leap forth and they light the shadows below me. I am one who was lost in the crowd, whom the fizzing lights made dizzy, a zero who saw everything about him reduced to mockery. Passed me men and women ignited with sulphur, porters in calcium livery opening the jaws of hell, fame walking on crutches, dwindled by the skyscrapers, chewed to a frazzle by the spiked mouth of the machines. I walked between the tall buildings towards the cool of the river and I saw the lights shoot up between the ribs of the skeletons like rockets. If I was truly a great human being, as she said, then what was the meaning of this slavering idiocy about me? I was a man with body and soul, I had a heart that was not protected by a steel vault. I had moments of ecstasy and I sang with burning sparks. I sang of the Equator, her red-feathered legs and the islands dropping out of sight. But nobody heard. A gun fired across the Pacific falls into space because the earth is round and pigeons fly upside down. I saw her looking at me across the table with eyes turned to grief; sorrow spreading inward flattened its nose against her spine; the marrow churned to pity had turned liquid. She was light as a corpse that floats in the Dead Sea. Her fingers bled with anguish and the blood turned to drool. With the wet dawn came the tolling of bells and along the fibres of my nerves the bells played ceaselessly and their tongues pounded in my heart and clanged with iron malice. Strange that the bells should toll so, but stranger still the body bursting, this woman turned to night and her maggot words gnawing through the mattress. I moved along under the Equator, heard the hideous laughter of the green-jawed hyaena, saw the jackal with silken tail and the dick-dick and the spotted leopard, all left behind in the Garden of Eden. And then her sorrow widened, like the bow of a dreadnought and the weight of her sinking flooded my ears. Slime-wash and sapphires slipping, sluicing through the gay neurones, and the spectrum spliced and the gunwales dipping. Soft as lion-pad I heard the gun-carriages turn, saw them vomit and drool: the firmament sagged and all the stars turned black. Black ocean bleeding and the brooding stars breeding chunks of fresh-swollen flesh while overhead the birds wheeled and out of the hallucinated sky fell the balance with mortar and pestle and the bandaged eyes of justice. All that is here related moves with imaginary feet along the parallels of dead orbs; all that is seen with the empty sockets bursts like flowering grass. Out of nothingness arises the sign of infinity; beneath the ever-rising spirals slowly sinks the gaping hole. The land and the water make numbers joined, a poem written with flesh and stronger than steel or granite. Through endless night the earth whirls towards a creation unknown ...

To-day I awoke from a sound sleep with curses of joy on my lips, with gibberish on my tongue, repeating to myself like a litany—*"Fay ce que vouldras! ... fay ce que vouldras!"* Do anything, but let it produce joy. Do anything, but let it yield ecstasy. So much crowds into my head when I say this to myself: images, gay ones, terrible ones, maddening ones, the wolf and the goat, the spider, the crab, syphilis with her wings outstretched and the door of the womb always on the latch, always open, ready like the tomb. Lust, crime, holiness: the lives of my adored ones, the failures of my adored ones, the words they left behind them, the words they left unfinished; the good they dragged after them and the evil, the sorrow, the discord, the rancor, the strife they created. But above all, *the ecstasy!*

Things, certain things about my old idols bring the tears to my eyes: the interruptions, the disorder, the violence, above all, the hatred they aroused. When I think of their deformities, of the monstrous styles they chose, of the flatulence and tediousness of their works, of all the chaos and confusion they wallowed in, of the obstacles they heaped up about them, I feel an exaltation. They were all mired in their own dung. All men who over-elaborated. So true is it that I am almost tempted to say: "Show me a man who over-elaborates and I will show you a great man!" What is called their "over-elaboration" is my meat: it is the sign of struggle, it is struggle itself with all the fibres clinging to it, the very aura and ambiance of the discordant spirit. And when you show me a man who expresses himself perfectly I will not say that he is not great, but I will say that I am unattracted . . . I miss the cloying qualities. When I reflect that the task which the artist implicitly sets himself is to overthrow existing values, to make of the chaos about him an order which is his own, to sow strife and ferment so that by the emotional release those who are dead may be restored to life, then it is that I run with joy to the great and imperfect ones, their confusion nourishes me, their stuttering is like divine music to my ears. I see in the beautifully bloated pages that follow the interruptions the erasure of petty intrusions, of the dirty foot-prints, as it were, of cowards, liars, thieves, vandals, calumniators. I see in the swollen muscles of their lyric throats the staggering effort that must be made to turn the wheel over, to pick up the pace where one has left off. I see that behind the daily annoyances and intrusions, behind the cheap, glittering malice of the feeble and inert, there stands the symbol of life's frustrating power, and that he who would create order, he who would sow strife and discord, because he is imbued with will, such a man must go again and again to the stake and the gibbet. I see that behind the nobility of his gestures there lurks the spectre of the ridiculousness of it all—that he is not only sublime, but absurd.

Once I thought that to be human was the highest aim a man could have, but I see now that it was meant to destroy me. To-day I am proud to say that I am *inhuman,* that I belong not to men and governments, that I have nothing to do with creeds and principles. I have nothing to do with the creaking machinery of humanity—I belong to the earth! I say that lying on my pillow and I can feel the horns sprouting from my temples. I can see about me all those cracked forbears of mine dancing around the bed, consoling me, egging me on, lashing me with their serpent tongues, grinning and leering at me with their skulking skulls. *I am inhuman!* I say it with a mad, hallucinated grin, and I will keep on saying it though it rains crocodiles. Behind my words are all those grinning, leering, skulking skulls, some dead and grinning a long time, some grinning as if they had lock-jaw, some grinning with the grimace of a grin, the foretaste and aftermath of what is always going on. Clearer than all I see my own grinning skull, see the skeleton dancing in the wind, serpents issuing from the rotted tongue and the bloated pages of ecstasy slimed with excrement. And I join my slime, my excrement, my madness, my ecstasy to the great circuit which flows through the subterranean vaults of the flesh. All this unbidden, unwanted, drunken vomit will flow on endlessly through the minds of those to come in the inexhaustible vessel that contains the history of the race. Side by side with the human race there runs another race of beings, the inhuman ones, the race of artists who, goaded by unknown impulses, take the lifeless mass of humanity and by the fever and ferment with which they imbue it turn this soggy dough into bread and the bread into wine and the wine into song. Out of the dead compost and the inert slag they breed a song that contaminates. I see this other race of individuals ransacking the universe, turning everything upside down, their feet always moving in blood and tears, their hands always empty, always clutching and grasping for the beyond, for the god out of reach: slaying everything within reach in order to quiet the monster that gnaws at their vitals. I see that when they tear hair with the effort to comprehend, to seize this, forever unattainable, I see that when they bellow like crazed beasts and rip and gore, I see that this is right, that there is no other path to pursue. A man who belongs to this race must stand up on the high place with gibberish in his mouth and rip out his entrails. It is right and just, because he must! And anything that falls short of this frightening spectacle, anything less shuddering, less terrifying, less mad, less intoxicated, less contaminating, is not art. The rest is counterfeit. The rest is human. The rest belongs to life and lifelessness.

When I think of Stavrogin for example, I think of some divine monster standing on a high place and flinging to us his torn bowels. In *The Possessed* the earth quakes: it is not the catastrophe that befalls the imaginative individual, but a cataclysm in which a large portion of humanity is buried, wiped out for ever. Stavrogin was Dostoievski and Dostoievski was the sum of all those contradictions which either paralyze a man or lead him to the heights. There was no world too low for him to enter, no place too high for him to fear to ascend. He went the whole gamut, from the abyss to the stars. It is a pity that we shall never again have the opportunity to see a man placed at the very core of mystery and, by his flashes, illuminating for us the depth and immensity of the darkness.

To-day I am aware of my lineage. I have no need to consult my horoscope or my genealogical chart. What is written in the stars, or in my blood, I know nothing of. I know that I spring from the mythological founders of the race. The man who raises the holy bottle to his lips, the criminal who kneels in the market-place, the innocent one who discovers that *all* corpses stink, the madman who dances with lightning in his hands, the friar who lifts his skirts to pee over the world, the fanatic who ransacks libraries in order to find the Word—all these are fused in me, all these make my confusion, my ecstasy. If I am inhuman it is because my world has slopped over its human bounds, because to be human seems like a poor, sorry, miserable affair, limited by the senses, restricted by moralities and codes, defined by platitudes and isms. I am pouring the juice of the grape down my gullet and I find wisdom in it, but my wisdom is not born of the grape, my intoxication owes nothing to wine. . . .

I want to make a detour of those lofty arid mountain ranges where one dies of thirst and cold, that "extratemporal" history, that absolute of time and space where there exists neither man, beast, nor vegetation, where one goes crazy with loneliness, with language that is mere words, where everything is unhooked, ungeared, out of joint with the times. I want a world of men and women, of trees that do not talk (because there is too much talk in the world as it is!) of rivers that carry you to places, not rivers that are legends, but rivers that put you in touch with other men and women, with architecture, religion, plants, animals—rivers that have boats on them and in which men drown, drown not in myth and legend and books and dust of the past, but in time and space and history. I want rivers that make oceans such as Shakespeare and Dante, rivers which do not dry up in the void of the past. Oceans, yes! Let us have more oceans, new oceans that blot out the past, oceans that create new geological formations, new topographical vistas and strange, terrifying continents, oceans that destroy and preserve at the same time, oceans that we can sail on, take off to new discoveries, new horizons. Let us have more oceans, more upheavals, more wars, more holocausts. Let us have a world of men and women with dynamos between their legs, a world of natural fury, of passion, action, drama, dreams, madness, a world that produces ecstasy and not dry farts. I believe that to-day more than ever a book should be sought after even if it has only *one* great page in it: we must search for fragments, splinters, toe-nails, anything that has ore in it, anything that is capable of resuscitating the body and soul.

It may be that we are doomed, that there is no hope for us, *any of us,* but if that is so then let us set up a last agonizing, blood-curdling howl, a screech of defiance, a war-whoop! Away with lamentation! Away with elegies and dirges! Away with biographies and histories, and libraries and museums! Let the dead eat the dead. Let us living ones dance about the rim of the crater, a last expiring dance. But a dance!

"I love everything that flows," said the great blind Milton of our times. I was thinking of him this morning when I awoke with a great bloody shout of joy: I was thinking of his rivers and trees and all that world of night which he is exploring. Yes, I said to myself, I too love everything that flows: rivers, sewers, lava, semen, blood, bile, words, sentences. I love the amniotic fluid when it spills out of the bag. I love the kidney with its painful gallstones, its gravel and what-not; I love the urine that pours out scalding and the clap that runs endlessly; I love the words of hysterics and the sentences that flow on like dysentery and mirror all the sick images of the soul; I love the great rivers like the Amazon and the Orinoco, where crazy men like Moravagine float on through dream and legend in an open boat and drown in the blind mouths of the river. I love everything that flows, even the menstrual flow that carries away the seed unfecund. I love scripts that flow, be they hieratic, esoteric, perverse, polymorph, or unilateral. I love everything that flows, everything that has time in it and becoming, that brings us back to the beginning where there is never end: the violence of the prophets, the obscenity that is ecstasy, the wisdom of the fanatic, the priest with his rubber litany, the foul words of the whore, the spittle that floats away in the gutter, the milk of the breast and the bitter honey that pours from the womb, all that is fluid, melting, dissolute and dissolvent, all the pus and dirt that in flowing is purified, that loses its sense of origin, that makes the great circuit toward death and dissolution. The great incestuous wish is to flow on, one with time, to merge the great image of the beyond with the here and now. A fatuous, suicidal wish that is constipated by words and paralyzed by thought.

It was close to dawn on Christmas Day when we came home from the Rue d'Odessa with a couple of negresses from the telephone company. The fire was out and we were all so tired that we climbed into bed with our clothes on. The one I had, who had been like a bounding leopard all evening, fell sound asleep as I was climbing over her. For a while I worked over her as one works over a person who has been drowned or asphyxiated. Then I gave it up and fell sound asleep myself.

All during the holidays we had champagne morning, noon and night—the cheapest and the best champagne. With the turn of the year I was to leave for Dijon where I had been offered a trivial post as exchange professor of English, one of those Franco-American amity arrangements which is supposed to promote understanding and good will between sister republics. Fillmore was more elated than I by the prospect—he had good reason to be. For me it was just a transfer from one purgatory to another. There was no future ahead of me; there wasn't even a salary attached to the job. One was supposed to consider himself fortunate to enjoy the privilege of spreading the gospel of Franco-American amity. It was a job for a rich man's son.

The night before I left I had a good time. About dawn it began to snow: we walked about from one quarter to another taking a last look at Paris. Passing through the Rue St. Dominique we suddenly fell upon a little square and there was the Eglise Ste. Clotilde. People were going to mass. Fillmore, whose head was still a little cloudy, was bent on going to mass too. "For the fun of it!" as he put it. I felt somewhat uneasy about it; in the first place I had never attended a mass, and in the second place I looked seedy and felt seedy. Fillmore, too, looked rather battered, even more disreputable than myself; his big slouch hat was on assways and his overcoat was still full of sawdust from the last joint we had been in. However, we marched in. The worst they could do would be to throw us out.

I was so astounded by the sight that greeted my eyes that I lost all uneasiness. It took me a little while to get adjusted to the dim light. I stumbled around behind Fillmore, holding his sleeve. A weird, unearthly noise assailed my ears, a sort of hollow drone that rose up out of the cold flagging. A huge, dismal tomb it was with mourners shuffling in and out. A sort of ante-chamber to the world below. Temperature about 55 or 60 Fahrenheit. No music except this undefinable dirge manufactured in the sub-cellar—like a million heads of cauliflower wailing in the dark. People in shrouds were chewing away with that hopeless, dejected look of beggars who hold out their hands in a trance and mumble an unintelligible appeal.

That this sort of thing existed I knew, but then one also knows that there are slaughterhouses and morgues and dissecting rooms. One instinctively avoids such places. In the street I had often passed a priest with a little prayer book in his hands laboriously memorizing his lines. *Idiot,* I would say to myself, and let it go at that. In the street one meets with all forms of dementia and the priest is by no means the most striking. Two thousand years of it has deadened us to the idiocy of it. However, when you are suddenly transported to the very midst of his realm, when you see the little world in which the priest functions like an alarm clock, you are apt to have entirely different sensations.

For a moment all this slaver and twitching of the lips almost began to have a meaning. Something was going on, some kind of dumb show which, not rendering me wholly stupefied, held me spellbound. All over the world, wherever there are these dim-lit tombs, you have this incredible spectacle—the same mean temperature, the same crepuscular glow, the same buzz and drone. All over Christendom, at certain stipulated hours, people in black are grovelling before the altar where the priest stands up with a little book in one hand and a dinner bell or atomizer in the other and mumbles to them in a language which, even if it were comprehensible, no longer contains a shred of meaning. Blessing them, most likely. Blessing the country, blessing the ruler, blessing the firearms and the battleships and the ammunition and the hand grenades. Surrounding him on the altar are little boys dressed like angels of the Lord who sing alto and soprano. Innocent lambs. All in skirts, sexless, like the priest himself who is usually flat-footed and nearsighted to boot. A fine epicene caterwauling. Sex in a jock-strap, to the tune of J.-mol.

I was taking it in as best I could in the dim light. Fascinating and stupefying at the same time. All over the civilized world, I thought to myself. All over the world. Marvelous. Rain or shine, hail, sleet, snow, thunder, lightning, war, famine, pestilence—makes not the slightest difference. Always the same mean temperature, the same mumbo-jumbo, the same high-laced shoes and the little angels of the Lord singing soprano and alto. Near the exit a little slot-box—to carry on the heavenly work. So that God's blessing may rain down upon king and country and battleships and high explosives and tanks and àeroplanes, so that the worker may have more strength in his arms, strength to slaughter horses and cows and sheep, strength to punch holes in iron girders, strength to sew buttons on other people's pants, strength to sell carrots and sewing machines and automobiles, strength to exterminate insects and clean stables and unload garbage cans and scrub lavatories, strength to write headlines and chop tickets in the subway. Strength . . . strength. All that lip-chewing and horn-swoggling just to furnish a little strength!

We were moving about from one spot to another, surveying the scene with that clearheadedness which comes after an all-night session. We must have made ourselves pretty conspicuous shuffling about that way with our coat collars turned up and never once crossing ourselves and never once moving our lips except to whisper some callous remark. Perhaps everything would have passed off without notice if Fillmore hadn't insisted on walking past the altar in the midst of the ceremony. He was looking for the exit, and he thought while he was at it, I suppose, that he would take a good squint at the holy of holies, get a close-up on it, as it were. We had gotten safely by and were marching toward a crack of light which must have been the way out when a priest suddenly stepped out of the gloom and blocked our path. Wanted to know where we were going and what we were doing. We told him politely enough that we were looking for the exit. We said "exit" because at the moment we were so flabbergasted that we couldn't think of the French for exit. Without a word of response he took us firmly by the arm and, opening the door, a side door it was, he gave us a push and out we tumbled into the blinding light of day. It happened so suddenly and unexpectedly that when we hit the sidewalk we were in a daze. We walked a few paces, blinking our eyes, and then instinctively we both turned round; the priest was still standing on the steps, pale as a ghost and scowling like the devil himself. He must have been sore as hell. Later, thinking back on it, I couldn't blame him for it. But at that moment, seeing him with his long skirts and the little skull cap on his cranium, he looked so ridiculous that I burst out laughing. I looked at Fillmore and he began to laugh too. For a full minute we stood there laughing right in the poor bugger's face. He was so bewildered, I guess, that for a moment he didn't know what to do; suddenly, however, he started down the steps on the run, shaking his fist at us as if he were in earnest. When he swung out of the enclosure he was on the gallop. By this time some preservative instinct warned me to get a move on. I grabbed Fillmore by the coat sleeve and started to run. He was saying, like an idiot: "No, no! I won't run!"—"Come on!" I yelled, "we'd better get out of here. That guy's mad clean through." And off we ran, beating it as fast as our legs would carry us.

On the way to Dijon, still laughing about the affair, my thoughts reverted to a ludicrous incident, of a somewhat similar nature, which occurred during my brief sojourn in Florida. It was during the celebrated boom when, like thousands of others, I was caught with my pants down. Trying to extricate myself I got caught, along with a friend of mine, in the very neck of the bottle. Jacksonville, where we were marooned for about six weeks, was practically in a state of siege. Every bum on earth, and a lot of guys who had never been bums before, seemed to have drifted into Jacksonville. The Y.M.C.A., the Salvation Army, the fire houses and police stations, the hotels, the lodging houses, everything was full up. *Complet* absolutely, and signs everywhere to that effect. The residents of Jacksonville had become so hardened that it seemed to me as if they were walking around in coats of mail. It was the old business of food again. Food and a place to flop. Food was coming up from below in trainloads—oranges and grapefruit and all sorts of juicy edibles. We used to pass by the freight sheds looking for rotten fruit—but even that was scarce.

One night, in desperation, I dragged my friend Joe to a synagogue, during the service. It was a reformed congregation and the rabbi impressed me rather favorably. The music got me too—that piercing lamentation of the Jews. As soon as the service was over I marched to the rabbi's study and requested an interview with him. He received me decently enough—until I made clear my mission. Then he grew absolutely frightened. I had only asked him for a hand-out on behalf of my friend Joe and myself. You would have thought, from the way he looked at me, that I had asked to rent the synagogue as a bowling alley. To cap it all, he suddenly asked me point-blank if I was a Jew or not. When I answered no, he seemed perfectly outraged. Why, pray, had I come to a Jewish pastor for aid? I told him naïvely that I had always had more faith in the Jews than in the Gentiles. I said it modestly, as if it were one of my peculiar defects. It was the truth too. But he wasn't a bit flattered. No, siree. He was horrified. To get rid of me he wrote out a note to the Salvation Army people. "That's the place for you to address yourself," he said, and brusquely turned away to tend his flock.

The Salvation Army, of course, had nothing to offer us. If we had had a quarter apiece we might have rented a mattress on the floor. But we hadn't a nickel between us. We went to the park and stretched ourselves out on a bench. It was raining and so we covered ourselves with newspapers. Weren't there more than a half hour, I imagine, when a cop came along and, without a word of warning, gave us such a sound fanning that we were up and on

our feet in a jiffy, and dancing a bit too, though we
weren't in any mood for dancing. I felt so goddamned
sore and miserable, so dejected, so lousy, after being
whacked over the ass by that half-witted bastard, that I
could have blown up the City Hall.

The next morning, in order to get even with these hos-
pitable sons of bitches, we presented ourselves bright and
early at the door of a Catholic priest. This time I let Joe
do the talking. He was Irish and he had a bit of brogue.
He had very soft, blue eyes, too, and he could make them
water a bit when he wanted to. A sister in black opened
the door for us; she didn't ask us inside, however. We
were to wait in the vestibule until she went and called for
the good father. In a few minutes he came, the good father, puffing like a locomotive. And what was it we
wanted disturbing his likes at that hour of the morning?
Something to eat and a place to flop, we answered inno-
cently. And where did we hail from, the good father
wanted to know at once. From New York. From New
York, eh? Then ye'd better be gettin' back there as fast as
ye kin, me lads, and without another word the big,
bloated turnip-faced bastard shoved the door in our face.

About an hour later, drifting around helplessly like a
couple of drunken schooners, we happened to pass by the
rectory again. So help me God if the big, lecherous-
looking turnip wasn't backing out of the alley in a limousine! As he swung past us he blew a cloud of smoke into
our eyes. As though to say—"*That* for you!" A beautiful
limousine it was, with a couple of spare tires in the back,
and the good father sitting at the wheel with a big cigar
in his mouth. Must have been a Corona-Corona, so fat
and luscious it was. Sitting pretty he was, and no two
ways about it. I couldn't see whether he had skirts on or
not. I could only see the gravy trickling from his lips—
and the big cigar with that fifty cent aroma.

All the way to Dijon I got to reminiscing about the
past. I thought of all the things I might have said and
done, which I hadn't said or done, in the bitter, humiliat-
ing moments when just to ask for a crust of bread is to
make yourself less than a worm. Stone sober as I was, I
was still smarting from those old insults and injuries. I
could still feel that whack over the ass which the cop

gave me in the park—though that was a mere bagatelle, a little dancing lesson, you might say. All over the States I wandered, and into Canada and Mexico. The same story everywhere. If you want bread you've got to get in harness, get in lock-step. Over all the earth a gray desert, a carpet of steel and cement. Production! More nuts and bolts, more barbed wire, more dog-biscuits, more lawn-mowers, more ball-bearings, more high explosives, more tanks, more poison gas, more soap, more tooth-paste, more newspapers, more education, more churches, more libraries, more museums. *Forward!* Time presses. The embryo is pushing through the neck of the womb, and there's not even a gob of spit to ease the passage. A dry, strangulating birth. Not a wail, not a chirp. *Salut au monde!* Salute of twenty-one guns bombinating from the rectum. "I wear my hat as I please, indoors or out," said Walt. That was a time when you could still get a hat to fit your head. But time passes. To get a hat that fits now you have to walk to the electric chair. They give you a skull cap. A tight fit, what? But no matter! It fits.

You have to be in a strange country like France, walking the meridian that separates the hemispheres of life and death, to know what incalculable vistas yawn ahead. *The body electric! The democratic soul! Flood-tide!* Holy Mother of God, what does this crap mean? The earth is parched and cracked. Men and women come together like broods of vultures over a stinking carcass, to mate and fly apart again. Vultures who drop from the clouds like heavy stones. Talons and beak, that's what we are! A huge intestinal apparatus with a nose for dead meat. *Forward!* Forward without pity, without compassion, without love, without forgiveness. Ask no quarter and give none! More battleships, more poison gas, more high explosives! More gonococci! More streptococci! More bombing machines! More and more of it—until the whole fucking works is blown to smithereens, and the earth with it!

Stepping off the train I knew immediately that I had made a fatal mistake. The Lycée was a little distance from the station; I walked down the main street in the early dusk of winter, feeling my way towards my destination. A light snow was falling, the trees sparkled with frost. Passed a couple of huge, empty cafes that looked like dismal waiting rooms. Silent, empty gloom—that's how it impressed me. A hopeless, jerk-water town where mustard is turned out in carload lots, in vats and tuns and barrels and pots and cute-looking little jars.

The first glance at the Lycée sent a shudder through me. I felt so undecided that at the entrance I stopped to debate whether I would go in or not. But as I hadn't the price of a return ticket there wasn't much use debating the question. I thought for a moment of sending a wire to Fillmore, but then I was stumped to know what excuse to make. The only thing to do was to walk in with my eyes shut.

It happened that M. le Proviseur was out—his day off, so they said. A little hunchback came forward and offered to escort me to the office of M. le Censeur, second in charge. I walked a little behind him, fascinated by the grotesque way in which he hobbled along. He was a little monster, such as can be seen on the porch of any half-assed cathedral in Europe.

The office of M. le Censeur was large and bare. I sat down in a stiff chair to wait while the hunchback darted off to search for him. I almost felt at home. The atmosphere of the place reminded me vividly of certain charity bureaus back in the States where I used to sit by the hour waiting for some mealy-mouthed bastard to come and cross-examine me.

Suddenly the door opened and, with a mincing step, M. le Censeur came prancing in. It was all I could do to suppress a titter. He had on just such a frock coat as Boris used to wear, and over his forehead there hung a bang, a sort of spitcurl such as Smerdiakov might have worn. Grave and brittle, with a lynx-like eye, he wasted no words of cheer on me. At once he brought forth the sheets on which were written the names of the students, the hours, the classes, etc., all in a meticulous hand. He told me how much coal and wood I was allowed and after that he promptly informed me that I was at liberty to do as I pleased in my spare time. This last was the first good thing I had heard him say. It sounded so reassuring that I quickly said a prayer for France—for the army and navy, the educational system, the *bistrots,* the whole *god-damned works.*

This fol-de-rol completed, he rang a little bell, whereupon the hunchback promptly appeared to escort me to the office of M. l'Econome. Here the atmosphere was somewhat different. More like a freight-station, with bills of lading and rubber stamps everywhere, and pasty-faced clerks scribbling away with broken pens in huge, cumbersome ledgers. My dole of coal and wood portioned out, off we marched, the hunchback and I, with a wheelbarrow, towards the dormitory. I was to have a room on the top floor, in the same wing as the *pions*. The situation was taking on a humorous aspect. I didn't know what the hell to expect next. Perhaps a spittoon. The whole thing smacked very much of preparation for a campaign; the only things missing were a knapsack and rifle—and a brass slug.

The room assigned to me was rather large, with a small stove to which was attached a crooked pipe that made an elbow just over the iron cot. A big chest for the coal and wood stood near the door. The windows gave out on a row of forlorn little houses all made of stone in which lived the grocer, the baker, the shoemaker, the butcher, etc.—all imbecilic-looking clodhoppers. I glanced over the rooftops towards the bare hills where a train was clattering. The whistle of the locomotive screamed mournfully and hysterically.

After the hunchback had made the fire for me I inquired about the grub. It was not quite time for dinner. I flopped on the bed, with my overcoat on, and pulled the covers over me. Beside me was the eternal rickety night table in which the piss pot is hidden away. I stood the alarm on the table and watched the minutes ticking off. Into the well of the room a bluish light filtered in from the street. I listened to the trucks rattling by as I gazed vacantly at the stove pipe, at the elbow where it was held together with bits of wire. The coal chest intrigued me. Never in my life had I occupied a room with a coal chest. And never in my life had I built a fire or taught children. Nor, for that matter, never in my life had I worked without pay. I felt free and chained at the same time—like one feels just before election, when all the crooks have been nominated and you are beseeched to vote for the right man. I felt like a hired man, like a jack-of-all-trades,

like a hunter, like a rover, like a galley-slave, like a ped-
agogue, like a worm and a louse. I was free, but my limbs
were shackled. A democratic soul with a free meal ticket,
but no power of locomotion, no voice. I felt like a jelly-
fish nailed to a plank. Above all, I felt hungry. The hands
were moving slowly. Still ten more minutes to kill before
the fire alarm would go off. The shadows in the room
deepened. It grew frightfully silent, a tense stillness that
tautened my nerves. Little dabs of snow clung to the
window-panes. Far away a locomotive gave out a shrill
scream. Then a dead silence again. The stove had commenced to glow, but there was no heat coming from it. I
began to fear that I might doze off and miss the dinner.
That would mean lying awake on an empty belly all
night. I got panic-stricken.

Just a moment before the gong went off I jumped out
of bed and, locking the door behind me, I bolted downstairs to the courtyard. There I got lost. One quadrangle
after another, one staircase after another. I wandered in
and out of the buildings searching frantically for the refectory. Passed a long line of youngsters marching in a
column to God knows where; they moved along like a
chain-gang, with a slave-driver at the head of the column.
Finally I saw an energetic-looking individual, with a
derby, heading towards me. I stopped him to ask the way
to the refectory. Happened I stopped the right man. It was
M. le Proviseur, and he seemed delighted to have stumbled on me. Wanted to know right away if I were comfortably settled, if there was anything more he could do
for me. I told him everything was O. K. Only it was a bit
chilly, I ventured to add. He assured me that it was rather
unusual, this weather. Now and then the fogs came on
and a bit of snow, and then it became unpleasant for a
while, and so on and so forth. All the while he had me by
the arm, guiding me towards the refectory. He seemed
like a very decent chap. A regular guy, I thought to myself. I even went so far as to imagine that I might get
chummy with him later on, that he'd invite me to his
room on a bitter cold night and make a hot grog for me.
I imagined all sorts of friendly things in the few moments
it required to reach the door of the refectory. Here, my
mind racing on at a mile a minute, he suddenly shook

hands with me and, doffing his hat, bade me good night. I was so bewildered that I tipped my hat also. It was the regular thing to do, I soon found out. Whenever you pass a prof, or even M. l'Econome, you doff the hat. Might pass the same guy a dozen times a day. Makes no difference. You've got to give the salute, even though your hat is worn out. It's the polite thing to do.

Anyway, I had found the refectory. Like an East Side clinic it was, with tiled walls, bare light, and marble-topped tables. And of course a big stove with an elbow-pipe. The dinner wasn't served yet. A cripple was running in and out with dishes and knives and forks and bottles of wine. In a corner several young men conversing animatedly. I went up to them and introduced myself. They gave me a most cordial reception. Almost too cordial, in fact. I couldn't quite make it out. In a jiffy the room began to fill up; I was presented from one to the other quickly. Then they formed a circle about me and, filling the glasses, they began to sing. . . .

> "L'autre soir l'idée m'est venue
> Cré nom de Zeus d'enculer un pendu;
> Le vent se lève sur la potence,
> Voilà mon pendu qui se balance,
> J'ai dû l'enculer en sautant,
> Cré nom de Zeus, on est jamais content.

> "Baiser dans un con trop petit,
> Cré nom de Zeus, on s'écorche le vit;
> Baiser dans un con trop large,
> On ne sait pas où l'on décharge;
> Se branler étant bien emmerdant,
> Cré nom de Zeus, on est jamais content."

With this, Quasimodo announced the dinner.

They were a cheerful group, *les surveillants*. There was Kroa who belched like a pig and always let out a loud fart when he sat down to table. He could fart thirteen times in succession, they informed me. He held the record. Then there was Monsieur le Prince, an athlete who was fond of wearing a tuxedo in the evening when he went to town; he had a beautiful complexion, just like a girl, and never touched the wine nor read anything that might tax his brain. Next him sat Petit Paul, from the Midi, who thought of nothing but cunt all the time; he used to say every day—*"à partir de jeudi je ne parlerai plus de femmes."* He and Monsieur le Prince were inseparable. Then there was Passeleau, a veritable young scallywag who was studying medicine and who borrowed right and left; he talked incessantly of Ronsard, Villon and Rabelais. Opposite me sat Mollesse, agitator and organizer of the *pions,* who insisted on weighing the meat to see if it wasn't short a few grams. He occupied a little room in the infirmary. His supreme enemy was Monsieur l'Econome, which was nothing particularly to his credit since everybody hated this individual. For companion Mollesse had one called Le Pénible, a dour-looking chap with a hawk-like profile who practised the strictest economy and acted as money-lender. He was like an engraving by Albrecht Durer—a composite of all the dour, sour, morose, bitter, unfortunate, unlucky and introspective devils who compose the pantheon of Germany's medieval knights. A Jew, no doubt. At any rate, he was killed in an automobile accident shortly after my arrival, a circumstance which left me twenty-three francs to the good. With the exception of Renaud who sat beside me, the others have faded out of my memory; they belonged to that category of colorless individuals who make up the world of engineers, architects, dentists, pharmacists, teachers, etc. There was nothing to distinguish them from the clods whom they would later wipe their boots on. They were zeros in every sense of the word, ciphers who form the nucleus of a respectable and lamentable citizenry. They ate with their heads down and were always the first to clamor for a second helping. They slept soundly and never complained; they were neither gay nor miserable. The indifferent ones whom Dante consigned to the vestibule of Hell. The upper-crusters.

It was the custom after dinner to go immediately to town, unless one was on duty in the dormitories. In the center of town were the cafés—huge, dreary halls where the somnolent merchants of Dijon gathered to play cards and listen to music. It was warm in the cafés, that is the best I can say for them. The seats were fairly comfortable, too. And there were always a few whores about who, for a glass of beer or a cup of coffee, would sit and chew the fat with you. The music, on the other hand, was atrocious. Such music! On a winter's night, in a dirty hole like Dijon, nothing can be more harassing, more nerve-racking, than the sound of a French orchestra. Particularly one of those lugubrious female orchestras with everything coming in squeaks and farts, with a dry, algebraic rhythm and the hygienic consistency of tooth-paste. A wheezing and scraping performed at so many francs the hour—and the devil take the hindmost! The melancholy of it! As if old Euclid had stood up on his hind legs and swallowed Prussic acid. The whole realm of Idea so thoroughly exploited by the reason that there is nothing left of which to make music except the empty slats of the accordion, through which the wind whistles and tears the ether to tatters. However, to speak of music in connection with this outpost is like dreaming of champagne when you are in the death-cell. Music was the least of my worries. I didn't even think of cunt, so dismal, so chill, so barren, so gray was it all. On the way home the first night I noticed on the door of a café an inscription from the *Gargantua*. Inside the café it was like a morgue. However, *forward*!

I had plenty of time on my hands and not a sou to spend. Two or three hours of conversational lessons a day, and that was all. And what use was it, teaching these poor bastards English? I felt sorry as hell for them. All morning plugging away on *John Gilpin's Ride,* and in the afternoon coming to me to practise a dead language. I thought of the good time I had wasted reading Vergil or wading through such incomprehensible nonsense as *Hermann und Dorotea.* The insanity of it! Learning, the empty bread-basket! I thought of Carl who can recite *Faust* backwards, who never writes a book without praising the shit out of his immortal, incorruptible Gœthe. And yet he hadn't sense enough to take on a rich cunt and get himself a change of underwear. There's something obscene in this love of the past which ends in bread-lines and dug-outs. Something obscene about this spiritual racket which permits an idiot to sprinkle holy water over Big Berthas and dreadnoughts and high explosives. Every man with a bellyful of the classics is an enemy to the human race.

Here was I, supposedly to spread the gospel of Franco-American amity—the emissary of a corpse who, after he had plundered right and left, after he had caused untold suffering and misery, dreamed of establishing universal peace. Pfui! What did they expect me to talk about, I wonder? About *Leaves of Grass,* about the tariff walls, about the Declaration of Independence, about the latest gang war? What? Just what, I'd like to know. Well, I'll tell you—I never mentioned these things. I started right off the bat with a lesson in the physiology of love. How the elephants make love—that was it! It caught like wildfire. After the first day there were no more empty benches. After that first lesson in English they were standing at the door waiting for me. We got along swell together. They asked all sorts of questions, as though they had never learned a damned thing. I let them fire away. I taught them to ask still more ticklish questions. *Ask anything!*—that was my motto. I'm here as a plenipotentiary from the realm of free spirits. I'm here to create a fever and a ferment. "In some way," says an eminent astronomer, "the material universe appears to be passing away like a tale that is told, dissolving into nothingness like a vision." That seems to be the general feeling underlying the empty bread-basket of learning. Myself, I don't believe it. I don't believe a fucking thing these bastards try to shove down our throats.

Between sessions, if I had no book to read, I would go upstairs to the dormitory and chat with the *pions*. They were delightfully ignorant of all that was going on—especially in the world of art. Almost as ignorant as the students themselves. It was as if I had gotten into a private little madhouse with no exit signs. Sometimes I snooped around under the arcades, watching the kids marching along with huge hunks of bread stuck in their dirty mugs. I was always hungry myself, since it was impossible for me to go to breakfast which was handed out at some ungodly hour of the morning, just when the bed was getting toasty. Huge bowls of blue coffee with chunks of white bread and no butter to go with it. For lunch, beans or lentils with bits of meat thrown in to make it look appetizing. Food fit for a chain-gang, for rock-breakers. Even the wine was lousy. Things were either diluted or bloated. There were calories, but no cuisine. M. l'Econome was responsible for it all. So they said. I don't believe that, either. He was paid to keep our heads just above the water line. He didn't ask if we were suffering from piles or carbuncles; he didn't inquire if we had delicate palates or the intestines of wolves. Why should he? He was hired at so many grams the plate to produce so many kilowatts of energy. Everything in terms of horse power. It was all carefully reckoned in the fat ledgers which the pasty-faced clerks scribbled in morning, noon and night. Debit and credit, with a red line down the middle of the page.

Roaming around the quadrangle with an empty belly most of the time I got to feel slightly mad. Like Charles the Silly, poor devil—only I had no Odette Champsdivers with whom to play stink-finger. Half the time I had to grub cigarettes from the students, and during the lessons sometimes I munched a bit of dry bread with them. As the fire was always going out on me I soon used up my allotment of wood. It was the devil's own time coaxing a little wood out of the ledger clerks. Finally I got so riled up about it that I would go out in the street and hunt for firewood, like an Arab. Astonishing how little firewood you could pick up in the streets of Dijon. However, these little foraging expeditions brought me into strange precincts: Got to know the little street named after a M. Philibert Papillon—a dead musician, I believe—where there was a cluster of whorehouses. It was always more cheerful hereabouts; there was the smell of cooking, and wash hanging out to dry. Once in a while I caught a glimpse of the poor half-wits who lounged about inside. They were better off than the poor devils in the center of town whom I used to bump into whenever I walked through a department store. I did that frequently in order to get warm. They were doing it for the same reason, I suppose. Looking for someone to buy them a coffee. They looked a little crazy, with the cold and the loneliness. The whole town looked a bit crazy when the blue of evening settled over it. You could walk up and down the main drive any Thursday in the week till doomsday and never meet an expansive soul. Sixty or seventy thousand people—perhaps more—wrapped in woolen underwear and nowhere to go and nothing to do. Turning out mustard by the carload. Female orchestras grinding out *The Merry Widow*. Silver service in the big hotels. The ducal palace rotting away, stone by stone, limb by limb. The trees screeching with frost. A ceaseless clatter of wooden shoes. The University celebrating the death of Gœthe, or the birth, I don't remember which. (Usually it's the deaths that are celebrated.) Idiotic affair, anyway. Everybody yawning and stretching.

Coming through the high driveway into the quadrangle a sense of abysmal futility always came over me. Outside bleak and empty; inside, bleak and empty. A scummy sterility hanging over the town, a fog of book-learning. Slag and cinders of the past. Around the interior courts were ranged the class rooms, little shacks such as you might see in the North woods, where the pedagogues gave free rein to their vices. On the black-board the futile abracadabra which the future citizens of the republic would have to spend their lives forgetting. Once in a while the parents were received in the big reception room just off the driveway, where there were busts of the heroes of antiquity, such as Molière, Racine, Corneille, Voltaire, etc., all the scarecrows whom the cabinet ministers mention with moist lips whenever an immortal is added to the waxworks. (No bust of Villon, no bust of Rabelais, no bust of Rimbaud.) Anyway, they met here in solemn conclave, the parents and the stuffed shirts whom the State hires to bend the minds of the young. Always this bending process, this landscape gardening to make the mind more attractive. And the youngsters came too, occasionally—the little sunflowers who would soon be transplanted from the nursery in order to decorate the municipal grassplots. Some of them were just rubber plants easily dusted with a torn chemise. All of them jerking away for dear life in the dormitories as soon as night came on. The dormitories! where the red lights glowed, where the bell rang like a fire-alarm, where the treads were hollowed out in the scramble to reach the educational cells.

Then there were the profs! During the first few days I

got so far as to shake hands with a few of them, and of course there was always the salute with the hat when we passed under the arcades. But as for a heart-to-heart talk, as for walking to the corner and having a drink together, nothing doing. It was simply unimaginable. Most of them looked as though they had had the shit scared out of them. Anyway, I belonged to another hierarchy. They wouldn't even share a louse with the likes of me. They made me so damned irritated, just to look at them, that I used to curse them under my breath when I saw them coming. I used to stand there, leaning against a pillar, with a cigarette in the corner of my mouth and my hat down over my eyes, and when they got within hailing distance I would let squirt a good gob and up with the hat. I didn't even bother to open my trap and bid them the time of the day. Under my breath I simply said: "Fuck you, Jack!" and let it go at that.

After a week it seemed as if I had been here all my life. It was like a bloody, fucking nightmare that you can't throw off. Used to fall into a coma thinking about it. Just a few days ago I had arrived. Nightfall. People scurrying home like rats under the foggy lights. The trees glittering with diamond-pointed malice. I thought it all out, a thousand times or more. From the station to the Lycée it was like a promenade through the Danzig Corridor, all deckle-edged, crannied, nerve-ridden. A lane of dead bones, of crooked, cringing figures buried in shrouds. Spines made of sardine bones. The Lycée itself seemed to rise up out of a lake of thin snow, an inverted mountain that pointed down toward the center of the earth where God or the Devil works always in a strait-jacket grinding grist for that paradise which is always a wet dream. If the sun ever shone I don't remember it. I remember nothing but the cold greasy fogs that blew in from the frozen marshes over yonder where the railroad tracks burrowed into the lurid hills. Down near the station was a canal, or perhaps it was a river, hidden away under a yellow sky, with little shacks pasted slap-up against the rising ledge of the banks. There was a barracks too somewhere, it struck me, because every now and then I met little yellow men from Cochin-China—squirmy, opium-faced runts peeping out of their baggy uniforms like dyed skeletons packed in excelsior. The whole god-damned medievalism of the place was infernally ticklish and restive, rocking back and forth with low moans, jumping out at you from the eaves, hanging like broken-necked criminals from the gargoyles. I kept looking back all the time, kept walking like a crab that you prong with a dirty fork. All those fat little monsters, those slab-like effigies pasted on the façade of the Eglise St. Michel, they were following me down the crooked lanes and around corners. The whole façade of St. Michel seemed to open up like an album at night, leaving you face to face with the horrors of the printed page. When the lights went out and the characters faded away flat, dead as words, then it was quite magnificent, the façade; in every crevice of the old gnarled front there was the hollow chant of the nightwind and over the lacy rubble of cold stiff vestments there was a cloudy absinthe-like drool of fog and frost.

Here, where the church stood, everything seemed turned hind side front. The church itself must have been twisted off its base by centuries of progress in the rain and snow. It lay in the Place Edgar-Quinet, squat against the wind, like a dead mule. Through the Rue de la Monnaie the wind rushed like white hair streaming wild: it whirled around the white hitching posts which obstructed the free passage of omnibuses and twenty-mule teams. Swinging through this exit in the early morning hours I sometimes stumbled upon Monsieur Renaud who, wrapped in his cowl like a gluttonous monk, made overtures to me in the language of the 16th century. Falling in step with Monsieur Renaud, the moon busting through the greasy sky like a punctured balloon, I fell immediately into the realm of the transcendental. M. Renaud had a precise speech, dry as apricots, with a heavy Brandenburger base. Used to come at me full tilt from Gœthe or Fichte, with deep base notes that rumbled in the windy corners of the *Place* like claps of last year's thunder. Men of Yucatan, men of Zanzibar, men of Tierra del Fuego, save me from this glaucous hog-rind! The North piles up about me, the glacial fjords, the blue-tipped spines, the crazy lights, the obscene Christian chant that spread like an avalanche from Aetna to the Aegean. Everything frozen tight as scum, the mind locked and rimed with frost, and through the melancholy bales of chitter-wit the choking gargle of louse-eaten saints. White I am and wrapped in wool, swaddled, fettered, ham-strung, but in this I have no part. White to the bone, but with a cold alkali base, with saffron-tipped fingers. White, aye, but no brother of learning, no Catholic heart. White and ruthless, as the men before me who sailed out of the Elbe. I look to the sea, to the sky, to what is unintelligible and distantly near.

The snow under foot scurries before the wind, blows, tickles, stings, lisps away, whirls aloft, showers, splinters, sprays down. No sun, no roar of surf, no breaker's surge. The cold north wind pointed with barbed shafts, icy, malevolent, greedy, blighting, paralyzing. The streets turn away on their crooked elbows; they break from the hurried sight, the stern glance. They hobble away down the drifting lattice-work, wheeling the church hind side front, mowing down the statues, flattening the monuments, uprooting the trees, stiffening the grass, sucking the fragrance out of the earth. Leaves dull as cement: leaves no dew can bring to glisten again. No moon will ever silver their listless plight. The seasons are come to a stagnant stop, the trees blench and wither, the wagons roll in the mica ruts with slithering harp-like thuds. In the hollow of the white-tipped hills, lurid and boneless Dijon slumbers. No man alive and walking through the night except the restless spirits moving southward towards the sapphire grids. Yet I am up and about, a walking ghost, a white man terrorized by the cold sanity of this slaughter house geometry. Who am I? What am I doing here? I fall between the cold walls of human malevolence, a white figure fluttering, sinking down through the cold lake, a mountain of skulls above me. I settle down to the cold latitudes, the chalk steps washed with indigo. The earth in its dark corridors knows my step, feels a foot abroad, a wing stirring, a gasp and a shudder. I hear the learning chaffed and chuzzled, the figures mounting upward, bat-slime dripping aloft and clanging with pasteboard golden wings; I hear the trains collide, the chains rattle, the locomotive chugging, snorting, sniffing, steaming and pissing. All things come to me through the clear fog with the odor of repetition, with yellow hangovers and gadzooks and whettikins. In the dead center, far below Dijon, far below the hyperborean regions, stands God Ajax, his shoulders strapped to the mill wheel, the olives crunching, the green marsh water alive with croaking frogs.

The fog and snow, the cold latitude, the heavy learning, the blue coffee, the unbuttered bread, the soup and lentils, the heavy pork-packer beans, the stale cheese, the soggy chow, the lousy wine has put the whole penitentiary into a state of constipation. And just when everyone has become shit-tight the toilet pipes freeze. The shit piles up like ant-hills; one has to move down from the little pedestals and leave it on the floor. It lies there stiff and frozen, waiting for the thaw. On Thursdays the hunchback comes with his little wheelbarrow, shovels the cold, stiff turds with a broom and pan, and trundles off dragging his withered leg. The corridors are littered with toilet paper; it sticks to your feet like fly-paper. When the weather moderates the odor gets ripe; you can smell it in Winchester forty miles away. Standing over that ripe dung in the morning, with a toothbrush, the stench is so powerful that it makes your head spin. We stand around in red flannel shirts, waiting to spit down the hole; it is like an aria from one of Verdi's operas—an anvil chorus with pulleys and syringes. In the night, when I am taken short, I rush down to the private toilet of M. le Censeur, just off the driveway. My stool is always full of blood. His toilet doesn't flush either but at least there is the pleasure of sitting down. I leave my little bundle for him as a token of esteem.

Towards the end of the meal each evening the *veilleur de nuit* drops in for his bit of cheer. This is the only human being in the whole institution with whom I feel a kinship. He is a nobody. He carries a lantern and a bunch of keys. He makes the rounds through the night, stiff as an automaton. About the time the stale cheese is being passed around, in he pops for his glass of wine. He stands there, with paw outstretched, his hair stiff and wiry, like a mastiff's, his cheeks ruddy, his moustache gleaming with snow. He mumbles a word or two and Quasimodo brings him the bottle. Then, with feet solidly planted, he throws back his head and down it goes, slowly in one long draught. To me it's like he's pouring rubies down his gullet. Something about this gesture which seizes me by the hair. It's almost as if he were drinking down the dregs of human sympathy, as if all the love and compassion in the world could be tossed off like that, in one gulp—as if that were all that could be squeezed together day after day. A little less than a rabbit they have made him. In the scheme of things he's not worth the brine to pickle a herring. He's just a piece of live manure. And he knows it. When he looks around after his drink and smiles at us, the world seems to be falling to pieces. It's a smile thrown across an abyss. The whole stinking civilized world lies like a quagmire at the bottom of the pit, and over it, like a mirage, hovers this wavering smile.

It was the same smile which greeted me at night when I returned from my rambles. I remember one such night when, standing at the door waiting for the old fellow to finish his rounds, I had such a sense of well-being that I could have waited thus forever. I had to wait perhaps half an hour before he opened the door. I looked about me calmly and leisurely, drank everything in, the dead tree in front of the school with its twisted rope branches, the houses across the street which had changed color during the night, which curved now more noticeably, the sound of a train rolling through the Siberian wastes, the railings painted by Utrillo, the sky, the deep wagon-ruts. Suddenly, out of nowhere, two lovers appeared; every few yards they stopped and embraced, and when I could no longer follow them with my eyes I followed the sound of their steps, heard the abrupt stop, and then the slow, meandering gait. I could feel the sag and slump of their bodies when they leaned against a rail, heard their shoes creak as the muscles tightened for the embrace. Through the town they wandered, through the crooked streets, towards the glassy canal where the water lay black as coal. There was something phenomenal about it. In all Dijon not two like them.

Meanwhile the old fellow was making the rounds; I could hear the jingle of his keys; the crunching of his boots, the steady, automatic tread. Finally I heard him coming through the driveway to open the big door, a

monstrous, arched portal without a moat in front of it. I
heard him fumbling at the lock, his hands stiff, his mind
numbed. As the door swung open I saw over his head a
brilliant constellation crowning the chapel. Every door
was locked, every cell bolted. The books were closed.
The night hung close, dagger-pointed, drunk as a maniac.
There it was, the infinitude of emptiness. Over the chapel, like a bishop's mitre, hung the constellation, every
night, during the winter months, it hung there low over
the chapel. Low and bright, a handful of dagger points, a
dazzle of pure emptiness. The old fellow followed me to
the turn of the drive. The door closed silently. As I bade
him good night I caught that desperate, hopeless smile
again, like a meteoric flash over the rim of a lost world.
And again I saw him standing in the refectory, his head
thrown back and the rubies pouring down his gullet. The
whole Mediterranean seemed to be buried inside him—
the orange groves, the cypress trees, the winged statues,
the wooden temples, the blue sea, the stiff masks, the
mystic numbers, the mythological birds, the sapphire
skies, the eaglets, the sunny coves, the blind bards, the
bearded heroes. Gone all that. Sunk beneath the avalanche from the North. Buried, dead forever. A memory.
A wild hope.

For just a moment I linger at the carriageway. The
shroud, the pall, the unspeakable, clutching emptiness of
it all. Then I walk quickly along the gravel path near the
wall, past the arches and columns, the iron staircases,
from one quadrangle to the other. Everything is locked
tight. Locked for the winter. I find the arcade leading to
the dormitory. A sickish light spills down over the stairs
from the grimy, frosted windows. Everywhere the paint is
peeling off. The stones are hollowed out, the bannister
creaks; a damp sweat oozes from the flagging and forms
a pale, fuzzy aura pierced by the feeble red light at the
head of the stairs. I mount the last flight, the turret, in a
sweat and terror. In pitch darkness I grope my way
through the deserted corridor, every room empty, locked,
moulding away. My hand slides along the wall seeking
the keyhole. A panic comes over me as I grasp the door-
knob. Always a hand at my collar ready to yank me back.
Once inside the room I bolt the door. It's a miracle which

I perform each night, the miracle of getting inside without being strangled, without being struck down by an axe. I can hear the rats scurrying through the corridor, gnawing away over my head between the thick rafters. The light glares like burning sulphur and there is the sweet, sickish stench of a room which is never ventilated. In the corner stands the coal-box, just as I left it. The fire is out. A silence so intense that it sounds like Niagara Falls in my ears.

Alone, with a tremendous empty longing and dread. The whole room for my thoughts. Nothing but myself and what I think, what I fear. Could think the most fantastic thoughts, could dance, spit, grimace, curse, wail—nobody would ever know, nobody would ever hear. The thought of such absolute privacy is enough to drive me mad. It's like a clean birth. Everything cut away. Separate, naked, alone. Bliss and agony simultaneously. Time on your hands. Each second weighing on you like a mountain. You drown in it. Deserts, seas, lakes, oceans. Time beating away like a meat-axe. Nothingness. The world. The me and the not-me. *Oomaharamooma.* Everything has to have a name. Everything has to be learned, tested, experienced. *Faites comme chez vous, chéri.*

The silence descends in volcanic chutes. Yonder, in the barren hills, rolling onward towards the great metallurgical regions, the locomotives are pulling their merchant products. Over steel and iron beds they roll, the ground sown with slag and cinders and purple ore. In the baggage car, kelps, fishplate, rolled iron, sleepers, wire rods, plates and sheets, laminated articles, hot rolled hoops, splints and mortar carriages, and Zorès ore. The wheels U-80 millimetres or over. Pass splendid specimens of Anglo-Norman architecture, pass pedestrians and pederasts, open hearth furnaces, basic Bessemer mills, dynamos and transformers, pig iron castings and steel ingots. The public at large, pedestrians and pederasts, gold-fish and spun-glass palm trees, donkeys sobbing, all circulating freely through quincuncial alleys. At the Place du Brésil a lavender eye.

Going back in a flash over the women I've known. It's like a chain which I've forged out of my own misery. Each one bound to the other. A fear of living separate, of staying born. The door of the womb always on the latch. Dread and longing. Deep in the blood the pull of Paradise. The beyond. Always the beyond. It must have all started with the navel. They cut the umbilical cord, give you a slap on the ass, and presto! you're out in the world, adrift, a ship without a rudder. You look at the stars and then you look at your navel. You grow eyes everywhere—in the armpits, between your lips, in the roots of your hair, on the soles of your feet. What is distant becomes near, what is near becomes distant. Inner-outer, a constant flux, a shedding of skins, a turning inside out. You drift around like that for years and years, until you find yourself in the dead center, and there you slowly rot, slowly crumble to pieces, get dispersed again. Only your name remains.

It was spring before I managed to escape from the penitentiary, and then only by a stroke of fortune. A telegram from Carl informed me one day that there was a vacancy "upstairs;" he said he would send me the fare back if I decided to accept. I telegraphed back at once and as soon as the dough arrived I beat it to the station. Not a word to M. le Proviseur or anyone. French leave, as they say.

I went immediately to the hotel at 1 *bis,* where Carl was staying. He came to the door stark naked. It was his night off and there was a cunt in the bed as usual. "Don't mind her," he says, "she's asleep. If you need a lay you can take her on. She's not bad." He pulls the covers back to show me what she looks like. However, I wasn't thinking about a lay right away. I was too excited. I was like a man who has just escaped from jail. I just wanted to see and hear things. Coming from the station it was like a long dream. I felt as though I had been away for years.

It was not until I had sat down and taken a good look at the room that I realized I was back again in Paris. It was Carl's room and no mistake about it. Like a squirrel-cage and shit-house combined. There was hardly room on the table for the portable machine he used. It was always like that, whether he had a cunt with him or not. Always a dictionary lying open on a gilt-edged volume of *Faust,* always a tobacco pouch, a beret, a bottle of *vin rouge,* letters, manuscripts, old newspapers, water colors, teapot, dirty socks, toothpicks, Kruschen Salts, condoms, etc. In the *bidet* were orange peels and the remnants of a ham sandwich.

"There's some food in the closet," he said. "Help yourself! I was just going to give myself an injection."

I found the sandwich he was talking about and a piece of cheese that he had nibbled at beside it. While he sat on the edge of the bed, dosing himself with his argyrol, I put away the sandwich and cheese with the aid of a little wine.

"I liked that letter you sent me about Goethe," he said, wiping his prick with a dirty pair of drawers.

"I'll show you the answer to it in a minute—I'm putting it in my book. The trouble with you is that you're not a German. You have to be German to understand Goethe. Shit, I'm not going to explain it to you now. I've put it all in the book . . . By the way, I've got a new cunt now—not this one—this one's a half-wit. At least, I had her until a few days ago. I'm not sure now whether she'll come back or not. She was living here with me all the time you were away. The other day her parents came and took her away. They said she was only fifteen. Can you beat that? They scared the shit out of me too. . . ."

I began to laugh. It was like Carl to get himself into a mess like that.

"What are you laughing for?" he said. "I may go to prison for it. Luckily, I didn't knock her up. And that's funny, too, because she never took care of herself properly. But do you know what saved me? So I think, at least. It was *Faust*. Yeah! Her old man happened to see it lying on the table. He asked me if I understood German. One thing led to another and before I knew it he was looking through my books. Fortunately I happened to have the Shakespeare open too. That impressed him like hell. He said I was evidently a very serious guy."

"What about the girl—what did *she* have to say?"

"She was frightened to death. You see, she had a little watch with her when she came; in the excitement we couldn't find the watch, and her mother insisted that the watch be found or she'd call the police. You see how things are here. I turned the whole place upside down—but I couldn't find the god-damned watch. The mother was furious. I liked her too, in spite of everything. She was even better-looking than the daughter. Here—I'll show you a letter I started to write her. I'm in love with her . . ."

"With the *mother*?"

"Sure. Why not? If I had seen the mother first I'd never have looked at the daughter. How did I know she was only fifteen? You don't ask a cunt how old she is before you lay her, do you?"

"Joe, there's something funny about this. You're not shitting me, are you?"

"Am I shitting you? Here—look at this!" And he shows me the water colors the girl had made—cute little things—a knife and a loaf of bread, the table and teapot, everything running uphill. "She was in love with me," he said. "She was just like a child. I had to tell her when to brush her teeth and how to put her hat on. Here—look at the lollypops! I used to buy her a few lollypops every day—she liked them."

"Well, what did she do when her parents came to take her away? Didn't she put up a row?"

"She cried a little, that's all. What *could* she do? She's under age. . . . I had to promise never to see her again, never to write her either. That's what I'm waiting to see now—whether she'll stay away or not. She was a virgin when she came here. The thing is, how long will she be able to go without a lay? She couldn't get enough of it when she was here. She almost wore me out."

By this time the one in bed had come to and was rubbing her eyes. She looked pretty young to me, too. Not bad looking, but dumb as hell. Wanted to know right away what we were talking about.

"She lives here in the hotel," said Carl. "On the third floor. Do you want to go to her room? I'll fix it up for you."

I didn't know whether I wanted to or not, but when I saw Carl mushing it up with her again I decided I did want to. I asked her first if she was too tired. Useless question. A whore is never too tired to open her legs. Some of them can fall asleep while you diddle them. Anyway, it was decided we would go down to her room. Like that I wouldn't have to pay the *patron* for the night.

In the morning I rented a room overlooking the little park down below where the sandwich-board men always came to eat their lunch. At noon I called for Carl to have breakfast with him. He and Van Norden had developed a new habit in my absence—they went to the Coupole for breakfast every day. "Why the Coupole?" I asked. "Why the Coupole?" says Carl. "Because the Coupole serves porridge at all hours and porridge makes you shit."—"I see," said I.

So it's just like it used to be again. The three of us walking back and forth to work. Petty dissensions, petty rivalries. Van Norden still belly-aching about his cunts and about washing the dirt out of his belly. Only now he's found a new diversion. He's found that it's less annoying to masturbate. I was amazed when he broke the news to me. I didn't think it possible for a guy like that to find any pleasure in jerking himself off. I was still more amazed when he explained to me how he goes about it. He had "invented" a new stunt, so he put it. "You take an apple," he says, "and you bore out the core. Then you rub some cold cream on the inside so as it doesn't melt too fast. Try it some time! It'll drive you crazy at first. Anyway, it's cheap and you don't have to waste much time."

"By the way," he says, switching the subject, "that friend of yours, Fillmore, he's in the hospital. I think he's nuts. Anyway, that's what his girl told me. He took on a French girl, you know, while you were away. They used to fight like hell. She's a big, healthy bitch—wild like. I wouldn't mind giving her a tumble, but I'm afraid she'd claw the eyes out of me. He was always going around with his face and hands scratched up. She looks bunged up too once in a while—or she used to. You know how these French cunts are—when they love they lose their minds."

Evidently things had happened while I was away. I was sorry to hear about Fillmore. He had been damned good to me. When I left Van Norden I jumped a bus and went straight to the hospital.

They hadn't decided yet whether he was completely off his base or not, I suppose, for I found him upstairs in a private room, enjoying all the liberties of the regular patients. He had just come from the bath when I arrived. When he caught sight of me he burst into tears. "It's all over," he says immediately. "They say I'm crazy—and I may have syphilis too. They say I have delusions of grandeur." He fell over onto the bed and wept quietly. After he had wept a while he lifted his head up and smiled—

just like a bird coming out of a snooze. "Why do they put me in such an expensive room?" he said. "Why don't they put me in the ward—or in the bughouse? I can't afford to pay for this. I'm down to my last five hundred dollars."

"That's why they're keeping you here," I said. "They'll transfer you quickly enough when your money runs out. Don't worry."

My words must have impressed him, for I had no sooner finished than he handed me his watch and chain, his wallet, his fraternity pin, etc. "Hold on to them," he said. "These bastards'll rob me of everything I've got." And then suddenly he began to laugh, one of those weird, mirthless laughs which makes you believe a guy's goofy whether he is or not. "I know you'll think I'm crazy," he said, "but I want to atone for what I did. I want to get married. You see, I didn't know I had the clap. I gave her the clap and then I knocked her up. I told the doctor I don't care what happens to me, but I want him to let me get married first. He keeps telling me to wait until I get better—but I know I'm never going to get better. This is the end."

I couldn't help laughing myself, hearing him talk that way. I couldn't understand what had come over him. Anyway, I had to promise him to see the girl and explain things to her. He wanted me to stick by her, comfort her. Said he could trust me, etc. I said yes to everything in order to soothe him. He didn't seem exactly nuts to me— just caved-in like. Typical Anglo-Saxon crisis. An eruption of morals. I was rather curious to see the girl, to get the lowdown on the whole thing.

The next day I looked her up. She was living in the Latin Quarter. As soon as she realized who I was she became exceedingly cordial. Ginette she called herself. Rather big, raw-boned, healthy, peasant type with a front tooth half-eaten away. Full of vitality and a kind of crazy fire in her eyes. The first thing she did was to weep. Then, seeing that I was an old friend of her Jo-Jo—that was how she called him—she ran downstairs and brought back a couple of bottles of white wine. I was to stay and have dinner with her—she insisted on it. As she drank she became by turns gay and maudlin. I didn't have to ask her any questions—she went on like a self-winding machine. The thing that worried her principally was—would he get his job back when he was released from the hospital? She said her parents were well off, but they were displeased with her. They didn't approve of her wild ways. They didn't approve of him particularly—he had no manners, and he was an American. She begged me to assure her that he would get his job back, which I did without hesitancy. And then she begged me to know if she could believe what he said—that he was going to marry her. Because now, with a child under her belt, and a dose of clap besides, she was in no position to strike a match—with a Frenchman anyway. That was clear, wasn't it? Of course, I assured her. It was all clear as hell to me—except how in Christ's name Fillmore had ever fallen for her. However, one thing at a time. It was my duty now to comfort her, and so I just filled her up with a lot of baloney, told her everything would turn out all right and that I would stand godfather to the child, etc. Then suddenly it struck me as strange that she should have the child at all—especially as it was likely to be born blind. I told her that as tactfully as I could. "It doesn't make any difference," she said. "I want a child by him."

"Even if it's blind?" I asked.

"Mon Dieu, ne dites pas ça!" she groaned. *"Ne dites pas ça!"*

Just the same, I felt it was my duty to say it. She got hysterical and began to weep like a walrus, poured out more wine. In a few moments she was laughing boisterously. She was laughing to think how they used to fight when they got in bed. "He liked me to fight with him," she said. "He was a brute."

As we sat down to eat a friend of hers walked in—a little tart who lived at the end of the hall. Ginette immediately sent me down to get some more wine. When I came back they had evidently had a good talk. Her friend, Yvette, worked in the police department. A sort of stool pigeon, as far as I could gather. At least that was what she was trying to make me believe. It was fairly obvious that she was just a little whore. But she had an obsession about the police and their doings. Throughout the meal they were urging me to accompany them to a *bal musette*. They wanted to have a gay time—it was so lonely for Ginette with Jo-Jo in the hospital. I told them I had to work, but that on my night off I'd come back and take them out. I made it clear too that I had no dough to spend on them. Ginette, who was really thunderstruck to hear this, pretended that that didn't matter in the least. In fact, just to show what a good sport she was, she insisted on driving me to work in a cab. She was doing it because I was a friend of Jo-Jo's. And therefore I was a friend of hers. "And also," thought I to myself, "if anything goes wrong with your Jo-Jo you'll come to me on the double-quick. Then you'll see what a friend I can be!" I was as nice as pie to her. In fact, when we got out of the cab in front of the office, I permitted them to persuade me into having a final Pernod together. Yvette wanted to know if she couldn't call for me after work. She had a lot of things to tell me in confidence, she said. But I managed to refuse without hurting her feelings. Unfortunately I did unbend sufficiently to give her my address.

Unfortunately, I say. As a matter of fact, I'm rather glad of it when I think back on it. Because the very next day things began to happen. The very next day, before I had even gotten out of bed, the two of them called on me. Jo-Jo had been removed from the hospital—they had incarcerated him in a little château in the country, just a few miles out of Paris. The *château,* they called it. A polite way of saying "the bughouse." They wanted me to get dressed immediately and go with them. They were in a panic.

Perhaps I might have gone alone—but I just couldn't make up my mind to go with these two. I asked them to wait for me downstairs while I got dressed, thinking that it would give me time to invent some excuse for not going. But they wouldn't leave the room. They sat there and watched me wash and dress, just as if it were an everyday affair. In the midst of it, Carl popped in. I gave him the situation briefly, in English, and then we hatched up an excuse that I had some important work to do. However, to smooth things over, we got some wine in and we began to amuse them by showing them a book of dirty drawings. Yvette had already lost all desire to go to the château. She and Carl were getting along famously. When it came time to go Carl decided to accompany them to the château. He thought it would be funny to see Fillmore walking around with a lot of nuts. He wanted to see what it was like in the nuthouse. So off they went, somewhat pickled, and in the best of humor.

All the time that Fillmore was at the château I never once went to see him. It wasn't necessary, because Ginette visited him regularly and gave me all the news. They had hopes of bringing him around in a few months, so she said. They thought it was alcoholic poisoning— nothing more. Of course, he had a dose—but that wasn't difficult to remedy. So far as they could see, he didn't have syphilis. That was something. So, to begin with, they used the stomach pump on him. They cleaned his system out thoroughly. He was so weak for a while that he couldn't get out of bed. He was depressed, too. He said he didn't want to be cured—he wanted to die. And he kept repeating this nonsense so insistently that finally they grew alarmed. I suppose it wouldn't have been a very good recommendation if he had committed suicide. Anyway, they began to give him mental treatment. And in between times they pulled out his teeth, more and more of them, until he didn't have a tooth left in his head. He was supposed to feel fine after that, yet strangely he didn't. He became more despondent than ever. And then his hair began to fall out. Finally he developed a paranoid streak—began to accuse them of all sorts of things, de- manded to know by what right he was being detained, what he had done to warrant being locked up, etc. After a terrible fit of despondency he would suddenly become energetic and threaten to blow up the place if they didn't release him. And to make it worse, as far as Ginette was concerned, he had gotten all over his notion of marrying her. He told her straight up and down that he had no in- tention of marrying her, and that if she was crazy enough to go and have a child then she could support it herself.

The doctors interpreted all this as a good sign. They said he was coming round. Ginette, of course, thought he was crazier than ever, but she was praying for him to be released so that she could take him to the country where it would be quiet and peaceful and where he would come to his right senses. Meanwhile her parents had come to Paris on a visit and had even gone so far as to visit the future son-in-law at the château. In their canny way they had probably figured it out that it would be better for their daughter to have a crazy husband than no husband at all. The father thought he could find something for Fillmore to do on the farm. He said that Fillmore wasn't such a bad chap at all. When he learned from Ginette that Fillmore's parents had money he became even more indulgent, more understanding.

The thing was working itself out nicely all around. Ginette returned to the provinces for a while with her parents. Yvette was coming regularly to the hotel to see Carl. She thought he was the editor of the paper. And little by little she became more confidential. When she got good and tight one day, she informed us that Ginette had never been anything but a whore, that Ginette was a bloodsucker, that Ginette never had been pregnant and was not pregnant now. About the other accusations we hadn't much doubt, Carl and I, but about not being pregnant, that we weren't so sure of.

"How did she get such a big stomach, then?" asked Carl.

Yvette laughed. "Maybe she uses a bicycle pump," she said. "No, seriously," she added, "the stomach comes from drink. She drinks like a fish, Ginette. When she comes back from the country, you will see, she will be blown up still more. Her father is a drunkard. Ginette is a drunkard. Maybe she had the clap, yes—but she is not pregnant."

"But why does she want to marry him? Is she really in love with him?"

"*Love?* Pfooh! She has no heart, Ginette. She wants someone to look after her. No Frenchman would ever marry her—she has a police record. No, she wants him because he's too stupid to find out about her. Her parents don't want her any more—she's a disgrace to them. But if she can get married to a rich American, then everything will be all right. . . . You think maybe she loves him a little, eh? You don't know her. When they were living together at the hotel, she had men coming to her room while he was at work. She said he didn't give her enough spending money. He was stingy. That fur she wore—she told him her parents had given it to her, didn't she? Innocent fool! Why, I've seen her bring a man back to the hotel right while he was there. She brought the man to the floor below. I saw it with my own eyes. And what a man! An old derelict! He couldn't get an erection!"

If Fillmore, when he was released from the château, had returned to Paris, perhaps I might have tipped him off about his Ginette. While he was still under observation I didn't think it well to upset him by poisoning his mind with Yvette's slanders. As things turned out, he went directly from the château to the home of Ginette's parents. There, despite himself, he was inveigled into making public his engagement. The banns were published in the local papers and a reception was given to the friends of the family. Fillmore took advantage of the situation to indulge in all sorts of escapades. Though he knew quite well what he was doing he pretended to be still a little daffy. He would borrow his father-in-law's car, for example, and tear about the countryside all by himself; if he saw a town that he liked he would plank himself down and have a good time until Ginette came searching for him. Sometimes the father-in-law and he would go off together—on a fishing trip, presumably—and nothing would be heard of them for days. He became exasperatingly capricious and exacting. I suppose he figured he might as well get what he could out of it.

When he returned to Paris with Ginette he had a complete new wardrobe and a pocketful of dough. He looked cheerful and healthy, and had a fine coat of tan. He looked sound as a berry to me. But as soon as we had gotten away from Ginette he opened up. His job was gone and his money had all run out. In a month or so they were to be married. Meanwhile the parents were supplying the dough. "Once they've got me properly in their clutches," he said, "I'll be nothing but a slave to them. The father thinks he's going to open up a stationery store for me. Ginette will handle the customers, take in the money, etc., while I sit in the back of the store and write—or something. Can you picture me sitting in the back of a stationery store for the rest of my life? Ginette thinks it's an excellent idea. She likes to handle money. I'd rather go back to the château than submit to such a scheme."

For the time being, of course, he was pretending that everything was hunky-dory. I tried to persuade him to go back to America but he wouldn't hear of that. He said he wasn't going to be driven out of France by a lot of ignorant peasants. He had an idea that he would slip out of sight for a while and then take up quarters in some outlying section of the city where he'd not be likely to stumble upon her. But we soon decided that that was impossible: you can't hide away in France as you can in America.

"You could go to Belgium for a while," I suggested.

"But what'll I do for money?" he said promptly. "You can't get a job in these god-damned countries."

"Why don't you marry her and get a divorce, then?" I asked.

"And meanwhile she'll be dropping a kid. Who's going to take care of the kid, eh?"

"How do you know she's going to have a kid?" I said, determined now that the moment had come to spill the beans.

"How do I know?" he said. He didn't quite seem to know what I was insinuating.

I gave him an inkling of what Yvette had said. He listened to me in complete bewilderment. Finally he interrupted me. "It's no use going on with that," he said. "I know she's going to have a kid, all right. I've felt it kicking around inside. Yvette's a dirty little slut. You see, I didn't want to tell you, but up until the time I went to the hospital I was shelling out for Yvette too. Then when the crash came I couldn't do any more for her. I figured out that I had done enough for the both of them. . . . I made up my mind to look after myself first. That made Yvette sore. She told Ginette that she was going to get even with me. . . . No, I wish it were true, what she said. Then I could get out of this thing more easily. Now I'm in a trap. I've promised to marry her and I'll have to go through with it. After that I don't know what'll happen to me. They've got me by the balls now."

Since he had taken a room in the same hotel with me I was obliged to see them frequently, whether I wanted to

or not. Almost every evening I had dinner with them, pre-
ceded, of course, by a few Pernods. All through the meal
they quarrelled noisily. It was embarrassing because I had
sometimes to take one side and sometimes the other. One
Sunday afternoon, for example, after we had had lunch
together, we repaired to a café on the corner of the Boulevard Edgar-Quinet. Things had gone unusually well this
time. We were sitting inside at a little table, one alongside
the other, our backs to a mirror. Ginette must have been
passionate or something for she had suddenly gotten into
a sentimental mood and was fondling him and kissing
him in front of everybody, as the French do so naturally.
They had just come out of a long embrace when Fillmore
said something about her parents which she interpreted as
an insult. Immediately her cheeks flushed with anger. We
tried to mollify her by telling her that she had misunder-
stood the remark and then, under his breath, Fillmore said
something to me in English—something about giving her
a little soft soap. That was enough to set her completely
off the handle. She said we were making fun of her. I said
something sharp to her which angered her still more and
then Fillmore tried to put in a word. "You're too quick-
tempered," he said, and he tried to pat her on the cheek.
But she, thinking that he had raised his hand to slap her
face, she gave him a sound crack in the jaw with that big
peasant hand of hers. For a moment he was stunned. He
hadn't expected a wallop like that, and it stung. I saw his
face go white and the next moment he raised himself
from the bench and with the palm of his hand he gave her
such a crack that she almost fell off her seat. "There!
that'll teach you how to behave!" he said—in his broken
French. For a moment there was a dead silence. Then,
like a storm breaking, she picked up the cognac glass in
front of her and hurled it at him with all her might. It
smashed against the mirror behind us. Fillmore had already grabbed her by the arm, but with her free hand she
grabbed the coffee glass and smashed it on the floor. She
was squirming around like a maniac. It was all we could
do to hold her down. Meanwhile, of course, the *patron*
had come running in and ordered us to beat it. "Loafers!"
he called us. "Yes, loafers; That's it!" screamed Ginette.
"Dirty foreigners! Thugs! Gangsters! Striking a pregnant

woman!" We were getting black looks all around. A poor Frenchwoman with two American toughs. Gangsters. I was wondering how the hell we'd ever get out of the place without a fight. Fillmore, by this time, was as silent as a clam. Ginette was bolting it through the door, leaving us to face the music. As she sailed out she turned back with fist upraised and shouted; "I'll pay you back for this, you brute! You'll see! No foreigner can treat a decent Frenchwoman like that! Ah, no! Not like that!"

Hearing this the *patron,* who had now been paid for his drinks and his broken glasses, felt it incumbent to show his gallantry toward a splendid representative of French motherhood such as Ginette, and so, without more ado, he spat at our feet and shoved us out of the door. "Shit on you, you dirty loafers!" he said, or some such pleasantry.

Once in the street and nobody throwing things after us, I began to see the funny side of it. It would be an excellent idea, I thought to myself, if the whole thing were properly aired in court. *The whole thing!* With Yvette's little stories as a side dish. After all, the French have a sense of humor. Perhaps the judge, when he heard Fillmore's side of the story, would absolve him from marriage.

Meanwhile, Ginette was standing across the street brandishing her fist and yelling at the top of her lungs. People were stopping to listen in, to take sides, as they do in street brawls. Fillmore didn't know what to do— whether to walk away from her, or to go over to her and try to pacify her. He was standing in the middle of the street with his arms outstretched, trying to get a word in edgewise. And Ginette still yelling: *"Gangster! Brute! Tu verras, salaud!"* and other complimentary things. Finally Fillmore made a move towards her and she, probably thinking that he was going to give her another good cuff, took it on a trot down the street. Fillmore came back to where I was standing and said: "Come on, let's follow her quietly." We started off with a thin crowd of stragglers behind us. Every once in a while she turned back towards us and brandished her fist. We made no attempt to catch up with her, just followed her leisurely down the street to see what she would do. Finally she slowed up her pace and we crossed over to the other side of the street. She was quiet now. We kept walking behind her, getting closer and closer. There were only about a dozen people behind us now—the others had lost interest. When we got near the corner she suddenly stopped and waited for us to approach. "Let me do the talking," said Fillmore, "I know how to handle her."

The tears were streaming down her face as we came up to her. Myself, I didn't know what to expect of her. I was somewhat surprised therefore when Fillmore walked up to her and said in an aggrieved voice: "Was that a nice thing to do? Why did you act that way?" Whereupon she threw her arms around his neck and began to weep like a child, calling him her little this and her little that. Then she turned to me imploringly. "You saw how he struck me," she said. "Is that the way to behave towards a woman?" I was on the point of saying yes when Fillmore took her by the arm and started leading her off. "No more of that," he said. "If you start again I'll crack you right here in the street."

I thought it was going to start up all over again. She had fire in her eyes. But evidently she was a bit cowed, too, for it subsided quickly. However, as she sat down at the café she said quietly and grimly that he needn't think it was going to be forgotten so quickly; he'd hear more about it later on . . . perhaps to-night.

And sure enough she kept her word. When I met him the next day his face and hands were all scratched up. Seems she had waited until he got to bed and then, without a word, she had gone to the wardrobe and, dumping all his things out on the floor, she took them one by one and tore them to ribbons. As this had happened a number of times before, and as she had always sewn them up afterwards, he hadn't protested very much. And that made her angrier than ever. What she wanted was to get her nails into him, and she did, to the best of her ability. Being pregnant she had a certain advantage over him.

Poor Fillmore! It was no laughing matter. She had him terrorized. If he threatened to run away she retorted by a threat to kill him. And she said it as if she meant it. "If you go to America," she said, "I'll follow you! You won't get away from me. A French girl always knows how to get vengeance." And the next moment she would be coaxing him to be "reasonable," to be *"sage,"* etc. Life would be so nice once they had the stationery store. He wouldn't have to do a stroke of work. She would do everything. He could stay in back of the store and write—or whatever he wanted to do.

It went on like this, back and forth, a seesaw, for a few weeks or so. I was avoiding them as much as possible, sick of the affair and disgusted with the both of them. Then one fine summer's day, just as I was passing the Credit Lyonnais, who comes marching down the steps but Fillmore. I greeted him warmly, feeling rather guilty because I had dodged him for so long. I asked him, with more than ordinary curiosity, how things were going. He answered me rather vaguely and with a note of despair in his voice.

"I've just gotten permission to go to the bank," he said, in a peculiar, broken, abject sort of way. "I've got about half an hour, no more. She keeps tabs on me." And he grasped my arm as if to hurry me away from the spot.

We were walking down towards the Rue de Rivoli. It was a beautiful day, warm, clear, sunny—one of those days when Paris is at its best. A mild pleasant breeze blowing, just enough to take that stagnant odor out of your nostrils. Fillmore was without a hat. Outwardly he looked the picture of health—like the average American tourist who slouches along with money jingling in his pockets.

"I don't know what to do any more," he said quietly. "You've got to do something for me. I'm helpless. I can't get a grip on myself. If I could only get away from her for a little while perhaps I'd come round all right. But she won't let me out of her sight. I just got permission to run to the bank—I had to draw some money. I'll walk around with you a bit and then I must hurry back—she'll have lunch waiting for me."

I listened to him quietly, thinking to myself that he did need someone to pull him out of the hole he was in. He had completely caved in, there wasn't a speck of courage left in him. He was just like a child—like a child who is beaten every day and doesn't know any more how to behave, except to cower and cringe. As we turned under the colonnade of the Rue de Rivoli he burst out into a long

diatribe against France. He was fed up with the French. "I
used to rave about them," he said, "but that was all literature. I know them now . . . I know what they're really
like. They're cruel and mercenary. At first it seems wonderful, because you have a feeling of being free. After a
while it palls on you. Underneath it's all dead: there's no
feeling, no sympathy, no friendship. They're selfish to the
core. The most selfish people on earth! They think of
nothing but money, money, money. And so god-damned
respectable, so bourgeois! That's what drives me nuts.
When I see her mending my shirts I could club her. Always mending, mending. Saving, saving. *Faut faire des
économies!* That's all I hear her say all day long. You
hear it everywhere. *Sois raisonnable, mon chéri! Sois
raisonnable!* I don't want to be reasonable and logical. I
hate it! I want to bust loose, I want to enjoy myself. I
want to *do* something. I don't want to sit in a café and
talk all day long. Jesus, we've got our faults—but we've
got enthusiasm. It's better to make mistakes than not do
anything. I'd rather be a bum in America than to be sitting pretty here. Maybe it's because I'm a Yankee. I was
born in New England and I belong there, I guess. You
can't become a European overnight. There's something in
your blood that makes you different. It's the climate—and
everything. We see things with different eyes. We can't
make ourselves over, however much we admire the
French. We're Americans and we've got to remain Americans. Sure, I hate those puritanical buggers back
home—I hate 'em with all my guts. But I'm one of them
myself. I don't belong here. I'm sick of it."

All along the arcade he went on like this. I wasn't saying a word. I let him spill it all out—it was good for him
to get it off his chest. Just the same, I was thinking how
strange it was that this same guy, had it been a year ago,
would have been beating his chest like a gorilla and saying: "What a marvellous day! What a country! What a
people!" And if an American had happened along and
said one word against France Fillmore would have flattened his nose. He would have died for France—a year
ago. I never saw a man who was so infatuated with a
country, who was so happy under a foreign sky. It wasn't
natural. When he said *France* it meant wine, women,

money in the pocket, easy come, easy go. It meant being a bad boy, being on a holiday. And then, when he had had his fling, when the tent-top blew off and he had a good look at the sky, he saw that it wasn't just a circus, but an arena, just like everywhere. And a damned grim one. I often used to think, when I heard him rave about glorious France, about liberty and all that crap, what it would have sounded like to a French workman, could he have understood Fillmore's words. No wonder they think we're all crazy. We *are* crazy to them. We're just a pack of children. Senile idiots. What we call life is a five-and-ten-cent store romance. That enthusiasm underneath—what is it? That cheap optimism which turns the stomach of any ordinary European? It's illusion. No, illusion's too good a word for it. Illusion means something. No, it's not that—it's *delusion*. It's sheer delusion, that's what. We're like a herd of wild horses with blinders over our eyes. On the rampage. Stampede. Over the precipice. Bango! Anything that nourishes violence and confusion. On! On! No matter where. And foaming at the lips all the while. Shouting Hallelujah! *Hallelujah!* Why? God knows. It's in the blood. It's the climate. It's a lot of things. It's the end, too. We're pulling the whole world down about our ears. We don't know why. It's our destiny. The rest is plain shit. . . .

At the Palais Royal I suggested that we stop and have a drink. He hesitated a moment. I saw that he was worrying about her, about the lunch, about the bawling out he'd get.

"For Christ's sake," I said, "forget about her for a while. I'm going to order something to drink and I want you to drink it. Don't worry, I'm going to get you out of this fucking mess." I ordered two stiff whiskies.

When he saw the whiskies coming he smiled at me just like a child again.

"Down it!" I said, "and let's have another. This is going to do you good. I don't care what the doctor says—this time it'll be all right. Come on, down with it!"

He put it down all right and while the *garçon* disappeared to fetch another round he looked at me with brimming eyes, as though I were the last friend in the world. His lips were twitching a bit, too. There was something he wanted to say to me and he didn't quite know how to begin. I looked at him easily, as though ignoring the appeal and, shoving the saucers aside, I leaned over on my elbow and I said to him earnestly: "Look here, Fillmore, what is it you'd *really* like to do? Tell me!"

With that the tears gushed up and he blurted out: "I'd like to be home with my people. I'd like to hear English spoken." The tears were streaming down his face. He made no effort to brush them away. He just let everything gush forth. Jesus, I thought to myself, that's fine to have a release like that. Fine to be a complete coward at least once in your life. To let go that way. Great! Great! It did me so much good to see him break down that way that I felt as though I could solve any problem. I felt courageous and resolute. I had a thousand ideas in my head at once.

"Listen," I said, bending still closer to him, "if you mean what you said why don't you do it ... why don't you go? Do you know what I would do, if I were in your shoes? I'd go to-day. Yes, by Jesus, I mean it ... I'd go right away, without even saying good-bye to her. As a matter of fact that's the only way you can go—she'd never let you say good-bye. You know that."

The *garçon* came with the whiskies. I saw him reach forward with a desperate eagerness and raise the glass to his lips. I saw a glint of hope in his eyes—far-off, wild, desperate. He probably saw himself swimming across the Atlantic. To me it looked easy, simple as rolling off a log. The whole thing was working itself out rapidly in my mind. I knew just what each step would be. Clear as a bell, I was.

"Whose money is that in the bank?" I asked. "Is it her father's or is it yours?"

"It's mine!" he exclaimed. "My mother sent it to me. I don't want any of her god-damned money."

"That's swell!" I said. 'Listen, suppose we hop a cab and go back there. Draw out every cent. Then we'll go to the British Consulate and get a visa. You're going to hop the train this afternoon for London. From London you'll take the first boat to America. I'm saying that because then you won't be worried about her trailing you. She'll never suspect that you went via London. If she goes searching for you she'll naturally go to Le Havre first, or Cherbourg. . . . And here's another thing—you're not going back to get your things. You're going to leave everything here. Let her keep them. With that French mind of hers she'll never dream that you scooted off without bag or baggage. It's incredible. A Frenchman would never dream of doing a thing like that . . . unless he was as cracked as you are."

"You're right!" he exclaimed. "I never thought of that. Besides, you might send them to me later on—if she'll surrender them! But that doesn't matter now. Jesus, though, I haven't even got a hat!"

"What do you need a hat for? When you get to London you can buy everything you need. All you need now is to hurry. We've got to find out when the train leaves."

"Listen," he said, reaching for his wallet, "I'm going to leave everything to you. Here, take this and do whatever's necessary. I'm too weak. . . . I'm dizzy."

I took the wallet and emptied it of the bills he had just drawn from the bank. A cab was standing at the curb. We hopped in. There was a train leaving the Gare du Nord at four o'clock, or thereabouts. I was figuring it out—the bank, the Consulate, the American Express, the station. Fine! Just about make it.

"Now buck up!" I said, "and keep your shirt on! Shit, in a few hours you'll be crossing the channel. Tonight you'll be walking around in London and you'll get a good bellyful of English. To-morrow you'll be on the open sea—and then, by Jesus, you're a free man and you needn't give a fuck what happens. By the time you get to New York this'll be nothing more than a bad dream."

This got him so excited that his feet were moving convulsively, as if he were trying to run inside the cab. At the bank his hand was trembling so that he could hardly sign his name. That was one thing I couldn't do for him—sign his name. But I think, had it been necessary, I could have sat him on the toilet and wiped his ass. I was determined to ship him off, even if I had to fold him up and put him in a valise.

It was lunch hour when we got to the British Consulate, and the place was closed. That meant waiting until two o'clock. I couldn't think of anything better to do, by way of killing time, than to eat. Fillmore, of course, wasn't hungry. He was for eating a sandwich. "Fuck that!" I said. "You're going to blow me to a good lunch. It's the last square meal you're going to have over here— maybe for a long while." I steered him to a cosy little restaurant and ordered a good spread. I ordered the best wine on the menu, regardless of price or taste. I had all his money in my pocket—oodles of it, it seemed to me. Certainly never before had I had so much in my fist at one time. It was a treat to break a thousand-franc note. I held it up to the lights first to look at the beautiful watermark. Beautiful money! One of the few things the French make on a grand scale. Artistically done, too, as if they cherished a deep affection even for the symbol.

The meal over, we went to a café. I ordered Chartreuse with the coffee. Why not? And I broke another bill—a five-hundred-franc note this time. It was a clean, new, crisp bill. A pleasure to handle such money. The waiter handed me back a lot of dirty old bills that had been patched up with strips of gummed paper; I had a stack of five and ten-franc notes and a bagful of chicken feed. Chinese money, with holes in it. I didn't know in which pocket to stuff the money any more. My trousers were bursting with coins and bills. It made me slightly uncomfortable also, hauling all that dough out in public. I was afraid we might be taken for a couple of crooks.

When we got to the American Express, there wasn't a devil of a lot of time left. The British, in their usual fumbling, farting way, had kept us on pins and needles. Here everybody was sliding around on castors. They were so speedy that everything had to be done twice. After all the checks were signed and clipped together in a neat little holder, it was discovered that he had signed in the wrong place. Nothing to do but start all over again. I stood over him, with one eye on the clock, and watched every stroke of the pen. It hurt to hand over the dough. Not all of it, thank God—but a good part of it. I had roughly about 2,500 francs in my pocket. Roughly, I say. I wasn't counting by francs any more. A hundred, or two hundred, more or less—it didn't mean a god-damned thing to me. As for him, he was going through the whole transaction in a daze. He didn't know how much money he had. All he

knew was that he had to keep something aside for
Ginette. He wasn't certain yet how much—we were going
to figure that out on the way to the station.

In the excitement we had forgotten to change all the
money. We were already in the cab, however, and there
wasn't any time to be lost. The thing was to find out how
we stood. We emptied our pockets quickly and began to
whack it up. Some of it was lying on the floor, some of
it was on the seat. It was bewildering. There was French,
American and English money. And all that chicken feed
besides. I felt like picking up the coins and chucking
them out of the window—just to simplify matters. Finally
we sifted it all out; he held on to the English and American money, and I held on to the French money.

We had to decide quickly now what to do about
Ginette—how much to give her, what to tell her, etc. He
was trying to fix up a yarn for me to hand her—didn't
want her to break her heart and so forth. I had to cut him
short.

"Never mind what to tell her," I said. "Leave that to
me. How much are you going to *give* her, that's the thing?
Why give her anything?"

That was like setting a bomb under his ass. He burst
into tears. Such tears! It was worse than before. I thought
he was going to collapse on my hands. Without stopping
to think, I said: "All right, let's give her all this French
money. That ought to last her for a while."

"How much is it?" he asked feebly.

"I don't know—about 2,000 francs or so. More than
she deserves anyway."

"Christ! Don't say that!" he begged. "After all, it's a
rotten break I'm giving her. Her folks'll never take her
back now. No, give it to her. Give her the whole damned
business. . . . I don't care what it is."

He pulled a handkerchief out to wipe the tears away. "I
can't help it," he said. "It's too much for me." I said
nothing. Suddenly he sprawled himself out full length—I
thought he was taking a fit or something—and he said:
"Jesus, I think I ought to go back. I ought to go back and
face the music. If anything should happen to her I'd never
forgive myself."

That was a rude jolt for me. "Christ!" I shouted, "you

can't do that! Not now. It's too late. You're going to take
the train and I'm going to tend to her myself. I'll go see
her just as soon as I leave you. Why, you poor boob, if
she ever thought you had tried to run away from her
she'd murder you, don't you realize that? You can't go
back any more. It's settled."

Anyway, what *could* go wrong? I asked myself. Kill
herself? *Tant mieux.*

When we rolled up to the station we had still about
twelve minutes to kill. I didn't dare to say good-bye to
him yet. At the last minute, rattled as he was, I could see
him jumping off the train and scooting back to her. Anything might swerve him. A straw. So I dragged him
across the street to a bar and I said: "Now you're going
to have a Pernod—your *last* Pernod and I'm going to pay
for it . . . with *your* dough."

Something about this remark made him look at me uneasily. He took a big gulp of the Pernod and then, turning
to me like an injured dog, he said: "I know I oughtn't to
trust you with all that money, but . . . but. . . . Oh, well, do
what you think best. I don't want her to kill herself, that's
all."

"*Kill herself?*" I said. "Not her! You must think a hell
of a lot of yourself if you can believe a thing like that. As
for the money, though I hate to give it to her, I promise
you I'll go straight to the post office and telegraph it to
her. I wouldn't trust myself with it a minute longer than
is necessary." As I said this I spied a bunch of post cards
in a revolving rack. I grabbed one off—a picture of the
Eiffel Tower it was—and made him write a few words.
"Tell her you're sailing now. Tell her you love her and
that you'll send for her as soon as you arrive. . . . I'll send
it by *pneumatique* when I go to the post office. And to-
night I'll see her. Everything'll be Jake, you'll see."

With that we walked across the street to the station.
Only two minutes to go. I felt it was safe now. At the gate
I gave him a slap on the back and pointed to the train. I
didn't shake hands with him—he would have slobbered
all over me. I just said: "Hurry! She's going in a minute."
And with that I turned on my heel and marched off. I
didn't even look round to see if he was boarding the train.
I was afraid to.

* * *

I hadn't really thought, all the while I was bundling him off, what I'd do once I was free of him. I had promised a lot of things—but that was only to keep him quiet. As for facing Ginette, I had about as little courage for it as he had. I was getting panicky myself. Everything had happened so quickly that it was impossible to grasp the nature of the situation in full. I walked away from the station in a kind of delicious stupor—with the post card in my hand. I stood against a lamp-post and read it over. It sounded preposterous. I read it again, to make sure that I wasn't dreaming, and then I tore it up and threw it in the gutter.

I looked around uneasily, half expecting to see Ginette coming after me with a tomahawk. Nobody was following me. I started walking leisurely towards the Place Lafayette. It was a beautiful day, as I had observed earlier. Light, puffy clouds above, sailing with the wind. The awnings flapping. Paris had never looked so good to me; I almost felt sorry that I had shipped the poor bugger off. At the Place Lafayette I sat down facing the church and stared at the clock tower; it's not such a wonderful piece of architecture, but that blue in the dial face always fascinated me. It was bluer than ever to-day. I couldn't take my eyes off it.

Unless he were crazy enough to write her a letter, explaining everything, Ginette need never know what had happened. And even if she did learn that he had left her 2,500 francs or so she couldn't prove it. I could always say that he imagined it. A guy who was crazy enough to walk off without even a hat was crazy enough to invent the 2,500 francs, or whatever it was. How much was it, anyhow, I wondered. My pockets were sagging with the weight of it. I hauled it all out and counted it carefully. There was exactly 2,875 francs and 35 centimes. More than I had thought. The 75 francs and 35 centimes had to be gotten rid of. I wanted an even sum—a clean 2,800 francs. Just then I saw a cab pulling up to the curb. A woman stepped out with a white poodle dog in her hands; the dog was peeing over her silk dress. The idea of taking a dog for a ride got me sore. I'm as good as her dog, I said to myself, and with that I gave the driver a sign and

told him to drive me through the Bois. He wanted to
know where exactly. "Anywhere," I said. "Go through
the Bois, go all around it—and take your time, I'm in no
hurry." I sank back and let the houses whizz by, the jagged roofs, the chimney pots, the colored walls, the urinals, the dizzy *carrefours*. Passing the Rond-Point I
thought I'd go downstairs and take a leak. No telling
what might happen down there. I told the driver to wait.
It was the first time in my life I had let a cab wait while
I took a leak. How much can you waste that way? Not
very much. With what I had in my pocket I could afford
to have two taxis waiting for me.

I took a good look around but I didn't see anything
worth while. What I wanted was something fresh and
unused—something from Alaska or the Virgin Islands. A
clean fresh pelt with a natural fragrance to it. Needless to
say, there wasn't anything like that walking about. I
wasn't terribly disappointed. I didn't give a fuck whether
I found anything or not. The thing is, never to be too
anxious. Everything comes in due time.

We drove on past the Arc de Triomphe. A few sight-
seers were loitering around the remains of the Unknown
Soldier. Going through the Bois I looked at all the rich
cunts promenading in their limousines. They were whiz-
zing by as if they had some destination. Do that, no
doubt, to look important—to show the world how smooth
run their Rolls Royces and their Hispano Suizas. Inside
me things were running smoother than any Rolls Royce
ever ran. It was just like velvet inside. Velvet cortex and
velvet vertebrae. And velvet axle grease, what! It's a
wonderful thing, for half an hour, to have money in your
pocket and piss it away like a drunken sailor. You feel as
though the world is yours. And the best part of it is, you
don't know what to do with it. You can sit back and let
the meter run wild, you can let the wind blow through
your hair, you can stop and have a drink, you can give a
big tip, and you can swagger off as though it were an everyday occurrence. But you can't create a revolution. You
can't wash *all* the dirt out of your belly.

When we got to the Porte d'Auteuil I made him head
for the Seine. At the Pont de Sèvres I got out and started
walking along the river, toward the Auteuil Viaduct. It's

about the size of a creek along here and the trees come right down to the river's bank. The water was green and glassy, especially near the other side. Now and then a scow chugged by. Bathers in tights were standing in the grass sunning themselves. Everything was close and palpitant, and vibrant with the strong light.

Passing a beer garden I saw a group of cyclists sitting at a table. I took a seat nearby and ordered a *demi*. Hearing them jabber away I thought for a moment of Ginette. I saw her stamping up and down the room, tearing her hair, and sobbing and bleating, in that beast-like way of hers. I saw his hat on the rack. I wondered if his clothes would fit me. He had a raglan that I particularly liked. Well, by now he was on his way. In a little while the boat would be rocking under him. English! He wanted to hear English spoken. What an idea!

Suddenly it occurred to me that if I wanted I could go to America myself. It was the first time the opportunity had ever presented itself. I asked myself—"do you want to go?" There was no answer. My thoughts drifted out, towards the sea, towards the other side where, taking a last look back, I had seen the skyscrapers fading out in a flurry of snowflakes. I saw them looming up again, in that same ghostly way as when I left. Saw the lights creeping through their ribs. I saw the whole city spread out, from Harlem to the Battery, the streets choked with ants, the elevated rushing by, the theatres emptying. I wondered in a vague way what had ever happened to my wife.

After everything had quietly sifted through my head a great peace came over me. Here, where the river gently winds through the girdle of hills, lies a soil so saturated with the past that however far back the mind roams one can never detach it from its human background. Christ, before my eyes there shimmered such a golden peace that only a neurotic could dream of turning his head away. So quietly flows the Seine that one hardly notices its presence. It is always there, quiet and unobtrusive, like a great artery running through the human body. In the wonderful peace that fell over me it seemed as if I had climbed to the top of a high mountain; for a little while

I would be able to look around me, to take in the meaning of the landscape.

Human beings make a strange fauna and flora. From a distance they appear negligible; close up they are apt to appear ugly and malicious. More than anything they need to be surrounded with sufficient space—space even more than time.

The sun is setting. I feel this river flowing through me—its past, its ancient soil, the changing climate. The hills gently girdle it about: its course is fixed.

Bibliography

Chadwick, Whitney and de Courtivron, Isabelle, eds. *Significant Others: Creativity & Intimate Partnership* (New York: Thames and Hudson, 1993).

Dearborn, Mary V. *Henry Miller: A Biography* (New York: Simon & Schuster, 1991).

DeSalvo, Louise. *Conceived with Malice: Literature as Revenge in the Lives and Works of Virginia and Leonard Woolf, D. H. Lawrence, Djuna Barnes, and Henry Miller* (New York: Dutton, 1994).

Durrell, Lawrence and Miller, Henry. *The Durrell-Miller Letters, 1935–1980*. Edited by Ian S. MacNiven (New York: New Directions, 1988).

Ferguson, Robert. *Henry Miller: A Life* (New York: W. W. Norton, 1991).

Fitch, Noel Riley. *Anaïs: The Erotic Life of Anaïs Nin* (New York: Little, Brown and Company, 1993).

Jong, Erica. *The Devil at Large: Erica Jong on Henry Miller* (New York: Turtle Bay Books, Random House, 1993).

Kennedy, J. Gerald. *Imagining Paris: Exile, Writing, and American Identity* (New Haven: Yale University Press, 1993).

Knapp, Bettina L. *Anaïs Nin* (New York: Frederick Ungar Publishing Co., 1978).

Mailer, Norman. *The Prisoner of Sex* (New York: New American Library, 1971).

Martin, Jay. *Always Merry and Bright: The Life of Henry Miller; An Unauthorized Biography* (Santa Barbara: Capra Press, 1978).

Miller, Henry. *Crazy Cock*. Foreword by Erica Jong; Introduction by Mary V. Dearborn (New York: Grove Weidenfeld, 1991).

———. *Letters to Anaïs Nin*. Edited and introduced by Gunther Stuhlmann (New York: Paragon House, 1965, 1988).

———. *Letters to Emil*. Edited by George Wickes (New York: New Directions, 1989).

———. *Moloch, or This Gentile World* (New York: Grove Press, 1992).

———. *My Life and Times* (New York: Playboy Press, n.d.).

———. *Quiet Days in Clichy* (New York: Grove Weidenfeld, 1956; 1965).

———. *The Rosy Crucifixion: Book One; Sexus* (New York: Grove Weidenfeld, 1965).

———. *The Rosy Crucifixion: Book Two; Plexus* (New York: Grove Weidenfeld, 1965).

———. *The Rosy Crucifixion: Book Three; Nexus* (New York: Grove Press, 1965).

———. *Tropic of Cancer.* Introduction by Karl Shapiro. Preface by Anaïs Nin (New York: Grove Weidenfeld, 1961).

———. *Tropic of Capricorn* (New York: Grove Weidenfeld, 1961).

Nin, Anaïs. *The Diary of Anaïs Nin: 1931–1934,* Volume One. Edited and with an Introduction by Gunther Stuhlmann (New York: Harcourt Brace Jovanovich, 1966).

———. *Henry and June: From the Unexpurgated Diary of Anaïs Nin* (New York: Harcourt Brace Jovanovich, 1986).

———. *Incest: From A Journal of Love; The Unexpurgated Diary of Anaïs Nin, 1932–1934.* With an Introduction by Rupert Pole and Biographical Notes by Gunther Stuhlmann (New York: Harcourt Brace Jovanovich, 1992).

———. *Ladders to Fire,* in *Cities of the Interior* (Athens: Swallow Press/Ohio University Press, 1959, 1974).

Nin, Anaïs and Miller, Henry. *A Literate Passion: Letters of Anaïs Nin and Henry Miller, 1932–1953.* Edited and with an Introduction by Gunther Stuhlmann (New York: Harcourt Brace Jovanovich, 1987).

Perles, Alfred. *My Friend Henry Miller: An Intimate Biography* (New York: John Day, 1956).

Perles, Alfred and Durrell, Lawrence. *Art and Outrage: A correspondence about Henry Miller between Alfred Perles and Lawrence Durrell (With an intermission by Henry Miller)* (London: Village Press, 1973).

Porter, Bern, ed. *The Happy Rock: A Book about Henry Miller* (Berkeley: Packard Press, 1945).

Tytell, John. *Passionate Lives: D. H. Lawrence, F. Scott Fitzgerald, Henry Miller, Dylan Thomas, Sylvia Plath—In Love* (New York: Carol Publishing, 1991).

Wickes, George. *Americans in Paris* (New York: Doubleday, 1969).

Wickes, George, ed. *Henry Miller and the Critics.* With a Preface by Harry T. Moore (Carbondale: Southern Illinois University Press, 1963).